GENTLEMEN

GENTLEMEN
A NOVEL

KLAS
ÖSTERGREN

TRANSLATED BY TIINA NUNNALLY

CANONGATE
Edinburgh · London · New York · Melbourne

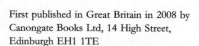

First published in Great Britain in 2008 by
Canongate Books Ltd, 14 High Street,
Edinburgh EH1 1TE

First published in the US in 2007 by
MacAdam Cage, 155 Sansome Street, Suite 550,
San Francisco, CA 94104

Originally published in Sweden as *Gentlemen* by Bonnier (ScanBook AB, Falun) in 1980

1

The publisher acknowledges subsidy from the Scottish Arts Council towards the production of this book

Scottish
Arts Council

British Library Cataloguing-in-Publication Data
A catalogue record for this book is available on
request from the British Library

ISBN 978 1 84195 816 3

Typeset by Palimpsest Book Production Limited, Grangemouth, Stirlingshire
Printed and bound by in Great Britain by Mackays of Chatham Ltd, Chatham

www.canongate.net

CONTENTS

GENTLEMEN

(Stockholm, Autumn 1978)

Presumably it's a quiet spring rain that can be heard drizzling over Stockholm at the moment, in the Year of the Child, the election year of 1979. I see none of it, nor do I have any intention of taking a look. The curtains are closed tight in front of the windows facing Hornsgatan, and this flat seems lugubrious, to say the least. It's been days since I've seen any daylight, while outside all of Stockholm is probably walking around in the very last springtime delirium of the seventies, but I don't give a damn.

This grand flat is like a museum to some kind of glory, an ancient ideal, or maybe some vanished chivalry. The library is silent and permeated with smoke, the service corridors with their gloomy sideboards and tall cabinets are terrifying, the kitchen is filthy, the bedrooms haven't been made up, the living room is cold. On either side of the fireplace – where we spent so many hours sitting on the Chippendale furniture, drinking toddies and entertaining each other with peculiar anecdotes – stand two Parian figurines made by the Gustafsberg Company towards the end of the nineteenth century. The pieces are about one and a half feet tall, and the porcelain looks exactly like the real marble they're meant to imitate. One of them represents 'Truth' and is depicted as a muscular man without a stitch of clothing on his body, with exquisitely sculpted features that nevertheless fail to conceal something indeterminate and evasive in his eyes. The other Parian figure represents, appropriately enough, 'Falsehood' – a jester leaning casually on a wine barrel, holding a stringed instrument and bubbling with *esprit*, no doubt in the midst of telling some risqué story about a shepherd.

It's not in the least difficult to make certain associations with the two men who until quite recently resided here in this flat. They abandoned it as hastily as if an air-raid siren had sounded. Everything stands untouched; indeed, this whole museum-like home is filled with such extraordinary objects, things from bygone eras. My thoughts are inevitably drawn back to the past.

Repulsive is what I am. Under this ridiculous English tweed cap my shaved and battered head is slowly trying to regain its former dimensions – as far as that's even possible. I've already aged with astonishing speed during this Year of the Child and the Swedish elections of 1979. I've acquired new wrinkles and some sort of tic or twitch under my eyes. It gives my face a certain haggard, though not entirely unattractive, look. Although only twenty-five, I'm already ageing like a Dorian Gray. I wouldn't have believed it was possible to burn out or to wither so cruelly in the preservative, antiquated darkness that has always been a terrifying possibility in this flat. At any moment, summoning the last of my strength, I could clear away the barricaded door in the hall – I dragged over an enormous, solid mahogany cabinet to make myself feel secure – and get out of here. But I don't. There's no going back. I suspect that this whole thing has driven me crazy.

I've got a wound on my skull and enemies at my throat. Everyone has some petty enemy, but I share mine with my friends, and my friends have disappeared. They never pointed out my enemy, and I don't know what he or she or it looks like. I can only hazard a guess. This is probably not going to be so much a portrait of an enemy, a description of Evil, as it is a portrait of my friends, a description of what is good and all its possibilities. It's going to be a dark story, because I'm inclined to believe that what is good in fact lacks possibilities. We must allow ourselves to despair, at least once in a while. If you've been the victim of an assault and serious abuse and almost lost your life as a result, at the very least it's excusable.

With regard to my own condition – my head is not to be subjected to any major stress, according to the recommendations of the doctors after they treated me – and considering the times, which seem increasingly unbearable, I'd better get started at once. I'm thinking of erecting a temple, a monument to the Morgan brothers. That's the least I can do for them, wherever they happen to be now.

———

To stand in front of a mirror in the Europa Athletic Club near Hornstull in Stockholm on an autumn evening in 1978 and nonchalantly whistle the solo of an old tune blaring from a plastic record player while at the same time

4

meticulously tying a Windsor knot in his tie was bad enough. But then, in the doorway on his way out, to shout in his booming voice: 'So long, girls!' – that was really going too far.

No one said a thing. Only Juan laughed, and Willis, of course. Juan wasn't his real name, but he had a basketball jersey with a big yellow 7 on it, and since he was Yugoslav and looked like a Spaniard, he was called Juan. He laughed at almost everything, not because he was trying to ingratiate himself but because, in his dark eyes, there was plenty to laugh about in this country. Willis also had a real sense of humour. He stood there sniggering in his office. He'd been the head of the Europa Athletic Club since it was founded, and he personally knew the man who had gone too far.

But everyone else at the Europa took it quite hard. A stranger had come and called them girls, and that was hitting below the belt, that was just not done. It was especially too much for Gringo. He'd been the uncrowned king of the Europa the past few years, and he'd largely been left in peace to rule undisturbed. No one dared challenge him. Except on this particular evening, when he'd been run through the wringer by the stranger. They'd started sparring, mostly just for fun, thinking they'd go three rounds. Gringo had calmly started popping in his famous right hooks – which at one time had won him a Swedish Championship – but then the stranger answered with a totally unorthodox style of boxing: inventive and varied, as if in a fourth dimension that no one had ever thought of before, until Gringo felt compelled to break off, justifying it by saying that his opponent had such damn bad breath. There was an odour of garlic surrounding the stranger, so Gringo couldn't move in close with his famously lethal right hooks. Gringo had capitulated to a little garlic! Everyone just about died laughing.

That was merely an excuse, anyone could see that, because even in the second round, Gringo had been in trouble. The rankings were chalked up and now Gringo sat on the bench under the clothes hooks, and in spite of a shower and plenty of cold water, he looked like he'd taken a beating. Both his cheekbones were red and swollen, and he had unwrapped the gauze from his hands with ill-concealed pain. For once he wasn't saying a thing. He was silent, but he'd get back at the man, everyone knew that. Gringo was brooding over his revenge.

'Who the hell was that?' asked one of the little guys, one of the featherweights who had stood glued to the ropes when Gringo was beaten by a totally untrained stranger who seemed born to box.

'That,' said Willis as he came out of the office with its glass doors and all the boxing portraits, 'that was Henry. One of my old lads. Henry Morgan. One of my best boys some twenty years ago. He's been gone a long time. He's a piano player. But he's been away.'

The little guys listened in amazement and then started pummelling the heavy sandbags, trying to punch exactly the way Morgan had, but it just wasn't the same. Now they had something else to talk about; otherwise Ali vs Spinks was all that mattered. Everyone was talking about the Match down at the Europa Athletic Club. The rematch between Ali and Spinks.

———————

Of course I couldn't help committing the name 'Henry Morgan' to memory. It was one of those special names to which your mind has a certain predisposition, and I wonder whether I didn't take the man to heart as well, even on that first evening. I don't think I was the only one.

Several evenings later I was down at the Europa again – I was awfully bored in the evenings and couldn't stand the thought of sitting in my ransacked flat. I needed to kill time and pound my depression into a punch bag.

The man named Henry Morgan came down at about the same time to say hello to Willis and 'the girls'. And in the glance that he exchanged with the boss, there was so much of that father–son relationship that Willis shared with only the few chosen lads he really believed in, the ones on whom he pinned all his hopes. He would do anything for them.

So this Henry Morgan had been gone for God knows how many years – he'd quite simply 'been away', as Willis had phrased it – because boxers come and go, and Willis had probably realised long ago that this guy would come and go exactly as he pleased.

I started skipping rope, and sadly enough the rope is the thing I've mastered the best in my whole routine. Henry Morgan was also skipping, and gradually we started dancing around in a sort of rope duel with crossed arms and double bounces at quite a furious pace.

It was already late and after an hour we were practically the only two left, besides Willis of course. He was sitting in the office behind the glass doors, hustling to get a few of his lads into the next competition.

'You're looking a little down in the dumps, kid,' said the guy named Morgan.

'I *am* a little down in the dumps,' I said.

'Apparently it's not just governments that get the blues this time of year,' he said.

'I have nothing against the time of year, per se,' I said.

The man named Henry Morgan stepped onto the scales and read off his weight, muttering something about 'light heavyweight'. After he'd put on a pair of brown slacks, a pinstriped shirt, burgundy pullover, and a houndstooth tweed jacket, he went over to the mirror to fix his tie in that complicated Windsor knot. He carefully combed his hair and peered into the mirror for a long time. His reflection showed the image of the perfect gentleman, a mysterious anachronism: hair cut short and parted, a powerful jaw, straight shoulders and a body that seemed both solid and supple at the same time. I tried to estimate his age, but it was difficult. He was a grown man with the look of a boy. He reminded me a bit of Gentleman Jim Corbett, whose picture was taped on the glass door of Willis's office. Or Gene Tunney.

After he stopped admiring his own appearance he began to study me as I sat there on the bench, gasping. It was clear that he saw something unusual, because he raised his eyebrows and said, 'Damn, to think I didn't notice it before!' And then he fell silent and continued to scrutinise me.

'What is it?' I asked.

'You're a hell of a lot like my brother, Leo. I could use you.'

'Is Leo Morgan your brother?' I said. 'The one who's the poet?'

Henry Morgan nodded silently.

'I thought that was a pseudonym.'

'How'd you like a part in a film?' he asked all of a sudden.

'As long as it pays,' I said.

'I'm serious. Would you like a part in a film?'

'What's it about?' I asked.

'Get dressed and we'll go out and talk about it over a beer,' he said. 'Damn, to think I didn't notice it at once!'

I threw on my clothes as Henry Morgan went back to admiring himself in the mirror.

'You're going to have to stand me a round,' he said.

'I had a feeling.'

The man named Henry Morgan let loose a roar of laughter and extended his hand.

'Henry Morgan's the name.'

'Klas Östergren,' I said. 'Pleased to meet you.'

'Don't be so sure about that,' he said, and roared again.

The Europa Athletic Club was located on Långholmsgatan near Horn-stull, diagonally opposite Café Tjoget, but that's not where we went because it's easy to get too drunk in that place, and we were both determined to take it easy. It was a completely ordinary, rainy Thursday in September 1978, and there was no special occasion, according to the calendar, to go on a binge. We ended up in Gamla Stan, the old town area, and went into the Zum Franziskaner pub. We each ordered a Guinness, and then, with aching legs, sat down on a bench.

Henry offered me a Pall Mall from a very elegant silver cigarette case and lit it with a fat, scratched old Ronson lighter. Then he began cleaning his nails with a little penknife that he kept in a burgundy leather case in his jacket pocket. I hadn't seen such a battery of paraphernalia in a very long time and was quite amazed.

But the cigarette was strong, and I glanced out at Skeppsbron where the rain was falling gently, making the streets slippery, shiny, gloomy and melan-choly. I said as much to Henry Morgan, that I was feeling down in the dumps and glum and I had every reason to feel that way. I had been robbed of nearly everything I owned.

––––––––––

To be robbed of practically everything you own is a very special existential situation, and a great moralist such as William Faulkner certainly might have said that the person who is robbed wins what the robber loses – the victim proceeds to drown blissfully in the perfect righteousness and complacency of innocence, the victim is suddenly forgiven all his own previous sins, and grace descends like an unwritten clause in an insurance policy with imme-diate divine effect.

So I was feeling very bitter but absolutely righteous that rainy Thursday in early September. But perhaps I should go further back in time. I'm not saying back to the beginning, because I don't believe that a story has any beginning or end; only fairytales begin and end at certain points, and this one is definitely no saga, even though it may sound like one.

Even back in that most beautiful, seductive May – at the beginning of 'the most coquettish of times' as the poet Leo Morgan said – I was broke. The bank had given me the cold shoulder, and I had nothing to sell. I was anticipating with dread an entire summer without money, which meant working. Even though it might appear otherwise, work didn't scare me. What felt ominous was a whole summer of being broke.

Feeling slightly desperate, I tried to pound out a few short stories for a couple of journals and weekly magazines, but the editors were up to their ears in submissions. They politely rejected my wares, and deep inside I wasn't surprised. They were shoddy goods.

After that I tried, rather more desperately, to offer my wares to the daily papers. I ferreted out a little controversy here and a little controversy there and threw myself full-force into debates about subjects and concerns to which, up until then, I had never given a thought or known anything about. This was in the spring of '78, exactly a decade after the legendary Revolutionary Spring. So it was high time for ennobled rebels (who were already starting to go grey) to raise their voices in an anniversary chorus that sounded awfully out of tune. Some of them wanted to re-evaluate the Revolution, which had completely lost its direction, by turning it into a playground for academic punks. Others saw it as a golden age rife with political *festivitas*. The long and the short of it was that our own era took the form of a time that was both waking up and falling asleep, depending on what condition a person had been in during the previous decade.

I knew quite well that an entire mafia existed that made its living by sniffing out controversies and throwing itself into the public debate. And often with great success. Occasionally the controversy would go on for months, spreading like some sort of intellectual rabies among the cultural journalists. Everybody was suddenly infected and on top form.

But that was obviously not my style. I never managed to get a handle on the controversy. Hitting below the belt was completely acceptable, but to take back anything, to say the opposition had been right, that was the same thing as committing hara-kiri in front of millions of readers. I needed a new profession.

My solution was to swear off writing for a couple of months, and just then Errol Hansen, my friend from the Danish embassy, rang and very conveniently happened to mention that they needed some help at the popular country club where he went for diversion.

'Wijkman, he's the one in charge of the whole place,' said Errol. 'He'd like to see someone show up with a recommendation. They've had problems with the groundskeepers before, guys who just lay about sleeping when

9

they had the whole fairway to mow. They don't look on that very favourably, you see. But I could recommend you if you like.'

'What would I have to do?' I asked.

'All you have to do is sit on the tractor and mow the grass. It's a real easy gig, a life of leisure, you know. Plenty of sunshine, fresh air and cute girls at the clubhouse.'

I was in a vulnerable state at the time, and I needed money and a job, so it wasn't hard to persuade me. The very next day I was standing in Mr Wijkman's office on Banérgatan to check in.

As soon as I set foot in that luxurious office – it was an accounting firm – I was accosted by a chic woman in her forties who was the secretary.

'Finally!' she cried, and I couldn't understand how I could be in such demand. 'Where *have* you been?'

I glanced at my watch to see if it was possible that I was horribly late, but that wasn't the case at all. I was actually five minutes early, but I didn't have a chance to think much about it before the chic secretary started loading me up with stacks of papers. Being the helpful gentleman that I am, I accepted one stack after another as she piled them on, twittering all the while.

'*This* time there's more than ever,' said the secretary. 'We've been on holiday and all, you know, so people have built up quite a backlog, but I hope you can handle this as quickly as always, I'm sure you can, *ten* copies of each, as usual, be a dear . . .'

'I'm afraid there's been some mistake,' I finally managed to say. 'I have an appointment with Mr Wijkman about applying for a job as a groundskeeper.'

The secretary was quite startled, and at that very moment the man who turned out to be Mr Wijkman, the managing director, came out of his office. Naturally he assumed the look of a large, sun-tanned question mark when he saw us in that situation, so difficult to interpret. A misunderstanding had occurred. The secretary had thought that I was from the company that made copies of dossiers, under strict confidentiality.

Both Mr Wijkman and the secretary apologised profusely. Of course I claimed to have known all along what was going on, and I think they both realised that they were dealing with a real little joker. It's a part of my daily life. I'm regularly mistaken for someone else, and people are always apologising to me profusely, which often gives me an advantage. Sometimes it's the beginning of quite an interesting acquaintance. It's an excellent position to be in when applying for a job, as in this case, if your future boss has to start off with an apology. It feels invigorating.

After this little farce – a fine example of the type of complication that Molière made his trademark – Mr Wijkman invited me into his elegant office. We immediately began discussing life in Stockholm in early summer, sailing, golf, his daughter and taxes.

Mr Wijkman and I hit it off at once, even though he thought it was a bit strange that I didn't have a job and wasn't a student either. That didn't really add up for him, but we were certainly not going to talk politics.

The meeting ended with me getting the job, and I was supposed to show up at the golf course the first week of June, when the regular groundskeeper would be on holiday. My temporary position would last all summer long. The salary didn't exactly make me fall on the floor in paroxysms of glee, but on the other hand the job did include meals and lodging in a little bungalow a stone's throw from the clubhouse. It sounded promising. Wijkman also intimated – an extremely discreet intimation, man-to-man – that a certain amount of high life went on at the club, in which I, with my alert mind and polished style, surely could participate and enjoy particular benefits.

———————

The first week of June started off splendidly. The weather was glorious and all of Stockholm was panting in the heatwave. The pavement cafés were full, and everyone was waiting for Midsummer, when they could finally get out of the city, which was nevertheless displaying a remarkable, though arguable, charm at the time. Everyone complains about the heat, and yet they love it, as long as they can go out and lie on the grass in the park. Sitting indoors in an office or standing in a workshop in the worst heat is absolutely unbearable. I myself was quite pleased to be moving out to the country, over twelve miles north-east of Stockholm, to a bungalow on a golf course.

The girl who lived next door to me was going to take care of my plants and post, and everything was packed up and ready. Errol gave me a lift out there in his high-class Mercedes with the diplomatic number plates. His golf clubs were casually tossed on the back seat, and the boot was full of my luggage. I had brought along work clothes, ordinary gear, and some nicer things for relaxing summer evenings at the country club.

'The danger is that you might drink up your whole salary at the club,' said Errol. 'That's easy to do.'

'Can't I get some sort of discount?' I asked optimistically.

'Possibly. But the bartender is a really tough customer. The cold type.'

'Damn. Well, never mind. I'm sure I'll figure something out. I'm planning to spend a lot of the evenings reading and working.'

Errol laughed his Danish laugh.

'Is it your books that weigh so much?'

'They're probably a good couple of stone,' I said.

'Two stone,' repeated Errol. 'Right, well, I think you'll be happy if you even manage to read the newspaper.'

'You know nothing about my moral tenacity,' I said.

Out at the club I was introduced to the rank and file, the servants. There were a few of Wijkman's subordinates, whose duties seemed quite loosely defined, the waiters and kitchen workers at the restaurant, as well as the bartender who, true to reputation was an insolent, cold man named Rikard but known as 'Rocks'.

After the tour of the estimable clubhouse, it was time to have a look at the machinery. I was escorted around by an up-and-coming young guy in his thirties, a real Young Turk, whose name I didn't even bother to remember. All he had on his mind was everything I was *not* allowed to do. His manner of speaking was like one long negation of existence, filled with prohibitions and felonies. I was not supposed to mow this way or that, or mow here or there, or drive too close to the club, or disturb the guests. And I was absolutely forbidden to lie down and sunbathe in full view up in the rough beyond the fairway. Also typical of this Young Turk was the fact that he didn't know a single thing about how the machinery functioned. There were two big Westing tractors that pulled a mower system for the fairway, a small Smith & Stevens tractor with very wide, soft tyres for the greens, as well as a couple of push mowers for various special purposes.

Grass, and golf-course grass in particular, is a whole science unto itself, as I soon realised, and my only task was to mow it. If I discovered bare patches or other mysterious phenomena I was immediately supposed to contact the consultants – experts in the field who would provide the appropriate remedies.

After the machinery, the tour finally headed for the celebrated bungalow which would be my lodgings. It turned out to be quite an elegant building, long and low, nestling on a gentle slope behind the club itself. A few of the rooms were occasionally used by the employees, or 'the staff', as the very American Young Turk liked to call the rank and file. But most of them commuted from the city to the club, so for the most part I could count on peace and quiet.

My room faced east, had sunlight most of the day, and offered a magnificent view of the little hollow where the deep green fairway undulated towards the fifteenth hole. A short hole requiring a four-iron, according to the Young Turk. He had almost made a hole-in-one at that very green. At any rate, it was a beautiful, serene view, and I had high hopes for the summer.

It took no more than a few days before I was completely into my job. I learned to worship the grass and despise the golfers. Their whole attitude got on my nerves. They were assaulting my grass. But it's no use talking about them. The grass was green, at any rate. I was soon sitting like some little hotshot racer behind the wheel of my deluxe three-gear Smith & Stevens tractor, wearing shorts and a T-shirt, and getting as tanned as an Adonis; I was feeling great. In the beginning I did quite a decent job, wanting to make a good impression, as they say. I developed an admirable style on the machines, learning all the special little quirks of the various models that gave them each a unique personality. They seemed as personal and individual as horses in a stable – though to the uninitiated they may appear quite anonymous. With one machine the trick was to kick a certain spot; another machine required shifting gears precisely this way or that at just the right moment to achieve the most perfect and docile pace. Back when I was a teenager, I knew everything there was to know about American dragsters. I had meticulously studied three years' worth of *Start & Speed*, and now I was reaping the benefits.

But by the second week I was already starting to take things more easily. A sense of 'mañana, mañana' began to settle in. There was a time for everything. It was hot and muggy, and a groundskeeper, a golf proletarian, needed to take a siesta when the sun was at its zenith. No one could find fault with that. Nor did anyone find fault with the way I was doing my job, since I did it well.

For a number of evenings a fine, tranquil, liberating rain fell, making me feel delicately attuned and harmonious as well. Naturally the rain was balm for my beloved grass, but it also cast a certain lyrical vitality over the landscape. A strangely colonial mood suddenly seemed to hover over the grounds between the club and my bungalow, as if it were a British country club in some Asian tea colony. There was a limestone path lined with rosebeds, along with lilacs and jasmine. In the drizzling rain, I sat on a bench near that path for hours, wanting fully to imbibe the refined and lofty atmosphere along with a cup of Oriental Evening tea and an unfiltered Camel cigarette.

It was idyllic, and anything idyllic is always in a state of stasis. I wondered what the opposite might be called. I couldn't come up with any antonyms for something idyllic other than war, physical violence and misery; any sort of physical change per se. I came to a certain self-realisation, perceiving that I myself, as a physical organism, was tremendously conservative. As a child I never washed until I was told that the warts on my fingers were caused by a lack of hygiene. Of course that wasn't true at all – after having scrubbed my hands fifty times a day, I was finally sent off to the hospital, where the warts were very painfully burned off. I still feel sick washing in cold water in the morning. And I always shave in the evening. I suffered from car-sickness until I was nearly grown-up. I actually hate to travel, and I never go anywhere near an aeroplane. My body is immensely conservative, perceiving even the slightest change as an assault. I would prefer, above all, to live in a termite mound – in which the temperature is exactly the same all year round. I detest any extreme changes in light or sound. At the cinema I often feel sick, and I try to avoid people with shrill voices or strong body odour. My whole being is, so to speak, predisposed to the idyllic. Yet as soon as I find myself lying in a hammock or sitting in a lilac bower, which may well be called idyllic, I start getting tics and spasms and have to flee as fast as possible. But I happen to know deeply rootless and restless individuals who rarely do anything other than sit in just these types of bowers among flowering bird-cherries and lilacs to inhale the idyllic fragrance of sweet blossoms and freshly brewed coffee.

I soon went crazy sitting there on that bench, and I lacked the peace of mind to tackle all the books I had planned on reading. I went over to see Rocks in the bar at the club. He could make an obliterating Singapore Sling, and that quickly put an end to any ambitions or intentions for the evening.

The threat of cruel change is one of the fundamental conditions of human existence, and considering how often the threat becomes reality, there is every reason to call that existence basically tragic. This would soon become evident to me personally, with all due clarity.

———————

The summer would turn out to be anything but idyllic. In early July I went up to the Young Turk's office to ask for some time off. He was lounging at his desk, talking on the phone about some company board that he was apparently going to join. When he was finished with the conversation he offered me a seat, saying, 'Sit down, dammit all. What the hell was your name?'

I told him my name, but I couldn't help laughing because I hadn't learned his name either. The Young Turk laughed along, just to be on the safe side, and asked me what I wanted.

'I'm going to a concert in Göteborg next week. I need to take a couple of days off.'

'That's going to be tricky . . .' the Young Turk started off, rubbing his jaw and trying to look harried. 'We're damned pleased with you, I want you to know that, but . . .'

Maybe it was because it was such a hot day; maybe it was because I hadn't had enough sleep. Whatever the reason, I wasn't about to be bullied, and I immediately went on the offensive.

'Look here,' I said, my voice icy cold, 'I've got tickets to Bob Dylan, and I don't care whether you like it or not. I'm going next week. That's how it is. You should be glad that I'm giving you fair notice.'

The Young Turk tapped his chin and nodded.

'Well, all right then. If that's the way it is.'

That's the way it was, and it turned out to be a splendid trip to Göteborg. Half of Stockholm had come to the west coast. Göteborg's trams were full of old hippies, beatniks, little Bob Dylans and Scandinavia's whole protest-song elite. It was like one big carnival.

And it was a grand festival. The myth had succeeded in killing his own myth, and he almost sounded like a new rock star. At the end everybody lit matches, like candles in a huge cathedral, making it feel as if we were in complete unity and inviolable.

I ended up next to a skinny guy who sat completely motionless for several hours. He didn't move a muscle. I recognised him from Stockholm, because he'd been showing up at events for a long time, wherever anything was

15

happening. I might have seen him first at the event to save the elm trees in Kungsträdgården, the King's Garden, in 1971. One of the protest singers who was going to perform said hello to this guy, and maybe that's why I noticed him. He was always alone, although everyone said hello to him. I didn't know his name.

But even though it was a great concert, the rest of my time off took the sheen off the Dylan experience. The day after the show, I hitchhiked to Stockholm. I had promised the Young Turk that I'd be back as soon as possible; a promise to him didn't mean much, but I didn't want to abandon the grass.

I went up to my flat in Lilla Essingen to get a change of clothes and to ask the girl who lived next door, who had promised to water my plants, if anything interesting had turned up with the post.

There wasn't the slightest mark on the front door, but as soon as I opened it I could feel the vibrations left behind by the thieves. No doubt it's the same for anyone who comes home to find that uninvited guests have been inside. Maybe it's the trembling guilt of the fingerprints, maybe burglars secrete a special sort of fluid, a previously unknown theft-adrenaline that comes out in their sweat, giving the room a unique atmosphere. Or maybe it's simply the fact that the unconscious is able to register every little change and thus prepare the conscious mind, issuing forewarnings and alarms before the Big Shock sets in.

As soon as I entered my flat, I confirmed what had already sparked my suspicions: my beloved home had been emptied of practically every single thing that might bring a few kronor on the black market. Not that I owned much of value, but when I did the estimate for the insurance company afterwards, it still amounted to quite a bit.

I instantly lit a cigarette and proceeded to look around. It felt exactly like receiving the news of a death. At first you just want to pinch yourself to wake up from the nightmare; later you refuse to comprehend anything, but you force yourself to sample small portions of the truth until a defensive reaction sets in as solace.

I matter-of-factly concluded that citizen Östergren was now in possession of an empty space totalling approximately forty-seven square yards, completely bare walls, a cleaned-out kitchen, and a bookshelf that had been ransacked of anything of value by the burglars' excellent sense of judgement and literary taste. All that remained were my desk and my two typewriters. How nice and humane, I thought. But to add insult to injury, the thieves had put a piece of paper in one of the typewriters and typed the words: 'Hope Dyllan was good. We'll leave you the tools of your trade so you'll be able to earn an income.' – just like some greedy bailiff who didn't know shit about how a rock star spells his name.

Only then did I pull out the desk drawer where I kept all my valuable documents. My passport and ID papers were gone, but the burglars had left behind a few items of purely sentimental value.

Roaming around in my flat, which had been cleaned out lock, stock and barrel, gave me the strongest sense of despair that I've ever felt. I definitely didn't feel angry, not yet. Instead I was tremendously surprised at the way a couple of hard-working thieves could haul out an entire removal van full of stuff without any suspicious citizen intervening. People knew me in the building, after all; I'd lived at that address nearly all my life.

I went out to the landing and rang my neighbour's doorbell. She wasn't home, but she was above suspicion. Then I aimlessly wandered up to the attic, just to make sure that the burglars hadn't gone up there and swiped my skates. There they still were, hanging from a hook behind the door, and that made me happy. My old skates had suddenly acquired a priceless value for me, and I pictured myself falling apart completely if they had been gone. I stubbed out my cigarette on the cement floor of the attic, peered out through the dormer window, and saw that it had started to rain again.

Since the burglars had even taken my telephone, I had to go over to another neighbour's flat. I told the whole story to an astounded and even more shocked fellow citizen and then rang the police and insurance company.

So it was a very upset groundskeeper who returned to the golf course. The whole bureaucratic investigation had been kicked into gear, and both the police authorities and the insurance representatives had informed me that it could take time. Summertime burglaries were nothing new; the investigators were overworked this time of year.

I tried to push aside the whole tragedy, burying myself in my work and mowing one hell of a golf course, raking all the paths and re-digging all the flower-beds in a blind fury. After a couple of days the worst of the shock had subsided, and in certain bright moments I was actually filled with a dizzying sense of freedom and independence. There was no longer anything keeping me in my place in the world. I could do whatever I felt like doing, provided I had a little money. But the next instant this euphoria would be replaced by the deepest sorrow. It felt like some sort of penance.

Days and weeks passed in this manner. In early August a small bright spot occurred: I was commissioned to write a book. This coincided with a couple of different anniversaries. First of all, the club was celebrating its tenth anniversary, with flags flying and much pomp and circumstance. After a great deal of solemn planning, palavering and arguing, they had arranged a fun little tournament for juniors, ladies, semi-pros and old-boys in mixed teams that would conclude with cocktails at a festive gathering in the evening. A big crowd of people turned up, and anyone of importance who had ever sunk a ball in any of the club's eighteen holes was on hand. It was a splendid evening and the whole publicity stunt looked as if it would be a memorable success.

Of course I too, in the democratic spirit of the day, had been invited. By that time I was feeling quite at home with the people who frequented the club. Most of them were disgusting, but it was still possible to have a good time with them, as long as you had no expectations. I went over to the club in the evening and took up a casual position at the poolside with a drink in my hand as I chatted with Mr Wijkman about the summer. He expressed his deep and solemn regrets about the burglary and seemed genuinely concerned. He told me that he wanted me to continue working at the club; I could simply move out there for good, or at least for the rest of the year. But I let him know that I now had to get back to my writing.

'Fan*tas*tic,' exclaimed Wijkman, who had grown a bit tipsy, and he slapped me on the back. 'It's fan*tas*tic that you can just sit there and write like that. You know, I have always ad*mired* people who be*lieve* in something . . .' he went on in a familiar manner.

While Wijkman kept on spouting off about life in general and writing in particular, I tried to scan the sea of people with all the celebrities. No one attracted me much, and I assumed it was going to take a lot of drinks for the evening to shape up into anything at all.

Eventually Wijkman's wife and enormous daughter joined us as we stood there trying to converse by the pool. I had never met them before, but they were just as suntanned, wore just as much make-up, and had exactly the sort of low-cut necklines you might expect.

'Now Klas here,' said Wijkman, introducing me, 'he's somebody for the

18

two of you. He's actually an *au*thor. He's a *se*cretive devil, ha, ha, ha,' he chuckled and disappeared into the crowd.

The ladies seemed instantly intrigued and asked me what I had written. They hadn't heard of my books, but they thought they definitely sounded interesting. They promised to order them from their bookshop at once.

'And yet you have to mow grass all summer long just to survive . . .'

'I'm not complaining,' I said.

'I suppose it's rather nice to do different sorts of jobs. You meet a lot of people, don't you?' said the mother, tilting her head to one side.

'Oh yes. My next book is going to be set on a golf course.'

Both the mother and the daughter laughed, and then the mother was clearly struck with an idea, apropos earning money.

'Wait here a minute,' she said, and she made her way through the guests.

I followed her with my eyes and watched her corner a middle-aged man wearing jeans and a sweater. He looked slightly bohemian, like an advertising guy who made tons of money and only came out to the club to hit a bucket of balls now and then and enjoyed having a drink in the bar. Mrs Wijkman exchanged a few words with the man, who hiccuped, and then they both looked in my direction. He nodded affirmatively and came back with her.

'This is Torsten Franzén,' said Mrs Wijkman as they approached.

'How do you do?'

We shook hands, and Mrs Wijkman explained that she and Torsten had been friends since school and that he knew of me because he was the publisher of a well-known company, and he always had loads of ideas.

Torsten Franzén put his arm around my shoulders and led me away; on our way out to the periphery of the crowd we grabbed a couple more drinks.

'Everybody is so fucking stuck-up in this place,' said Franzén. 'Don't you agree?'

I nodded and lit a cigarette.

'You need a job?'

'Money, first and foremost,' I said.

'That's right,' said Franzén. 'You should never work for nothing, even if you're a writer. You see, I really like your work, and I've got an idea that might interest you.'

'Let's hear it.'

Franzén told me in confidence about the second planned celebration, meaning the hundredth anniversary of the publication of August Strindberg's novel *The Red Room*. Franzén's idea was that someone – such as myself, for instance – should sit down and rewrite the book, but set it in the present day. The book was still hot stuff, but adapted to the present it could be dynamite. It was Franzén's hope that a young talent with a bold style could do something brilliant with it.

'The idea does appeal to me,' I confessed.

'Don't be so damned reticent, like all the others,' said Franzén. 'Either you're hot for the idea or you're not, that's the question.'

'Let me have a few minutes to think it over. This isn't the best setting for conducting this sort of business.'

'OK,' said Franzén, giving me another slap on the back. 'I'll give you fifteen minutes, then I'm going to throw you in the pool. Maybe it'll help if you know that I'm prepared to put ten grand on the table as soon as you sign the contract.'

Franzén took aim for the nearest table with drinks and set off. I was now alone in a corner on the other side of the pool, and the club and all of life seemed far away. I smoked a cigarette as I pondered the proposal in silence. The idea was quite appealing, and I was actually looking for a new project. Rewriting *The Red Room* with a present-day setting was undeniably tempting; there were plenty of people to skewer, and besides, it was a genre that I hadn't attempted before.

Ten grand on the table certainly didn't make the offer any less attractive.

Before long I headed for a drinks table, downed a dry, sharp little shot in a single gulp and paused to see how it felt. It went down nicely, and then I made up my mind. I went looking for Franzén and said, 'You've got a deal!'

Franzén stuck out his mitt and looked relieved. The deal was made, and we drank a toast to *The Red Room*.

'This could be your breakthrough if you can pull it off,' he said.

'As long as no one else does it first.'

'You'd better get started tonight, for God's sake. We need the manuscript before Christmas.'

'It'll work out.'

'It *has* to work out. You're the perfect guy for the job.'

'Thanks.'

'Oh hell,' said Franzén in the middle of everything. 'Do you see who's just arrived over there?'

I scanned the crowd by the entrance but couldn't see any big celebrity worth noting.

'Who?' I asked.

'Sterner, Wilhelm Sterner. He's the one wearing the light-blue jacket, with that Chinese woman, or whatever she is. They're over there, talking to Wijkman.'

I had a hard time picking out the man in question, but I did see Wijkman, who was wagging his tail like some clever little puppy dog.

'Who the hell is he?' I asked, because I'd never heard of Wilhelm Sterner.

Franzén looked at me with both contempt and sympathy, and maybe a touch of forgiveness thrown in.

'If you're going to set *The Red Room* in the present, you've got to know who the hell Wilhelm Sterner is. He's a big shot, one of the biggest. He seldom shows up at these low-level functions,' said Franzén emphatically. 'Look carefully, because this could be the first and last time you'll ever see him.'

'So what's his game in life?'

'He's the man behind this golf course,' muttered my new publisher out of the side of his mouth, because he didn't want to let the behemoth out of his sight for even a second. 'He's the man behind almost all Swedish business today, let me tell you. Ten years ago he took over the Griffel Corporation. Pretty soon he'll be as big as Wallenberg. He trained with Wallenberg, actually. The old man himself taught him. You can tell. He's growing into the suit. And it's about time. The old man's suit. Wilhelm Sterner – he exists but he's invisible.'

'*Non videre sed esse*,' I interjected.

Franzén gave a start and fixed his eyes on me briefly.

'*Exactly*,' he said. 'That's right, my boy. To exist, but not be seen. That's his motto, and Wallenberg's. The government is about to fall apart, I'd bet a thousand kronor on it. Things are rough right now. But next year is another election. Then they'll start looking for new, fresh ministers. There aren't many competent fellows around, people who haven't already been compromised. But Sterner has never been part of any government.'

'So he's clean?'

'*Clean?*' exclaimed Franzén, once again making me feel like an idiot. 'Is there any heavyweight who's *clean*? But he knows how to tidy things up, Sterner can sure do *that*. He can *tidy things up* after himself. He recently drove two of his department heads to their death. One guy's ticker gave out, and the other one found a rope. And I don't suppose anyone remembers the 'Hogarth Affair' anymore. People dropped like flies; I don't really know much about it myself. But Sterner is a devil, my boy. A real wolf in sheep's clothing. Good-looking clothing.'

So I did my best to home in on this financial behemoth who trod on corpses, but I found that it was actually quite difficult to do. He was standing over near the entrance in his impeccable light-blue club blazer, beige trousers and brogues, his skin attractively tanned. His iniquity, of course, was of international scope.

He might have been pushing sixty, but that was only a guess. If I wasn't mistaken, he played tennis with other magnates to keep himself fit. He was a typical serve-expert who slammed away and ground people down, smashing his opponent to smithereens with his serves like Tanner, imbued with all the stubbornness and recalcitrance that every big shot absolutely has to have. He was certainly difficult to pin down, this man, with his aura of equal parts charm and malice. Stout and solid, as befits a magnate with a world presence, yet at the same time light and resilient. In general he was as unreal and vague as a Ken doll, merely emanating precision and an odourless physical clout. His jacket moved freely in space, floating like a Zeppelin without touching the ground.

All the small fry and their wives wanted at any cost to go over and touch the Evil One, to shake hands with the big shot. Before long Franzén was over there too, shuffling his feet. Like an American senator, Sterner very dutifully shook everyone's hand as his escort, the woman with the Asian appearance, looked on, nodding left and right and handing out smiles of recognition, both high and low. She had got hold of a martini and was elegantly sipping her drink in the behemoth's shadow. She seemed accustomed to the whole thing, looking exactly as blasé as was permitted; she gave the impression that the party was dreary, without appearing to be bored to death. She also looked as if she'd been a really hot number when she was young. By now she was middle-aged, but she had no need to regret a single day. If I'd had another half-hour, I could have been bewitched by her, but I didn't. Not this time.

The big finance king Wilhelm Sterner and his dazzling lady-friend thought it best to withdraw early that evening, and that showed good judgement because it turned out to be quite a damp party. I helped pull at least five fully dressed guests out of the pool. Including my new publisher, Franzén.

That was more or less the state of my situation in the early autumn of 1978. That was also approximately what I told Henry Morgan at the Zum Franziskaner, as a way of introducing myself. He actually heard a good deal more, but that doesn't really belong in this account.

The story of the burglary made a strong impression on Henry. He was deeply moved and even had tears in his eyes.

'You poor boy!' he exclaimed. 'You remind me so damned much of my brother,' he added with great emphasis. 'You both belong to an ill-starred lot. Are you a Pisces too?'

'Of course.'

'I might have guessed! I'm quite psychic, you know. I can sense things in my bones. I knew you were a Pisces.'

That's when the thirst set in. We had been talking for several hours, and we'd run out of cash, so there was nothing to do but leave.

'We can go up to my place,' said Henry. 'I'm sure I can find something to offer you.'

'I really ought to be getting home,' I said because I recognised the pattern. The plug had been pulled, and we could easily keep going all night long, even though it was a completely ordinary Thursday. No saints had either died or been born on that day, or if they had, it was in vain because it was never recorded on our calendar. Or maybe Luther had sacked those saints.

'I really ought to go home now. It's only Thursday, for God's sake.'

'No arguments,' said Henry. 'I haven't yet told you about your role, your role in the film.'

'All right then,' I said. 'But you'll have to make it brief.'

It turned out that Henry Morgan lived on Hornsgatan. Right across from Puckeln Hill, in one of those dilapidated old buildings, between the newly renovated façades that look so unreal, like sugar cubes topped with cream.

We went into the foyer, which was adorned with a hunting mural dated 1905.

'Wait here,' he said, standing in front of the lift as he took out a key ring. 'I live on the top floor, but I have to get us something to drink.'

23

Henry selected a key and opened a door in the foyer. Then he disappeared behind a curtain and silence descended. The light went out, and I fumbled my way to the switch. The silence continued for several more minutes. Finally I heard a couple of doors opening and shutting behind the curtain and out stepped Henry Morgan with a half-full bottle of Doctors whisky.

'It's nice when people trust you,' he muttered with satisfaction and opened the doors to the lift. 'Just don't ask any questions.'

The sixth floor consisted of a single flat with two entrances, and I assumed that it was a luxury residence, but Henry didn't want to show me much that night. Instead he shushed me by placing his index finger to his lips.

'We have to be quiet! People are sleeping here.'

'Do you have a family?'

'Everyone's asleep, everyone's asleep!' he whispered. 'We'll have to stay in the kitchen.'

We tiptoed out to a big, rectangular kitchen with both a gas and a wood stove, smudged old cupboards stretching up to the firmament, wood panelling on the walls and an impressive sideboard made of dark wood. Henry lit a couple of candles and took out some sturdy-looking glasses.

'Sit down, kid,' he hissed, pointing to a chair. 'Yes, by God, someone else lives here. It's a bit chilly, isn't it?'

'That's OK. We could have a little pick-me-up, couldn't we?'

Henry poured a couple of healthy pick-me-ups and started talking about the film role I was supposed to get. It turned out that he wasn't exactly the director but something more along the lines of an extra, though he had in fact once played a starring role. It was in *Calle Learns the Crawl*, a training film about swimming from 1953, when that fine swimmer, the ten-year-old Henry Morgan, made his debut on the big screen. He wondered if I remembered the film, but I didn't. I was too young.

So Henry Morgan was an extra, one of the best. All the extras were part of one big family, and I learned that it was almost always the same bunch who appeared in all the films made in Sweden. There were thick folders filled with photos and data on all the extras, and Henry was going to see to it that I ended up in just such a folder, because that was as important as being on the housing waiting list.

He claimed to have shot at wagons and fought and fenced and sat in speakeasies in historical films; he had stood in employment queues and taken buses and waved farewell from train platforms in modern films. The next time I saw any Swedish film made after '68 I ought to think of him, because it was highly likely that he was somewhere in the background.

The film now in question was a story from the early sixties, the first film by a new director.

'They need a skinny guy in a thin nappa leather tie and nylon shirt, and you'd be perfect for the part,' said Henry. 'I play the piano – I'm a pianist, after all – and we're supposed to be rehearsing a couple of tunes in the background, and then a chick and a guy start arguing in front of us. It's bound to be fun. Can you sing?'

'Not really.'

'That's OK. I can train you. You see, if we do this right, we'll get more offers. That's how it works in this business.'

I wasn't especially keen on becoming an extra, standing there with plastered-down hair wearing a nappa tie and nylon shirt and singing off-key. That wasn't at all what I had in mind. If I was going to be in a film, it had to be a proper role right from the start.

But I managed to voice only feeble objections. Henry Morgan was an enthusiast, and he had phenomenal powers of persuasion. Maybe the whisky also played a part. At any rate, some time in the wee hours of the morning – after we had sat there whispering our way through a dozen of our favourite films – I finally gave in and promised to go with Henry the very next day to visit the film company and get registered as a prospective extra.

'That's fucking great!' Henry bellowed.

'Shh!' I hissed. 'We don't want to wake up the others.'

'What others?' he said.

'The ones asleep in the flat.'

Henry Morgan looked a little puzzled at first, but then he started laughing, a booming, jovial laugh, the kind that rises up from the diaphragm the way only truly happy or drunk people can do it. He laughed for a long time, then wiped his eyes and pulled himself together.

'There's no one else here,' he said. 'I'm here all alone. I just thought it might be fun to drink quietly for a change.'

I was starting to think this man was a real idiot. It didn't help matters that he went over to the kitchen window, opened it and began shouting into the autumn night:

'Spinks! Spinks! Spinkssss!'

At that point I was convinced that the man truly was an idiot and that we'd have the police after us. Henry kept on yelling into the night:

'Spinks! Spinks! Spinkssss!'

It took a few minutes before a pair of eyes emerged from the depths of the night and onto the windowsill jumped a black cat. He was so black that his fur verged on blue. Henry picked up the big fellow in his arms. The cat instantly started purring and then meowed when he caught sight of me.

'This is Spinks, the black cat from Nowhere,' said Henry. 'He roams around on the roof, and I don't know who he belongs to. If a cat can really belong to anyone, that is.'

'Hi Spinks,' I said.

Spinks came over to say hello. Henry poured some cream into a dish, and the big fellow noisily lapped it up.

'He showed up here on the night when Spinks beat Ali, so there was never any doubt what to call him.'

Henry sat and prattled with Spinks for a bit while I attempted to find my way to the toilet. When I came back to the kitchen a faint light was coming from the other end of a narrow corridor connecting a number of rooms. Clinking tones came from there, crisp, light notes from a piano. I headed back towards the room and there, behind a pair of tall, mirrored doors, sat Henry Morgan, playing a shiny black grand piano. It filled half the room, while the rest – from what I could see on that occasion – contained several palms on pedestals and an old-fashioned sofa with tassels. It was a very tasteful room, filled with a special spiritual aura as Henry sat there at the piano, playing several ethereal chords. Spinks and I sat down on the sofa with the black tassels and sank into the atmosphere.

I must have dozed off, because I gave a start at the sound of a fiery dissonance and Henry's voice.

'Don't fall asleep now, kid. We have to practise tonight.'

'What's the rush?'

'There's no time to waste. Come over here and stand next to the piano!'

I shuffled over to the piano, but I was having a hard time staying on my feet. What I really wanted was to go to sleep, but Henry started tapping out an old hit tune to encourage me, so I cleared my throat and joined in on the refrain.

'Since you're a writer, you ought to be able to write some lyrics for me,' said Henry. 'I've tried with Leo, but he's too serious. I'll bet you're different. We could become a new variety team, writing couplets. You really ought to try everything in life.'

'One thing at a time,' I said.

'Have you heard "The Drop Drips" by Alice Babs and her daughter? We'll start with that. A complicated round. The drop drips and the drip dropped,' he began singing. 'When I get to the "p" in "the drop", that's when you come in. Get it?'

'Yes, I get it,' I said. 'But it's such a damned ridiculous tune,' I objected. 'Couldn't we try something more sedate right now, in the middle of the night?'

'Who cares what time it is. Now, let's go . . . The drop drips and the drip dropped . . . hang on a minute . . . The drip dropped. Let's take it from the top . . .'

I took a deep breath on 'drips' and started singing, even though it was one of the worst songs I'd ever heard. Besides, it wasn't easy to sing something that was almost hopelessly difficult at three in the morning after a lot of beer and whisky. But Henry was bull-headed and, as I mentioned, he possessed phenomenal powers of persuasion.

By five in the morning on a perfectly ordinary Friday, we were actually able to sing 'The Drop Drips and the Drip Dropped' almost as well as Babs and her daughter. Henry sat there revelling in the results, and with good reason. He was an excellent teacher.

'OK, that's enough for today,' he said at last. 'You're looking a bit peaky.'

'That doesn't even come close to what I am.'

'You can crash here if you like.'

'I could sleep anywhere.'

Henry showed me to a room at the other end of the long corridor, which was as dark as a passageway to Hell. He threw open the door and the only thing I really took in was a big bed, onto which I collapsed full-length without even taking off my shoes.

'There's just one thing you should know,' said Henry.

'What's that?'

'That's Göring's old bed you're lying on. Good night.'

On a perfectly ordinary Friday in early September I woke up around eleven a.m., feeling sick and not really sure where I was. Slowly my consciousness started functioning again, blowing life into my memories of the night before, and I scanned the room with bleary eyes until I located myself in the bed that had supposedly once belonged to Göring.

It was a sunny day, and the room faced the courtyard to the east; the sun blasted down on the galvanised roof, blinding me. And in fact, it was rather a pleasant room with light-coloured wallpaper and thin curtains, a tile stove, a mahogany bureau, several wardrobes, a couple of copperplate engravings depicting scenes from Shakespeare's plays and a Persian rug. The bed that was supposedly Göring's had an enormous bedstead with knobs carved from walnut. Against all the odds I'd slept quite well in that bed.

I got up, feeling cold even though I'd slept in my clothes and had wrapped myself up in the coverlet. Out in the kitchen Henry was in the midst of a substantial breakfast of eggs, bacon and fried potatoes. The mere smell made me feel instantly sick, but I was actually very hungry. I felt as if I were on board a ship.

'Morning,' said Henry. 'Did you sleep well?'

'Like the dead.'

'There's a Réveil waiting for you,' he said, pointing to a big whisky glass containing a pale, slimy liquid.

'What is it?'

'A Réveil? It's an eggnog, an eye-opener, a hair-of-the-dog, plain and simple.'

I sniffed at the drink and immediately wanted to know what was in it, because I didn't trust the cook.

'An egg yolk, grenadine, a dash of cognac, nutmeg and milk,' said Henry, rattling off the five ingredients as he held up one finger after another. 'It's extremely nourishing and fortifying; it'll revive the old spirits.'

After breathing deeply I took a swallow, and the drink was actually good, even though I've never put much store in hair-of-the-dog concoctions; they've always seemed a bit *too* depraved for my taste. But Henry refused to give me any breakfast until I downed the entire Réveil, so it was just as well to pick up the glass and empty it. And it did the trick. After the substantial breakfast, my old spirits actually were fully revived, and it was a glorious sunny day. I felt like a sultan.

'You'll have to tell me the story about Göring's old bed sometime,' I said later, because I couldn't get it out of my mind.

'I'll do that,' said Henry. 'But not right now. I have to shave and make a good job of it. We need to go over to see the film people and get your picture taken. You're not backing out, are you?'

'Backing out? Me? Never!'

'Good. Go ahead and take a look round the place while I shave. You should be glad your whiskers don't grow as fast as mine do.'

I did as Henry said and took a tour of the flat. It really surprised me. I couldn't figure this man out. Whenever you meet a stranger, you always try to put labels on him, but in Henry's case none of the labels fit. His flat alone made it a hopeless endeavour.

It was a very old double luxury flat, cold and gloomy. From the big hallway a long corridor led to four rooms in a row. There were two bedrooms, a library and a living room with a fireplace. At one end of the corridor was the room with the grand piano, and at the other end the bedroom with Göring's old bed. The corridor also gave access to a separate section of the flat, but I was stopped by a locked door.

After my tour I went back to the kitchen and washed the dishes; it was the only thing I felt like doing. Washing dishes is a pleasant activity if you put your heart and soul into it. Then it serves the same function that I imagine is served by meditation. Afterwards you feel as clean and sparkling as the china.

Henry came back after shaving – he had done a good job of it – and putting on proper clothes. He was wearing a new, pinstriped blue shirt, a burgundy tie and pullover, a houndstooth jacket with leather patches on the elbows, brown trousers and walking shoes.

'So, shall we pop over there?' he said. 'I've already given them a ring. It's a go.'

'OK,' I said.

'Thanks for washing up, by the way.'

'No problem. I enjoy washing dishes.'

'Good, I'll remember that.'

We strolled across the locks at Slussen to Gamla Stan where the small film company had their offices. Henry waltzed inside without ringing the doorbell, and people greeted him cheerfully, exactly as if he were a real star. I was introduced to an efficient woman in early middle-age; her name was

Lisa and she was in charge of production. She gave me a long, slow look, as if in her mind she were already taking off my clothes and dressing me in uncomfortable Terylene trousers, a nylon shirt and a leather tie.

'I've seen you somewhere,' she said. 'Have you been in a film before?'

'I don't believe so,' I said.

'What's your name?'

I told her my name, and her face lit up like a sun. I thought that maybe she'd read one of my books.

'That's it!' she said. 'You were in *Remorse Comes Gently*, right?'

'No,' I said with a sigh. 'I've never been in a film.'

Henry gave me a furious look, because that was not a good thing to harp on about.

'You might still be good,' said Lisa after a long pause. 'Can you sing?'

'Yes, yes, of course he can,' Henry chimed in, and suddenly he was Henry *the manager*. 'His voice is perfect for the part. He's got fantastic material. We only practised for a few minutes, and it fit him like a glove.'

'OK, then let's take a few pictures,' said Lisa, and she took a few shots with a Polaroid camera. After she wrote down my name, social security number and address it was time to make our exit.

'Don't worry about all that,' said Henry out on the street. 'You have to learn to handle those kinds of people the right way. You can't be shy or hesitant; you have to assume a confident manner. It's the same in all walks of life.'

'I see,' I said. 'OK, I get it.'

'Now we'll go over to Kristina for some coffee.'

We ordered a pot of coffee at the Café Kristina on Västerlånggatan and lit our first cigarettes of the day. I instantly felt sick again. My heart began pounding in my chest and I stubbed out the cigarette. Henry was being unusually quiet. Without saying a single word he meditatively smoked two cigarettes in a row while I browsed through the selection on the jukebox across from our table.

Henry was looking mournful. He surveyed the room, lit another Pall Mall, and ran his hand over his newly shaven face. His mood could change from white to black in no time. Two nostalgic lines of a song could make him bitter and sentimental at the same time, just as he was finishing telling a funny story.

He gave me a long look as I lit another cigarette and thought about going home. I could always hope for something pleasant and uplifting in the post. Maybe a payment from my publisher Franzén, or new decisions from the insurance company.

'How'd you like to move in with me?' Henry asked abruptly.

I was surprised and didn't know what to say.

'We . . . we don't really know each other very well,' I said.

'All the better,' he said. 'But for God's sake, I'm psychic. I think I know exactly what you're like. You're like my brother Leo, except without his faults.'

'And what is he like?'

'No rhetoric now. I'm serious. There's plenty of room for you up there. You can work in the library and sleep in Göring's old bed. We don't need to get in each other's way.'

I willingly admitted that I was tired of my own flat, and that it had also been stripped of anything of value. I could easily move everything over in a cab.

'Well, I haven't got much to lose,' I said.

'Neither do I,' said Henry. 'And besides, it'll be cheaper if we join forces. I assume that neither of us is especially well-off.'

'You're right about that.'

'So? You should never hesitate for long when it comes to making important decisions. I often make snap decisions. And then whatever will be, will be. It's been up and down. But I'm still alive, even though I'm feeling a bit lonely.'

'What about your brother Leo? Doesn't he live with you?'

'That can always be worked out. He's in the States right now, in New York. I got a postcard the other day. He won't be back for a long time.'

'What the hell,' I said. 'Let's try it.'

'It's a deal then.'

Henry stretched his hand across the table. The deal was done. I would go home immediately, pack up the few belongings that the thieves had left me out of sheer humanity, have my post forwarded, and try to find a trustworthy person to sublet the place. It could all be arranged in an afternoon.

And it was. One of Errol Hansen's respectable friends from the Danish embassy needed a little pied-à-terre in a central location, and so the problem was solved.

In the middle of my flat there now stood two large suitcases containing my clothes, next to two typewriters and a couple of boxes of books and papers and items of purely sentimental value: a fox skull that I'd found in the woods, a crab shell I got from some fishermen in the Lofoten Islands, several rocks, and an ashtray in the shape of a gaping satyr. You flicked the ashes into his mouth.

Autumn sunlight poured through the dirty windows, turning the whole room white, and I silently took a few drags on an unfiltered Camel. The smoke circled around in thin wisps like cirrus clouds high overhead.

I was feeling melancholy. The flat seemed so lugubrious in the state it was in. I had endured such genuine anguish in this space, and now I was going through some kind of separation anxiety. I had loafed around and worked here, loved and hated in this place, and I'd become part of the atmosphere. I had actually written my best lines in this place. Now a few stray ideas and characters flitted across the bare floor like fleeing phantoms. The years became compressed into a few details, a couple of isolated incidents. I was melancholy. A whole new life was about to start, and I had no idea where it might take me. No doubt that was fortunate.

The lift doors slammed and Henry Morgan came tramping through the door of the flat.

'Frey's Removal Service, good afternoon,' he said, shoving a peaked cap back from his forehead.

'What kind of hat is that?'

'It's a genuine mover's hat. Is this all?'

'It's all I've got left. Everything I have to my name.'

Henry stared at the modest pile of suitcases and boxes, and the two typewriters in the middle of the room. He shook his head.

'Whoever did this was awfully thorough.'

'It's fucking Dylan's fault, the whole thing.'

'Don't be so down about it, my boy. You're going to start over in whole new digs. Soon you'll get the insurance money and you can buy all new things. We can go over to the shops in Söder and buy back every single item.'

'I don't want all that shit back,' I said. 'I'm starting a new life now.'

'So be it. Let's get going.'

We carried everything out to the landing, into the lift, and over to the Volkswagen van that Henry had borrowed from the Furniture Man shop. It didn't take more than an hour. A new life was ready to begin.

Henry had obviously thought through all the details. I would have two rooms at my disposal, to do with more or less as I pleased. The bedroom with Göring's old bed and the library. I carried my two typewriters into the library, noting that there was reading material of the highest order for several years to come. Henry lugged my suitcases into the bedroom. He had cleaned out the wardrobes and scrubbed them with soap. It almost smelled like spring.

'So what do you think?' he asked.

I sat down on the window-seat and looked out. The arrangement suited me perfectly.

'This is better than I've ever had it before,' I said.

'It's going to get cold; you need to be prepared for that. We have to go out and get wood and keep the stoves going even in October. The fuses in the cellar blow out if you switch on even one radiator.'

We took a tour of the flat, and Henry told me about his grandfather, because this place had once been his. He'd been dead for ten years now. His name was Morgonstjärna and he was of noble blood. Today the lineage was dying out. There was a seal in the House of Knights with the family crest on it, but little else was left. Grandfather Morgonstjärna had only one son, Henry's father, who was also deceased. The only remaining family members were Henry, his mother Greta and his brother Leo. But their name was Morgan.

'Have you ever heard of the Jazz Baron?' asked Henry as we went into the billiard room.

'The Jazz Baron?' I repeated, and it did sound somewhat familiar.

'That was my father,' said Henry. 'His name was Morgonstjärna, of course, but he was a pianist, a jazz pianist. He was very well known. When he started playing properly, he couldn't keep the name Morgonstjärna because it didn't fit in in those circles. He needed a name that sounded a bit more American, so he changed it to Morgan. That was back during the war, I think. Grandmother was sick with rage, and she broke off all contact with my father. He died when Leo and I were little. Grandmother died not long afterwards. This was once her room. Grandfather turned it into a billiard room straight after her death.'

Henry's paternal grandfather had always been a real dandy, a *bon vivant*. The fact that he eventually married didn't seem to make much difference. This was evident from the furniture; there was something aristocratic and

33

coquettish about it all. The library was filled with marvellous books, heavy, beautifully bound volumes that were in pristine condition. There was an oppressive, smoke-permeated atmosphere in that particular room. I immediately felt at home.

The living room was like some sort of museum. Persian rugs on the parquet floor with sedate and ingenious patterns. A Chippendale arrangement consisting of a sofa and two armchairs made of rattan and mahogany. They had supposedly once belonged to Ernst Rolf. Like the variety star, Morgonstjärna had had a penchant for gaming and gambling, and one night back in the merry thirties they were playing poker together. Rolf lost and was forced to give up a pawn ticket to pay off his debts. When Morgonstjärna redeemed the pawn ticket for a very small sum, he found himself in possession of some tip-top Chippendale furniture; he'd made a good deal.

There were also a number of small oak and mahogany tables, some with tops made of a yellowish marble from Africa, called *giallo antico*, according to Henry. And on the tables stood scores of small plaster busts and porcelain statues, as well as rocks and unknown minerals that the dandy had collected during his feverish travels around the globe.

He was a globetrotter, you see, a cosmopolitan with weighty dignity, and his travelling trunks up in the attic were covered with decals from every little backwater in the world, any place that could offer a decent bar and a British country club. In reality he was the permanent secretary for the society of the WWW – Well-travelled, Well-read, Well-heeled – a small, jocular club of older, cultivated gentlemen who played billiards and cards and drank whisky.

'I'm especially proud of this television,' said Henry, patting an unwieldy set with doors that could be closed in front. 'Grandfather was one of the very first to have a TV. We would make a pilgrimage over here on Saturday nights to witness the miracle. He never got a new one. It still works perfectly, though only on the state channel, One. But that doesn't matter. I've never been interested in the other channels.'

The rest of the flat was decorated in the same heavy, dull, dark style in which turn-of-the-century wallpaper, Biedermeier chairs, functional lamps made of stainless steel, Persian rugs and huge pieces of furniture made of walnut and rattan and leather swallowed up the sunlight coming through the windows. Anyone who lived here needed no predisposition to depression. In a mere minute you could dash from room to room and draw the thick curtains to create your own night-time at any hour of the day, any season of the year. Henry said that it sometimes made him feel anxious.

'Night exists in this flat as a perpetual possibility,' he said. 'All you have to do is draw the curtains and pretend, that's all that's required.'

I remember that he sounded uneasy, uncomfortable.

Henry mostly made use of his bedroom and the Studio, which was the name of the room with the grand piano. It was an old Malmsjö piano, and the sound was supposedly as fine as that of a Bösendorfer Imperial, or so he assured me. Maybe it was the acoustics that did it. As I mentioned, there was nothing more in there than a couple of pedestals with palms and a sofa with black tassels. The sound could roll around as it pleased.

I went back to my bedroom and started hanging my clothes in the wardrobe. I made up Göring's old bed with my own linens and hung up a couple of photographs of myself and my family. I realised that I needed to phone my family and tell them that I had moved.

The dawn was gentle and indulgent; it rose up over the galvanised roof, and Henry had called in Spinks, who was now sitting on his knee and purring.

'My God,' said Henry, 'what a match. There's going to be a lot of talk from Willis now. He's met Ali. He went with the club and watched Ali train in the summer. He has his autograph on a shirt in his office. What a lot of harping there's going to be at the Europa after this.'

Henry was utterly elated after the Match. It was now mid-September, and we'd gone to the Royal Tennis Hall to watch the televised transmission of the Ali vs Spinks fight. The master had put Spinks, the title-holder, in his place, making use of all the rules of the game. He led off with a jab, kept him at a distance, and picked up point after point the way a magician brings in the applause. There was no shuffling, no rope-a-dope, just pure boxing, a show without tricks. The only secret was practice and expertise.

I was already completely exhausted from all the preliminary matches and we'd had a couple of beers before the main event, and now, at dawn after the Match, fatigue had given way to sheer desperation. But Henry didn't seem ever to have heard of exhaustion; he just kept talking and talking.

'Did you see his left hook? I mean, did you really *see* it? I didn't. It was just too *fast*, pure and simple. It's unbelievable that Spinks could even stay on his feet!'

'No, I didn't see the left hook,' I said. 'But pretty soon I'm going to be seeing stars.'

'There's going to be a lunar eclipse tonight,' said Henry. 'That's what the Cigar Seller said, at any rate. We'll have to check it out.'

'Of course we will. But first I need to get some sleep.'

So on the night after the Match there was a lunar eclipse. When it was properly dark we went up to the attic. It was a big attic with a high ceiling and separate storerooms for each flat. Henry had his own sawhorse in his attic area where we could saw wood.

A ladder led up to a hatch in the roof, and we climbed up in the light of a torch. Henry opened the hatch and clambered out onto the roof.

'Careful now, my boy,' he urged me.

'Don't worry, I'm scared of heights.'

'All writers seem to be. My brother, Leo, gets dizzy just looking at a globe. It's true! He's ready to pass out at any moment.'

We climbed up onto the roof and looked at the moon. It seemed eerie and terribly huge. As we sat up there on the roof, shivering, the moon disappeared completely behind the earth's shadow. Only a faint yellowish-red outline remained, and it was easy to imagine how that sort of natural phenomenon could drive people insane in the past.

'In the past?!' exclaimed Henry. 'Isn't it driving you insane right now?'

'Not entirely,' I said.

'I think it's eerie, damned repulsive,' said Henry, and he began howling when the eclipse was at its worst.

Henry howled long and loud, just like a real moon-lunatic would sound, while I tried to shush him, but without success. After a while Spinks came padding over to us, peering at Henry in bewilderment and taking several careful steps to the side.

But it's true, at any rate, that a lunar eclipse can make anyone a bit anxious. It seems so final and monumental.

———————

The autumn got off to a flying start in mid-September, but I was having a hard time getting myself going. I was having big initial problems with the pastiche of *The Red Room*, and I was already feeling a bit stressed. Franzén, the publisher, rang up now and then to give me a push. True to his word, he had plunked down ten grand on the table, so at least I had money to live on for some time to come.

Henry did everything in his power to make me feel at home. He kept to his part of the flat most of the day, walking around in dirty overalls and whistling. He was good at whistling in overalls, and that's why he wore them, or so he claimed. In reality that turned out not to be true at all, but everything in its proper time. More about Henry's overalls later.

I tried to install myself in the old dandy's library, but I couldn't seem to settle down properly. Henry and I were consciously trying to keep the world at a distance, to lock ourselves in – he had a very clear vision of the two of us as a couple of creative dynamos who needed all manner of peace and quiet in order to generate the vital Art – but the doors were too thin.

One day in September the police decided to storm the buildings occupied by squatters in the Mullvaden district, and since I had friends there, I went over to watch.

The police had blocked off Krukmakargatan, which runs the length of the Mullvaden district, and there were cops in every doorway, talking to people who loved cops or hated cops or just wanted to talk.

Towards evening people began surging forward en masse, pushing against the police barrier. It turned into a real circus. Fire-eaters and troubadours were in charge of the entertainment, reporters trotted about interviewing surly constables and outraged sympathisers collected rubbish and lit a fire. The fire department and mounted police were instantly on the spot, and all of a sudden the whole neighbourhood seemed to be invaded by scores of imitators from *King of the Royal Mounted*. Horses trampled their way through the seated crowds and hysteria began to spread.

As I mentioned, it was a chilly evening; autumn had really taken hold. I went up to the flat to have some soup and warm up before the battles later that night. Henry was home, staring at the old TV set. He was watching a programme about Jean-Paul Sartre, and in a number of scenes they showed the old existentialist at demonstrations. Henry started bragging about Paris in '68, when he personally saw Sartre on the street. He had even asked the Oracle a question.

'Don't you want to come over to Mullvaden instead?' I asked him.

'Are they still trying to clear them out?'

'It's a damn circus with tons of cops and fakirs. Don't you want to come along?'

'I've had enough of cops.'

'Are you a *coward*?'

'A *coward*? *Me*?'

'That's what it seems like,' I said and went out to the hall to bundle up in a couple of layers of warm clothes. 'It's obvious that we have to support the occupation,' I shouted towards the sitting room where Henry was slouched in front of Sartre.

'You go ahead and take care of the practical side; I'll look out for the theoretical,' he muttered sullenly, because he didn't like being accused of cowardice. Though he'd never be much of a theorist.

So I went back to the Mullvaden district just as *King of the Royal Mounted* launched a raid on the peacefully seated crowds, and a girl I knew had a tooth kicked out by an agitated gelding. A horse's hoof smashed right through the guitar belonging to a troubadour, who went totally berserk and started jabbing at the horse's arse with the splinters that remained of his dear old Goya guitar. The crowd surged across the street, bodies moving between the legs of the horses, police whips cracking, batons flailing. It was starting to look like an actual riot. Flashbulbs went off on all the cameras. The reporters were licking their lips.

After several minor skirmishes, the situation returned to the status quo. The police went back to their positions, and the demonstrators sat still. The whole neighbourhood reeked of horse droppings.

And it went on like that, hour after hour, in the long waiting period before the final confrontation, which didn't happen until much later. In the meantime, the Opposition racked up one point after another. The police could do nothing but stay back. From a moral point of view, the passive resistance was superior.

I couldn't help thinking about *The Red Room*. Olle Montanus was inside one of those occupied buildings, shivering. He was going to live on in my version of *The Red Room*, or maybe it would be a son, a hunched little lad who is the spitting image of his father. He arrives in the capital from the country to attend his father's funeral. My pastiche of *The Red Room* was going to start where Strindberg's novel ended. It would be 1978–79, and Olle's boy Kalle Montanus would be lounging inside an occupied flat in the Mullvaden district. That was brilliant! He would be sleeping soundly, that boy, sleeping and dreaming about a better world and not worrying about a thing, until a pimply provincial imbecile from his own home town came storming through the door to wake the idler lying on the sofa. They would recognise each other and start arguing about an old loan. That's how it would start.

'Tea with rum,' said someone behind me, giving me a poke in the back. My musings about *The Red Room* were abruptly cut off, and I turned around to see Henry in full battle attire. 'Tea with rum,' he said again, and handed me a thermos cup of the aromatic drink.

'So you came after all!'

'Sartre is so heavy. He's too damned heavy in the long run. I think I'm actually more the practical type.'

We had been diligently practising 'The Drop Drips' and several other popular tunes, and we knew our repertoire almost too well. It sounded too professional, not amateurish enough, and Henry feared that we'd deliberately have to mess things up a bit in order to sound truly authentic.

The day had now arrived for our part in the film. Following concise instructions from Lisa at the film company, we took the train up to Söderhamn one morning, arriving around noon.

According to Henry, the stars were in our favour. He had read in his horoscope that something great and overwhelming was going to happen that very day. 'Be careful, because you're playing with powerful forces.' That's what it said, and Henry had interpreted it as unequivocally in his favour.

A whole new world opened to me: the frantic and glamorous world of film. Henry was a stickler for etiquette, and he saw to it that we were received in a manner befitting the real giants. True to form, he was wearing clothes that made him fit in perfectly with his role, *à la naturelle*, so to speak. The props department found nothing to add or remove or polish up with regard to his appearance. To top it all off, he had recently gone to the barber and had his hair cut in that boyish style with a parting, which he had sported ever since the early fifties.

Things were much worse for me. Henry cheerfully left me in the hands of the make-up artist, but first he took her aside and had a minor quarrel with her.

'But I *can't*. You know that,' she kept repeating, while Henry kept insisting and nagging at her until finally she gave in and promised him something. I could only guess what it might be. They had known each other for years.

The make-up artist was naturally a bit annoyed when she returned to lowly me and my hair. In a matter of minutes she managed to cut my hair down to the very beginning of the sixties, before the Beatles got rich and hairdressers got poor.

After this assault on my head, I had to put on the disgusting grey Tery-lene trousers, the uncomfortable nylon shirt and string vest, the nappa tie and the pointy shoes that I had dreaded right from the start. But if you're in a film, that's what you do. Some actors starve themselves for weeks to play a lean character. Some directors torture their actors, alternately criti-cising them and flattering them to achieve just the right effect. A little hard-ship was all part of the job. Movie stars didn't just sit in directors' chairs with their names printed in gold on the back, drinking champagne. Garbo was probably the only one who slipped out of a cab, perfectly dressed and made-up just before the clapperboard signalled the start of a scene. At least that's what Birger at the Furniture Man shop claimed, and he was a Garbo aficionado. But more about that later.

'Sharp!' said Henry about my new look. 'You're punk. Ask them if you can keep those duds. You look really with it.'

Henry moved around the studio as if he'd never done anything else, conversing with the film-makers, the lighting crew, the technicians, and all the other extras, whose family he had belonged to for so many years. Everyone respected him, and they laughed and nodded their heads as soon as he approached.

'So here's Klasa, my new discovery. A real natural talent,' he said, pushing me in front of the director, whose name was Gordon and who proved to be disappointing. He didn't match my expectations at all. I've always imagined directors as egocentric demons who whip and abuse their co-workers. But this Gordon was a totally different type, and presumably of the new school. Gordon padded around whispering, and he seemed ashamed of the fact that it was his insignificant self who happened to be in charge of the whole show. He had a hesitant, awkward and excessively sweaty handshake, and he thought I would be perfect.

'You, you, you . . . look exactly like one of my childhood friends,' he said. 'They, this . . . this film is, in a way, damned personal, you know. I need to get, get hold of this piece of myself,' he went on until someone else demanded his attention.

Henry seemed to share my opinion of Gordon, but we didn't let on and roamed about the old auditorium, checking out the girls. This particular scene was supposed to depict preparations for a school dance, with the atmos-phere a bit agitated and nervous. Nervousness and anticipation were precisely the words for the mood that Gordon was spreading around him. No one knew anything, and if Lisa hadn't been the type of person she was, the film would undoubtedly never have been made.

After nearly four hours of waiting and whispering, it was time for the first take. The stars, professionals who were the box office draw, were not in the least bit annoyed. They were experienced actors who knew that making a film means waiting. One of my favourite actors was playing the principal of the school. He emerged from his dressing room with great dignity. Everybody fell silent in his presence and lowered their eyes. And even though he was downright repulsive in his sovereignty, people flocked to him as if to a dangerous precipice that they simply couldn't resist peering over.

Gordon whispered a few instructions, moving everyone into the proper groupings, and Henry and I took our places on the stage where we were supposed to pretend to practise 'The Drop Drips' and other obsolete hits.

The first take was a disaster. Henry and I performed perfectly, but the dress of the young leading actress flipped up in the back. Gordon thought it was actually a damn fine effect, but the skirt was a bit crooked. After about five more takes of this scene, the dress finally sat the way it should.

'I think it's a wrap, by God,' said Gordon, and so the whole thing was over.

I hadn't even really got into the mood yet. We'd been practising for weeks, after all, and then the scene took only a paltry few minutes.

'So that's the life of an extra,' said Henry. 'Now we'll go and pick up our wages.'

We collected our wages from a harried factotum and discovered that our modest contribution added up to a couple of thousand kronor.

'And half the scene will end up getting cut. In the best case we'll end up flickering past like a couple of phantoms in the background. But that's how it is. You have to be humble if you're an extra. You're there, but you're invisible.'

'*Non videre sed esse,*' I said.

Henry gave a start and looked at me with incomprehension. Then he launched into a monologue about the innermost being of an extra, which was something incredibly remarkable. It's often some extra or a stupid little minor role that you remember most from a film. There was something magnificent about that, in Henry's opinion, and he wondered if he ever ought to accept a real role. He was truly thriving in the background. It was there that he could create music so beautiful that it was destructive.

43

At the time I didn't understand him, but it could be that I understand him better today, much later. Henry was so aggrieved about various things that he tried to pretend he didn't care in the least. Life was a shrug of the shoulders, a click of the heels. But that was undoubtedly just a defiant reaction. In reality he was so indignant that he could hardly stand it, and you can only be truly indignant when you care deeply about something. To endure this heavy burden of moral responsibility, he had to pretend that he had no sense of responsibility at all. Every time someone demanded something from him, he would grow frightened and feel himself under fire. He promptly went on the defensive. He wanted to exist but not be seen.

I didn't understand him at all as we sat in the dressing room, smoking cigarettes from his fancy case. He cleaned his fingernails with the little pen-knife from the burgundy leather case which he always carried with him. I didn't understand him, and I was in a bit of a daze. Mostly I wanted to know what he thought of my debut.

'You were good, Klasa,' said Henry as he finished his manicure. 'You were fucking great.'

'Thanks,' I said in a maudlin tone. 'I could never have done it without you.'

'You know what,' said Henry, 'I'm going to go over to see Karin for a while.'

'Who's Karin?'

'The make-up artist. We've got some things we need to talk about. I'll meet you down at the station at 2:15 a.m. That's when the train leaves for home.'

Henry disappeared into the hubbub with Karin, and I said goodbye to the film crew, giving them my thanks. The stage manager said they would let me know if anything else came up for me. That sounded promising, and just as I was about to leave, I ran into the Star and got what felt like an electric shock. He was charged with unreality, unnatural power, imbued with what people call charisma, like a magnetist or an influential magnate who exists but isn't seen. I had grown up with that star on TV, but he now seemed only half as tall as he ought to be. In spite of his modest height, his spiritual stature was fully on a par with Caesar's, if we're to believe the historians. I myself felt as if I were standing at the very pinnacle of my life. This was the sort of thing that my children would get sick of hearing about. Too bad I was too shy to ask for his autograph.

Söderhamn was no metropolis, except for the motorbike riders. There was a biting wind that cut right through me, and I was feeling rather downhearted. I tried to warm up by thinking about the pillaging the Russians had done – that was all that I knew about this coastal town in Norrland – and about all the fires they had set here in the eighteenth century. The place must have been as dazzlingly beautiful back then as it was grey and devoid of charm today. I went inside the central train station, sank down onto a bench, smoked a cigarette, and read the evening paper. I realised that I hated Söderhamn.

Henry arrived punctually, a few minutes before the train's departure, and we were soon on our way home. Henry wasn't feeling particularly upbeat either. Maybe it was the anticlimax that had brought both of us down. We'd been preparing for this part, charging ourselves up to high voltage, and now we'd been discharged and paid off. It felt like a New Year's Day when you can't really remember the clock striking twelve or any of your new resolutions.

Henry stared out the window, looking at the dreary, dimly lit landscape, not saying a word.

'So what happened with Karin?' I asked.

'We talked. Just talked.'

'Did you screw her?'

'No, dammit,' said Henry. 'I've never screwed Karin.'

He didn't sound especially thrilled about this, as if it were something that he would like to do but never had.

The conductor clipped our tickets, and I tried to sleep but without success. Henry was still silent and dejected, staring out at the insipid landscape. He didn't say a word until Gävle.

'I had such a strange feeling,' he said in a low voice, almost to himself. 'All those people, dressed in the clothes from the past. It was as if I had no distance from all that. It felt like a dream. I was part of that era, playing in a school band and going to those sorts of dances. It was almost eerie, like a dream.'

Eighteen miles or so south of Gävle Henry said, still as if to himself, 'I have to see Maud again. I have to see Maud.' And then, speaking straight out, in a loud, resounding voice, with a remote look in his eyes for God, Satan, me and the whole world, he said:

'That's what my horoscope meant! I have to go and see Maud.'

The neighbourhood was nicely situated between Mariakyrka church, with its magnificent collection of graves – where Lasse Lucidor 'the Unfortunate', Stagnelius and Evert Taube distinguished themselves as pilgrimage destinations – and the now redeveloped and respectable square, Mariatorget. The buildings were marked by a worn beauty, although they were merely counterparts to those at Puckeln in Söder, newly renovated eighteenth-century structures infested with potters, gallery owners and an endless number of troubadours, at least according to the guy by the name of Henry Morgan.

Small enterprises were flourishing once again. From the corner of Bellmansgatan it was possible to count no fewer than a dozen small businesses that might not be considered particularly solid, but there was life in them all the same. There was the Primal Café in the old apothecary shop, a haberdashery, a framing shop, a cigar seller, a second-hand bookshop, a stamp collectors' shop, a greengrocer, along with a number of galleries and second-hand shops selling clothing and, of course, the Furniture Man.

The doorbell rang and the sound cut right through my breakfast. It was my fifth breakfast all alone. I hadn't heard a peep from Henry since the night we came back from filming in Söderhamn. He had come home, taken a shower, made a phone call and then left. That was the meaning of his horoscope. He was going to be away for a few days.

Now I went out to open the door, and on the landing stood a delivery boy from Egon's Laundry, holding a package of shirts and linens wrapped in brown paper.

'Is that for here?' I asked.

'Morgan, ten shirts and four sheets, pillowcases and towels. That's what it says on the note. A hundred and twelve *riksdaler*, please,' said the delivery boy.

'All right,' I said with a sigh, and went to get the money.

'Do you have anything for collection?' asked the delivery boy.

'Collection?' I said. 'Oh, I see. I don't know. I'll check.'

Then we exchanged dirty laundry for clean and said thanks and goodbye. I put Henry's clean shirts on his bed, thinking it was rather pretentious of him to be sending out his laundry, but that was his business. Though I had to pay for it. All the same, it made me feel a little better because I took it as a sign that he was still alive.

Otherwise there wasn't much to feel good about just then, except for the absolute decline and total collapse of the bourgeois coalition government, just as my crafty publisher, Franzén, had predicted six months earlier at the country club. The flat felt a bit empty and gloomy when Henry decided to take off, and I forced myself to start working properly and extremely systematically on my pastiche of *The Red Room*. At any rate, I turned out about a dozen pages that looked as if they might hold up.

I was attempting to get to know the others in the building, and had already succeeded quite well with the Cigar Seller. He was a very correct gentleman in late middle-age, always dressed in a suit with a bow-tie, and he was well-informed about current events and what went on in the neighbourhood. He served as my informant as long as my host was away.

The Cigar Seller also had a very interesting assistant helping out in his shop. She was a *femme fatale*, about thirty-five, who was at least as elegant as he. She wore a long dress, and her face was heavily plastered with pancake make-up, mascara and fiery red lipstick. As far as I knew, she had never spoken to a single customer, and no one was sure whether it was even permissible to speak to her. At any rate, she would listen to what was said in the shop and then dash into the storeroom, quick as lightning, if something was wanted. She would purse her lips if you looked unhappy. No doubt her only real task was to stand there looking generally pretty. Perhaps she was also supposed to lead the customers' thoughts to the substantial selection of porn magazines and erotica – everything from *The Marquis* to *Love 1*, and so on – which the Cigar Seller had for sale. So there were plenty of opportune reasons for boycotting the shop, provided you had no sense of curiosity or any interest in gossip. Unfortunately, I've never been that sort of person.

Naturally the Cigar Seller kept me informed of everything of importance going on in the neighbourhood.

'I can certainly see,' he said to me confidentially as he leaned across the counter, 'that *you're* a good sort of chap. And I don't think Morgan would let just anybody live in his flat. He's a proper gentleman. But these galleries here . . . They attract a lot of . . . well, you know, odd types of people, if you know what I mean.'

I had no idea what he meant, and I cast a quick glance at the woman, who gave me an arch smile.

'But you ought to go over to the Furniture Man. They're good folks. You should definitely get to know them.'

'I suppose I should,' I said, not saying a word about the fact that I was afraid of finding my own old furniture and belongings as soon as I approached any shop selling second-hand goods.

A man called the Flask walked past and waved through the window. The Flask was also a good chap, according to the Cigar Seller. The Flask had taken early retirement because of a bad back, and he supplemented his pension by collecting empty bottles in the parks.

'And you know . . .' said the Cigar Seller, lowering his voice, 'I think he has . . .' and he licked his thumb and forefinger and rubbed them together as he winked at me.

'From empty bottles?' I said in surprise.

'Oh yes! Oh *yes!*' exclaimed the Cigar Seller. 'He has a platform on his bike and he comes home after a day in the sunshine with bottles worth two hundred kronor! Tax-free. He's someone who has money under his mattress, I can promise you that. But he's not the sort you want to mess with – you'd be wise to stay out of his way.'

'I believe you.'

'Yes, watch yourself, my boy. A couple of junkies came in one day and started waving a pistol around, and *that gal* over there,' he said, jabbing his thumb towards the pin-up girl who immediately gave him a smile, 'she dived down behind the counter, scared out of her wits. But someone had to try to calm those lunatics down because I could tell that they wanted to get their hands on the day's take. Then the Flask came through the door, just like this,' he said as he walked through the door himself, trying to stick out his chest the way the Flask had done. 'And he was all over them like lightning, let me tell you, tossing one guy after another out the door and telling them to go to hell, and I damn well think that they did! Ha, ha, ha!'

'That's quite a story,' I said. 'You must have seen quite a few things . . .'

'You'd better believe it,' said the Cigar Seller with satisfaction. 'And then there's Wolf-Larsson. Do you know him?'

'No,' I said. 'I don't know Wolf-Larsson either.'

'Morgan is the one who dubbed him Wolf-Larsson. A real eccentric, you know. If you're ever out at night in the pubs around here, I'll be damned if you won't run into Wolf-Larsson. He's always out with his German shepherd, an incredibly splendid dog. He does, actually, look like a wolf . . .'

'Morning, boys!' said Henry Morgan as he stepped through the door.

'Hello, hello!' I said, and we shook hands. Henry winked, looking pleased and well-rested.

'Hello, Dolly!' Henry said to the woman behind the counter, and as usual she smiled back, chastely, a holy smile filled with piety.

Henry was there to turn in the bets. He had a regular betting system going on the football pool with Greger and Birger at the Furniture Man. It cost exactly twenty kronor.

'That guy is a sly devil,' said Henry as we went up in the lift. 'Watch out for him. Whatever you say to the Cigar Seller, half the town will know about it within the hour. He's leaky as a sieve. He's got a direct line to TT, the Central Wire Service.'

'I don't have any secrets,' I said.

'No, but *I* do,' said Henry. 'Though she's damn fine, that filly of his.'

Henry had been visiting Maud on Friggagatan and hadn't had any breakfast. He was hungry and needed food. I didn't intend to ask him any questions. We were supposed to respect each other's personal privacy, that was the plan.

Henry's breakfasts were noteworthy, to say the least. Health-food nuts, calorie counters and vegetarian followers of Are Waerland would have gasped and counted for hours, finally ending up with the very essence – in lengthy formulas – for a new suicide recipe if they were to use his ingredients. People like to picture bachelors of Henry's age downing a cup of Nescafé made with lukewarm tap water while standing up and smoking a hasty cigarette. But that was definitely not the style of Henry *le gourmand*. He'd acquired the habit during his prolonged youth spent on the Continent. I don't know whether his breakfasts should be pronounced Continental – and in that case,

50

whether Danish, English, German or French – but they were in any case monumental.

Henry donned a greasy apron and at a furious pace, keeping time with the radio's pop tunes, his bartender arms began flailing around the kitchen like drumsticks as he set the table with whatever his meagre pantry had to offer. First a couple of glasses of murky but nourishing guava juice to take the worst edge off his appetite. Then a couple of slices of home-baked French bread, toasted so that the salted butter would run properly, the Emmenthaler cheese would melt and the Wilkin & Sons gooseberry conserve would dissolve. Then a glass of carrot juice, half a packet of bacon and a fried egg with German cinnamon ketchup, washed down with plenty of orange juice. On top of all that he shovelled in a bowl of kefir with whipped sour cream and muesli, ending with a cup of chicory coffee crystals dissolved in hot, full-fat milk. The coffee had the strength that many vulgar marketing types would call 'abortive', and after a quick visit to the bathroom, he was back at the table to read the two morning papers, not for the sake of obtaining a balanced viewpoint but for the sheer pleasure of it.

I could probably put away only a quarter of all that food, but we did share the same passion for the daily papers. Henry and I both read at least four daily papers as well as a number of weeklies down at the Cigar Seller's shop. This assiduous reading of the papers – and the chicory coffee, which he bought at an indoor marketplace – was something that Henry had picked up during his days in Paris. That was when he was the young *Henri le boulevardier*, running around the cafés and constantly in search of new discoveries. In some ways he was still the same as ever, and I never stopped being surprised at his persistent indignation and flood of emotion as soon as he started reading a daily paper. Henry was easily moved, and he would be quite beside himself if there was anything depressing in the paper. It wasn't even a matter of the inevitable end of the world or the cold statement from the Institute for Futurology that humanity had at most a total of twenty-five years at its disposal before the final catastrophe. It might just be an article about a simple cat killer or a new influenza from the Far East. Henry would feel instantly blue and call on Zeus and Spinks to calm himself down, or he would take his temperature using a strange strip with liquid crystals. He would press the strip to his forehead and read the results in the mirror.

While reading the news and grumbling and complaining, he'd start wringing his hands in the deepest anguish at all the cruelty and evil in the world, then, as suddenly, the crisis would be over. It ran right off him like water off a duck's back. For the eternally starry-eyed Henry, the prime minister was still Tage Erlander and the king was Gustav VI Adolf. Ola Ullsten was just some little fussbudget, and Carl XVI Gustaf was and would remain Tjabo, the crown prince. Moreover, he was extremely delighted with the crown prince's bird, Silvia, a damn fine pin-up girl, a real *Nussika*, as Astrid Lindgren's character Karlsson-on-the-Roof would have said. Henry's entire world view was harebrained and chaotic, and crumbling away.

One morning we read about a horrible accident on the roof of one of the skyscrapers in New York. A crowd of people was standing on the roof, waiting to be transported to Kennedy Airport. As the helicopter was about to land, a gust of wind seized hold of the aircraft, making the blades swing down towards the waiting crowd on the roof. Some people were sliced right down the middle, others were cut in half and some were quite simply decapitated. It was said that a head landed on the pavement several blocks away, making people faint. An Orthodox Jew had a vision, went mad and began tearing out his beard, while an enterprising businessman made the biggest coup of the year by immediately selling old binoculars to all the rubbernecks who wanted a look at the head.

All this proved to be too much for Henry.

'Can't you just *picture* it?!' he shouted, pacing back and forth in the kitchen. 'A head comes plummeting down to the pavement right at your feet! A decapitated head. What an expression on the face. I can damn well guarantee you that it clobbered Leo before it landed. I can damn well guarantee it because he's always attracting all sorts of misfortune. You don't know him, but I do.'

Henry's face was turning bright red with excitement, and nothing short of a cold shower could calm him down. But then it all seemed to vanish into thin air.

'Apropos Leo,' he said quite calmly, 'We have to decide on the weekly move. He's playing chess by post with a fellow called Hagberg in Borås.'

'Oh right, that guy.'

'He's a chief accountant and chess fanatic, and apparently he has games going on in countries over at least half the globe. I think that's all the man lives for. On the other hand, he's the only bastard that Leo even pays much attention to, and now that he's away I have to keep the show going. I'm a damned terrible chess player.'

'Me too.'

'I thought as much,' muttered Henry. 'Dammit all. Oh well, two are better than one. So let's go in and decide on the next move.'

We went into the sitting room. Next to the TV was a beautiful table made of jacaranda wood. We pulled up a couple of chairs and sat down at the table. Henry read out the brilliant move by Hagberg, the chess fanatic and citizen of Borås. Then we moved his black knight and found ourselves in a very grim situation.

'God only knows what I had in mind before,' said Henry with embarrassment. 'By the way, Hagberg has no idea that I've been playing for Leo. If he knew, he'd probably die of scorn. He has only raised objections twice so far.'

'This is hopeless,' I said, discouraged.

'Nothing is hopeless, my dear Klasa,' said Henry. 'Have you got a smoke?'

We each lit a cigarette and stared ourselves blind at that damned black knight. But after a little fretting and grumbling we agreed that the rook was our only chance in this situation. Henry typed up the move – his childish handwriting had made the accountant suspicious – and then put the letter in the hall, where outgoing post went.

After that we each went our own way, retreating to our separate sections of the flat. Henry went off to practise on the piano while I settled down in the library to read a cheap paperback of *The Red Room*, making liberal use of a red pen. I was determined to do a proper analysis of the task.

That's how the morning hours often passed, until we would meet in the hall before lunch. There Henry might pull out a drawer in the bureau, which inevitably contained a thick booklet of luncheon vouchers, the kind many Swedish companies provide their employees with.

'Look but don't ask any questions,' he might say, handing me a booklet of luncheon vouchers. 'One booklet a week, no questions asked and no alcohol.'

'On my word of honour,' I was allowed to swear.

We often went down to Costa's lunch place on Bellmansgatan. There the whole gang showed up at lunchtime: the Fence Queen and Greger and Birger from the Furniture Man, several gallery owners, the Cigar Seller and the Flask. The mood was excellent, as was the food, which the tourist guides would no doubt rate with a single star.

———

In October I regained my identity, or so they claimed. The police investigation and the insurance company's own reconnoitring had led to approximately the same propitious conclusions in the case of Klas Östergren, a.k.a. 'the Burgled'. A lively agent from the insurance company rang me up to tell me that I would be receiving a partial payment of 10,000 kronor for the time being. I also heard from the police authorities, and I was able to collect new identity papers, a passport, an ID card and other documents to replace those that had disappeared from my home and no doubt ended up on the black market.

A certain share of the insurance money went to back taxes and other pressing debts, but there was still a tidy sum left over. We organised a celebration. There were lobsters available at the indoor marketplace. Henry went off to see a shopkeeper he knew and came back with two real whoppers, alive and black as dung, aggressive and with furious antennae whipping back and forth in the little wooden box.

Henry made a broth with vegetables, beer and spices and then boiled the lobsters, which instantly turned bright red. Around seven that evening we were ready. I had set an inviting table with elegant china and tall crystal glasses along with a couple of bottles of Ruffino Toscano Bianco, dry and cool.

We ate the lobsters warm with a couple of pats of butter and toast. We ate in silent reverence, because warm lobster, perfectly prepared, is one of the best things this world has to offer. Afterwards we had coffee in the sitting room, each of us dozing in an armchair by the fire. The idea was that we would recharge and then go out on the town — we had been living a miserly and dreary existence for some time now — but the delicacies took their toll on our strength, and the Italian wine didn't make us nearly as Italian as we had hoped.

Henry put on an old jazz record, but that didn't make us any livelier either. I longed more than ever for an old rock album — it didn't matter which one as long as it rocked and got me going again. But all my records had been stolen, and for Henry rock and pop had never existed. It might be something he would sit and sing along with in a pub, but that was all. I had now been living in his flat for a month, and I was starting to miss my music. Henry claimed that I was going through withdrawal. He was going to get me to listen to real music.

He suggested that we write a song together. It would be about two gentlemen, a showy, peppy little tune with a refrain that stayed with you, a perfect hit.

If the girls leave you flat
And they don't have a five or a ten
Then forget about that
We'll dream ourselves fat, we are gentlemen

That's what Henry dictated, because he was no stranger to that type of handi-
work. It's what the average serious composer prefers to regard as a type of
prostitution. But with his great art, which he regularly talked about, Henry
was absolutely uncompromising. He wasn't about to sell out.

However, we didn't get very far with 'Gentlemen' that evening. Nor did
we behave like gentlemen. A cool saxophone brought all our impulses down
to the ground, and we sank even deeper into our armchairs, if that were
possible. It was raining outside, and neither of us had any further desire to
lay waste to the town.

'I don't even feel like this is a celebration,' I yawned.

'Me too,' said Henry drowsily in English, using incorrect grammar. 'I think
we ate a little too fast. Lobster has to be eaten slowly. And we should have
invited some women over, then we would have pulled ourselves together.'

'I've got nothing left in me,' I said.

'Me too,' Henry repeated, still incorrectly. 'Sometimes life is just so incom-
parably tedious.'

It remained a mystery how two lively and talented boxers could fade so
easily on an evening after a lobster dinner and a few bottles of dry Italian
white wine. But at least it wasn't work that had worn us out.

K eeping a secret requires a certain technique, maybe even a certain talent. But what's beyond all doubt is that Henry Morgan lacked both the talent and the technique. Some time in late October I was initiated into Henry's Secret, which explained a great deal.

He had no job; he was an artist, after all, exactly like Olle Montanus in *The Red Room*, and at times he could end up totally destitute. But he always managed to find a way out. That was how it had been ever since he'd returned home from the Continent. He had his small inheritance – an appanage which arrived once a month and was strictly controlled by an attorney's office – and occasionally he would sell a few valuable but unreadable books from his library. Now and then he would take some odd job in the city or down at the harbour. Everything always worked out one way or other.

But strangely enough, he was such a damned energetic and enterprising man, in the very prime of his life. He roared around in that flat clad in a pair of filthy overalls, and he didn't seem the least bit like a sensitive pianist practising for the breakthrough of his career.

Henry had plans to hire the Södra Theatre for a night to present his major work for solo piano: 'Europa, Disintegrating Fragments'. He had been working on it for close to fifteen years, and he thought it was high time to make his debut in a serious fashion. I actually agreed with him, and the idea of hiring the Södra Theatre wasn't a bad plan at all. The phenomenal Hungarian had rented the Dramaten Theatre a number of years earlier, and it was a big success. Why should Henry Morgan expect anything less? It would only cost four or five thousand kronor, including staff, and there were always a few days available in the spring. Invitations had to be sent out – in some fancy, mincing typeface, as he said – to the entire Music Establishment, which meant critics and producers and arrangers. How could it possibly fail?

The plan was rather ambitious, but beneath the clouds there was a world thirsting for culture. It took some snazzy efforts to get noticed at all in that field. I supported Henry 100 per cent. He had the whole piece scribbled out in an enormous notebook and all he needed, he claimed, was to practise a couple of hours each day to polish the subtler nuances. But it looked as if the actual amount of time he practised was at most fifteen minutes; then came a clutch of pop tunes, a coffee break, lunch, more coffee and endless dashing around the flat.

It was this endless dashing around and the loud slamming of doors that made me both dubious and curious. Henry was always going around – during work hours, that is – in his filthy overalls, claiming that he could whistle better when he wore them.

'A pair of overalls with suspenders and button-fly instils harmony,' he said. 'Try it yourself and you'll see!'

No sooner said than done. I jumped into his warm overalls, which, granted, were a bit too big, but I had to admit they were extremely comfortable. Of course I had done work wearing overalls before, but I'd never imagined that you would automatically start to whistle just by putting overalls on – but now it seemed quite natural. And they do make you whistle well, no matter what aria you attempt.

'Damn,' I said, 'I think I'll buy myself a pair.'

'Of course you should,' said Henry, putting them back on. 'You can get them over at Albert's Menswear. Quite cheap. They also give you the feeling that you're doing something useful. You become a little more of a cultural *worker* wearing overalls!'

We were in total agreement about the matter, but the question remained: why did his clothing end up getting so damned filthy, even downright *muddy*, whenever he went out for a while in the middle of the day? As far as I knew, there was no sandbox down on the street.

Henry was fully aware of how puzzled I was, and it was now, at the end of October, after I'd been living with him for about a month, that he thought I had passed muster, so to speak. I could be initiated into Henry's Secret. In his opinion I had proven myself to be trustworthy, loyal and highly reliable. It was high time for me to be admitted to the circle of the chosen few, the initiated. On top of all that, I knew how to work, how to put my back into it; that was something he had undoubtedly noticed.

———————

It was an amazing story, to say the least. Henry had spent a large part of his youth in Europe, on the Continent. He had deserted from his military service and gone into exile. His adventurous exile lasted all of five years, or so he claimed, and didn't come to an end until the rebellious spring of '68. At that time he was in Paris, in the very thick of events, as always, when he received a letter from home, from his mother Greta back in Sweden. It brought news of a death. In the midst of the revolutions, old Grandfather Morgonstjärna had plodded up the long staircase over on Hornsgatan – the newfangled lift never penetrated his consciousness – and then collapsed on the landing with a ruptured heart.

Henry was of course summoned home from his proud exile – the military authorities had forgotten all about him long ago – to attend the burial at the family grave in Skog Cemetery. Old Morgonstjärna was deeply mourned, and the remaining members of the WWW Club were all present, contributing a magnificent wreath. The burial took place in the utmost silence, according to the wishes of the deceased.

There was also a last will and testament. The surviving members of the family received their allotted shares, and it was with the greatest curiosity that Henry received his. It consisted of two envelopes. One was purely a financial matter, consisting of a monthly allowance of fifteen hundred kronor 'so that my grandson Henry Morgan might cultivate his music without regard for market conditions or insipid, modern-day circumstance . . .' as the old man expressed it. The money was to be paid out by an attorney's office, and it was linked to the cost-of-living index and so slyly calculated that the heir would never be able either to squander his inheritance or to live a life of luxury.

The second envelope was even more surprising, if that were possible. It was labelled 'The Crew' in pen, and 'For Henry Morgan' in pencil. Perhaps the old man was uncertain right up to the very end who should be entrusted with the very special contents of that envelope.

Henry found a bundle of yellowed papers, one of them particularly fragile; it was faded, much-handled and soiled. It was an old map. He read through the story about how one night the old dandy – who was a devoted gambler and had won many things, not just the fine Chippendale furniture from Ernst Rolf – was playing poker with several gentlemen from the WWW (Well-travelled, Well-read, Well-heeled) Club. They were 'university-educated men and scholars'. One of these gentlemen was evidently a historian, and he had done research on the neighbourhood of Rosendal Större, where Morgon-stjärna lived. The historian had made some astonishing discoveries. He had reconstructed the mysterious old Bellman passageways, and via a number of other historians he had found a map to hidden treasure.

There were multitudes of myths about the Bellman passageways. Everyone who lived in the Rosendal Större district knew someone else whose brother had been down in the passageways trying to uncover their mysteries. But if you asked where this brother, this eyewitness, was today, you would be met with a look of horror, a sigh and utter silence, or with slippery evasions. It was said that in the forties an adventurer had gone searching through the passageways, through the old, now-razed building on Bellmansgatan. Enticed by his pernicious hunger for knowledge he went further and further under-ground until he was finally swallowed up by the earth. After a week his supporters above ground started getting worried, so they sent down a doctor and a nurse, who both met the same fate. In more recent times, after the so-called Bellman building had fallen into disrepair, the cellars were used as a sanctuary for devil worshippers whose bloody rituals spread horror through all of Söder. A number of vagabonds and other drifters had also lived there until the building was finally torn down in the mid seventies.

But the historian-member of the WWW Club had a different theory about the Bellman passageways. According to him, the story went like this: King Adolf Fredrik ordered an escape route to be constructed for himself and his family from the Royal Palace. He anticipated a siege against Stockholm, though it was unclear who the enemy would be, and he had ordered an under-ground passageway to be dug beneath all of Gamla Stan. This escape route was to be linked to a passageway under Södra Malmen, though how this would be done was never actually established; the historian assumed that the construction of the Stockholm underground railway made any investigation virtually impossible.

But – and this was where the Rosendal Större neighbourhood came into the picture – the passageway would by necessity lead to the area around Maria-kyrka and the present-day Mariatorget. Located there, in addition to a warehouse with a stable under constant guard, were a full assortment of horses, wagons and other military and civilian equipment. This was the district where old Mr Morgonstjärna lived and where Henry Morgan and I now resided.

The gambler-historian had bet a good deal of money, and in the end even his secret map became part of the poker game that night. And then he lost it all, and quite rightly so. He had apparently been researching the matter as a hobby, more or less, but no one found any reason to doubt his claims. Upon closer examination, the whole thing sounded like some sort of childish dream, but the fact that the scholar and poker-game loser committed suicide after very honourably relinquishing his map and notes, seemed to acknowledge a certain underlying truth. He had been planning to make a big killing on the whole thing.

The point was that at a certain underground spot along this now presumably filled-in escape route, there was supposedly a grotto where the king had deposited a large number of valuables. He would never have been able to flee the royal palace with more than his personal regalia, and so he had stored, in advance, a number of chests filled with gold and riches.

After Morgonstjärna *the gambler* had acquired this valuable treasure map, he began, slowly but surely, to develop a treasure-hunting crew in the building. Down in the cellar were a number of unused rooms, and one in particular actually revealed a walled-up doorway in the foundation that could be dated back to the seventeenth century. Tapping on the doorway had revealed a hollow space behind it. Late one night in October 1961, Mr Morgonstjärna started knocking down the wall, and to his great satisfaction he found a passageway leading straight down into the depths. A parallel to the Berlin Wall might easily be drawn – during periods of unrest, people often concern themselves with walls of various types.

But back then, in 1961, Mr Morgonstjärna was already an old, worn-out man. He needed help, and he actually managed to rope a number of underlings into the project. They set up a form of limited partnership, and by taking a vow of absolute silence they could buy a part of the presumed find, the gold treasure that was hundreds of years old. The capital they invested was their own labour.

Seven years later, that is, when Henry's paternal grandfather departed this life and left behind his strange testament, the 'crew' had grown to include half a dozen people. In addition to the old man and dandy himself, there was the Philatelist, Greger and Birger from the Furniture Man, the Flask and

Wolf-Larsson. By then they had dug their way approximately five and a half yards due south, seven and a half yards due east, where the passageway turned 180 degrees, and continued due west. No gold had been found, but nobody doubted that they were on the right track, because there had been no lack of auspicious signs.

'Surely you can't expect me to believe all that,' I said to Henry after he told me about the treasure, as excited as a little Boy Scout.

It was a raw and blustery autumn day, and we were having our afternoon coffee in the sitting room. Henry had really warmed to his tale of the treasure-hunting project, and he said that what he had told me was strictly confidential, not to go beyond these walls, for our eyes only, man to man, and whatever else you might say. I had been entrusted with a confidence, but I had also been given occasion to wonder once again whether Henry Morgan might actually be out of his mind. It sounded undeniably like some story in a lousy children's book.

'You *can't* really expect me to believe you,' I repeated.

'I'll let you see the map if you like,' said Henry, annoyed. 'Though I'm not thrilled about showing it to anyone.'

Looking more than a little miffed, he went to his room and came back at once with the map. It was in fact an extremely detailed illustration of the entire area, showing the various cellars, both real and hypothetical, and the passageways linking them to form an entire underground network. Somewhere in this maze there was supposed to be an opening to the correct passageway, the king's escape route with the enormous hidden treasure.

In silence I carefully studied the map. Henry sucked contentedly on a cigarette, and I could sense that he was thinking: I told you so, you bastard.

'Huh,' I said. 'So how far have you got?'

'Up to here,' said Henry, setting his stubby index finger in about the middle of the neighbourhood, under the pump in the courtyard. 'The passageway branches off in two directions, one heading west and the other one east. We're going to continue east, to start with. We must be getting close to the church.'

'Well, well,' I said. 'But it does seem a bit childish.'

'*Childish*,' repeated Henry. 'Of course it's childish. It's fucking childish, the whole thing! It's just as childish as watching a football match. But just wait until you go down there, then you won't have even a second of doubt. I guarantee it!'

Henry turned out to be right. Naturally I insisted on inspecting the excavations at once, and Henry couldn't very well refuse. We went down to the cellar through the door in the hallway that led to the Philatelist's flat. It was the door that Henry had opened on my first night there, when we'd been to the Zum Franziskaner and drunk a good deal and then got thirsty and wanted more. He had taken a bottle of whisky from the Philatelist, who sat there boozing with his buddies practically every night.

We went through the Philatelist's storeroom and down the stairs to the cellar. If you moved quietly, no one in the whole building would notice a thing. It was very cunningly arranged.

From a small cellar room — filled with tools, shovels, pickaxes and hoes, sledgehammers and crowbars, as well as a wheelbarrow — the first passageway angled straight down into the depths. Several lamps produced a faint light, and it was cold, raw and damp. The passageway wound its way towards the fork that my guide had mentioned.

'So here it branches off,' said Henry when we reached the spot. 'Are you scared?'

'Scared?'

'That it might cave in. It *could* actually collapse. We had a little cave-in last year. But nobody got hurt. As luck would have it, no one was down here. If you look closely you can see that they're very old posts. This really is an ancient passageway.'

I studied a thick post that supported a crossbeam and scraped its surface with a stone. The wood was grey all the way through and starting to rot. It smelled of mould and earth, like a swamp.

'I believe you,' I admitted. 'This is definitely a fucking ancient passageway. But I do have my doubts about the gold.'

'Well, all right,' said Henry with a sigh. 'Of course you can have your doubts. Of course you might wonder what we're really doing down here. But what purpose will that serve? It's important to try. You have to believe in *something*.'

'But nobody's working today?'

'I think this is Greger's day. But he might have something going on. He works for the Fence Queen.'

'The woman who owns the Furniture Man shop?'

'Yes. Nice bird. She's Greger's and Birger's boss, and she could find gold with a bowie knife. All she has to do is touch something, and estates, junk and rubbish all turn to gold. An enterprising girl!'

'Do *they* believe in all this?'

'They're behind it 100 per cent. Birger and Greger and I do most of the work. Wolf-Larsson and the Flask mostly sit around and drink down here. But something always gets done.'

'But don't they want to see some sort of results? It beats me how you can get them to keep believing in this stuff.'

'Faith can turn mountains into rubble. But *I'm* not the one who's making them dig. They've got faith in this, and I damn well do too. Besides, sometimes we have a party. At my invitation. We're going to have one in November, by God; I forgot about that. I've got to rustle up some cash to pay for the party.'

It's difficult to say precisely what it was, but there was something that made me believe Henry. He always sounded so damned convincing as soon as he started talking about a project; his enthusiasm was infectious, like an extremely virulent disease. It was obvious that in Mr Morgan the business world had missed out on a salesman who could have had a brilliant future.

Consequently, I did exactly as he said – I went down to Albert's Menswear and bought a sturdy pair of overalls. Henry was right about the fact that wearing overalls made you a good whistler. There is something tranquil and harmonious about the pose that you automatically assume in a pair of overalls: your hands stuck deep in the pockets, snuff and cigarettes in other convenient pockets, while there's plenty of room for tools and books and anything else you may want to have with you.

It didn't take long before I was fully assimilated into the 'crew'. I was introduced to the Philatelist – a ratty little gentleman with bifocals, very knowledgeable in his field – and the whole crowd from the Furniture Man. The Fence Queen was also a veritable authority in her profession. She merely had to cast a swift glance at any object to estimate its market value down to the last öre, and she always got the price she asked. She moved about among all the junk, wearing a dress, her hair in a French roll, with an air of almost spiritual dignity.

Greger was rather stupid and lacking in independence. He tried to copy Birger, who in this company was considered quite elegant – as far as it went. He looked like the toy-maker Gepetto in my childhood book about Pinocchio, although a bit younger. He too always told the truth.

Birger was a real charmer. He kept up with fashion and he often went down to Albert's Menswear to buy himself a new outfit as the spirit moved him. He was always freshly shaven, with his hair oiled and his clothes newly pressed. Birger was a well-mannered connoisseur and a fair poet, a third-rate rhyme-master. He rarely had time for customers.

Wolf-Larsson and the Flask were also part of the project. Neither of them was particularly talkative; they simply went about their work without uttering a word. God only knows what they would have spent their time on otherwise. They were both retired.

The autumn had really begun to take hold by the time I started working down in the passageway. My days seemed to take on a more structured routine. After an early breakfast, the morning was devoted to Art in the library with *The Red Room*. After much hesitation my pastiche had finally taken off; the analysis was shaping up, and I thought that certain unmistakable flashes of genius were emanating from my typewriter. Thanks to Licentiate Borg in Strindberg's novel – his coarse and cynical penchant for speaking his mind, that is – I had found a natural catalyst. Borg already had an intense relationship with Arvid Falk, after all, and he could stand off to one side and comment on events in a natural way. Borg was absolutely invaluable, but I was still having a hard time accepting the idea that the story would work without Olle Montanus, so I was sticking with the idea that his previously unknown son from the country village, a boy named Kalle Montanus, aged eighteen, had to be lying asleep on a kitchen bench in the neighbourhood taken over by squatters. It was unthinkable to write a Stockholm story without including the rebels, the so-called counter-citizens. Arvid was just going to have to tear himself away from his dreary schoolmistress and abandon himself to uninhibited bohemianism, maybe in the company of a gypsy girl from Mullvaden. That sounded brilliant.

Well, one page gave birth to another, the book had finally started to flow, and my publisher, Torsten Franzén, sounded very pleased, although a bit stressed. After a couple of hours of diligent work in the library during those clear, lofty autumn mornings, it would be time for lunch. We would go to Costa's lunch bar on Bellmansgatan, making use of Henry's inexhaustible supply of luncheon vouchers. Having promised never to ask where the vouchers came from, I still don't know, even today.

After lunch there would be several hours of toil down in the passageway. We often worked alone; it could easily get a bit crowded down there. We hacked our way forward through mud and sand and dirt by turns. The work could quickly become a bit monotonous and boring, but you could always dream about what you were going to do with the money.

Then it would be time for dinner, and we took turns cooking. Henry was a real wizard with food, and he had at his disposal a considerable library of cookbooks – everything from exotic Balinese delicacies to simple fare for Swedish treasure hunters.

After dinner we were generally rather tired, the physical and mental labour having taken its toll. We would play some billiards, watch TV, read a good book, or converse. Henry took his stories from the Continent while I – who wasn't nearly as worldly or experienced as Mr Morgan – was given advice about how *The Red Room* of today ought to be furnished.

We had undeniably made a success of things – we had arranged our life precisely the way life should be arranged. It was a question of a balance between body and soul. Without doubt, the only thing lacking was women.

Artists are sensitive souls, eternal gypsies. Henry Morgan was no exception. With one stroke his grand piano could be out of tune; not only that, it could be totally unplayable. It was the worst grand piano in the whole damn world, and how was he supposed to be able to reach the top echelons with that swine of an instrument? Even a deaf person would vomit at the mere sight of it, in the opinion of the sensitive musician.

This scene was played out at regular intervals, and then Henry would head down to the cellar to dig his way out of the worst of his rage. He could be gone for almost an hour and then come back even more annoyed, if that were possible. There might be a boulder in the way that had to be pried loose, and for that he'd need reinforcements.

'Don't bury yourself down there right now,' I said on one of these occasions, trying to sound light-hearted. 'Let's pop over to the Europa and box for a while. I'm sure that'll help.'

'Good idea,' said Henry with a sigh. 'This day is cursed, I could see that in my horoscope. Nothing but non-stop obstacles.'

The depressed-but-always-psychic Morgan had seen very clearly that this day would offer adversity, but taking the offensive is always the best method of defence. We would be defiant, and so we decided to top off the day (a Friday), and the whole week, by going into town for a little dancing. It seemed a great idea.

We were determined to be in good spirits. We packed up our sports gear and walked down Hornstull and Långholmsgatan over to the Europa Athletic Club. It was a Friday afternoon, and the boys were taking it rather easy – all except Gringo.

'Hi, girls!' bellowed Henry, as usual.

Everyone except Gringo, the uncrowned king, said hello, and Willis came out of his office to have a little chat about Ali vs Spinks. He never got tired of talking about that match, and of course he had his own theories about Ali's strategy. He would make comparisons with Joe Louis, who had also had to abdicate in 1949, undefeated, because that was the only thing Ali could do in the current situation.

Gringo, on the other hand, was in a fighting mood that day. He was a real 'Hotspur' just then, sparring with Juan, who had a fight in a couple of days and needed a good workout.

'Easy! Easy!' shouted Willis. 'Take it easy, Gringo! Juan's got a match on Monday; he's got to look pretty. Save your ammunition!'

Gringo was at least two stone heavier than the little Yugoslav, who looked like a Spaniard. Hotspur had a terrifying right hook which he wasn't really supposed to use when he was sparring. It was a lethal weapon that had knocked out at least twenty-five boxers in the past.

The scene was set for revenge that day. Henry had really taught Gringo a lesson a while back, but he'd had so much going on – as he always said to Willis – that he hadn't had time to do much training lately.

Gringo wanted Henry to get in the ring, and Henry couldn't very well refuse. He muttered something about being out of shape while the feather-weight guys crowded round one corner of the boxing ring. Sure enough, Henry was headed for an eye-popping beating. Gringo had worked himself up and instantly went on the offensive. Henry, countering very mechanically, barely managed to avoid being beaten.

Afterwards – Henry said he'd had enough after two rounds – I thought the man would be absolutely furious after a whole day of constant adversity. But my fears turned out to be groundless. Henry was in excellent spirits, in spite of the fact that his whole body must have been bruised and aching after being worked over by Gringo's insane right hook.

'Thanks, Gringo,' said Henry, sticking out his red fist. 'You pounded the devil and all hell right out of me.'

Gringo was satisfied and elated after his legitimate revenge and allowed himself a handshake and a smile.

After a couple of hours at the Europa, we headed home by way of the state off-licence. We bought ourselves a couple of bottles of wine, a grilled chicken and some big potatoes to bake in the oven.

It was already dark and gloomy by the time we reached home. The huge flat could seem gloomy enough in the daytime, but at twilight it was as desolate, silent and oppressive as a medieval castle. It was essential to go round and turn on a countless number of small lamps to shatter that depressing, disheartening chiaroscuro.

'Night exists in this flat as a perpetual possibility,' Henry had said. 'It's just a matter of drawing the curtains and pretending, that's all we need do . . .'

He sounded a bit uneasy or out-of-sorts.

The evening was shaping up nicely. After dinner we started sprucing ourselves up for a night filled with *festivitas*.

'We need to shave,' said Henry, 'and make a decent job of it. That's very important . . .'

So we shaved, and did it properly. Henry always turned these ordinary procedures into acts of finesse and sophistication. He was forever talking about the Art of Cooking, the Art of Cleaning and the Art of Shaving. It was pure drama to watch Henry shave with soap, shaving brush, straight razor and strop.

Then it was time to put on our 'confirmation' suits. Henry chose a dark flannel outfit while I took out my old magical black suit. I borrowed a noose from Henry's collection, and in the end I looked quite presentable.

Henry had decided that we should go down to Baldakinen. He said it was a respectable joint. I had no idea how to conduct myself, but he assured me that was no problem.

'The girls in the Pillar Hall are smart and experienced. They know exactly what to do. You don't have a thing to worry about,' said Morgan.

We took the underground downtown, strolled along Vasagatan to Norra Bantorget, and arrived at Baldakinen right on time. I had nothing to worry about, according to Henry, so I wasn't worried. We were in top form, and my legs started moving as soon as I heard the stamping on the dance floor.

We got a decent table in the midst of the sea of people, and we each ordered a whisky.

'We've definitely earned this, Klasa,' said Henry as he lit a cigarette with a somewhat exaggerated flourish of refinement. 'We can look back on a week of work well done.'

'I've churned out a lot,' I said. 'At least twenty-five pages.'

'Things are going well for me too,' he said. 'It was lucky that you moved in with me, don't you think? It's worked out perfectly.'

'I agree,' I said. 'I've never lived as splendidly as I do now.'

'Watch out, my boy,' Henry said suddenly, giving me a kick under the table. 'Pretty soon it's going to be ladies' choice. You're going to be asked to dance by a black-haired woman in her forties wearing a blue Charleston dress.'

'You're out of your mind!'

'Don't turn around,' said Henry. 'Do *not* turn around! She's got her eye on you, her little lamb, her quarry. Soon she'll have her claws in you. I guarantee it! Bet you fifty kronor!'

'Done!' I said. 'Fifty kronor!'

We clinked our whisky glasses and surveyed the room.

'Oh yes, by God, have a look. You're all set. She's already turned down a fat accountant. She's just sitting there, waiting. I wonder what I should do. I'm too old to pin my hopes on the ladies' choice.'

By now my curiosity was being sorely tested, and I was forced to pretend that my neck was hurting and turn to get a look at that woman in the blue Charleston dress. It was true that she had her dark eyes fixed on me, and she looked quite stylish. She gave me a smile and at the same time Henry kicked me under the table.

'Fifty kronor!' he muttered with satisfaction.

The dance band was pounding out its steady, comforting 'dunka-dunk' beat, and people were jumping around on the dance floor in transports of joy. I was feeling a little nervous because I hadn't danced in a very long time. Henry had his radar turned up high and was homing in on practically every woman in the place. It was rather slim pickings, and the more attractive-looking girls had already been claimed by enterprising salesmen wearing checked jackets with enormous knots in their ties tucked under their chins like big bread rolls.

I didn't realise that it was ladies' choice until I felt a tap on my shoulder. I turned around and sure enough, there was the black-haired woman in the blue Charleston dress.

'Would you like to dance?' she asked me simply.

'If I can,' I said, once again feeling Henry's damned shoe striking my shin. 'I hope it's a slow dance.'

Fortunately the band played a tender tune with 'heart' and 'soul', and the singer's phrasing had that nasal sound, rolling all his 'r's. He had a sort of standard Swedish enunciation, dance-band style, the plainest of dialects. I couldn't help laughing at his rolled 'r's, and the woman I was dancing with asked me what was so damn funny. I explained it to her, but she didn't find it at all amusing.

But the dancing part was going well. We glided smoothly and easily across the floor, managing to avoid any collisions with a bunch of louts who were romping about, shouting and yelling to each other.

The woman's name was Bettan, and we leisurely danced five long dances in a row. We were hot and a little sweaty when we went back to our table. Henry was evidently out on the prowl. I asked Bettan if she'd like to sit down for a while, and she said yes. We chatted a little about this and that, and Bettan turned out to be a very pleasant woman. She was single at the moment. She had two children and lived on Dalagatan. Not far from here, she said.

Henry soon returned to the table. He'd been playing roulette and had won, so he promptly offered us drinks. He introduced himself to Bettan with the greatest courtesy, clicking his heels and kissing her hand, and the lady accepted. She wanted a gin fizz.

Henry immediately struck up a conversation with Bettan, like the proper gentleman he was. He found out all sorts of things about her, without appearing to be either curious or indiscreet. Bettan liked Henry too, and it turned out to be a marvellous evening. She danced with both of us – she loved to dance – and she had a stamina that nearly killed us two reasonably fit boxers.

Later in the evening Henry also managed to find a female companion on that sultry autumn night – I couldn't really see who it was – and Bettan and I were feeling the urge. She had no time for circumlocutions, insinuations or diffident, semi-articulated phrases about sleep and bed and good night. It was straight to the point and full steam ahead:

'You're coming home with me now, aren't you?' she said, as if a refusal would be unimaginable, an insult.

'Of course I am,' I said. 'I just have to tell Henry.'

My good friend was in the middle of some intense groping with an enormous woman in a sequined dress. I shouted in his ear that I was leaving.

'Sure,' he said, giving me a wink. 'See you in the morning.'

'Here's fifty kronor!' I said, stuffing a banknote in his pocket.

Bettan worked as a secretary for a big company, and she had green fingers. Plants were her hobby, and the whole flat smelled like a jungle in the tropics. It was filled with plants, and she knew the name and price of each of them.

71

I've forgotten all the names, but I did learn that plants could be bloody expensive. She claimed that she could sell some of them for several thousand. Maybe she meant the full-grown palms flanking the sofa group in the living room.

'Would you like anything? Tea or wine, or . . . ?'

'A cup of tea would be nice,' I said, following Bettan out to the kitchen.

On the wall was a pinboard with a school lunch schedule tacked up along with addresses and messages for the kids. There was also a picture of some lads that I liked at once. The boys were in their early teens, as punk-looking as they come. One of them had carrot-coloured hair; the other's was purple. They looked like little trolls.

'Lovely boys,' I said.

'They're not as bad as they look,' said Bettan.

'Do they play in a band?'

'Of course,' said Bettan. 'It's called The Piglets.'

'Great name,' I said. 'I'd like to see them.'

'We can look in on them, if you want.'

We opened the door a crack to the punk trolls' room, and there they lay, sleeping with their bushy purple and carrot-red hair, which stuck out like gauze from their heads. The one with the carrot hair looked almost like an albino, with his pallid skin and pale eyelashes.

'Could I buy one of them from you?'

Bettan started to laugh and closed the door so as not to wake the trolls.

'You wouldn't be able to stand it. You should hear them practising here at home. The only solution is to flee.'

We had tea in the jungle in the living room, and Bettan talked about her plants, or rather *to* her plants. Then it was time for bed.

'You're the youngest lover I've ever had,' said Bettan in the bedroom.

'*Am* I a lover?'

'Of course, what did you think?' said Bettan, undressing me as if she were my mother.

'You have sons and lovers,' I said.

'I have to, otherwise I couldn't stand it,' said Bettan. 'Just take it easy now.'

'I promise.'

Henry *le charmeur* had just shaved – to keep up a proper appearance he had to do it several times a day – when I arrived home on Saturday. The kitchen table was cluttered with the remains of breakfast for two. I poured myself a cup of lukewarm coffee, sank down on a chair and leafed through the newspaper.

'So how was your night?' asked Henry during a pause in his merry whistling serenade.

'Excellent,' I said. 'Although there was a hell of a commotion this morning.'

'Did her old man come home?'

'Not at all. There isn't any old man,' I said.

But it had been a bad morning, all the same. It started when I woke up to a hellish noise when the two punk trolls started practising on electric bass and drums, making the whole building shake. Bettan was already dressed and made-up, alert and lively. She wanted to drag me along into town to do some shopping, but I had such a fucking headache from the punk rock music that I couldn't even eat breakfast.

'OK then,' said Bettan. 'Just give me a call sometime,' she said, kissing me on the lips. She wasn't the least bit sentimental, and I suppose that women of her age don't have many illusions. That's just how it was.

'How about your night?' I asked Henry.

'I'm in love again,' he sang in English, looking starry-eyed and amorous. 'She's in the bathroom, putting on her make-up.'

'I see,' I said. 'A Valkyrie?'

'Yes, sir.'

We didn't have a chance to exchange any more code words before Henry's new love appeared in the kitchen. She was a good-sized morsel in the middleweight class, about thirty-seven years old, wearing a long dress with sequins, high-heeled shoes and thick baroque make-up.

'Hi,' she said, sticking out her hand. 'Lola Lilac.'

'Hi, Lola,' I said. 'Nice name you have. My name is Klas.'

'Hi, you little cutie, ha, ha, ha,' roared Lola, her voice shrill and sexy, to put it mildly.

Now it looked as if the night's activities had given Lola and Henry some diffuse sort of telepathic connection, because it took only a single exchange of glances for them to start giggling discreetly at something. I had no clue what it was. They were just like two teenagers who had been necking out in the cloakroom and were now extremely proud of their exploits and wanted everyone to know about it, though they didn't come right out and say so. Everything was implied, using little gestures and long, pining looks.

But Lola wasn't one of those overly romantic types, and she came steam-rollering into the kitchen to take over.

'All right, boys,' she said, pushing Henry away from the sink. 'I see you're a couple of typical bachelors,' she went on as she started gathering up the dishes. 'I'll take care of this.'

Lola rushed around the whole kitchen like a white tornado swathed in sequins, scolding Henry and cursing me for being so messy.

'Oh, you damn bachelors,' Lola kept repeating over and over again.

Now and then she would take a break in her important duties to plonk herself down on Henry's lap and give him a kiss. They sat there cooing like two turtledoves, giggling and pinching each other on the cheek.

'My little rooster,' said Lola.

'My little lambkin,' said Henry, pinching her flesh, which made the woman jump up with a howl.

All that cooing was making me feel a little sick, so I left them to it. Even though I closed two doors, I could still hear Lola Lilac's voice echoing from the kitchen as she, filled with meddlesome officiousness, proceeded to give Henry advice and tips on how everything in a household should be handled.

'Oh yes, you damn bachelors,' she said over and over again.

After a while there was silence and a couple of doors slammed. They had gone into Henry's bedroom, and after a few more minutes I once again heard her voice.

'Ohhh, Hennnryyyy . . . oh . . . oh . . . ,' she cried lasciviously from the bedroom, piercing four doors.

They must have gone at it for a couple of hours, until it was time for Lola to run home. By that time I had ensconced myself in the library to work for a few hours; it was the only way to ease my hangover. But it wasn't easy while Lola Lilac's randy panting was thundering through the whole flat, even though I had turned on the radio.

Finally Lola stuck her hairsprayed head in the door and shouted, 'Toodle-oo, cutie', and disappeared, delighted and satiated by her lover Henry Morgan.

When peace was at last restored, Henry *the sybarite* came in and said that he was in love, head over heels in love. He even looked younger, in spite of a sleepless night. He was clean-shaven, and the bags under his eyes had paled, erased by Lola's torrents of kisses.

'And she has such a beautiful name,' said Henry. 'Lola Lilac . . .' he repeated a few times, as if tasting the words, reliving the memory of her fleeting kisses. 'I'm going to write a little song for her,' said the man in love as he carefully closed the door. 'A sweet little song', I heard faintly from the corridor.

I was actually rather sceptical about Henry's passion. Lola Lilac was a bit too crude, and I assumed this was a matter of a short-lived aberration. Later the man would wake up from his intoxicated state, regretting what he had done, said and promised, and she would be extremely difficult to deal with. Henry Morgan was just that sort of man – it was no surprise.

By noon Henry's song was finished. It was called 'Lovely Lola Lilac', and when I heard the light, breezy melody and the mincing, coquettish lyrics, I had great difficulty picturing the meddlesome middleweight tornado in the long sequinned dress, high heels and thick make-up who only a couple of hours earlier had blown through our flat.

'Nice tune,' I said. 'Very nice tune. Although I wonder if you're not being a little bit *too* romantic. Lola seems . . . to have both feet on the ground, so to speak, like—'

'Don't bring me down, Klasa,' said Henry, sounding disappointed. 'Why do you always have to bring me down?'

'I have no intention of bringing you down. Maybe I'm just too hungover.'

Henry draped himself over the grand piano and groaned. He sighed heavily, and I could see that it was already over. Henry had buried his face in his arms resting on the piano, and I could hear him crying, sobbing quietly, in resignation. The keys were wet between C and F.

I sat down on the sofa and sighed too. This was truly a day of fuming and fretting in a hung-over vale of tears.

'Please forgive me if I was a little insensitive,' I said. 'I suppose I should have held back a bit.'

Henry nodded.

''Sallright to mmmtend hmmmmwhile . . .' he grunted down at the piano.

'I can't understand a word you're saying.'

Henry raised his head and looked out of the window at the dirty grey of Hornsgatan. He turned towards me and tears were running down his cheeks.

'It's all right to pretend once in a while,' he repeated. 'Surely we're allowed to pretend once in a while.'

'Of course,' I said.

Henry pulled out a newly pressed handkerchief, blew his nose, and then in the middle of it all, he started chuckling.

'They're all so ruthless,' he said, snuffling. 'They're all so damned honest and forthright . . .'

'Who do you mean?'

'Lola said that she was married and that she loved her husband and her kids more than anything else on earth. She wasn't lying – I could tell she wasn't. No, by God, I'm never going to fall in love again. And by the way, I'm not in love now either. I was just pretending, to see how it felt, you know. It's been such a long time.'

'Same here,' I said. 'It's been a fucking long time.'

Henry started plinking at the piano again, significantly more calm and composed, with less feigned delight. It sounded as if Mozart were trying his hand at the blues. Henry was playing much more honestly, and I sank back in the sofa, closed my eyes and listened.

'I'm in the mood for Maud,' Henry sang in a low voice. 'I'm in the mood for Maud,' he wailed like some genuine black blues singer.

I realised that he was going to be gone for a while. He would take off that very evening. Lola Lilac was merely a reminder of Love.

Another period of diligent work ensued in the sanctuary that we had tried to create in the flat: several hours at the typewriter, a few hours in the passageway and then quiet, chilly autumn evenings in front of the fireplace. I voluntarily kept to my schedule, in spite of the fact that Henry was away visiting Maud for a couple of days.

Now and then I would go down to the passageway to dig. Greger and Birger were on duty but, as I mentioned, they did very little work. Mostly they sat around bickering and drinking dessert wine. Birger was in the middle of a long new poem, and he had a hard time concentrating. Greger had to push the wheelbarrow.

'A person has to live too,' said Birger when I came down to the cellar one afternoon. 'A person has to live even when he's working, don't you agree?'

I concurred.

'Greger is a simple man, you know,' said Birger as Greger moved off, groaning as he pushed a full wheelbarrow. 'He's a bit naïve, but damn pleasant. He's always willing to help out, you know. Always. But he's a simple man.'

'Nobody I've ever met has been particularly simple,' I said.

'No, that's true,' said Birger amicably. 'Exactly, and that's what I say in my new poem. "Simplicity is just Maja's way / of scattering the black marsh / as twilight overtakes the day / and life appears so harsh,"' Birger read aloud.

'Neat rhyme,' I said. 'Pure Hjalmar Gullberg.'

'Thanks,' said Birger, sticking out a grimy hand.

'Is there any left?' asked Greger when he came back.

'Left of what? If it's dirt you mean, there's plenty more!'

'Of the sweet stuff. That's what I mean,' said Greger.

Birger poured another glass of dessert wine, and we had a little nip in reverent silence.

'So, have you made any progress?' I asked.

'Dammit, my boy,' said Birger emphatically, 'we've done more than half a yard this morning alone.'

'We've been working like dogs,' said Greger. 'The only problem is that we get so filthy, and it hurts my spine, right here, in the small of my back . . .'

'Just listen to him!' said Birger. 'It hurts your spine! You're just putting us on; you're a damn actor, that's what you are, Greger! A fucking Garbo!'

And so it was that Birger told me about the time he had spent with Garbo. He claimed, you see, to have lived in the same building at Blekingegatan 32 where Greta Gustafsson once lived. The fair Greta had pushed Birger in his pram during that great year of peace, 1918, and he remembered her perfectly because she was both a bit shy and quite forward all at the same time. Greta took little Birger over to the church, Allhelgonakyrka, and sat down on a bench in the cemetery to lick a lollipop, and the little tyke got to lick it too. Birger had licked the same lollipop as Greta Garbo! Later, of course, he could never recognise his nursemaid in all those films that Hollywood made with the girl from Blekingegatan. She was transformed, ruined, spoiled. There was nothing left of the girl with the lollipop at Allhelgonakyrka. The time is out of joint.

'But I'll tell you this,' said Birger. 'As soon as we find the gold treasure, someone is going to pop right over to America to pay a visit to Greta! Make no mistake about it. She'll remember me – she has to.'

'You've been saying that for fifty years now,' said Greger.

'All things come to he who waits . . .' said Birger.

The guys brushed off the dust and dirt from their clothes and turned over the shift to me, all the while fervently palavering about whether Garbo was recognisable or not up on the cinema screen. Presumably they continued that discussion for the rest of the day.

A few more days passed in this manner, and then Henry came back from his sojourn with Maud. One morning he was suddenly standing in the hallway, nodding and asking me whether there were any letters for him.

'Just from Hagberg in Borås, I think.'

'Have you come up with the next move?'

'I think we'd better do it together.'

Lennart Hagberg in Borås was apparently feeling threatened by that ingenious castling, and generally we could feel quite pleased with our strategy.

'Leo is going to owe you a big debt of gratitude after such a brilliant game,' said Henry. 'Chess is the only thing he has ever mastered in his life.'

———————

It was the All Saints' Day holiday, and we were supposed to mourn our dead. Or rather: we were supposed to *honour* our dead, as Henry expressed it.

I've never been much of a churchgoer, although I'm very religious, which is a different thing altogether. Henry's face fell when I told him that I had never been confirmed, had never attended a church service, and that I had also withdrawn my name from the state church. He couldn't comprehend how anyone could live such a thoroughly secular life. He was no first-rate theologian, but as an arch romantic and eschatologist, he did have some feel for the liturgy. I was in complete agreement that there was a certain emotion to the rituals, but for my part that wasn't enough.

'And Luther was a surly devil,' I asserted. 'He got rid of a whole lot of holidays—'

'You don't say!' said Henry, giving me another one of those pop-eyed indignant looks. 'Well, I'll be damned. I never thought about that . . . It's true that in France I thought a good deal about converting, although it seemed so incredibly ambitious. I'm not really that type . . .'

'I just don't like Luther, that's all there is to it,' I said.

'And that's something worth thinking about,' said Henry.

This conversation took place on the bus heading for Skog Cemetery – we were going out there to light our respectful candles. Dusk descended over the highway as Henry lapsed into pangs of anguish about Luther.

'Don't think about him now,' I said. 'Don't let him ruin the day!'

Out at Skog Cemetery the graves were already lit up. We were caught up in a deeply spiritual and ritualistic mood as we purchased our pine torches at the entrance. Everyone was quiet, talking in low voices, and not even the flower-sellers seemed especially high-spirited, even though they were doing a brisk business in candles and spruce boughs.

'Impressive,' said Henry at the gates. 'It makes you feel all weak at the knees.'

The torches and candles cast their flickering light over the headstones, making names emerge from the dark, from the silence, and from oblivion.

Candles burned on the ground, over the hills and gullies, in the forest and in the glades. The candles rippled into infinity – for a brief time a solemn eternity surrounded the individual names and factual data. For a few hours on that November evening, the stone-carvers' work glittered like the undying light in our prayers.

People were wandering like disembodied overcoats along the paths between the graves. Everyone spoke in hushed and subdued voices, lighting their candles, meditating with clasped hands, their faces shimmering, the headstones glittering and their breath swirling away in prayers and frost.

We stood there a long time, staring out at all that splendour, until we found the right pathway, the one leading to the Morgonstjärna family monument. It was a well-tended affair, with a tall stone displaying an eroded family crest.

Henry lit the torch with his Ronson lighter – turned up high like a blowtorch – and set it at the base of the headstone. He read all the names in a loud and clear voice, ending with his father, Gus Morgan, 1919–1958, and his grandfather, Morgonstjärna, 1895–1968. After he'd read the names, he stood perfectly still for a long time with his hands in his coat pockets. It was cold and a nasty wind was sweeping in from the Hungarian steppes. His cap was pulled down so he could meditate in peace and quiet. Of course I couldn't feel the same deep emotion, but I was even more touched by that undulating sea of flickering flames moving through the woods and into eternity itself.

'Hi everybody!' said Henry abruptly, shattering the solemn mood. 'I hope you're all doing well, wherever it is that you are.'

He stared down at the light, the headstone and the little frozen trellis rose climbing up over the gilded names.

'All of you must think it's a rather trivial and comical ritual, what we're doing down here, or up here, however you look on the matter from wherever it is that you are. I suppose it *is* banal, but what's a person to do?'

He turned to face me and repeated, 'What's a person to do?'

'We have to carry on,' I said. 'That's our only chance – to carry on.'

'At moments like this,' said Henry, looking out at the sea of lights, 'at moments like this it's so easy to have doubts about the whole thing. Everything seems so meaningless . . . It seems so petty to toil and rush around in the few brief years that are allotted to us; it's so seldom that we pause to look around us and take stock of what we're really doing . . . It's a judgement, a harsh judgement, a penance . . .'

'You shouldn't look at it that way.'

'No, that's exactly it. A person shouldn't give in. That's what the others have done, who . . .'

An icy wind swept through the cemetery, and we started shivering in the cold.

'It's cold on Earth,' said Henry, as if presenting an excuse to leave.

'You sound so odd,' said a voice from the darkness next to the grave. 'Just like a real pastor.'

A girl, or rather a woman, appeared from behind the headstone. She smiled and continued to extol Henry's eloquence.

'I couldn't help listening,' she said. 'You sounded like a real pastor, and it was so beautiful that I almost started to cry.'

The woman now emerged on the pathway, and she turned out to be an elegant lady of twenty-five or so, dressed entirely in black and with a mourning ribbon on the collar of her coat.

'My father died a month ago.'

Henry took out his cigarettes and offered them to us. We each took one, saying nothing. She was the first to break the silence.

'Are you going into town?'

We both nodded, shivering.

'Do you have a car? If not, I can give you a lift.'

'Thank you very much, my defenceless child,' said Henry, in the hope that the paternal pastor-like tone would strike home. But it didn't really. As it turned out, the woman in question was definitely not some sort of defenceless little lamb. She had a glaring yellow van with PICKO'S emblazoned on the sides. She was one of those girls who was clearly not born yesterday. The type who races around the city in a Picko's delivery van. I think hers was number 8, just like a certain successful basketball player.

Henry completely lost his head when the woman led us over to the glaringly bright vehicle.

'You drive a *delivery van*?!' he exclaimed in surprise. 'That's the . . .'

'Hop in, boys!' she said. 'What are your names, by the way?'

Henry introduced himself very properly, as usual, with a handshake and a click of his heels, and he nodded at me and told her my name without expounding any further.

'I'm Kerstin Bäck,' she said.

'All right, Kerstin,' said Henry. 'Just take it easy now. The roads are probably slippery.'

Kerstin drove like an angel, shifting as eagerly as a racing-car driver. She had an amazing feel for the pedals, and Henry alternated between surreptitious glances at the speedometer and at the lively play of the pedals. Or maybe it was her knees; I had my suspicions.

'It's true what you were saying,' said Kerstin when she got the van up to speed. 'What you said about things being meaningless. It can feel so absurd, all this . . . this striving that we get involved in. I don't really know what all that striving is for.'

'Who does know?' Henry interjected.

'But you've got to keep fighting. You can't just see emptiness in everything.'

'A person has to pretend,' said Henry. 'A person has to pretend all the time that there's something beyond the mountains. Otherwise everything becomes empty and cursed . . .'

But in fact Kerstin didn't seem exactly paralysed by a fear of death either. She came very close to sending all three of us back to Skog Cemetery with a number of death-defying manoeuvres to overtake other cars.

'What are you going to do now?' she asked us near Slussen.

'I don't really know,' said Henry. 'Maybe go and get some coffee.'

'Good,' said Kerstin. 'Gamla Stan?'

Without waiting for our assent, she stepped on the gas and headed up Slottsbacken, manoeuvred the van into a parking space intended for motorbikes and disabled drivers and jumped out.

We trotted over to the Kristina Café and ordered three coffees with cinnamon rolls and biscuits. It was very crowded and noisy, and our reverent mood was soon sent packing. Life had once again seized hold of us with its thirst, appetites and desires. But Henry couldn't resist adopting that sermonising tone – I'm convinced that he still thought Kerstin could be softened up that way – and he said that he respected women dressed in mourning; in his opinion they had a special dignity about them.

'I'm going to take off this mourning ribbon soon,' said Kerstin. 'I can't stand hearing any more condolences.'

'Are you all alone now?'

'Yes, my mother died five years ago. I thought I'd never get over it. But I did. Pappa took it even harder than I did. And now he's gone too. I can't really picture him as . . . as dead. He was so great.'

Our coffee arrived, and Henry offered us another round of cigarettes. Out of sheer delicacy of feeling he kept quiet for a change.

'My father was so full of ideas,' said Kerstin. 'He started a private betting company; that was back in the twenties. In Göteborg . People were betting like crazy. Then times got hard and the state started its own Football Betting Service, and he had to come up with something new. So he turned to bicycles and cars. Pappa was one of the first car dealers in town. I wish you could have met him; it would have been an experience you never forgot.'

'That's what it sounds like,' said Henry.

Kerstin was sad again, and she started to cry. She buried her face in her hands and wept and sniffled.

'I . . . can't . . . help . . . Oh . . ,' she sobbed.

'There, there,' said Henry, handing her a newly pressed handkerchief.

'Thanks,' said Kerstin, blowing her nose hard. 'Whoops! Oh shit!' she shouted. 'SHIT!'

'What's wrong?' Henry and I asked in unison.

'I've lost a lens,' said Kerstin. 'The contact lens in my right eye. SIT STILL, SIT ABSOLUTELY STILL, DON'T MOVE!'

Henry and I sat at the table as if frozen, not even daring to breathe as Kerstin cautiously unfolded Henry's handkerchief and examined every little fold. Then she inspected herself, her mourning clothes, the table, the chairs and the floor. Cautiously she got down on the floor and crawled around on the carpet like a near-sighted pooch, swearing her head off.

'Fuck these lenses to hell,' she cursed, and Henry sniggered. 'They cost over five hundred kronor each, these fucking lenses!'

Kerstin finally found the lens in her coffee cup. She fished it out with a spoon and went to the ladies' to wash it off as best she could.

'Strange bird,' said Henry. 'A really strange girl.'

'I'm speechless,' I said.

'I'm in love,' said Henry demurely. 'I'm in love again,' he sang softly.

I didn't dare tell him that I was too. Maybe not head over heels, but at least a little lukewarm, halfway there, at least up to my shoulders.

Of course this turned into a song too. It wasn't until Henry received my lovingly rhymed lyrics to 'The Girl with the Contact Lenses and Mourning Ribbon' that he realised that I too had fallen for her. She had given Henry her phone number in the café in Gamla Stan, and she had said that she definitely wanted to see us again, and soon. Henry was on cloud nine all the way home. I kept my love to myself, although the song that I wrote and handed over to Henry so that he could set it to music spoke for itself. There was no doubt about the matter – only a poet who was truly in love could write like that.

Henry sat at the piano for an hour with the new song and then summoned me, giving me a smirk as soon as I appeared.

'These are powerful lyrics, Klasa,' he said. 'Fucking powerful.'

'Thanks, Hempa. I'm really glad you think so,' I said, sitting down on the sofa with the black tassels to smoke a cigarette.

'But I'm getting a sense that the songwriter himself has very hot feelings for the subject, if I may say so . . . It's pure adulation.'

I was embarrassed and blew smoke towards him, swine that he was, sitting at the piano.

'That could be,' I said.

'Woo-hoo,' Henry hollered into the piano. 'I guess we'll have to share her. Chastely and innocently. Jules and Jim . . .' he went on as he started playing that Jeanne Moreau song, and he even knew half the words.

'Be serious!' I said, annoyed because I didn't want him to make fun of my tender song of praise. 'Play it properly.'

'OK, forgive me,' said Henry, pulling himself together. 'Here goes.'

And he played the song, which was the best one the two of us had written so far. A rather melancholy ballad about a girl with contact lenses and a mourning ribbon who is grieving for her father, a betting-pool king from Göteborg. It was so easy and rewarding to make up rhymes for that city.

The goose banquet was without a doubt the high point of the year for the treasure hunters. One day in early November Greger came up to ask about the arrangements – he had been sent by Birger, of course – and Henry informed him that the arrangements would be exactly the same as usual. Greger was given the task of relaying the invitation to the other guests.

The fact that the arrangements were going to be exactly the same as always signified a very ceremonious event with the so-called black soup (made from goose giblets), a couple of nicely roasted geese, a suitably heavy wine, dessert and cognac with the coffee. It was a costly party, and consequently Henry suggested that I select a number of volumes from the library that we could sell for a couple of thousand kronor.

Since I often frequented antiquarian bookshops and always read the reports in *Book Auctions* magazine, I had an inkling about what the market prices might be. I chose a number of reference and speciality books and went back and forth, calculating, adding and subtracting. I rang up dealers and got tips on some absolutely unfindable French books, *L'histoire de la Comédie Française* in four thick volumes.

But then I came up with a brilliant choice – *The Swedish Tourist Bureau's Annual Report*, collected and in perfectly preserved condition from its very beginning in 1886 up until 1968. It was a fine collection, two yards of shelves about Swedish terrain, history, cultural miscellany, canoe expeditions and bicycle trips throughout the realm. I was sure we could get at least fifteen hundred for it.

Excellent, brilliant, in Henry's opinion, and we loaded the eighty-two volumes into a couple of empty boxes and went over to the Furniture Man to borrow a vehicle. We didn't have to go far to get a nice offer, but Henry wanted to try a really high-class and respectable antiquarian shop, so we headed for Ramfalks on Hamngatan.

'A thousand,' said the man behind the counter as he leafed through a couple of the books.

'You know what?' said Henry *the salesman*. 'We had an offer of two and a half on the phone. Although that was in Uppsala. And I'll be damned if I'm going to drive out in the country just for a couple of hundred extra. Seventeen fifty is what I want . . .'

'I don't know . . . ,' the bookseller fussed. 'That sounds like a lot. But of course . . . they're fine-looking volumes . . .'

'*Fine-looking* volumes?' Henry repeated. 'They're *first-rate* volumes, for God's sake! No one has ever even touched them. Well? Shall we say two thousand even?'

There was not much more arguing – the bookseller acquiesced because he really had no choice when confronted with Henry *the salesman*, who quickly got him to realise that an antiquarian bookshop without the *Swedish Tourist Bureau's Annual Report* going back to 1886 was not an antiquarian bookshop worth mentioning.

With those two delightful banknotes in hand we took off and headed straight for the Hötorg indoor marketplace, where Henry had a buddy who sold meat and wild game. He was a hefty guy weighing over fifteen stone, with the brawny arms of a bouncer and wearing a bloody apron. It turned out that he'd been a boxer in the past, and a very good one.

'Nice to see you, kid,' said the meat-seller. 'So did you see Ali vs Spinks? What a fucking fight! Geese? Two of them? You should have rung ahead, Hempa. I never could figure you out. Two geese?! On the spur of the moment! No way.'

'What the hell?!' cried Henry, his face pale. But the meat-seller merely laughed and shook his head. Then he pulled two nice-looking birds out of the cooler and flung the goods onto the counter with such force that it shook.

'Flew up from Skåneland yesterday all by themselves, ha, ha, ha,' chuckled the meat-seller.

'Nice going,' muttered Henry. 'Nice going for an idiot like yourself.'

After this exchange of pleasantries we made a good number of other purchases at the marketplace, and we returned home with the Furniture Man's van packed full with six big boxes. It had cost us just over fourteen hundred kronor, and Henry was very pleased.

Roasting a goose is no job for a novice, and roasting two geese is no job for two novices. But with common sense, a good cookbook and an endless amount of patience, we managed to complete the task successfully. Henry had done all this before, but he always forgot how to do it from one year to the next.

Some time around three in the morning we were done. There sat two splendidly roasted geese, stuffed with innards and bread crumbs, dripping with grease and emanating such a heavy aroma that just inhaling it made us feel full.

The goose banquet turned out to be a memorable event. We put a long table in one of the cellar rooms that looked like a regular medieval vault with its walls roughly plastered white, little niches for burning candles, and benches fastened to the side walls. We set the table with a coarse linen cloth, rolled napkins and fine china.

The kitchen up in our flat was total chaos. Henry was flailing his bartender arms around, his apron covered with goose fat, gravy, giblet soup, spices and flour. He was in high gear, having the time of his life. I thought it best to keep out of the way and take care of the other arrangements, the atmosphere or ambiance, down in the cellar.

The ceremonies were to begin as soon as the chef gave the signal. The table was set and the candles were lit in the candelabras, their light shimmering on a couple of bouquets of red tulips, heralding Christmas. Everything looked extremely impressive down there in the cellar.

'I was told seven, and seven it is,' said Greger, the first to show up.

'Welcome, Greger,' said Henry. 'May I offer you a drink?'

'Yes, please,' said Greger, and assumed a diffident pose, with the drink in his hand.

He was dressed in his very best, and he even had a red rose in his buttonhole.

Then the rest of the gang arrived very punctually: the Flask wearing a jacket and checked shirt; Wolf-Larsson in a checked blazer, parking his German shepherd in the corner; the Philatelist in an old grey suit; Birger wearing a bow-tie; and finally the Fence Queen, who drew a whistle and a muted round of applause. The evening's queen wore a long black skirt with a glittering Lurex top, a pearl necklace and long earrings.

Everyone was quickly in high spirits, thick clouds of smoke swirled round the vaults, and Birger gave a long, magisterial evaluation of Henry's welcome punchbowl. He totted up full marks – he was a connoisseur of most things, after all – and Greger's eyes sparkled with admiration.

Henry slipped upstairs to the kitchen while the rest of us warmed up with drinks and some rather gluttonous small talk. The Philatelist had made a few excellent deals that autumn, and the Furniture Man was doing better business than ever. Things were looking up for the shop-owners in the Rosendal Större neighbourhood, and we all drank a toast to the good times ahead.

'Dinner is served!' Henry bellowed as he came downstairs with the steaming black soup, fresh from the stove. 'Please sit down, everyone!'

A minor commotion ensued, of course, as all these gentlemen had to be seated at the table. The Fence Queen was given a place of honour, right across from the host, so that everyone could have a good view of her. The rest of the gang sat down wherever they could find a place. I ended up between Wolf-Larsson and Birger.

The black soup was delicious, the wine loosened our tongues even more and the guests uttered long sighs over the soup's aroma, which was both bitter and delicate at the same time. Birger was one of those stylish types who spooned his soup the opposite way, just to appear a bit more refined. He seemed to be moving his spoon away from him the whole time.

'Look at him and his fancy manners,' said Wolf-Larsson.

'You say that every year,' replied Birger.

'No fighting now, boys,' said the Fence Queen, who never lost control of her admirers.

'No, cheers and welcome, one more year,' said Henry, raising his glass.

'*Skål*, counts and barons!' said Birger.

'*Skål!*' roared everyone in unison.

Then the host and I disappeared as soon as it was high time for the goose, the main course, which was crackling away in the oven upstairs. We were met with thunderous applause when we placed the two geese on the table and the delicious aroma began wafting through the cellar.

'Hooray!' shouted Greger.

'You two are amazing!' said the Fence Queen.

'*Bravissimo!*' said Birger.

Henry carved the geese and distributed an equal share of the morsels to one and all. Served with baked potatoes, apple sauce, Brussels sprouts, four different kinds of jelly, carrots, peas and a gravy made from dripping and two litres of reduced cream, the dinner was a gourmand's delight without equal. We shovelled down the food, sighing, groaning, bemoaning the limitations of our stomachs, sighing even more, and enjoying ourselves to the hilt. The toasts became more frequent, the heat more oppressive; ties were loosened, jackets removed and sweat poured from our brows. The sweat became mixed with shiny goose fat, and the sighs were interrupted by clacking jaws, smacking lips and the constant gurgling of the wine.

Greger was the first to unfasten his belt; the rest of us followed his lead, and by the third round the Fence Queen was the only one behaving in a somewhat dignified manner. She handled her liquor well even though all the men, of course, wanted to drink a toast to her.

Birger had, naturally, put together a poem in honour of the celebratory occasion, and as soon as he was feeling a bit tipsy, he tapped his glass. Everyone began shushing each other in order to establish a semblance of order and attentiveness.

'I have written a little homage to . . . to the goose and the chef . . .' he started off, slurring his words.

'Let's hear it!'

'Shh . . . I will recite it from . . . from memory. "What role do the words of the poet play / when a goose graces the table on St Morten's Day . . ."' Birger began. I've actually forgotten the rest because by that time no one was particularly lucid.

The wine, the heat and the food had made me drowsy, and I couldn't really keep up with everything anymore. But Birger was bemoaning – and this much I dare assert with certainty – the paucity and inadequacy of words when confronted with a table set for a goose feast, and he didn't waste the opportunity to find rhymes for *goose* and *gravy* and *giblets*. At that point someone pointed out that he did the same thing every year, and that the rhymes actually belonged to the singer, Povel Ramel.

Birger was a bit upset by this inconsiderate response, but he kept his good humour. Glasses were raised to toast one thing after another, and the gentle glow of reconciliation settled over the cellar vaults. During the pause between the goose with wine and the coffee with cognac, all of us lads went out to the courtyard to take a leak in the fountain under the maple tree. It was a mild, starry evening in late autumn. The fresh air felt good, and we could see a little patch of the star-strewn heavens above the courtyard, a small corner of the universe, framed by the façades of four buildings. If you stood there staring long enough, you felt as if you were flying up from the courtyard, into eternity. That's what the Flask claimed he had once done.

'I stood here for half an hour, staring straight up at the sky. Then I lost my footing and just seemed to fly upwards. I woke up in the bicycle shed several hours later. But of course, it was fucking late at night . . . ha ha ha . . .'

We laughed our heads off at the Flask's Ascension and then went back down to the Inferno to stuff ourselves from a stockpile of pickled ginger on top of all that goose fat.

We were all sitting there sipping our cognac, in the best of moods. The table, as is customary, had taken on the look of a battlefield, cluttered with coffee cups, glass platters, ashtrays, toppled empty wine bottles and soiled napkins. Abruptly an icy wind blew through the room, a gust from the outside world, as a lost angel threw open the door and swept away the haze, the smoke, the alcoholic fumes, the laughter and the atmosphere – the whole mood, plain and simple.

He was suddenly just standing there in the vaulted room. I didn't know who he was, of course, but I instantly recognised him because I'd seen him plenty of times in the city – all the places where anything was happening. He had been at the Gärdet Festivals and the Elms demonstration, he had hung out at the art school in Stockholm and turned up at all sorts of events. And I remembered him from the Bob Dylan concert in Göteborg in the summer. We had ended up sitting next to each other – this skinny introverted guy had merely sat there, his eyes half-closed, motionless and preoccupied.

Of course I had no idea what this man was doing here at our private goose banquet in the cellar. My first guess was that he had heard sounds coming from the courtyard and had come in search of a drink. But it turned out I was completely wrong.

'Leo?!' said Henry in surprise. 'Leo?!' he said several more times until he got up from the table to shake hands with his brother and welcome him home. 'But *how in hell*?!' he wondered, looking like one big question mark.

Leo was not at all how I'd imagined him. According to Henry, we were supposed to be so alike. But I didn't think that seemed true at all. Leo was much taller than Henry and seemed almost emaciated. His cheeks were hollow and he had the grey skin of a heavy smoker, stretched tight over his cheekbones. His eyes flickered nervously beneath the curly black hair hanging over his forehead. His response to Henry's welcome was quite restrained.

So this was Leo Morgan, the child prodigy who became the cherished poet of the youth movement in the early sixties – the Provie, occupier of the student union building, avant-garde musician, author and exposer of the most rotten forces in society. What he was now, at the present time, I had no idea. And that was probably fortunate for me.

The rest of the gang all knew Leo Morgan well. They greeted him with a respect that was hard to fathom, as if he were some sort of social inspector. Leo gave me a nod when Henry explained who I was.

Henry seemed suddenly a bit dispirited and subdued by this interruption, because it had come as such a surprise. He hadn't been expecting Leo to come back home. They sat down at one end of the long table, talking quietly and sensibly to one another. No one could hear what they were talking about. I assumed that Leo had a great deal to report from America, although the scene didn't look as you'd imagine when someone comes home from a long trip and starts telling tall tales about his adventures in faraway lands. Usually you'd expect wild gestures and loud laughter, but this conversation looked more like a discussion in some political party headquarters about future strategies for a debate.

The two brothers spent a long time talking together, and the party soon took off on its own; one *skål* to the counts and barons followed another. Henry had been scrupulous about purchasing several bottles of Grönstedts Extra, a very fine cognac, which soon lent extra pep to the celebration. The boys got caught up in fiery discussions about the world situation, and the Fence Queen really cut loose and began tap-dancing to prove that she had once been a dancer.

It was late by the time Leo finally ended up sitting next to me at the table. He'd had quite a lot to drink; he looked composed but worn-out and tipsy. He wanted to know how I was doing and what I was working on. I told him that I was writing a modern version of *The Red Room*, that it was going splendidly and that I was doing fucking great.

'So how was it in New York?' I asked him. 'Henry has been on the lookout for letters, but none ever arrived . . .'

Leo's expression turned dark and gloomy, both menacing and absolutely vacant. He fixed his eyes on the candelabra on the table. He didn't speak for a long time.

'Hmm, well,' he said. 'It was intense. Fucking intense. The buildings were full of magma, as if the whole city were built on top of a volcano. It glowed and throbbed in all the windows and shopfronts, and I kept thinking that it would leak out somewhere. I spent most of my time at the cinema . . .'

'I see,' I said, a little bewildered. 'I see.'

'Do you believe that?' Leo asked without taking his eyes off the candles.

'What?' I said. 'Believe what?'

'The part about the buildings,' said Leo with a smile.

'Why shouldn't I?'

'Because I've never been there,' said Leo. 'I've never been to America.'

I sniggered, feeling a bit of a fool, because I didn't know what was wrong with this man.

'What the hell are you laughing at?' he said sullenly.

'I have no idea,' I said.

'I was locked up in an asylum,' said Leo. 'I was locked up in an *asylum* . . .'

BROTHERS

HERBARIUM

(Leo Morgan, 1948–59)

'My heart no longer strikes / it strikes back . . .' That was what it said in a fragment that I found in Leo's two-room quarters, redolent with incense, a couple of days ago. And there's reason to doubt that his heart is striking at all today. As poetry, the words bear the unmistakable signature of Leo Morgan, a stamp that guarantees Royal Purveyances to Hell – that is the life-blood of Morgan the demiurge, the shaman and the wizard, incised like the revelatory code, the final signal for all our psychic forces to go on the attack, brandishing our consciences, loaded with live cartridges, all over our innermost cavern walls, dripping with cold sweat from the stalactites of our tears.

Like all present-day magicians, the man ended up spending some time in an insane asylum. At Långbro Hospital, on the outskirts of Stockholm, there is a file on the patient Leo Morgan, born 28 February 1948, with an allegedly complete record of the case. Naturally I haven't had access to the document. Unlike the case history of that Nazi and idiot Hermann Göring, Leo's records are still confidential, but I'm neither stupid nor without contacts. I've been able to ascertain that in this instance it's a matter of something that without exaggeration might be called a 'whitewashed account' – a medical account that has been corrected and censored after the fact. For that reason I venture to call it an 'allegedly' complete report.

To reveal right now why someone went in and changed the report would, of course, be getting ahead of my story; it would also give this account an inappropriate anticlimax. This is by no means some sort of thriller; nor is it a psychiatric dissertation. Actually, I have only a vague idea of who might have had an interest in intervening by censoring and altering the facts, which upon cursory examination hardly seem to warrant such a serious offence. But then, nothing is what it seems to be upon cursory observation.

Leo Morgan was thus taken in hand and admitted for psychiatric treatment at Långbro Hospital in May 1975. The doctors' first diagnosis was catatonia. This meant, among other things, a total inability to act, a type of petrifaction or mutism, an utter lack of communication with the outside world.

Catatonia display similarities with autism. A psychosis may underlie the symptoms, some form of trauma, one or more experiences that have never been sensibly explained or given full expression. The soul accumulates questions, hatreds and passions, ultimately channelling everything into a total or partial passivity.

A number of doctors have given their opinion regarding the Leo Morgan case, and some state in the medical record that in his childhood the patient was latently autistic but that he had intuitively sought out channels and outlets for the traumatic energy. It was when these outlets stopped functioning, or as one doctor formulated it, 'when the channels became once again silted up with the rubble of frustration' – some doctors are true poets! – that his illness would erupt in full force.

Maybe there was some reason for all this. Doctors are generally competent people, and what I've found out on my own shows a number of similarities with the 'whitewashed report'. But, strangely enough, only one of four doctors looked in the patient's poetic work for the key to Leo's petrified door. This testifies to a lack of imagination on a grand scale, as well as wholesale failure on the part of the psychiatric hospital. I myself view his poems as self-explanatory, not to mention an inescapable and essential part of his case history.

But what are undeniably the most important and crucial elements are the facts that have been whitewashed, censored by some higher-up, a doctor in the hands of a disembodied Power. The Leo Morgan case is just one small episode in a multifaceted and, for a novice such as myself, immensely comprehensive story which, among those in the know, is called the *Hogarth Affair*. The history of Sweden in the twentieth century boasts of a number of 'affairs' in which royal swindling, military espionage or corporate manipulation were uncovered, brought to light – at least in convenient proportions – only to be later added to events labelled 'scandals'. These types of affairs and scandals occur at regular intervals in all societies, civilised and corrupt alike. There is something inevitable about it and, in some sense, desired. And when the whole thing is over – which means when the convenient scapegoats have been publicly pilloried or placed under lock and key – the most zealous defenders of justice and democracy start pounding their chests and raising shrill, boastful voices to praise their own and the system's magnificent capacity for self-purification. That's part of the picture when it comes to a scandal: one hand washes the other, preferably to the tune of a national anthem.

But the Hogarth Affair is different from other affairs by virtue of the fact that it has not yet been brought to light; time after time it has been hushed up. And according to the suspicions that have been communicated to me, it has been kept secret at the cost of three human lives and a couple of million Swedish kronor in bribes, as well as at least one case of insanity. And that's where Leo Morgan comes into the picture, even though, as I mentioned, he stands on the outermost periphery of the whole thing.

The central figures in the Hogarth Affair – incidentally, it got its name from one of the members of the Well-travelled, Well-read, Well-heeled Club, the journalist Edvard Hogarth – are either deceased or highly active potentates and magnates within the business world and public administration. Presumably it is there, in the whirlwind of corruption and effective blackout, that we need to begin the search for the people who intervened to censor Leo Morgan's medical account. The trail ought to end, at any rate, at the Griffel Corporation's palace, in the room where CEO Wilhelm Sterner himself reigns. But this is a job for a journalist with a cast-iron stomach and nine lives; not for me.

What I have to say about my friend Leo Morgan starts off quite innocently, like any other reverent biography of a poet. But it gets better, as arsonists supposedly say. That too is undoubtedly just a pack of lies.

———————

Measles, scarlet fever, German measles, chicken-pox, whooping cough, croup – all those long, drawn-out vaccination processes for so-called childhood diseases with their hallucinogenic peaks of fever, their prickling rashes, itching pustules and devastating instructions . . . Shouldn't every biography begin with just such a list of illnesses when the little creature, for the first time, makes real contact with a state other than what we call normal? The manner in which every person endures his childhood illnesses is highly individual. The patient that the family doctor – the eternally old, reliable, huffing-and-puffing Dr Helmers – examined, Leo Morgan, displayed exactly the same symptoms for every type of illness: an irregular pulse, weakness bordering on death and an absolutely non-existent will to get better.

Henry on the other hand required restraints and a straitjacket to keep him in bed; he screamed and howled for exactly twenty-four hours until the fever subsided, and then he was well again, no matter what illness had felled him. He wanted to go back to school, even though he never managed to make up the lessons that he had missed.

But little Leo lacked the *will* to get well. Nevertheless, he would usually be two weeks ahead of his classmates in his homework because he was an extremely gifted child prodigy. His glassy eyes greeted Dr Helmers with neither entreaties, impatience nor satisfaction. His gaze was quite simply desolate and empty, indifferent. Leo had escaped to another world, and by the time he was eight he already knew what death meant. Ten years later, in a famous poem, he would define every human endeavour and breath as 'a war against death', in which death was both the goal and the means. He was then caricatured by a critic as the 'anarchist with bombs in his own pockets'. And that presumably signalled the absolute apex of that critic's career.

Leo Morgan was marked by death, fixated on death, and he studied death with the inexhaustible frenzy that only someone who is deathly afraid can display. In reality, the little boy was scared out of the very wits which he turned to his benefit. His entire life was a prolonged attempt to find his way back from the valley of the shadow of death, but it was a long road, and he lacked any sort of reliable map.

A melancholy, almost tragic downpour was drenching the city. It sounded like an absent-minded and cautious plinking, as if a pianist with gigantic hands were pawing at the galvanised roof.

Henry was sitting in the dormer window of the laundry room up in the attic. Greta had a day off from her job at the Community Sewing Room down on Mariatorget, where people could come to get help with their sewing. It was her laundry day, and Henry had promised to help her wring out the sheets and hang them up.

A nice warm steam was coming from the very modern Husqvarna washing machine. In the winter the windowpanes would be covered with mist, and you could conjure up the street below by wiping them clean, or you could print letters, numbers and dates in the condensation. If Henry had done that, he would presumably have written 7 April, 1959, since that's the date we're describing in our chronicle.

It wasn't especially cold outside, and he opened the window to look out across the green, red and yellow rooftops rippling like crumpled paper in the Brännkyrkagatan district. He liked the view. If he leaned out of the window he could peer over the eaves and catch a glimpse of the street below. When he was a kid that had made him feel dizzy. But Henry was no longer a child; he was sixteen, went to the Södra Latin school, played Dixieland jazz, and was a decent boxer.

Right now he sat there looking out of the window, whistling a tune that they were practising in the band. Greta sighed and groaned and wondered what had happened to the sheets. She had put the sheets in the spin-dryer, but when they were nearly dry and she took them out, the sheets were completely covered with tiny black hairs.

She wondered out loud what could have happened to the sheets. Henry went over to the spin-dryer and looked down, with due respect for the machine. He had never liked spin-dryers because when he was a kid and looked inside them, he would always feel dizzy, just like when he peered down at the street six storeys below.

He could see that there were tiny hairs inside. Greta sighed, thinking it was very strange. She started cleaning out the spin-dryer.

Henry, in an almost embarrassing manner, had become aware of his manhood up there in the laundry room. He wasn't really sure what had prompted this feeling, whether it was the warm, damp, caressing air, or whether it was the fragrance of clean laundry. Whatever it was, he was filled with lust. He told Greta that he was thinking of taking a tour around the attics for a bit. He promised to come right back.

Henry was planning to find some secluded spot where he could rid himself of his importunate lust. There was a place where he and a couple of other boys from the neighbourhood, in the greatest secrecy, had stored a number of issues of *Pin-Up*, *Top-Hat* and *Cavalcade*. It was a dim corner of an empty attic storeroom where they could individually or together wreck their spines, impair their minds and ruin any chance of leading a respectable life.

This attic was undoubtedly one of the biggest in all of Stockholm. The corridors seemed to cover an entire neighbourhood, leading first to the right, then to the left, branching out in several directions at once, leading to dead-ends and completely new, endless networks. You almost needed a map to find your way if you failed to take proper notice of the numbered arrows. But even as a child Henry had despised maps; he put his trust in his instincts, his intuitive feeling for the points of the compass. Since this had won him first place in orienteering, surely it should be good enough for him to find his way in a simple attic.

It might be surmised that on this occasion the boy, taking a circuitous route to that particular attic storeroom, raced along with a pounding pulse. On his way he happened to pass a couple of other storerooms that were also empty and abandoned. But he caught sight of a strip of light seeping into the dark from a thin slit in a boarded partition. He was curious, of course, and stopped at once to sneak cautiously over to the wall. He heard voices that were not at all difficult to identify: Leo and Verner, the chess genius. Henry couldn't fathom what they were doing there.

He opened the door slightly to the abandoned attic storeroom, causing the boys to jump in fright – they had been caught red-handed.

Verner was the chess genius who was no longer such a genius. Henry had outgrown him, so Verner now had to settle for Leo's company. They still played childish games, although they did so solemnly and doggedly, not as heedlessly as other children. They collected stamps, played chess, came up with inventions and performed experiments. Verner had the sternest mother in town; she protected her son as if he were a haemophiliac. He was seldom allowed out after dinner, he was never permitted to fight and he always had to have his lessons down cold. He was forced to study on Sundays as well, and even now, as a young boy, he was a bit odd because of this state of things. He had started a club at school for Young Inventors, but so far there were no members because he mostly kept to himself, picking his nose. He couldn't seem to spend time with other boys unless a club were instantly formed to identify what they would be doing. Everything had to be organ-ised, with a chairman, a board, membership cards and rules to make sure that nothing unexpected would occur. If it wasn't organised, Verner couldn't stand it. He was about as spontaneous as the leader of a political party.

On that April day in 1959 when Henry entered Leo and Verner's secret attic storeroom, he was mildly shocked – the boys had created a small scientific laboratory up there. They had nailed blankets and cloths over the walls to mute the sound and to prevent the light from their torches from seeping out and disclosing what they were up to. From some orange crates they had taken a few boards that at the moment were clearly functioning as autopsy tables. In the centre of one of the planks lay a dead kitten that Verner had cut open with a scalpel. Leo was studying little pieces of flesh under a microscope.

Verner and Leo sat there as if paralysed until Verner found his tongue to protest their innocence. They had found the dead cat; they weren't the ones who had killed it. It didn't take Henry long to put two and two together. The cat hair in the spin-dryer was of course the remains of the hooligans' latest party. There was a gang that stole cats in the springtime and broke into laundry rooms to spin the animals to their death amid wild shouting.

Henry believed the boys, even though he still thought they were nuts. He started screaming that they were both crazy, sitting there and staring at the body of a dead cat. Why were they doing that? It was disgusting!

Henry was absolutely furious. Verner and Leo were dumbfounded. They couldn't say a word. They couldn't explain why it was so amazing to look at dead tissue under a microscope. It just was.

Well, Henry finally calmed down, and then he suddenly remembered why he'd come to this part of the attic in the first place. He asked Verner for a laboratory flask, struggling to keep from laughing. Embarrassed, Verner handed over a flask, and then Henry left and headed for his own secret storeroom. Filled with fury combined with lust, he leafed through an old issue of *Pin-Up* until the sweetest moment of the divine sexual act sent shivers racing through his whole body and, in a highly tangible temporal confirmation of success, it also sent a measured white, sticky fluid, a secretion, an essence, the very mystery of life out across the cold floor of the attic. Fortunately, a small portion of this magnetic mass landed in the laboratory flask. Quite pleased, Henry rushed back with the results in a considerably more amicable state of mind.

He shoved Leo away from the microscope, slipped out the piece of cat flesh, and slid his own quivering sample into place. He adjusted the instrument and immediately saw tiny, cocky sperm cells merrily swimming around in our world, wriggling and jostling their way across the Baltic Sea, down through the North Sea, across the English Channel, through the Strait of Gibraltar into the hot salt of the Mediterranean, east to the Suez Canal, out to the Arabian Sea, straight down the Indian Ocean, around the Cape of Good Hope, right across the Atlantic Ocean, around Cape Horn and up through the Pacific towards the Bering Sea, where the cold made them a bit stiff in the tail.

Henry cheered at this dizzying odyssey through the oceans of the world. A number of mates looked tired and feeble right from the start, some were misshapen with crooked tails, but most of them were big, fat, strong chaps that merrily wriggled towards a non-existent goal. As so often before, they had been tricked.

He shouted to Verner and Leo that here was something worth looking at. It was much more exciting than dead cats. But when he tore his eyes away from the lens of the microscope, he found himself all alone in the secret laboratory. Verner and Leo had run off. They never took part in this remarkable discovery of Henry's, Henry *the inventor*.

And Greta, of course, never learned the reason for the mysterious little hairs on her sheets. Henry was certainly not one to keep silent, but no doubt he thought she'd had enough of death and misery; he didn't want to worry her unnecessarily.

I, on the other hand, heard the story approximately twenty years later. It was very much like a lot of other things that I know about Leo. The story stems from Henry, from his perspective, because Leo was a professional silent type. He had an unusual, extremely strange way of speaking. Leo spoke slowly, sucking on the words like boiled sweets until he spat them out. He used words rather like a small child who finds a smashed piece of chewing-gum on the pavement, pries it loose with an ice-cream stick and stuffs it into his mouth. With a ruminative expression he chews the gum until it's soft, only to spit it out again when the taste is revived from its fossilised slumber. It took time to listen to Leo, once he started talking at all. I concluded as much on that very first evening when he joined us at the goose banquet in the cellar. I surmised that his manner of speaking was caused by some sort of shattered relationship with language, and words in general.

It's unlikely that anyone today would remember the poet Leo Morgan, other than those who are most in the know. He was never an Evert Taube, even though at one time in his fair youth he found himself quite close to Gösta Nordgren, known as Snoddas.

There are three books that admit him to the eternity of libraries, now that human memory is starting to fail. He made his debut with *Herbarium* (1962), followed by *Sanctimonious Cows* (1967), and finally *Façade Climbing and Other Hobbies* (1970).

As a rule, three such impenetrable, heavy poetry collections would give a poet more than a certain reputation among the initiated, but Leo was not the type to publicise his own work, or to promote himself at all the right parties, or to stay on good terms with the right critics. There are plenty of examples of such lone wolves and outsiders but, regrettably, there are even more examples of just the opposite.

Citizens possessed of a good memory may recall Leo Morgan as the child prodigy who read poems on the TV show *Hyland's Corner*. That must have been in the autumn of 1962, because Henry claimed to have seen the programme when he was doing his military service, and he was damn proud. No one knows who 'discovered' Leo, but he had just made his book debut, only fourteen years old, with the poetry collection *Herbarium*, and he'd won notice as a minor celebrity. Many critics said they were astonished that a teenager could come up with such exquisite and luscious rhymes, because the boy, like so many 'amateurs', insisted on writing rhymed verse. No subverted modernism here. One critic had even mentioned the equally youthful Rimbaud, although without making any further comparisons, but still . . . Perhaps it was a bit of an exaggeration, even though there was something evasive and indefinable about *Herbarium* which, for lack of a better term, might be called *brilliant*. Perhaps it was the fact that there was often something flawed about the poems, a slipping away, an ambiguity, that made the reader uncertain and hesitant – it was questionable whether the young boy actually knew all the meanings and connotations of the words.

The critics, at any rate, were quite favourable, and maybe it was this critical success of the poems, as well as the poet's uncommonly young age that prompted *Hyland's Corner* to invite the child prodigy to read on TV. Child stars have always been highly favoured by the entertainment industry.

At the rehearsals before the evening broadcast of the *Corner*, Leo conducted himself perfectly. He was well-groomed, conscientious and well-mannered, maybe a little *too* well-behaved. But the studio crew were a forbearing lot, and they took good care of the discovery, making sure that he got to shake hands with the TV stars Lill-Babs, Lasse Lönndahl and Gunnar Wiklund. He stuffed their autographs into his wallet, in the compartment behind his little Bakelite comb.

But later, after dinner, when it was time for his entrance and Leo was standing in the wings and listening to Lennart Hyland bellow out his name as he introduced the precocious discovery as the son of the Jazz Baron, the popular jazz pianist and welcome guest on many a *Corner* show, the boy began to shake. A jaunty studio man with enormous teeth and wearing a white jacket slapped Leo on the back and wished him luck. And all of a sudden Leo was standing there, dazzled by the spotlights, his lips dry and knees shaking. Greta was sitting somewhere in the audience, and in their homes sat several million people staring at him. Verner, his classmates, his teachers and others who knew Leo were sitting there right now, this very second, staring at him. It was impossible to comprehend a single word of what Uncle Hyland was babbling about over there in his armchair. He said something, nodded and drew a round of applause – no doubt for Leo – and just as the boy was thinking of starting to read, that damn Jack-in-the-box popped up and drew another round of applause. But after that there was silence at last, and the cameras moved on their trolleys, and Leo realised that it was now time. With shaking hands he picked up his book and leafed through it a couple of times, exactly as if this were the very first time he had seen the book, or as if he were searching for a word on a list. The audience didn't notice at all that the young boy was nervous – the next day the newspapers reported on 'Leo Morgan's sophisticated pauses, his indefinable stage presence' – and at last he started reading the poem 'So Many Flowers'.

I've extracted from the poem several of what I consider the best verses. It's a very long ballad that suffers from a certain unevenness.

> So many flowers have I gathered
> that no one can count them all.
> They were the medallions of June
> from the most coquettish of times.
>
> The fairest of flowers
> blooms for all eternity.

The strongest of beauties
grows in solitude.

So many flowers have I given
to all those who save them.
They were all my childhood friends
from the most cruel of times.

The fairest . . .

So many songs have I written
to all those who sing.
There is no one left I know
from the most banal of times.

In the rest of the poem he further develops this theme, which is also the
theme of the entire collection. It is only seemingly an homage to flowers, to
nature. Beneath this floral splendour lie the thoughts of the Artist, the one
who protects nature, the one who shows people how beautiful the world
really is. According to the young Leo Morgan, these experiences have to be
transformed, reshaped by the artist in order for anyone to be capable of
seeing the underlying reality. A quote ascribed to Nietzsche will no doubt
spill from the lips of an educated person: 'Art is not merely an imitation of
the reality of nature but in truth a metaphysical supplement to the reality of
nature, placed alongside it for its conquest.' It's most unlikely that this quote
would have been known to the young Morgan, but he probably would have
understood from a purely intuitive standpoint that it dealt with conquest –
he had to conquer himself.

So the pervasive theme is dried plants, the herbarium that the young boy
collects during long walks, carrying his vasculum across resplendent meadow-
lands in the early morning hours of the month of June, 'the most coquettish of times', when the flowers are at their most beautiful, the dew still
covers the fields, and the plants are lovely and fresh. But the *skald* never
enjoys nature's splendour as much as when he presses and dries his plants,
determines their species and name and puts them in the herbarium, arranged
according to the systems of Linnaeus.

Life is at its most beautiful when compressed and dried out into pale, crisp symbols on rough paper. Not until life ends up in a herbarium does it acquire meaning and significance; it becomes catalogued and registered as language – the plants have become symbols, calligraphy, and printed words.

Herbarium is consequently a poetry collection filled with Latin names, acute observations and items that bear witness to a profound intimacy with nature. The strange thing is the way in which this cogency, this taut and restrained form does not become a rhyming prison for such a young and inexperienced *skald*. Leo Morgan strides boldly through the syntax like an accomplished poet – the reader can't help but surrender to his adolescent charm.

By the way, perhaps it should be added that the magical repetition of 'cruel times', 'banal times' and 'coquettish times', etc., is a stylistic element that permeates all of Leo Morgan's work. He seems possessed by the magic of words, repetitions and ambiguities, just like certain manic individuals.

But to return to the set of *Hyland's Corner* . . . Leo Morgan made his way through 'So Many Flowers', reading verse after verse and making use of what seemed convincingly like trained phrasing, pausing and beautiful diction. The studio audience was beside itself with delight. Hyland's eyes sparkled; he flashed his choppers and bellowed like never before. 'That was fan*ta*stic, Leo Morgan, you wonder boy!' Hyland shouted, gleaming and gurgling with pleasure. In the wings the jaunty studio man in the white jacket slapped Leo on the back and said that the kid had made a breakthrough. The fact is that the studio man was right – Leo was a hit in viewers' living rooms. Sweden had a new darling that the weekly press could tout for a couple of weeks until people got tired of him, found someone new and tossed the old on the rubbish heap.

———————

As a result of Leo's performance on *Hyland's Corner*, a new print-run of the poetry book *Herbarium* was ordered, and a lot of foolish journalists came over to Brännkyrkagatan to interview the young poet. Some of the poems were also set to music by a well-known modern composer and recorded by a great opera diva.

In other words, success was his, although Leo Morgan was not the sort to let it go to his head. He remained perfectly serene. For that matter, as a young child he had already distinguished himself as an exceptional bookworm, as opposed to his sanguine brother, who could barely even spell his own name.

But Leo was still the little boy who collected plants, even now that these plants had become symbols and words in a celebrated poetry book. In spite of this loyalty to his own childhood, the very act of writing signalled an equally precocious and bitter farewell to 'the most banal of times'. Leo had realised that he would never recapture that time. This was the bitter insight that forced him constantly, through the magic of words, to relive what had been lost, because there was sorcery in the words. It had to do with the creation of a human being, that moment when the child becomes a person. When it comes right down to it, children are not considered people in our culture. Children are dwarfs, creatures, gnomes, mysterious and inexplicable. For that very reason every adult must strain to speak in the artificial, hopeless sort of prenatal polyglot which is supposed to have an ingratiating effect on children. The only things children want to know when they talk to people are names and facts, and it's important to give children these names and facts in order to stimulate their curiosity – adulthood, at least as seen from the outside, is a way of putting a muzzle on curiosity and any desire for discovery.

Leo had learned – perhaps unconsciously – to control his curiosity, and yet he still had a long way to go before the final leap into the complete opposite of curiosity: indifference. But one day that's where Leo would end up, and maybe it was to emphasise even further how different he was from Henry, one of the world's most inquisitive individuals.

Herbarium was just a small step towards the petrifaction of the adult world, but it was a step nevertheless. Leo had entered the world of language, the sphere of listeners, and it's significant that he had acquired his own short-wave radio a few years before *Herbarium* came out.

It was a marvellous radio, a Philips with magnificent oak panels and lots of buttons and knobs made of ivory-coloured Bakelite. Leo loved to sit in bed at night when all the lights were turned off and look at the illuminated dial with all the place names in the world: Lahti, Kalundborg, Oslo, Motala, Luleå, Moscow, Tromsö, Vasa, Åbo, Rome, Hilversum, Vigra, Brussels, Belfast, London, Prague, Athlone, Copenhagen, Stuttgart, Munich, Riga, Stavanger, Paris, Warsaw, Bodö and Vienna.

Leo's paternal grandfather had given him the radio. His grandfather claimed to have been to almost all those places because he was a member of the Well-travelled, Well-read, Well-heeled Club. To become a member you *had* to have travelled to all parts of the world that would fit on a radio dial. Leo would sit there in the dark room at night, turning the knobs with the feverish fingers of an eleven-year-old, making the needle slide onto Hilversum – a pleasurable glide between Rome and Vigra – where some lady was singing opera. There was always some plump, clear-voiced lady singing opera in Hilversum. Leo imagined that his grandfather had met this stout opera diva in Hilversum and presented her with flowers because she sang so beautifully. All grown-ups thought that opera was beautiful. Or at least so they said.

The names on the radio dial sounded magical, faraway and exotic. And later in life Leo could never see any of those names without thinking about his grandfather, the WWW Club or long and exciting journeys. Strangely enough, Leo would never leave Sweden, not even to set foot on the island of Åland. A number of the names on the dial, such as Vigra and Moscow, sounded Russian, grey and dreary like Nikita Khrushchev. Others sounded more festive, such as Copenhagen and Paris. That's where Leo's father, the Jazz Baron, had played. He had told them a lot about those cities, about Tivoli, the Eiffel Tower and amazing castles. But that was a long time ago now, and Leo tried not to think about his father. Everyone told him that he shouldn't brood so much about his father, and maybe that was why he had been given the radio.

Sometimes he would listen until late at night, and he often fell asleep in the warm yellow light coming from the radio dial. Henry had to come up and switch it off. Henry may not have been outright jealous of Leo because he'd been given the marvellous Philips radio. It was more likely that Henry was damned curious about what it was like inside. One afternoon he came up with the idea that he would be Henry *the engineer*, specialising in radio technology, just to impress his little brother and to satisfy his own damned curiosity.

Without warning Henry began taking apart the whole marvellous Philips apparatus, using a screwdriver. He claimed that he was just going to have a little look inside. He would remove the oak panel and take a look. Leo was concerned, of course, but he knew that he didn't have a ghost of a chance of stopping Henry.

The engineer sat there, whistling, as he took out a lot of screws, washers and nuts. It was amazing how much a radio could hold: valves, cords, resistors, soldered circuit-boards, speakers, more resistors and washers and valves, until he ended up with a whole pile of loose parts. Henry sat there for a good three hours, unscrewing and adjusting and tinkering and examining and taking things apart, discovering that a radio, like a Chinese box, had more and more hidden parts.

Leo sat sobbing in the room he shared with his brother. He wept silently, not wanting Henry to notice. Leo had his pride. He kept his tears to himself, burying them deep inside and leaving a big patch of spittle in the middle of Henry's pillowcase.

When Greta came home for dinner from her job at the Community Sewing Room down on Mariatorget, she found Henry sitting at the kitchen table, which was completely covered with hundreds of parts from what had once been a radio from Philips in Holland. She was furious, of course. She didn't hesitate to give Henry a proper scolding, and when she found Leo dissolved in tears on his bed, she almost lost all composure. Henry promised to put the radio back together at once. In reality he was just trying to adjust it a bit so that it would sound better. First-rate radios always required *service*. But it was clear that the engineer had lost his head long ago. When Henry *the failed radio technician* had finally – long after bedtime, and he hadn't even stopped to eat dinner – put all the parts back in the box and stuck the plug in the outlet, not even the slightest hum came out of Leo's marvellous Philips radio. It cost over a hundred kronor to have the set repaired.

––––––

From the herbarium's careful arrangement of families, genera and species – so neatly and decoratively arranged by the young Leo Morgan, who because of his handy examination method never flinched at even the most peculiar of plants for fear of not being able to determine its classification – arose a magnificent solitary plant whose power seemed to shine even brighter after days and weeks of drying in the press. It was the Storm bluebell, the pride of Storm Island, a particular variety of the large bluebell, *Campanula persicifolia*. It was the absolute majesty of the meadows, a towering sovereign over the cretins that were always creeping around down in the dirt and thickets. In both colour and stature *Campanula persicifolia* was vastly superior to its subjects. The plant could shoot up nearly one and a half yards above sea level, and its colour was as clear as the deep blue sky. From time immemorial people on Storm Island had recognised that this particular species of the large bluebell was something very special; it was in their damp meadows that it flourished best, after all. It had come to them as solace – the sky-blue Storm bluebell was said to start chiming miraculously all over Storm Island to warn of malevolent winds, bad weather and danger. Very old islanders

109

also claimed to have heard the bells chime just before ominous storms. Strangely enough, they were often right. But praise for the large bluebell's magnificence was not merely provincial boasting and bluster. It had all been confirmed when the famed nineteenth-century botanist Häggdahl made his grand tour of Sweden's outlying archipelago in order to write his magnum opus, the maritime-orientated *Flora Along the Coasts of the Kingdom of Sweden*. He couldn't help focusing his attention on that very plant from Storm Island, ' . . . a windswept but nonetheless sparsely populated island on the far eastern edge of the Stockholm archipelago where the climate seems most beneficial for *Campanula persicifolia*, which occurs there in a particularly beautiful and majestic form in the somewhat marshy meadows in the middle of the island, located in an enormous long valley that resembles a bowl, providing the vegetation with shelter from the wind, which otherwise freely ravages the skerries . . .'

Leo Morgan had naturally heard the legends about the Storm bluebell and was aware of Häggdahl's enthusiastic description. The first time that he, with a feeling of disconsolate shame in his body, cut down one of these sacred plants, it was nearly as tall as he was. He considerately apologised for his act, but on the other hand he could promise this particular flower a form of eternal beauty in his herbarium. Of course there were other beautiful plants in Storm Island's flower-filled meadows. Among the favourites were the deep-rose-coloured German catchflies and Swedish oregano, the blue forget-me-nots and dog violets, the yellow rock-roses and babies'-slippers, and, of course, the reddest of all flowers, the treacherously beautiful and deadly dangerous long-headed poppy. Magnificent examples of all of them were gathered, carefully picked at the height of their bloom. Then they were lovingly pressed and, with the greatest piety, inserted into the Linnaean–Darwinian system. People came from all over to catch a glimpse of the herbarium, this impressive work documenting all of Storm Island's flora, from the simplest grass plant on the shoreline to the monumental Storm bluebell from the divinely graced meadows – which in Leo's dried state would shimmer with what appeared to be undiminished power and, in popular parlance, assumed a touch of magic and sorcery. There was something special about that Leo Morgan.

———

The poetry book *Herbarium* is also a homage to life on Storm Island in the Stockholm archipelago, to childhood summers spent in a type of paradise far out in the archipelago. We won't say much here about Storm Island, that speck of rock in the middle of the Baltic Sea, located almost in the right-angle of a triangle formed by Rödlögam, the Björkskär archipelago and Svenska Högarna. Perhaps the purely anthropological remark should be made that the island – up until the mildly explosive nineteenth century – served only as an overnight spot for those fishermen who lived in the inner archipelago and were headed east to hunt seal. Later the island was populated by a number of families who, in the early twentieth century, reached their highest census before returning today roughly to the population figure of the Middle Ages, which was all of seventeen individuals.

Families come and families go. In 1920 a girl was born on Storm Island, and she was given the name Greta. Her parents, who were perhaps not wild with enthusiasm – this daughter was their seventh child – bore the surname of Jansson and were part of what might be called the original population. A certain inbreeding had provided Storm Island's populace with a disproportionately large number of idiots and fools, although there was nothing wrong with this girl. She developed well, with a strong back, lovely teeth and clear blue eyes. No one could say anything but that she was sweet. It was not just her name that made people think of that other Greta who had become a star in Hollywood – a place so lustrously bright, even Storm Island was caught by its glow.

With an openness of mind, Greta Jansson assimilated the meagre measure of knowledge about the world that was available in such a backwoods locale under the auspices of a perennially drunk schoolteacher. By the age of eighteen she already felt that she had outgrown Storm Island; there was nothing on those rocks that would be inscribed in the history of the twentieth century. On a warm day in May in the late thirties, she allowed herself, like most of her older siblings, to be rowed across the bay and over to Kolholma, where the steamboat was docked. There she boarded the ship and went off to Stockholm. After taking several different types of jobs, she ended up as an assistant at the Community Sewing Room on Mariatorget. That was the place where she felt most at home. Later on she would be promoted to head seamstress, and she has continued to work there up to the present day.

So it was this seamstress whom the Jazz Baron met at Bal Tabarin on a merry evening in 1940. It was as merry an evening as could be expected in that year, although the Jazz Baron didn't allow himself to worry. He was a lively, carefree soul. And the son that Greta gave birth to three years later seemed to have inherited all the sunshine that the Jazz Baron had inside him. Henry, of course, was the child in question.

But at that time the lives of Greta and the Jazz Baron were anything but carefree. When the jazz pianist introduced himself as Gustaf Morgonstjärna, the girl from the archipelago could hardly believe her ears – his name sounded so inexplicably noble. And when the Jazz Baron later introduced his fiancée as Greta Jansson from Storm Island in the Stockholm archipelago, she was naturally not at all what his snobbish mother had in mind. To her Aryan eyes, Beelzebub herself had sunk her claws into her beloved only son. The boy's piano playing had gone too far; nothing had turned out as expected. In those days Mrs Morgonstjärna would have liked to see her son as a stylish cadet. Instead the good-for-nothing shambled about wearing a slovenly trench coat with sheet music spilling out of his pockets. A Negro musician – that was what her son had become. A messenger of the devil who played music that made people go wild. Mr Morgonstjärna, the former dandy, libertine, *bon vivant* and globetrotter, as well as the perennial secretary of the WWW Club, was sufficiently well-travelled, well-read and well-heeled not to give a damn what sort of girl his son took a liking to and married. Just as long as she was sweet and nice, and a healthy amount of love was part of the picture.

Now, this may sound like the prelude to some truly smarmy manor-house novel about a man of noble birth and a girl of the people – in spite of the fact that it has been stripped of any overly garish overtones from the account that Henry related to me. In his version – filled with sentimentality, laments and banalities – all of life became one long serial novel in a ladies' magazine.

Sweet young Greta Jansson from Storm Island now became a familiar sort of watershed. The Jazz Baron was head over heels in love with her, and he received his father's blessing but his mother's curse. Mrs Morgonstjärna – in a pompous farewell sermon – repudiated her son Gustaf, along with the Devil and Louis Armstrong. Her son was no longer welcome in her home; only over her dead body would he be able to return to claim the inheritance which she unfortunately could not deny him. Nor did she have any legal right to withhold it, since the modest inheritance which would eventually fall to her son consisted of a stock portfolio from the paternal side of his family.

It was in the midst of all this that the Jazz Baron changed his name for good, to the even greater annoyance of his self-serving mother. Gustaf Morgonstjärna disappeared forever from the registry of nobility, and into the Swedish jazz world stepped Gus Morgan, alias the Jazz Baron.

That's how it was. At Midsummer in 1940 – as the well-oiled German war machine occupied Denmark and Norway, having just marched into Paris – the couple went out to Storm Island. Gus and Greta Morgan were married by a pastor who had come over from Kolholma, and on Midsummer's Eve a party was held that presumably would require a titan of Strindberg's calibre to describe.

———————

It was out there on Storm Island that the boys spent all their summers when they were young. This paradise island became exactly the same 'flower-basket in the sea' for the poet Leo Morgan as Kymmend Island was for Strindberg. Greta spent all her holidays on her home island while the Jazz Baron mostly travelled around the country on various tours that never seemed to end. In the early fifties he was at the height of his career as a musician. There is a photo showing him as part of a group standing around Charlie Parker, who made a whirlwind tour of Sweden at that time. The picture was taken in a cellar in Gamla Stan, late at night in the middle of a jam session, a night that was said to be one of Parker's best. Presumably it was also one of the Jazz Baron's best. He could br found on the periphery of the circles surrounding Halberg, Domnérus, Gullin, Svensson, Törner, Nonin and other greats. He was among the first to welcome bebop to Sweden. He cheered when Gillespie visited in 1948, though he realised that it would take a while for the general public to come around. He would never be able to make a living playing bebop in Sweden. For the sake of money and food he had to stick with the dance-band tours and settle for sitting in with the house band at occasional sessions. Nevertheless, he was always a welcome guest when they played. He could be found on the periphery of the circles surrounding Halberg, Domnérus, Gullin, Svensson Törner, Norin and other greats. He was often on the radio because he was an easy sort of guy to deal with; he wasn't that spontaneously combustible type that so many jazz musicians could be. The Jazz Baron was joy incarnate, and that was apparent in his tone; it lacked that aggressive edge. It was bebop on Midsummer's Eve – more lyrically seductive than fiercely demonic, a quality that did not escape a certain amount of attention from *Estrad, Orchesterjournalen*, and other leading publications. A brilliant future was predicted for the Jazz Baron. He was still quite young, the father of two boys and full of vitality and energy.

Henry turned ten in 1953, and by then the Jazz Baron had already started training the boy. Henry had a real talent for the piano and was given classical instruction – by a woman on Götgatan – as well as lessons in modern music by his father. Occasionally Henry was allowed to accompany the Baron on tours during holidays, and that was the best thing the boy could imagine. He would sit for hours listening to the jazz musicians, though the best part of all was actually listening to them talk rather than play. Jazz musicians had a way of talking like nobody else. They had their own language, full of strange, mysterious words – and Henry would have blushed if he had understood them.

This was the way Henry preferred to remember his childhood, as part of the baggage on his father's tours (which were as successful as they were endless), from Ystad to Haparanda. Leo, on the other hand, was much too young to go along. He was born in 1948, skinny, anaemic, whiny, constantly sick and in bed, with no interest in either listening to his father or going with him to concerts. Leo liked lying in his sickbed under some heavy, dusty book that looked as if it would crush his birdlike chest, which would hardly have filled a thimble with air, much less an instrument.

But during the summer they would go out to Storm Island, and there it was left to the maternal grandparents to take care of the boys. They never had any problems with Leo; he mostly sat indoors, idling away the time with his books or collecting plants. Worse was their responsibility for Henry, since only by mustering all the patience that he had could the lad sit still long enough to put away a glass of milk and a warm cinnamon roll.

The Leo we meet in *Herbarium* is probably also the same one that his maternal grandmother and grandfather took care of out there on Storm Island. He was a slender little boy who got up early in the morning to throw on his clothes and head out to the meadows in search of rare plants. Of course he had a proper vasculum, which was his most cherished possession. The little botanist would set out for the fields before the dew had disappeared, and he would stay out there for hours, collecting plants with all the persistence and concentration of an adult. When Leo did something, he always made a thorough job of it. Henry, on the other hand, could never focus on anything. In his whole life he never even learned to spell properly. But Leo would set to work, silently and purposefully completing everything he undertook. He would be back for lunch with the round metal box filled with flowers, which he then dried in the press, mounted on pieces of cardboard in various albums and entered into a catalogue of different families, genera and species.

The boys' grandmother saw something very religious in all of this. A normal child would never be able to produce with such a tranquil state of mind this sort of magnificent and extraordinary collection of plants. Leo was 'otherwise', different, as they said in the north. And he was clearly different. Leo was divinely gifted; he 'had contact'. According to his grandmother, those people who distinguished themselves from the masses by virtue of exaggerated zeal or bigoted piety 'had contact'. And this contact was naturally of the vertical kind. God was keeping an eye on Leo, and the old woman never had to worry about him.

He never even went out if it was sunny. When Leo was an infant the sun brought him out in a rash, and when he was a child, strong sunlight hurt his eyes. While the other children dived into the waves from the docks, Leo would sit in the shade and read. He hated swimming and never went into the water. He had learned to hate the water in school. Water and a young child's unexpressed but discerning knowledge about terror were inextricably linked.

Even in elementary school swimming had been part of the curriculum. This had gone on for many years, during every single term, until the boys in every class could swim the unofficially mandatory thirty feet under water. This goal had been established, completely outside any regulations, by a fascist swimming instructor named Aggeborn, who had a crew-cut and wore wooden clogs with white perforated tops. He refused to be satisfied until all the boys had passed the water test and got hair between their legs. The programme was decidedly torturous, even for the ruffians in the class.

On bleak, freezing cold, weary winter evenings they had to go to the swimming hall; there they were forced to take a dip in temperatures that rarely rose above 15°C. The process was as loathsome as it was ritualistic. After stripping off all their clothes, the boys would scrub their thin, shivering bodies clean in a washroom filled with miniature bathtubs. After a brief period of respite in the hot water of the tubs, the boys would line up to scrub each others' backs with rough brushes and a soapy solution that smelled of animals. Leo always had the misfortune to end up in front of one of the tough bullies in his class, who would scrub so vigorously that Leo's back would be striped for days afterwards. The room was cold and draughty, the boys were shivering and wanted to go home. But after that they were herded out to the swimming pool to stand on the freezing floor, whose sharp tiles cut into their skin as their cruel swimming instructor went through the leg movements. Those who failed to perform them properly, who didn't arch their feet correctly, received a kick from the white wooden clogs. Leo would forever associate the soft, warm bodies of the little boys in those cold, tiled rooms with the images he happened to see at about the same time from Nazi concentration camps in Poland. The pattern was exactly the same: naked people, stripped of every single ounce of dignity and subjected to arbitrary experiments by supposed superiors. In a poem – presumably written in the mid-sixties – Leo Morgan wrote in his most ferocious mood: 'Somewhere there is a radio / which sends only ciphers / burned into skin / from the clean rooms / where Nazis sat at typewriters / keeping impeccable ledgers of annihilation / about the final shower of entire families . . .' This was what nakedness and baths signified. To be naked meant becoming vulnerable. Leo wanted to remain clothed. He needed protection in this raw world.

'Looks like it's going to rain, said the boy, crawling in under her skirts.' That was one of the countless proverbs with which the old women on Storm Island faced the world. It could be an epitaph on Leo Morgan's headstone, since he spent nearly all his life indoors, poring over thick books. The boy read everything. By the age of ten, Leo wanted nothing to do with books for children and adolescents, brimming with excitement and adventures that could fill Henry with amazement. He wanted to know what the world looked like, how space looked, how the depths of the ocean looked. He read Brehm's zoological works, astronomy and descriptions of expeditions undertaken by Heyerdahl, Bergman and Danielsson. That was the sort of thing that interested a botanist, philatelist and gifted angel such as Leo Morgan.

It was worse with Henry. As far as swimming went, he was the best in the region. He could pass for a seal, even among the local residents, who were accustomed to the water – that was why he was selected to star in the training film, *Calle Learns the Crawl* – an effort that presumably coloured the rest of Henry's life.

Whenever the rain came pouring down – it could pour on Storm Island for weeks in the autumn – Henry *the outdoorsman* would walk around in his shirtsleeves, looking for worms for his fishing line, and it took more than one reprimand to get the boy to come indoors. He had some sort of chameleon system regulating his body temperature, just like his grandfather, the Boat Builder, who could stand outside in the middle of winter planing planks and ribs in the draughty boathouse, with no gloves on and only a tattered thermal bodywarmer over his shirt.

Henry was his grandfather's protégé. That was the way it had always been.

He was his grandfather's assistant in the boat-building shed. Wind and weather had no effect on either of them. They were men, and a man belonged on the sea. All summer long Henry would be out bobbing up and down in the sailing boat that his grandfather the Boat Builder had made. He never felt lonely, he was never afraid or lost. If he was out sailing for a week at a time without putting into port, he claimed that he still met a lot of people. In the middle of the open sea he would come upon a timber barge or a canoeist on his way to the Finnish archipelago. Once he claimed to have gone so far east that he could no longer get his bearings properly. Suddenly he ran into a solitary fisherman who was fishing for herring and spoke Russian. Then he had to turn around. Worst of all was when Henry *the sailor* sat all alone on a skerry at the outer edge of the archipelago and caught sight of a mermaid swimming towards a rock to polish her scales. At least that was what he tried to tell his little brother at night when they were supposed to be asleep and Henry had returned from the endless expanses of the sea.

From a very early stage Henry and his grandfather decided that they would build a big, proper ship together. They talked about it constantly, and the rare letters that Henry composed were all written during the winter when he was back home in the city, telling his grandfather about new ideas for their building project. In the summer they always went around fantasising about that extraordinary boat, outlining details, practical solutions and grand sailing routes through the exotic oceans of the world.

His grandfather had very few commissions at the time – mostly modest little rowing boats for summer visitors. Occasionally he might make small skiffs for yachtsmen. All the big jobs had vanished.

His grandfather was calmly waiting for retirement, when he and Henry would make good on their plans for that marvellous sailing vessel. The rough drafts and sketches gradually turned into proper drawings. Some time in the late fifties the drawings began taking shape as an exquisite oak keel from which the ribs rose, one after the other, with all the consummate cogency of the experienced boat-builder. People on the island started talking about Jansson and his Ark. But for his grandfather's part, there wasn't so much religion in the whole thing as there was retirement. For Henry's part, it had to do with a vision.

———

But *Herbarium* would nevertheless be a form of farewell to the idyll of Storm Island, the place where Henry and Leo Morgan grew up. The ingenuous sweetness of childhood – which actually, in Leo's case, wasn't really very sweet – would swiftly be replaced in the summer of 1958 with the serious brine of Life.

It was Midsummer's Eve, and on Storm Island this heathen holiday was celebrated in exactly the same manner as elsewhere, except that instead of wreaths, they hung two fish-shaped leafy boughs on the crossbar of the pole. For those who lived on the coast, this was a local tradition that they would never give up.

Including all the summer visitors, there were close to a hundred festively dressed, high-spirited, merry celebrants over in the meadow. They could buy juice and rolls and warm sausage at various stands, and the boys competed to see who could stuff down the most sausages. Leo never participated in such tests of strength. He didn't stand a chance, nor did he care. He was more interested in the dance of the morons. When it was the little tykes' turn, a couple of backward boys affected by the inbreeding on Storm Island would always play leapfrog as if the suppressed playfulness of an entire winter had to be let out all at once. The boys drooled and had a great time, and no one interfered; they were left in peace. Midsummer's Eve was their festival.

Later in the evening, of course, there was a party with herring and aquavit, with more grilled sausage for the children. It was always held in Norrängen in a barn that belonged to Nils-Erik, one of the big fishermen on Storm Island. The long tables quickly turned rowdy, and the Jazz Baron played the accordion as part of a trio. The evening was exactly as magical and alluring as it should be. The children played tag in the woods and danced around the bonfires, where they roasted sausages. Several of the old fishermen lay in the hay up in the loft, snoring, while a number of summer visitors ended up quarrelling with each other, and the inbred boys continued to play leapfrog between the tables in the barn.

Leo sat in his usual place on these occasions – on a barrel in a corner of the dilapidated barn. He liked that spot; he could take part without really getting involved. He could observe without participating, watch all the faces, all the hands moving about as they became more and more unruly, creeping into forbidden territory – picking their noses, stroking other people's breasts, scratching their own crotches, touching other people's thighs . . . Leo tried to imagine what would happen later that night – he wondered which people would be quarrelling, fighting and arguing when the Jazz Baron's accordion fell silent and the light returned to the meadows to reveal the escapades of the night.

Tonight, from his seat atop the old barrel, Leo could see Henry and one of Nils-Erik's brutish sons homing in on the same girl. Nils-Erik owned the most cabins on the island, and he rented them out to summer visitors. This particular girl was a summer visitor, and Leo knew that Nils-Erik's sons all stood in a shed masturbating whenever she turned up on the rocks wearing a bathing suit. Those lads were crazy about girls. There were a few girls on Kolholma, but rumour had it that they were going to move to the city. The lads had to seize every chance they could get.

Nils-Erik's boy was determined at any price to arm-wrestle with Henry, to pull fingers, shove beams, have a tug-of-war, or whatever the hell he could in front of the girl, as long as they came to some sort of decision. One of the boys had to eliminate the other, that was all there was to it. And the girl offered no objections.

Leo watched the drama from the top of his barrel and was moderately amused. He was afraid that Henry was headed for a beating because Nils-Erik's sons were robust creatures, and they had already started drinking aquavit. Late that evening the barn in Norrängen was one big chaos of drunken fishermen, cackling old crones, giggling girls, bickering summer visitors and people who had already fallen asleep, stretched out across tables or comfortably curled up in the loft. Henry and this fisherman fellow went out into the night to fight over the girl, and Leo didn't dare follow them to see how it went. He was positive that Henry would quickly be defeated.

When the Jazz Baron played the last waltz of the evening – there were actually some who still had the energy to dance, even to the very last number – Leo the little ten-year-old botanist slipped out of the barn. He went out into the bright Midsummer night, inhaled the saturated air, thick and damp, and wandered a short way into the woods. He wanted to be alone for a while, to think and brood over those things that a ten-year-old thinks about. Maybe he was trying to figure out what was wrong with the inbred boys, what sort of illness they had. Leo had seen pictures in medical books of misshapen people with enormous hydrocephalic heads, grotesque noses or no noses at all; people with no arms and extra-long legs, people with only one eye, and others who had no mouth. There were any number of variations, and Leo knew the names of many diseases, names that were given in tribute to learned doctors who had figured out the cause of the illness. They were always foreign names, German names. Perhaps Leo could find some special defect in the boys on Storm Island, Morgan's Disease, so that they too might be cured. Or he could discover some unknown flower, *Morgana morgana*, which would make his name world-famous, eternal, infinitely repeated for as long as stamens and pistils did their job and the soil was good.

Leo walked along dreaming his childishly ambitious dreams when he heard the air go out of the accordion far away in the barn. People would be hauling themselves home now, and giggling girls would be picking flowers to place under their pillows. He turned around, quietly heading back towards the barn and the site of the festivities. When he reached it all the guests had gone, the fire in the yard had died down and a thin column of smoke was rising up towards the sky, which was already light. He walked all alone from the meadow down towards the houses on the rocks. Here and there he could hear bursts of laughter and giggling, but he didn't pay any attention. He was not the object of their laughter.

He was sitting on a rock and staring at the sunrise with his precocious expression of interest when Henry and the girl came rowing past. They emerged from a dock shed in a tarred rowing boat. Henry was at the oars while the girl lay indolently stretched out on the bottom of the boat. So Henry had won. Nils-Erik's boy had been beaten, good and proper. Leo couldn't deny that he felt rather proud. Henry didn't see Leo on the rock. Right now Henry had eyes only for the girl, and he was trying to row like a real he-man. They were heading out towards the skerries.

On that particular night the children were allowed to stay out as late as they liked. A number of parents even seemed to insist that the children stay outside because the walls were so thin between the bedrooms. Leo stayed out a bit longer; he too had no desire to go home. He was wide awake and alert, happy in his solitude. No one intruded to ask him prying questions or tell him what to do. He was totally free. He could sit here on this flat slab for as long as he pleased and feel the sun slowly heating up the rock beneath him, dreaming whatever dreams he liked. He could watch the rowing boat with Henry and the girl glide across the bay – it was amazing how damned fast he could row all of a sudden, heading for some lonely place made for lover-boys like Henry. He had inherited all his father's charm, that Henry. At least that's what the women on Storm Island said. The Jazz Baron was well-liked on the island, especially on Midsummer's Eve, when he played the accordion and flirted with all the old ladies.

Leo followed the boat with his eyes as it moved across the quiet bay where an endlessly cautious breeze rippled the water and a few gulls silently began their morning fishing. Maybe they plan to put in at some skerry, thought Leo. Maybe they were going to row out to Snake Island (which was full of snakes) just so that Henry could show that he dared handle poisonous reptiles, because he certainly did. A few summers ago – Leo couldn't remember exactly when it was – Henry had kept his own snakes in a cardboard box, just to show that they wouldn't bite as long as you treated them kindly. Greta nearly went crazy when she found out about it. She threatened to throw the box in the sea, although nobody knew how she was going to do that, since she didn't dare go near it. But Henry promised to take the snakes out to Snake Island, and that was what he did.

Leo hated snakes too, and he was always afraid that a snake might be in the grass in the meadows where he gathered plants. That happened once, and Leo had stood there, completely hypnotised by the reptile basking in the sun. It was bright morning sunshine, and the snake seemed to stir in the heat, but Leo couldn't run away. He was incapable of taking even a single step. He stood absolutely motionless for an hour, until the snake quietly wriggled down into the grass and disappeared. Then the spell was broken, and Leo dashed home, refusing to go out for several days. Henry promised to take care of any snakes he saw, and Leo imagined that his brother had some sort of secret pact with all snakes, because they never did bite him. Many years later – when Leo was attending Södra Latin school and had started writing poetry – he felt an affinitiy with the famous writer of *The Snake*, Stig Dagerman, and it was probably no accident that one of his nicknames in school was *the Snake*. It was a provocative moniker – it's easy to spread fear, but difficult to do it nicely. A snake frightens by means of its enigmatic precision, its secretive cogency. A snake is a brindled ribbon, a cable loaded with poisonous terror that can paralyse an entire barracks of full-grown men. A snake is silent; no one can hear its heart or is moved by its eyes, because a snake has no need for solace.

Perhaps it was on this very Midsummer night that Leo pledged the snake his hate-filled devotion because he realised abruptly that he was inconsolable. Suddenly – without any warning except that a single Storm bluebell could be heard ringing to alert everyone to the disaster – this Midsummer's Eve became terribly bright and clear and permeated by a merciless light, as the inconceivable always is. Leo had just arrived home from the rocks when the alarm sounded. Suddenly people started screaming in loud, shrill voices for help. Leo heard a great wailing coming from the beach a short distance away, and he rushed over there. He could see his father's red, chrome-plated accordion gleaming in the morning sun from where it had been placed on a rock near the shore. He could see his grandfather and Nils-Erik and several women; they were dragging something out of the water. Greta was nowhere to be seen, but Leo heard everyone repeating her name. Someone had to go and find her. When Leo's grandfather caught sight of the boy, he shouted for him to stop, to stay where he was, or to go home or any damn place but here. 'The poor boy,' Leo heard one of the women say, and she came hurrying over to him. She picked him up in her arms and wept, saying that it was so dreadful, so terrible, and Leo noticed that the old woman smelled of coffee, freshly made coffee. She wept and sobbed against Leo's little shoulder, pressing her face against him, and in between sobs she talked about Leo's father, the Jazz Baron, and she said he *had been* such a fine man, so cheerful and all. And then Leo didn't hear another sound. Leo heard nothing and said nothing, but he saw everything that he shouldn't have seen as clearly as if it were all an illustration in *Gulliver's Travels*.

———————

Exactly twenty years later Henry Morgan and I stood in Skog Cemetery, lighting candles for the dead. It was All Saints' Day, and Henry told me that he had bellowed like a lost calf at the funeral. He had tried to be manly and hold back his tears, but without success. That was the end of a long period of hellish trials and tribulations. In a single moment that Midsummer night had become inexplicably clear as he rowed the girl home from the skerry, where they had used up a whole packet of condoms, lying on a sailcloth spread out on a slab of rock. He noticed as soon as they stepped ashore on Storm Island that something was wrong. He said goodbye to the girl who, with smudged make-up and stains on her clothes, stumbled home. Straight after that he found out what had happened while he was off on the skerry making love. Henry was overcome with such a sense of shame that he nearly went out of his mind. He ran amok in the boat-building shed and hacked off parts of the Ark, which stood there, a fraction of a dream realised. If his grandfather hadn't wrestled him to the ground and disarmed him, he might have managed to wreck the whole thing. After this intermezzo, Henry seemed to turn himself inside out, and he put even greater effort into repairing the damage. He chopped and sawed and scraped for over twenty-four hours without rest, trying to restore the vessel as best he could. The whole time, tears poured down his cheeks, which perhaps prevented him from making measurements and cuts and lines as exact as his grandfather's.

Leo, the little ten-year-old, reined in his own emotions and tried to console his mother as much as was possible. She clung to the little boy, calling him her angel. He stood in the very centre of the tragedy, even though it felt as though he found himself in the eye of a hurricane. He seemed untouched by the whole thing, as if he had won some share of perfection instead of losing something fragile and transient. Everyone agreed that the boy with the thin, aged face, with the sorrowful, solemn eyes, was worthy of admiration.

Grief quickly spread over the whole country, and Greta became a celebrated widow; there were many who shared her sorrow. Naturally there was some speculation about the premature death of the Jazz Baron. Certain malicious voices tried to claim that his death was no accident, but that was just spiteful gossip. The Jazz Baron was actually just entering his prime; he had glimpsed the light of the dawning of his life, and he had had no reason to feel despair.

'JAZZ BARON DEAD' was the headline in the biggest morning newspaper, and the well-known music critic devoted no less than twelve inches of column space plus a photo to the memory of Gus Morgan. In the article he praised the Baron's 'characteristic warm and lyrical tone, which for so many represented jazz itself in Sweden; a meeting between the violent nation to the west and our Nordic gentleness – proof both of the Baron's strong originality and the universality of the music . . .' The critic ended with words that were equally reverent and poignant: 'The Parnassus of Swedish jazz has lost its baron, its crown prince.'

THE COURTESAN

(Henry Morgan, 1961–63)

Everyone was talking about the Match down at the Europa Athletic Club. All of Stockholm, all of Sweden, maybe even the whole world was talking about the Match that day. Henry Morgan, as usual, was whistling 'Putti Putti', which was somewhere in the middle of the Top Ten, as he kicked the slushy, heavy, slippery snow off his shoes and greeted Willis, who was changing a light bulb. 'Now you're our only hope,' said Willis. 'It's going to be a while before we have a new champion.'

'If we ever do,' said Henry. 'Ingemar will never recover from this, never.'

Everybody had listened to the Match on their radios, the third and final encounter between Ingo and Floyd – the 'Decisive Moment', as the spectacle in Miami Beach was called. The knockout in the sixth round had come like a bolt of lightning out of a clear blue sky. The newspapers were talking about a fourth match, but people in the business knew that as far as Ingo was concerned, there could never be a rematch. He was too smart for that.

Henry had spent half the night lying in front of Leo's marvellous Philips radio. Leo himself was already asleep by the time the Match got started because he wasn't the least bit interested in boxing. Leo liked flowers.

In spite of Ingo's defeat, the lads were down at the Europa, training as usual. It was all a matter of becoming the new Ingo, as the posters said, and maybe it was only now that this had become clear to some of them. Because only now was there actually an 'old' Ingo.

'Come on now!' Willis urged as Henry put on his sparring gear. 'You need to get with the programme. You haven't been here in a while.'

'I've been studying,' said Henry in apology.

'I'm not going to fall for that studying excuse anymore,' said Willis. 'You'll have to come up with something better than that.'

'I will,' said Henry.

He smiled in a way that was both proud and embarrassed at the same time and then started to jab at the pads that Willis was wearing over his hands. Willis set great store by Henry Morgan because from the very first he could see that there was something special about this good-for-nothing. As if Henry had been born to box. He was no slugger; he was powerfully built in the neck and shoulders, but that didn't make him a palooka. He possessed a suppleness, a nimbleness, a mobility, as well as the proper amount of imagination – without those things he would have just been an ox, a bruiser. And besides, Henry had rhythm. His father, the Jazz Baron, had been pals with Willis because the old master's help was required by a number of less reputable pubs and dives to keep order at the door. The Jazz Baron played every pub in town. Willis was no jazz expert, but when the Baron played, he couldn't help listening. The Jazz Baron had something special. Everyone knew that he came from a posh family, but he was so unpretentious, like a regular person. It was a shock when he passed away. The newspapers wrote of an accident, and there was no reason for anyone to think otherwise.

Willis had taken on Henry and got him started on boxing in order to help him get over his father's death. When Henry put on the gloves, it was almost as if he was playing the piano – his whole style was harmonious and steady. There was nothing abrupt, desperate, strenuous or superficial about Henry's boxing style. Willis had never needed to go after him with the pruning shears, as he used to say. When greenhorns turned up at the Europa, he always took out the pruning shears. He had to trim and prune the lads down the way a gardener prunes his shrubs to give them the proper form.

But Henry Morgan was already trimmed and pruned; his gloves fit precisely the way they should. In his case there were other concerns, because he was not a trainee without problems. The problem with Henry was that as soon as he was scheduled to fight a match, they had to have a backup ready. Henry would train for a match, get charged up like never before and get into the best possible physical shape, but then when the fight was actually going to take place, he would frequently simply disappear, swallowed up by the earth. No one would know where Henry was, and the only thing to be done was to bring in the best available replacement, who always lost, causing the Europa Athletic Club to record yet another defeat.

But on those few occasions when Henry actually did go through with it, he would do his utmost. Of the dozen or so bouts that he fought, he lost only once. That was in Göteborg , against a guy from Redbergslid. It was a snobbish club.

'Come on, keep going!' bellowed Willis. 'You've got another minute to go!'

On the wall was a filthy egg-timer that Willis set for three minutes so the lads could train doing rounds. In the pauses Henry kept bouncing around with a springy step to keep his heart-rate up. He was feeling a bit heavy but tried not to show it because he'd been smoking too much, staying up late at night, and Willis didn't want to hear stuff like that. Henry refused to admit that he wasn't feeling good, because he didn't want to upset the old man. Another match was coming up.

'I have plans for you, Hempa,' said Willis. 'You should be able to fight in Göteborg again.'

'I don't like those Göteborgers,' said Henry. 'They fight all wrong.'

'Don't give me any of that damn whining,' said Willis sullenly. 'There's a tournament a few weeks from now. You can get in some tough sparring towards the end. Then we have the Swedish Championships in the autumn. I've signed you up, so you've got nothing to say about it, OK?'

'I suppose not,' said Henry and sighed.

After the training session, he knotted his tie as meticulously as usual in an elegant Windsor knot and studied himself in the mirror. He had a tiny scratch on his neck, extending down a few inches from his ear. He knew he hadn't got that from any glove.

It was dark and slushy out on the street, and it had started to freeze again. Snow was falling, heavy and muffled. The trams, cars and buses were struggling through the slush on Långholmsgatan where the number four was heading for Västerbron. Henry shoved his cap down a bit on his wet hair and pulled an elegant silver cigarette case from his jacket pocket. Using his equally elegant Ronson lighter, he lit a cigarette butt that didn't go with the stylish case. Only long, fresh, innocent cigarettes were intended to be inside that case, as they had been when it was in the possession of the man with the initials W.S.

Henry strolled along Hornsgatan down to Zinkensdamm, where he bought an evening paper, and then turned onto Brännkyrkagatan. In front of his building he picked up some wet snow, packed it into a ball and pitched it at Verner's window up on the third floor. Verner had already become a bit 'otherwise'. Henry waited for a while and then saw Verner's head appear in the window. Verner was shaking that head of his at being disturbed while he was labouring so assiduously over his homework. He didn't come back. Verner was not pleased.

Henry and Verner had been great pals when they were kids. Back then Verner's room – he had his own room because he was an only child and his mother was also on her own – reeked of Meta fuel-tablets from his steam-engine. He had been given a whopper of a steam-engine as a Christmas present. Being the inventor that he always was – although this was long before the pimply teenaged upstart Verner Hansson created the Association for Young Inventors at the Södra Latin school – he had constructed a number of different accessories that could be attached to the steam-driven apparatus. There were saws, planes, jingling bells and a whole lot of other totally meaningless equipment that basically just moved.

Henry was nowhere near as technically talented as Verner, but he had a real gift for tinkering with anything that moved. Verner and Leo, on the other hand, could carry on for days and weeks at a time, putting together lifelike models of buildings, aeroplanes and cars. It was precisely this obstinate tenacity that united them, although it also separated them from all the other impatient, glassy-eyed, noisy kids in the neighbourhood. Afterwards they would set the meticulously built models on their shelves, occasionally casting satisfied glances at their creations.

But Henry had no patience for such things. His models were always sloppy, half-finished monstrosities. The aeroplanes had to be tested no matter what the risk, tossed out the window from the fifth floor to be smashed to smithereens on the pavement below, always to Henry's great surprise. His model cars had to go out in the traffic, where they were pulverised beneath the tyres of real-life Fords, and consequently Henry didn't own a single model that he had put together himself. On the other hand, his creations weren't really worth saving. He always thought that it was all right to paint over unsightly joints and other mistakes that he made when he hastily and eagerly scraped, sawed and filed off either too much or too little by turns. But that only made the mess even worse. Paint and varnish, strangely enough, had the effect of making the mistakes stand out even more distinctly than before.

So Henry was quite a bungler and, from what I understand, he didn't get much better over the years. But if someone caught him, pointed out how he had cheated – it might be the woodworking instructor or some poker player – he could always wriggle his way out of a bind by talking; he could drive anybody crazy. Therein lay his great talent. Perhaps the Ark – that big ship that he had started building with his grandfather on Storm Island in the archipelago – was the only exception. But that boat was never finished either.

Verner was probably the only person who was absolutely immune to Henry's subterfuges and excuses. Verner could see right through him. That's why he never forgave Henry when he took apart his steam-engine to give it an unnecessary cleaning, and then never managed to make it run again. Verner was utterly furious and resolved never to forgive Henry, but that didn't bother Henry in the least. He just kept on fiddling with anything that moved. He had also discovered that there was something else that moved, and did so much better than a steam-engine. Henry had started playing Dixieland. He had formed a school band and won admirers who moved in a considerably more exciting way than a trivial and childish steam engine.

Henry arrived home just in time for dinner. Leo emerged from his room, leaving behind his homework or his stamp collection or his herbarium, and not saying a word of greeting to anyone. He had too much to keep track of in that head of his. Greta gave Henry a long look as he sat down at the kitchen table. She didn't need to say a word – he knew exactly what she wanted to hear, but he wasn't going to comply. She just wanted to hear a few words about where he was spending his time all those evenings when he didn't come home. Last night he'd come home in time for the match between Ingo and Floyd, and that was no doubt the only reason he came home at all. She simply wanted to hear a few meagre words confirming that he wasn't doing anything stupid at night. Lately so many stupid things were being done in town during the night-time. She had read in the papers about that horrible Spilta gang in Östermalm that assaulted people and stole things and snorted drugs and robbed people and got into all sorts of other mischief. In Björns Trädgård there was another gang, while the Subway Gang ravaged the underground system. It seemed as if the whole city had been taken over by gangsters. The police were at a loss and no longer seemed able to main-tain order. Things were so bad that even the rockers could hold their own hot-rod mass in the church on Liljeholmen.

Greta wanted some reassurance that Henry was watching his step, because she didn't want to find out about one thing or another through the grapevine. If anything was going on, she wanted to be the first to know. That was the least she could expect, as she had said over and over again ever since she had been left on her own with the boys. Henry had always promised to keep her informed. And for the most part he did, but lately he'd become less informative, and often he wouldn't come home in the middle of the week. She didn't like it.

Something had happened to Henry recently; he had become so grown-up all of a sudden. It now seemed a long time ago that he was the little boy with all those big ideas. He had always sold the most lottery tickets for the Athletic Association's Christmas Lottery, which started up in August. He had always distributed the most advertising circulars to letterboxes, and he had always collected the most empty bottles. He had organised the boys in his building to join forces to collect bottles, which was more efficient. They were allowed to use a storage space in the cellar for the hundreds of bottles they gathered until they filled several prams and went over to the state off-licence to turn them in for cash.

But that was all very long ago. Henry was still boxing, but he was undoubtedly more interested in Dixieland and girls. That much Greta could see. All of a sudden Henry had become a young man.

But on this particular evening in the late winter of 1961, he was eating like a horse, and that was enough to make any worried mother rest easy for a while. Henry had blithely shovelled down five stuffed cabbage rolls with lingonberry sauce and at least as many potatoes. Leo merely sat and picked at his food while a snorting Henry cut slices as thick as phone books from the soft cheese. But at least Leo did his homework. He was so smart that he had skipped a year in school.

'Just think if those two had been one boy,' their grandfather used to say. That horrendous thought said a lot.

'Eat your *hetvägg*, boys,' said Greta as she placed a few cream-filled buns and some warm milk on the oilcloth. She was probably the only person in all of Sweden, except for foreigners and those members of her family still living on Storm Island in the archipelago, who called cream buns *hetvägg* instead of *semla*. Henry stuffed them down as he listened to the radio and read the evening paper all at the same time. Everyone was commenting on the Match, but Henry merely shook his head. It was the end of Ingo, for good. And Henry hadn't fared much better. He was also done in, and he went to bed early. Leo did his homework in the kitchen, while Greta ironed shirts. She found one that Henry claimed to have bought. It had the initials W.S. inside the collar. Because she was thinking so hard, that particular shirt ended up being ironed with special attention. It would not surprise me if here and there the cotton were damp from her tears, although that may sound a bit too maudlin.

———————

'Everything took place just as it does on Earth . . . My handwriting was the same, even though my hands didn't weigh a thing. But I had to hold on tight to the notebook so that it wouldn't float away,' said Gagarin. It's the same with the Morgan brothers. You have to hold on tight to them, etch them into scenes so that they won't float away into memory and the everlasting ice-cold space of the mind – just like in some terrible nightmare from which you have to free yourself, over and over again.

Perhaps it was Henry's well-developed talent for attaching his life to great turning points in history that made him claim that he was lying in Maud's lap on that morning when the world learned that Yuri Alexeyevich Gagarin had orbited around the Earth in space. The two of them, at any rate, didn't give a damn about Gagarin.

Maud went over to the window, pulled up the shade, and looked out across Östermalmsgatan and Engelbrektskyrka, which was chiming nine o'clock. She lived in an English brick building covered with ivy on Friggagatan, in the Sånglärkan district. It was a beautiful flat, filled with erotic wooden figures from Indonesia.

'It's spring now, Henry,' she said. 'Listen!' She threw open the window. The birds were twittering, and the rooftops and pavement smelled exactly the way they should when warmed by the April sun. 'Pretty soon that icicle is going to fall,' she said, nodding at an enormous icicle that pointed towards the street like a lance. 'I'm afraid of icicles . . .'

'They're just water,' said Henry. 'They're great in drinks.'

'You're a real tough guy, aren't you?' said Maud.

'I can't deny that I do have a few muscles,' said Henry, kneading his right bicep. 'At any rate, I'm not scared of icicles. My brother Leo, on the other hand, he's really scared of icicles. He's scared of most things. Sometimes he has an absolute fit and lies in bed, raving all night long. My mum has to put cold flannels on his ankles and forehead to calm him down.'

'Just because of icicles?'

'Because of anything! It doesn't take much,' said Henry. 'A week ago he came running up the hall and then threw off his clothes and lay down on his bed, shaking with fever or cold, and he was raving too. He said that he was walking along the pavement on Hornsgatan behind a woman with a pram, and all of a sudden a whole load of icicles came plunging down. At least a ton of icicles, he said. And they all landed right on that pram. The whole thing was smashed to a pulp, and the woman was hysterically digging through all that ice to find her baby. And she cut her hands, which started to bleed and get numb, but finally she pulled out the baby. "He's alive!" she screamed, even though the baby was nothing but pulp.'

'Did he see the dead baby?!' said Maud, looking quite broken-hearted.

'There wasn't any baby,' said Henry. 'It was just Leo being delirious – he imagined the whole thing. I think he's starting to go bonkers. He's been doing too much homework.'

'I think you're the one who's nuts,' said Maud.

'In that case, we're both nuts,' said Henry. 'You and me, I mean.'

Maud sat in the spring sunshine, enjoying herself. Henry looked at her for a long time as she leaned out the window. She was the only female he had ever seen move around completely naked without seeming bashful or claiming that it was getting cold, as a pretext for covering herself up with something. She had a body that didn't really fit the usual perception of the female body, the perception that belonged to Rubens or Zorn – two names that she had taught Henry *the mongrel* – which was also shared by *Pin-Up* magazine – a name that Henry had learned all on his own. Maud didn't fit that mould at all. There was something Asian about her looks, with her small breasts and narrow hips, black hair and extraordinary cat-eyes, which looked good with any sort of make-up. The women that Henry had actually been with were few in number, when it came right down to it; they were also so shy that they never let him look at them in the way in which he, with his insatiable desire, would have liked. They were just childish girls from school who sat in front of the radio whenever the Top Forty was on; girls who knew by heart 'I'm Gonna Knock on Your Door, Ring on Your Bell', by Eddie Hodges; girls who mostly wanted to talk about school, settling down and having babies. Today they were all talking about Gagarin. Henry didn't give a damn about that. Everyone was talking about Gagarin except Maud and him.

She was now sitting on the window seat, letting the sunlight flood over her body. Henry could stay there in bed and look right inside her if he liked. She closed her dark eyes, turned her face towards the sun and let him stare as much as he pleased.

'The one thing about you that reminds me of Sophia Loren is your eyes,' he said.

'I don't give a damn whether I look like Sophia Loren or Aunt Fritzi or the Virgin Mary,' said Maud. 'Quit nagging at me!'

'But I'm the nagging type,' said Henry. 'I know that. But you remind me of all of them. Sophia Loren is the primal mother, Aunt Fritzi is the step-mother and the Virgin Mary is the womb. Although, in *reality*, you don't remind me of any of them.'

'I get along fine without any of them,' said Maud.

'That's exactly right,' said Henry. 'Have you got any cigarettes? I'm out.'

'"I'm out,"' Maud mimicked him with a laugh. 'It'll be a cold day in hell when you have any of your own.'

Maud got up and opened the cupboard under the window seat, which was filled with cartons of cigarettes with tax-free seals. W.S. bought them on his travels around the world. Henry knew that quite well even though he didn't say anything. As he had been told, Maud got along fine without being reminded of anything. She didn't want to hear any reminders at all when they were together. They were not going to talk about either W.S. or Gagarin.

Henry lit a king-size Pall Mall and took a few drags, blowing a couple of tight smoke rings towards Maud and using the saucer under the bed as an ashtray. 'With you, I can love all women in one,' he said, and he was totally serious. 'For me you're more of a human being than a woman. At one time I thought I was going to be gay.'

'That's what all little boys think before they grow up.'

'You have such small breasts . . .'

'If they're not good enough, you know where the door is. This flat is small too.'

'I have a friend,' said Henry, 'who woke up in terror one night. He'd been having a nightmare and he was in a cold sweat. He had dreamt about a hermaphrodite. He had met the most fabulous woman on earth, but when they were going to make love, he discovered that the broad had balls. He woke up in a panic and discovered that he was lying in bed with one hand on his girl's breast and the other between his own legs. Some sort of short-circuit had occurred in his dream.'

133

'All right, you'd better stop telling all these lies!' said Maud, laughing so hard that snot came out of her nose.

'Come here, Fritzi!' said Henry, stubbing out his cigarette.

'You're a strange one,' said Maud, crawling back under the covers.

As I said, they didn't say a word about Gagarin that morning. They didn't give a damn about Russian fools taking notes up there in space. For that matter, they didn't give a damn about W.S. either.

———————

The night they first met was now a few months in the past, and both of them already thought of it as swathed in a romantic glow, like in one of the new French films, or in a book by Salinger or in a really pleasant tune.

One night a few of the city's best school bands were asked to play at the Gazell in Gamla Stan, and Henry had shown up with a quartet that he wasn't at all pleased with, but it would have to do. This was his second quartet, and they had previously played a dozen tunes for a school dance. It was the standard combination of a piano, bass, drums and clarinet. At the school dance they had planned on playing a mix of songs, but everyone mostly wanted music they could dance to. Since they didn't want to disappoint their audience, the band had stuck to livelier tunes.

But at the Gazell they could really cut loose. The audience was older, more mature, and they wanted to hear the real cool numbers that they could get into and really dig. The people who went to the Gazell were deep. Henry thought that was great, and he tried to play some cool music, but the lads from school couldn't really follow. The clarinet sounded much too shrill and screechy, and it didn't work even when the soloist tried to imitate Acker Bilk. Henry yelled at his group and told them that they needed to think about styles other than Dixieland, because Dixieland could end up being out someday, no matter how odd that might sound.

Even so, their set at the Gazell went great – but then maybe the audience wasn't expecting much. Later in the evening the Bear Quartet was going to play. It was a group well-known to aficionados, those who were deep and truly wanted to get down into the jazz, to sit with their eyes shut, quietly swaying their heads, while they smoked a cigarette, drank a little red wine and so on. The Bear Quartet itself was known for being a group of very deep guys – at least in the interviews in *Orchesterjournalen*. They had all played bop and Dixieland

and were familiar with the full range. These days they were playing in a slightly avant-garde style, which mostly involved playing longer solos.

At any rate, there was an irrefutable air of mystery surrounding the guys who played in the Bear Quartet. Henry didn't know them personally, but he knew that his father, the Jazz Baron, had played a session with them, and he'd said that when their time came, those boys were going to be big. Maybe their time had now come.

It was undeniable that they looked deep. Two of them wore black berets, one of them had a beard and long hair down to his neck. But the fourth one wasn't there. Three quarters of the Bear Quartet were now sitting on stage: the drummer, bass player and tenor saxophonist, but the pianist was missing. He was somewhere in the club, but no one knew exactly where.

Suddenly the tenor-sax player, who was very tall, stood up and started moving among the tables and audience, heading straight for Henry, who was sitting with a Kornett beer, quenching his thirst after his set. 'So you're Henry Morgan, is that right?' said the guy wearing the shades.

'That's me,' said Henry.

'I knew your dad. We were thinking of playing a tune for him tonight. I liked him. He was one of the best.'

Henry didn't really know what to say. He didn't know what to do either until he was on his way back to the stage to sit in with the group.

'So the thing is,' the tenor-sax player began speaking from the stage, 'our pianist just got sick over in the bar, and he took off. We don't know where, but we've found someone to fill in for him, someone you saw earlier,' he went on. He was apparently the only member of the Bear Quartet who spoke to the audience. The drummer fumbled his brushes over the high-hat, while the bass player leaned meditatively on his bass. Henry was nervous that he might forget the changes that were scribbled on a piece of paper propped up on the piano. 'This is going to be a bit ad lib,' said the tenor-sax player to the audience. 'Improvised, you know. We're going to open with a tune called 'The Baron', and it's dedicated to the Jazz Baron.'

The sax player counted off for the quartet, and they started up. It went slow and sounded cool, exactly the way Henry wanted it to sound, and he got lost only once. After a long sax solo, he got to take over, and he played well. The audience was turned on and applauded heartily. Henry sat in with the Bear Quartet for the rest of the evening, taking it in like the breakthrough that it was.

The night didn't end until some time around two a.m. A handful of real enthusiasts were still there when the sax player with the beret and shades took his last solo, sounding as avant-garde as hell.

Henry was offered a Kornett beer, and he sat down at a table to unwind with a cigarette. He felt wiped out and couldn't really fathom the whole thing.

'That was fucking great, my boy,' said the tenor-sax player as he sat down next to Henry. 'My name's Bill.'

They shook hands, and the saxophonist named Bill laughed, revealing big white teeth in the middle of his unshaven face. Only now, outside the spotlight, did he take off his shades for a moment to press a cold lager to his eyelids.

'Great night, Bill,' said a girl from the darkness. 'Great night!'

'Sure,' said Bill. 'I don't think you know Henry Morgan,' he went on, nodding at Henry. 'He's the angel who came to our rescue tonight. This is Eva and Maud.'

The girl named Eva came over to the musicians' table, bringing along the girl named Maud. They looked to be about Henry's age, both of them; real Dixieland broads wearing tight black slacks and Icelandic wool sweaters. No doubt they also wear duffel coats when it's cold out, thought Henry.

'You look so funny in that tie,' said Eva. Henry was embarrassed and offended, and she noticed that at once. 'Don't feel bad about it. Bill doesn't look much better.'

'So, what shall we do now?' said Bill.

'We could go over to my place, if you want,' said the girl named Eva, looking around the table.

'Of course we do,' said Bill. 'What do you say, Henry?'

'Sure,' said Henry. 'I just to have to buy some cigarettes.'

They went over to the other quartet members who were sitting there with a bottle of wine, looking more deep than ever, and Bill set the time for the next rehearsal. Then he said something about Henry that no one else could hear.

That early March morning was bitterly cold and oppressive. Eva and Maud, as predicted, wore duffel coats, but they were still freezing. No buses or trams were running at that time of night, but as luck would have it, Eva lived near Odenplan, so they just had to walk up Drottninggatan. They were talking about Paris; all of them had been there – except for Henry.

'Paris is the place, all right,' said Bill, shivering. 'It's never this fucking cold in Paris. And if it does get cold at night, there are always plenty of bars where it's warm inside. Fucking warm.'

'I saw Sartre there one night last autumn,' said Eva. 'He was so short and sweet.'

'He's fucking powerful,' said Bill. '*Dirty Hands*, man, what a play! So powerful . . .'

'Have you read anything by Sartre?' asked the girl named Maud, who was leaning on Henry's arm.

'I hardly read anything,' he said. 'Maybe Damon Runyon. *Guys and Dolls*, I like that one.'

He could tell that Bill and these girls were not like the people he was used to. They had got so deep from reading that heavy Frenchman's books that the teachers were always talking about at school. Henry read *Guys and Dolls* and thought it was good, but he had never opened a book by Sartre. Nor did he think he ever would.

'*Guys and Dolls* is OK, I guess,' said Bill. 'But you ought to read Sartre. *Dirty Hands*. You'll get more what jazz is all about if you read Sartre.'

'Why's that?' said Henry, a little annoyed.

'Well, it's about fundamental things. Just like real jazz. Not Dixieland. You know, you have to choose between one thing and another. You're faced with a choice where several paths could be the right one, and you feel worried that right now you might not be able to tell which path to take. What seems right today might seem wrong tomorrow, and there you stand like an idiot, just staring. Provided you don't believe in God, of course.'

'I've got a stomach-ache,' said Eva. 'I've got such a damn stomach-ache.'

'It's just the cold,' said Bill, stuffing his hand inside her duffel coat. 'Give me Paris any day.'

Eva's flat was cold and old-fashioned. They immediately lit a fire in the stove, using empty sugar boxes. Bill started leafing through a bunch of books by Dostoyevsky, and Henry looked through the records. He instantly felt at home.

The girl named Maud brought in a tray with tea cups and biscuits and set it in front of the fire. 'What do you do when you're not playing?' she asked Henry.

'I'm still at school,' said Henry, drawing himself up.

'How old are you?' she asked, sounding surprised.

'I'll be eighteen in June.'

'A youngster!' shouted Bill. 'You've got your whole life ahead of you!'

'So how old are all of you?'

'That's not something you should ask a lady,' said Maud.

'These old girls are twenty-five,' said Bill. 'They're past their prime.'

Maud smiled and went out to the kitchen to tell Eva something. Henry assumed that it had to do with him, because they both started laughing out there. He definitely felt like a youngster in this crowd. But he felt at home.

After that, Bill put on a hot new record with, as he said, a fucking powerful tenor-sax player named John Coltrane. It was 'My Favourite Things', and it sounded like nothing else. All four of them lay down on the floor in front of the fire blazing in the stove and just listened, closing their eyes and digging this new John Coltrane, who blew as cool and smoky as it was possible to blow at that time of the morning. And Bill said that it sounded just like in Paris. Henry was almost asleep. He felt a hand running through his hair, but he didn't feel like finding out whose hand it was. He was peering into the landscape created by the embers inside the stove. It was a dark, glowing lava landscape, constantly pulsating and changing. And the air from Coltrane's horn fanned the coals into that white heat which makes the embers turn into nothing, into ashes.

———————

Dawn had already come and gone and Henry would have kept on sleeping if it hadn't been so damn cold. He was wakened by the chattering of his own teeth because it was draughty on the floor. Someone had put a blanket over him, but it wasn't enough.

He was lying on the floor alone. Bill and Eva had taken the bed. Bill was the only jazz musician that Henry would ever meet who wore longjohns.

Henry set about adjusting his tie. He hauled himself up off the floor, closed the damper on the stove and went out to the kitchen. For breakfast he drank some milk from a bottle in the pantry, then found his coat and left. Down on the street he ran into people on their way to work. The city was starting to huff and puff in the cold. Steamy clouds of breath were mingling above the pavements, and Henry felt full of life. A bit stiff in the back, but comfortably drowsy and tired.

He stuffed his hands in his coat pockets and started walking back towards Gamla Stan. In one pocket he suddenly felt a piece of paper that didn't belong there. He pulled out the paper and read: 'Rendez-Vous today at 1 p.m. Maud. P.S. You can keep wearing the tie, as far as I'm concerned.'

Henry had almost forgotten about Maud; he'd paid even less attention to when she left the flat. He had dozed off and slept soundly on the floor. Maybe she was the one who had put the blanket over him. It made him happy, at any rate, and he headed off for school at a brisk pace. He wondered where the Rendez-Vous was located and what sort of place it was. It sounded like a restaurant, and he didn't have much money. But no doubt he'd figure something out. 'Master is my name, though poverty oppresses me', said the beggar', as Henry's mother used to say. And that's what Henry said too.

————————

Henry was not the punctual type, but for once he was determined to show up on time. He leapt out of the tram near Norrmalmstorg, walked down Biblioteksgatan to the corner of Lästmakargatan, and turned up the hill towards the Rendez-Vous. He had found the address in the phone book at school.

Maud looked nothing like he had imagined her. It took him a while before he even recognised her. Last night she had looked like a teenage girl, but now she was wearing a brown suit with a pleated skirt. Her lips were painted a dark red, and her hair wasn't black at all; it was also quite straight. She was smoking a lot. There were already three cigarette butts in the ashtray, red from her lipstick.

Maud actually looked the way you might imagine a tough woman in luxury packaging would look, as a song might have described her. When Henry caught sight of her, she was holding a little round mirror and painting her lips as bright red as a tough woman in luxury packaging would do it.

Henry hadn't a clue where this meeting was going to lead. He hadn't a clue about most things in life; he wasn't the analytical type, like his precocious brother. Events happened to him the way they happened to a true defeatist – he merely had to accept the situation as a sentence without a trial.

But at least he was given a hint. Maud sat there, as absorbed as a narcissist staring into a pocket pond, and Henry had an inkling that this woman was totally concerned with physical appearances and not achievements. She might talk about Sartre and Art, but she wanted to turn great ideas and deeds into physical qualities instead of actions. Physical qualities were replaceable, just like a lipstick, or a scarf that according to a certain fashion trend, was supposed to stay fastened to the strap of a handbag.

'You're right on time,' she said, pushing out a chair with her foot.

'You're so dressed up!' Henry couldn't help saying.

'Dressed up?' said Maud.

'You didn't look like this last night.'

'I should think that's my own business,' said Maud curtly.

'Sure,' said Henry. 'But I just thought that . . .'

'You can order whatever you want. It's my treat,' said Maud, handing him a menu.

Henry had very definite ideas about how a gentleman should behave at a lunch with a lady, and he tried to insist on paying, even though he barely had enough money even for his own lunch. Maud pretended not to hear what he was saying, out of pure tactfulness, and Henry gave in without further argument.

Maud had thick, chestnut-coloured hair with a parting down the middle, cut quite short at the back, and with two points dangling down her cheeks. Sometimes she sucked on them when she was thinking. Otherwise she sucked on a cigarette. She smoked more than Henry did, and that was saying a lot. He had a hard time focusing on the menu choices; he was completely bewitched by this creature Maud. He mostly just sat and wondered if that beauty spot on her right cheek was real or had been painted on. He didn't dare ask.

That's how the whole lunch proceeded, under the astrological sign of Henry *the amateur* and his sense of awe. He was incapable of telling a single story about himself – not even about boxing, though Maud was incredibly fascinated – without stopping in the middle of a sentence to stare at her. Then he'd have to pick up the thread again. He didn't know whether this was some sort of love, hitherto unknown to him. But he tried to keep things together as best he could, until Maud placed her hand on his and said, 'Henry, you seem a little nervous.'

'I guess I'm just tired,' he said. 'I shouldn't have had wine with lunch. I didn't get enough sleep last night.'

'So I'm not making you nervous?'

'You're not the same as I pictured you.'

'Are you disappointed?'

'On the contrary.'

'Don't worry about it right now. Everything has its purpose.'

'So what should we do now?'

'We can go over to my place, if you like. I live nearby.'

Maud paid for everything, and then they sauntered over to Birger Jarls-gatan, where she slipped into Augusta Jansson's shop, as was her custom, to buy a bag of sweets for two kronor fifty. She loved salty liquorice. Henry thought she was marvellously childish.

Maud lived in one of the red brick buildings in Lärkstan, in a sparsely furnished two-room flat right under the eaves, with a view of Engelbrekt-skyrka.

'Put on a record,' she said. 'I'll get us something to drink.'

Henry hung his coat and cap on a coat-rack with four pegs. It almost tipped over, and ended up tilting against the wall. It always did that, as he would learn.

He went into the living room, which had mullioned windows and was furnished with a low sofa, a couple of armchairs, a TV and a small stereo bench with a turntable and records. The floor was covered with a wall-to-wall carpet, and this was the first time that Henry had ever set foot on a wall-to-wall carpet. It lent a special atmosphere to the room, a certain inti-mate and familiar atmosphere, seemingly relaxed and exciting at the same time, as a contemporary-furniture catalogue might express it.

There was a lot of modern jazz in the stack of records. MJQ, Miles Davis, Thelonious Monk, Duke Ellington, Charles Mingus, Arne Domnérus, Lars Gullin and Bengt Hallberg. At the very bottom were a couple of albums with Elvis the Pelvis. About half of the records were classical music, and Henry put on Sibelius. He didn't know much about Sibelius, except that the Finn had boozed a lot and died the year before his own father passed away. What more did he really need to know?

Maud came in from the kitchen carrying a tray with whisky, ice cubes, soda, gin and Grappo. He could choose whatever he wanted. Henry chose whisky.

————————

'Now I want to hear this one,' said Maud, getting up from the sofa. She had been lying with her head on Henry's lap, and they had listened to Sibelius, both of them almost falling asleep. Henry was feeling drowsy from the whisky, and he had forgotten to worry about his hands. When Maud lay down in his lap, he didn't really know what to do with his hands. Should he run them through her hair, pat her on the cheek or let them lie quietly on her breasts? But then he had dozed off, sinking into the music and feeling very peaceful.

'This is my favourite tune,' said Maud, and she put on 'Spin My World', by Jan Malmsjö. The song was already a hit, but it had never really turned Henry on; for that matter he'd never been to any cabarets or theatres where this sort of French singer performed. Those places were mostly frequently by intellectuals talking about Paris and Sartre, like Maud and Eva and Bill in the Bear Quartet.

Maud knew all the words by heart, and she sang along softly, looking at Henry without blinking. He lit a cigarette and thought the song was OK.

This time it was not dawn but twilight. They had fallen asleep in the bed, and Henry awoke as twilight set in. He cautiously pulled himself free from Maud, who was lying on his arm, lit a cigarette and looked out of the window.

It must have been about five in the afternoon. People were on their way home from work. Maud and Henry had eaten lunch, gone home, had a couple of drinks, listened to music and talked a little about skipping school. Then they had made love. All of this had taken less than four hours. That must be a record for me, thought Henry.

He blew smoke at the ceiling, feeling more antisocial than ever. He had skipped school plenty of times in his day, but that was in order to work extra hours, to box, or to rehearse with the school band. He had never in his life slept with a woman in the middle of the day, and it felt quite bohemian.

The beauty spot on Maud's right cheek was not genuine. Henry had kissed it right off.

'You have to leave,' said Maud as soon as she awoke and got up to put on a bathrobe.

'Leave?'

'Yes, leave,' she said curtly. 'Don't ask any questions right now. I'll explain later. You have to leave. It's already late.'

Henry had no idea what this was all about. He thought she was being awfully quick about changing moods. LEAVE! That sounded like an order. LEAVE! With a big exclamation mark. 'Are you married?' he asked as he pulled on his trousers.

Maud started to laugh. It wasn't a nervous or malicious sort of laugh; it sounded happy and warm. 'I didn't notice before,' she said as she kept on laughing. 'I didn't notice that you have a button fly!'

Henry chuckled along with her and started fumbling more than necessary with his fly.

'No, my young man,' said Maud, 'I'm not married.' She held up her left hand to show him that she wasn't wearing a ring. She had on several other beautiful rings, but no wedding band. 'I'm not married,' she went on, 'and I'm not going to get married either, not for a good long time.'

Henry sat down on the edge of the bed and pulled on his vest and shirt, buttoning it up more slowly than necessary.

'Are you disappointed?' asked Maud.

He looked at her back as she sat at the dressing table, brushing her hair. Her posture was erect, making her look like a straight-backed horsewoman in one of the paintings in his grandfather's flat on Hornsgatan.

'Of course I am,' said Henry. 'I don't like being thrown out.'

'You're not being thrown out, Henry. But you have to leave.'

'Can't you tell me why?'

'Not now. You wouldn't understand. Later. Some other time.'

'OK,' said Henry glumly. 'I'll leave, but . . .'

'But?'

'But I'm not coming back ever again.'

'Don't be silly!' said Maud, not sounding the least bit worried. The threat didn't work because Henry couldn't make it sound convincing, since he wasn't convinced himself.

'All right, that was stupid,' he admitted.

When he started knotting his tie, she turned around from her position in front of the mirror at the dressing table. 'That tie . . .' she began. 'I can give you a new one, if you like.'

'You have *ties* in your flat? And you're not married? You really are an eccentric, aren't you!'

Maud laughed again, that carefree laugh of hers. 'Look in that box,' she said, pointing to a box on the window seat facing the church. Henry discovered that the box was filled with ties, exclusive ties from Morris & Silvander, as well as from England and France. Expensive ties without the creases and wrinkles from knots that had stayed in place for several days.

'He must change his tie every day, at least,' said Henry. 'And he has excellent taste. A good salary, travels a lot, about one eighty in his stockinged feet.'

'Perry Mason was never jealous,' said Maud.

'I'm not either. I'm just curious, from a professional standpoint.'

He *was* curious, from a professional standpoint; he was also a notorious liar. Of course Henry was jealous, but he didn't feel that sharp pang in his chest that he had felt before. This time it was different. Maud was a full-grown woman, twenty-five years old, even though at any time she could make herself look like a teenager with a couple of well-chosen and carefully calculated lines with a brush, a few dabs with a lipstick and the right clothes. She could also behave like a little lady and a childish chick at the very same time. Henry couldn't make her out, nor could he understand how he felt about her. Love was hatred and jealousy, but he'd never been able to mobilise blind passion until they were both lying in her bed and she was writhing under him and he was watching her, as astonished as a child. Now all that was left was the taste in his mouth. She had abruptly changed again, into a very practical, rational and unsentimental creature.

'Well?' she said. 'Do you want a tie or not?'

Henry had sunk into a sort of pragmatic composure and insisted that he wasn't interested.

'I don't want any tie. My own is good enough. I don't want to go around wearing someone else's clothes. Especially *his*!'

'But your shirt is all ragged,' said Maud. 'Just look at that cuff!'

Henry studied the cuff above his wristwatch. It was undeniably worn. 'So what?' he said sullenly.

'Here!' said Maud, handing him a freshly ironed, nice-smelling shirt from the wardrobe. 'Take this one!'

It was an elegant, heavy cotton shirt with stripes, and Henry couldn't resist. He had always liked freshly ironed shirts, and in this instance the shirt seemed less personal than the ties. A tie is like a signature, a badge against the shirt. A tie says more about the owner than even the shirt front. Henry didn't notice that the initials W.S. were under the shirt collar, or that it was made in England and very exclusive.

'OK,' he said when he was fully dressed. 'I'm leaving now.'

Maud came out of the bathroom to give him a hug that was much too light and fleeting. He started nibbling on the back of her neck, but she pulled herself free from his arms.

'Can you come back on Sunday?'

'Will *he* be gone by then?'

'Let's not have any of that nonsense right now,' she said, annoyed. 'Don't think about him.'

'Sunday morning, then. Early.'

'Early,' Maud repeated. 'Wake me up and we'll have breakfast together.'

Out in the stairwell Henry quickly discovered something in one of his pockets. He pulled out a slim, oval cigarette case made of silver. It was filled with long cigarettes. The initials W.S. were engraved on the lid. She has a real thing about putting objects in people's pockets, thought Henry, lighting a tax-free Pall Mall. It tasted excellent.

———

Henry noticed that something unusual was going on as soon as he came out onto the street. He had quickly thrown on his clothes this Sunday morning so that he could have breakfast with Maud, not waking either Leo or his mother. He didn't want to be showered with a lot of questions, and he slipped quietly out of the door.

But there was a strange feeling on the street, and down at the Slussen underground station there was a great throng of people. Entire families were standing on the platform with food hampers, morning newspapers, bags and backpacks. The kids were yelling and shouting, holding footballs and skipping ropes. At first Henry assumed that they were on their way out on their usual Sunday excursions, since he couldn't even remember when he'd last been up this early on a Sunday morning.

The train arrived, and the carriage filled up with bellowing people. Henry was pressed into a corner by a smiling old woman who was lugging a good-sized hamper and had four grandchildren with her. 'We're leaving in good time,' said the old woman. 'Jumping the gun, so to speak,' she went on, nodding conspiratorially.

The whole car seemed rampant with Sabbath and conspiracy. Henry couldn't for the life of him fathom what was going on, what they were so excited about. Mostly he felt sleepy and almost dozed off for real because the train waited at the platform for a long time.

Finally the train began chugging out onto the bridge towards Gamla Stan at a snail's pace, and then, suddenly, the starting gun was fired, or the starting signal or whatever it should be called. The whole city started screaming and crying and roaring and whistling, and Henry was instantly wide awake. He didn't understand what was happening. He stood here gaping like a fool, staring out across Riddarfjärden in astonishment. Every single siren in the whole city was wailing at full blast. Air-raid sirens. They were shrieking of terror and war and black-outs and rationing. A respectable paterfamilias pulled down a window and stuck out his head because the train had now stopped in the centre of the bridge.

'Did they wake you with the phone alarm?' asked the old woman with the food hamper.

'Phone alarm?' said Henry.

'Well, then it must have been the loudspeaker van,' the old woman guessed, giving him that conspiratorial nod again. Henry was slowly starting to understand what was going on. This was long before the emergence of *Henri le boulevardier*, the newspaper reader and flaneur, the libertine and *bon vivant*. Henry had been walking around in a fog of desire and longing for Maud, dreaming his way through his school days, and plinking on the piano until late into the night. He hadn't really been keeping up with the times, and he hadn't realised that this particular Sunday was the day of the big evacuation exercise. All of Stockholm – as was intended and planned by the vice-governor and the managers at evacuation headquarters – was supposed to rush pell mell down to the shelters and underground stations and buses in order to evacuate out to the Uppland countryside. It was no longer 'If War Comes'. War had come. It was already a reality, or at least it was at evacuation headquarters. But the panic and terror of war were not particularly evident among the passengers in the underground carriage; it seemed more like a carnival, a publicity stunt and a free Sunday excursion. People crowded together with their footballs and food hampers and thermos bottles, talking and joking quite amiably.

When the train rolled into the station at Rådmansgatan, a murmuring passed over the platform and into the carriages. A rumour began spreading that the king, His Majesty King Gustav VI Adolf, and the ambassadors and dark-complexioned princes and princesses, were all on their way. It got even

146

more crowded inside the car, if that were possible. Henry was now pressed into his corner and, gentleman that he was, he was holding the little old woman's food hamper in his arms. He had noticed that all the men, meaning all the decent fellows, were being helpful and chivalrous towards the women and children, playing the expert and hero and criticising evacuation head-quarters for its poor planning. The men were telling preparedness stories, and they all thought that everything was moving too slowly; this would never work if the situation were ever for real.

'The *king*,' said the little old woman in amazement, her eyes sparkling. 'The *king* . . .'

'It's probably just a rumour,' said Henry.

'I suppose he's never taken the underground before.'

'I don't suppose he has,' said Henry. 'But I've got to get off now,' he went on, trying to give the food hamper back to the old woman.

'Get *off*?' said the woman, amazed again. 'But this train is going to Hässelby. From there we have to take a bus out into the country.'

'I have to get off at Odenplan,' said Henry, thinking that Odengatan led up to Lärkstan where Maud lived. He had no intention of going all the way out to Hässelby.

The door opened and the platform outside was teeming with people who surged forward to get on; no one was getting off. Henry couldn't move. He tried to wriggle and squirm his way forward, but he was wedged into a vice of evacuated flesh.

'What are you trying to do, kid?' asked a hero, paterfamilias and the proud owner of a bass voice.

'I want to get off here,' said Henry calmly.

'Off?!' said Bass Voice. 'Dammit, kid, we're going out to Hässelby and from there we take a bus out to the country. Nobody's getting off here!'

Henry was getting desperate. People kept crowding in from the platform, and he couldn't get off. When he realised that he was simply a prisoner in an evacuation manoeuvre, he took the food hamper back from the old woman and sighed deeply. The only thing he wanted, the only thing he had been thinking about for the last few days, was to see Maud. And just when he wanted to get off this damn train, the whole city had decided to play war, pretending that all of Stockholm had to be evacuated. Henry started laughing. He laughed so hard that sweat ran down his forehead, and the little old woman stared up at him uneasily while Bass Voice stared down at him and shook his head.

Henry stayed trapped in that carriage all the way out to Hässelby. By then the 'War' was in full swing. In silence he had gone through every imaginable swear word, and he was determined to take the first train back. As soon as he stepped out onto the platform, Bass Voice grabbed hold of him.

'Hey kid, could you give me a hand? Do you mind?' he said, pointing to the handle of an enormous suitcase that he had brought along on the underground.

'What do you have in there?' asked Henry.

'Clothes, kitchen utensils, essential items,' said Bass Voice solemnly. 'I'm doing a test.'

'I see,' said Henry.

Bass Voice looked so stern and surly that Henry didn't dare refuse to help him. Together they carried the heavy, cumbersome suitcase out to the square where scores of buses were waiting, their engines running. Bass Voice gave his wife and three children brief, precise instructions to go left, then right, steering them towards just the right bus. Apparently he liked giving orders. They shoved the suitcase into the luggage compartment of the bus, and Bass Voice exchanged a few words with the driver about the bus, and which particular features were not especially satisfactory. Bass Voice also liked buses.

'Is everybody here?' he rumbled, checking inside the bus. His whole family replied in unison, 'Yes!' All the other families immediately followed his lead, the fathers yelling and the children and wives answering. There was a hell of a lot of shouting.

Henry started heading back to the underground. Just outside the station, he saw Leo and Verner walking along. They had caught the train just after Henry, and they were equipped to the teeth. Verner was also taking this whole evacuation thing very seriously, while Leo was just following along. They waved a copy of the booklet *If War Comes*, and showed Henry that they had brought along every single thing you were supposed to have. They seemed very pleased with the whole operation and disappeared into the throngs of evacuees. Henry took the underground back to Odenplan. He was already very late.

Maud wasn't home. Henry rang the doorbell over and over again, but no one answered, and once again he worked himself into a sweat by swearing. He swore at all the damn pretend-wars and the pretend-heroes going around with suitcases filled with lead, and he hated all of Stockholm like the plague. He yearned to get away. To Paris. That's where he would go, sooner or later.

There they damn well didn't play war. If there was a war, it was the real thing.

Henry sighed for the twenty-fifth time that day and started walking down the stairs in resignation. But in the hallway luck was with him; he happened to hear voices coming from the cellar. Necessity is the mother of invention as well as of a certain genius. Henry put two and two together and realised that everyone in the building was, of course, down in the cellar, also playing war.

And right he was. Henry went down to the cellar, and there sat all the tenants, drinking coffee and eating buns and having a very pleasant time. Henry was welcomed heartily.

'This is all so exciting with the war,' said Maud in his ear. 'It feels as if we only have a few short hours together today before you have to go off to the front.'

'That's exactly how it is,' said Henry.

'Well, ladies and gentlemen,' said the building supervisor, raising his voice a notch. 'It all went very well, and we'd like to thank Mrs Lindberg for her wonderful buns and Mrs Bäck and Mrs Hagström for the coffee. We certainly hope that we never have to go through the real thing but that we'll see a little more of each other in civilian life. That's the most important thing we've learned.'

The coffee guests, that is, the evacuees, loudly applauded the supervisor's speech, and the manoeuvre was officially over. Maud and Henry went up to her flat. As Henry hung his coat on the coat-rack, which tilted against the wall, Maud was already on her way to the bedroom.

It was some time at the end of April in 1961 – the best of times for this odd alliance – and after breakfast Maud was sitting on the floor in front of the TV wearing her bathrobe, with a teacup between her legs. Henry was completely absorbed in watching the royal warship *Wasa* as she surfaced. The dive boss Fälting could be seen gasping for air through the hose, and the navy band struck up a tune with extra vigour. People were cheering and applauding. The TV cameramen at Lodbrok kept the cameras rolling.

For almost everyone, it represented a revelation from the historic depths of three hundred and thirty-three years ago – an oak hull dripping with sludge and water, filled with cannons, kegs of aquavit, copper coins, ceramic bowls, passglasses, cutlery and sculptures. And as she reached the surface, orders and corrections were released from the commander, shouted when she heaved onto her port side in the middle of the Thirty Years War in Stockholm. She began taking on water through her gun ports, and panic erupted in full force. The catastrophe was inevitable.

But for Henry, this was not a moment when something was being revealed. Not at all. For him it was quite the opposite. When the royal warship *Wasa* came to the surface that day, he was utterly absorbed in the historical event, but to his eyes something was not being dragged up out of the stinking muck. Instead, something was sinking, flooding, being consigned to history. He watched everything with his indefatigable curiosity, but his thoughts were far, far away. He was thinking about the Ark, the ship that he had tried to build out on Storm Island. His maternal grandfather, the Boat Builder, got the whole project started, and every summer they had worked on that ship, which they were going to sail around the world. Henry read about Joshua Slocum and Hornblower and escaped into his dreams. In his dreams he planed every plank, making the seams tighter and tighter, until disaster struck and everything came to an end out there on Storm Island.

The Ark was never completed. It was still out there in one of the boathouses, half finished, crumbling away and unreal, like some monumental elk skeleton that you come upon in a forest glade and the foxes have eaten it clean so that the ribs are pointing up towards the sky, just like the bare framework of a keel. The Ark lay out there on Storm Island, where the last remnants of his mother's family wandered around in bewilderment like degenerate fools, waiting for summertime visits and the post and fresh provisions. Henry had harboured a dream of going back, exactly as if nothing had happened, to get his grandfather drunk on aquavit, shake some life into the old man, dress him in his stinking longjohns, and lead him down to the boathouse to finish the Ark. But the water surrounding Storm Island would be forever poisoned. In the coves it was putrid and stagnating; the seaweed floated dead and decomposing down in the deep, in the dark deep. The Ark would remain an elk skeleton, nibbled bare by voracious hyenas so that its ribs pointed towards the sky like the framework of a keel, like an accusation, a reminder of sorrow and eternal unrest.

Only now, as Henry lay there in Maud's flat, watching the royal warship *Wasa* rise to the surface amidst the cheers of the crowd, could he drown the Ark, let it sink to the bottom, settle into the muddy grave vacated by the *Wasa*. The dream of the Ark belonged to his childhood, and Henry wanted to leave it behind because he was feeling strong and intoxicated with love.

Henry started laughing when the music suddenly ceased and the crowd fell silent. For one dizzying moment everyone was quiet and seemed to be wondering: *what have we really done?* Almost ashamed at having awakened a woman from her three hundred and thirty-three years of slumber, in which she most certainly should have been allowed to remain. Henry laughed loudly, and then his laughter changed to a quiet hissing; tears fell from his eyes, and he felt liberated, washed clean, exonerated.

The flat was full of daffodils, called Easter lilies in Swedish, and the flowers gave off a strong scent of martyrdom and vicarious suffering. Henry had suffered. He'd thought he would always suffer, that he'd never win a reprieve or solace from a great love. But now it had come to him as he sat there watching an ancient ship being raised from the sea floor. The daffodils' scent signified suffering, but Maud's scent signified life and desire.

She didn't notice that he was crying when he approached her from behind.

She was lying on the wall-to-wall carpet in front of the TV with her eyes fixed on the royal warship *Wasa* as Henry gently uncovered her body, the way only a figurehead of sea-drenched oak is otherwise uncovered.

Henry attended Södra Latin school. He had started there as a young pup several years after the suicide of its famous pupil, Stig Dagerman, and the panicked reactions to Alf Sjöberg's movie *Frenzy* and the book *The Snake* were still sending out their terror-filled shadows from the cast-iron banisters and over the walls. Henry had grown up there in the ranks of schoolmaster discipline at the boys' school, with queues of thick sweaters and suede jackets and well-scrubbed necks, which over the years got bulkier until the jackets were replaced with coats and the boys played at being young men, going to cafés and smoking. They hung around outside the girls' school on Götgatan, where elegant little ladies from the suburbs south of Söder peeked out, giggling behind the curtains and waiting for invitations to the dances at the boys' school. It was a boys' school full of discipline and manly rituals, and I assumed that Henry did quite well there. He was a pianist and boxer, but he was also the one to cheer the loudest when it became apparent that the first girl, under the new school ordinance and with full parliamentary rights, was going to set her dainty foot through the massive school doors to attend classes, which up until then had been reserved for males. That was in the autumn of 1961.

But in the spring of that year the boys' school was enjoying its last hurrah. Henry went around whistling 'Putti Putti', and he was sleeping more soundly than usual during his classes. He was living a hard life with a mature woman, that young Morgan.

His quartet had naturally been booked for the graduation parties. Henry couldn't fathom how he was going to endure another year of school as some half-baked loudmouthed graduates came trotting through the heavy doors, out onto the stairs under the school clock, drunk and merry, with tears mixing with powder, perfume and punch. Proud parents had given the quartet instructions about where to sit on the traditional flatbed lorry carrying the celebrating graduates through the city. The group had also been instructed not to start playing until such and such a moment, but Henry didn't give a damn about any of that. He was playing guitar because no one dared haul a piano up onto the flatbed lorry, which had pissed him off. That's why he didn't give a damn about whether the arrangements suited those who were paying for them or not. He had made up his mind that tonight he was going to eat a lot and drink a lot, free of charge and then head home to Maud. She was going away. She had wept and made Henry weep too. Maud was going away and would be gone all summer.

Henry's quartet went through the entire prescribed repertoire of gradua-tion songs, and no one heard how false they sounded, nor did anyone care. The graduate, a harmless type from Enskede, was giving a decent party at his home. The quartet played, and during the breaks Henry drank a great deal. He had a good-sized drink sitting behind the music stand on the piano the whole time. It was a typical assembly-line piano, mostly intended for show, that had been handed down and was out of tune.

After the banquet, there was going to be a dance, and everyone had agreed that they wanted to dance the swing and the foxtrot to Elvis, and so the quartet was dismissed. Henry received fifty kronor from the proud father who, sounding tearful and grateful and lofty all at the same time, tried to articulate a few polite phrases to thank the musicians and wish them good luck.

Henry got a lift to Hötorget from some equally tearful and sentimental relatives wearing their old graduation caps, yellowed with age. He took the route through Tunnelgatan, whistling 'Spin My World' in the tunnel. It echoed magnificently, as if heralding a decisive, final farewell.

Maud was wearing a suit, an elegant suit, and a polo jumper. Henry realised at once that 'He' had been there. Henry was a bit drunk and in despair, but he tried to hide it. He didn't want to ruin this evening, which would be their last one for an indefinite amount of time.

'But it's not "an indefinite amount of time",' said Maud, mimicking Henry's sullen tone. 'I'll be back in August or September.'

'You haven't even told me where you're going,' said Henry, sinking onto the sofa and paying no attention to the record player. He was tired of music, worn out, tired of any kind of sound at all.

'How did it go at the party, by the way?'

'Who cares?' said Henry with a groan. 'Have you got anything to drink?'

Maud went out to the kitchen and came back with gin and Grappo on a tray. 'Just don't drink too much,' she said.

Henry took out a pack of John Silvers, lit a cigarette and leaned back against the sofa.

'You're not using the cigarette case . . .' said Maud. 'Did you sell it?'

'I did *not* sell it,' said Henry, a little embarrassed. 'But I did pawn it. As soon as I get some cash I'll buy it back.'

'It doesn't matter,' said Maud. 'Maybe that was the point, anyway. At any rate, he knows about everything now.'

'And?'

'And he doesn't care. Or at least that's what he says.'

'Is he the one you're going away with?'

Maud nodded and poured herself a small drink. Henry wasn't particularly inquisitive in this condition. He merely felt a dormant sense of jealousy because he had been faced with an ultimatum right from the start, and he knew that he would never be able to have her all to himself. W.S. would always be there, like a shadow, an *eminence gris* that never left a calling card. Henry had already grown accustomed to this. He didn't love Maud in the passionate way that he imagined he should. He loved Maud in a totally different way, perhaps a deeper and more serious way that he didn't yet fully understand, nor would he ever understand it.

Maud had decided to lay all her cards on the table, to give Henry the facts of the case, to tell him who W.S. was and why she needed both of them.

Once upon a time, many years ago, a big American trunk and a couple of suitcases stood in a stifling hall, far, far away. Maud had very carefully labelled them with her name and then the word 'SWEDEN'. She had long wondered why she actually wrote 'SWEDEN', because it could just as well have said 'JAKARTA' or 'STATELESS', since that was actually how she felt. She had lived in so many different places that she no longer felt Swedish. But now the destination was 'SWEDEN' on this particular ill-fated day so long ago.

Maud and everyone else knew that her mother easily forgot things. That was because of the pills she took for her nerves. If you told her something in the morning, she would have forgotten it by lunchtime. Not always, but almost always. Right now she had forgotten where Maud's father was. Maud said that he was out at the Teahouse.

Her mother looked quite haggard even though she was still very lovely. She was the most beautiful of all the diplomat wives in Jakarta, including all the *femmes fatales* from the French delegation. In a way, Maud's mother been brought down by her own beauty; it had made her unhappy.

She asked Maud to pour her a drink, a weak one, because it was already two o'clock. She asked her daughter if she'd heard from Wilhelm.

Maud went over to the drinks trolley, which stood against the wall next to the window. She looked out but saw only rain, the monsoon rain that had been coming down without interruption for over a week. Of course she'd heard from Wilhelm. He was going out to the Teahouse with Father. They had gone out to purchase some china and would be back by three.

Maud's mother seemed out of sorts. She didn't know if it was because of the rain, but she assumed that it was. Her shoulders ached, and that was probably due to the dampness. She was out of sorts and wanted to go back to Stockholm too. It was springtime in Sweden, and you could order arti-chokes at the pavement cafés. She longed for Swedish vegetables.

Her mother babbled on, but Maud wasn't listening. She heard only the endless rain as she tried to sense whether she had travel fever and longed for 'home' in Sweden, whether she missed anything at all, though she couldn't really think what it might be.

At about the same time as Maud was hanging her clothes in the big trunk labelled 'SWEDEN' and putting small items in the suitcases, her father, who was the counsellor at the Swedish embassy in Jakarta, and his good friend Wilhelm Sterner were sitting out at the Teahouse talking. The Teahouse was the name of a small cottage, or rather a very meagrely constructed cabin which they had rented in order to get out of the city once in a while. It was located on a mountain slope on the outskirts of a small town about nine-teen miles south-east of Jakarta.

The view was magnificent, looking out over a long valley and an old, extinct volcano. The tropical rainforest clung to the volcano's slope in dull green colours; heavy clouds shrouded the top and hid a Buddhist monastery. They had sat there on many a night, listening to the animals, drinking whisky and talking.

Wilhelm Sterner and the counsellor were old school chums. They had both studied law, specialising in international law, and they had ended up in the diplomatic corps, the big time. Now, in the year 1956, Sterner was hoping for an offer of a good job in private industry. He was going to leave the diplomatic big time and return home to Sweden. But the counsellor planned to stay.

They were now sitting out at the Teahouse, talking about the tropical rain. It would undoubtedly go on for a couple more weeks, and Wilhelm Sterner had no objection to heading home. He promised to look after Maud. The counsellor expressed regret; he seemed to have lost contact with his family. Things were not as they should be.

Wilhelm Sterner felt a bit uncomfortable. No one could really tell whether the counsellor knew what everyone else knew – he was, in some ways, an idealist, like Dag Hammarskjöld. The counsellor and Hammarskjöld had met in New York, and Maud's father kept coming back to that meeting. He had a hard time explaining his true feelings. He had felt inferior and yet strong, as if he had found a kindred spirit in Hammarskjöld, as if their view of the world were exactly the same. Maud's father had always been both an open and a closed sort of person at the same time, a public figure but a very private individual. His wife couldn't take it; everyone knew that. She had sought out her own avenues, and it might seem as if he wanted and welcomed the weight of Christ's cross as soon as he found the opportunity to shoulder it.

He now confided to Wilhelm Sterner that he was thinking of seeking a position that had been advertised in Hungary. He wanted a change, and there might be a need for him in Hungary right now.

Wilhelm Sterner attempted to steer him towards other problems, such as the difficulties in his own home. He had to sort things out with his family, first and foremost. And he would certainly be needed in Jakarta as well. There were movements in all these islands, these three thousand fermenting volcanic islands, that wanted to see Sukarno's head on a platter. Then he'd have a chance to play the hero, if he liked. Sterner had talked to Maud, and she had wept – not because she was leaving but because she was scared and worried.

Wilhelm Sterner saw that the counsellor heard what he said but he wasn't really listening. Maud's father looked very focused, yet utterly preoccupied. Sterner was reminded of an animist trying to listen to the rain, to hear the raindrops speak, sing, and anticipate the crops.

Maud's father was obstinately staring out at the rain, claiming that he could do more good in Hungary. He was going to apply for the position.

It was already very late, and they had to go back to the city. Maud and Wilhelm Sterner were going to fly home to Sweden at dinner time. Their two cars were parked on the slope in front of the Teahouse. The counsellor had a heavy English car with big tractor tyres. Sterner had rented a jeep, an

157

old colonial jeep with a top. Driving on these roads required heavy-duty vehicles. The rain had penetrated into the soil, the ground was saturated with water, and in several places they had to drive through lakes a yard deep. In other spots the soil had started to give way in minor mudslides. The road out to the Teahouse was never the same; it was in a constant state of flux. No matter how often you drove there, you could never be entirely secure.

Maud's father had filled his car with East Indian china. He had bought all of it at a very advantageous price and was going to send home a box with Maud. It was best to take home valuable items in small lots.

Wilhelm Sterner was following behind but having trouble maintaining his speed. The car skidded and slid on the curves, and he was surprised that the counsellor was driving so fast. They were both good drivers, but in this terrain none of the usual rules applied. The road was totally unpredictable; in the middle of a curve a huge clump of foliage might be hanging over the road and slap against your windscreen, obscuring the ground, which was enough to throw anyone off balance.

It happened only about six miles or so outside Jakarta. Wilhelm Sterner had fallen behind and was crawling along at a snail's pace, approaching a curve, when he saw people screaming and waving in a disquieting and alarming manner up ahead. Some were leaping down a muddy, brush-covered slope, screaming and pulling at their hair, wailing and hollering.

Sterner stepped on the brakes with an ominous feeling about what had happened. He later claimed to have sensed it all along. Maud's father had been driving so damned fast, so unnecessarily fast, because they really had no reason to be in such a hurry.

His car had slid off the road, rolled down a slope, and finally came to rest at the base of a palm tree. His body was covered in bloody shards of East Indian china.

All summer long after the ceremonious funeral – as was befitting a departed counsellor – Maud's mother stayed at a sanatorium up in the area around Leksand in Sweden. She was consumed with guilt towards her betrayed and buried spouse. The hysteria which had been somewhat under control became an acute psychosis even before they left Indonesia, during those desperately hectic days as they tried to settle everything before their departure for home. Maud had been forced to take over all the arrangements and also keep an eye on her mother so that she wouldn't take too many pills.

Wilhelm Sterner was indispensable. He was the one who had brought them word of the death. He was also the one who made the preparations for their return home and arranged the funeral service, as well as their housing in Stockholm.

During that entire hot summer of 1956, Maud's mother stayed at the sanatorium in Dalarna province. Her psychosis underwent several stages, but at the bottom of everything was an absolutely irreparable and incurable guilt that had plagued her ever since her husband's death. Maud's mother – after the terrible shock – was convinced that she should die, was going to die. Sometimes she lay in bed all night, loudly moaning about the lumps of death she'd found in her shattered chest.

Thanks to a very patient psychiatrist and Maud's support, she was later released and able to begin a more or less respectable life in a moderately large flat on Karlavägen back in Stockholm. Maud had found a good job as a secretary at the foreign ministry. That was why she had planned to leave Jakarta in the first place, before the tragedy had intervened.

Wilhelm Sterner was also the one who arranged for the small two-room flat in Lärkstaden. He had lived there himself, as the incurable bachelor that he was, but over time and with higher-level positions, he needed more space. He had now been recruited by big business and – according to many rumours that were both persistent and unconfirmed – he had become a sort of Young Turk to Wallenberg.

Maud moved into the charming flat in the autumn of 1956. She redecorated it, creating a place to live that suited her particular needs. She furnished it in a spartan style but with exquisite taste, hanging wood carvings from the Far East on the walls, and putting in that unusual, exclusive wall-to-wall carpeting.

Maud was a modern young woman. She did quite well living on her own. She bought a record-player and was even so modern that she bought herself a TV. That was back during the first days of television, and watching TV may not have felt exactly like a solemn experience for a worldly young woman like Maud, but it was still quite extraordinary.

She was most likely watching TV on that autumn evening when she heard the front door open and someone come into the hall. She was terrified and undoubtedly didn't even have time to decide whether she should pretend she hadn't noticed and keep staring at the TV, or whether she should get up and start shouting.

It was Wilhelm Sterner who came into the living room. He said hello to the terrified Maud and explained that he had an extra key which he wanted to give to the rightful owner.

She exhaled and told him that he could have been good enough to ring the bell before he came in. Sterner apologised. His shoulders slumped and he looked generally distressed. He asked her for a cup of coffee.

Maud made coffee as Sterner sat on the sofa, still wearing his coat and looking dejected and distressed. Naturally she wondered what was going on, whether something special had happened.

Wilhelm Sterner looked at her with eyes that were melancholy and clear, yet demanded respect. He admitted that the damn key wasn't the reason he had come to see her at all. There was something more important.

Maud didn't even have time to light a cigarette before Wilhelm Sterner collapsed onto her lap, weeping despairingly. He confessed at once that he had been in love with her ever since Jakarta. He was prepared to do anything for her sake – sacrifice his career or do whatever she asked.

Strangely enough, Maud was not the least bit surprised. She didn't want anything from him. She'd had a hunch about this but didn't really know what to do. Sterner was already middle-aged, a man in the upper echelons of big business, and a good friend of her late father's. She had seen this man at regular intervals in various places around the world for as long as she could remember. No one knew whether she could think of him as anything but a substitute father.

She ran her hand through Sterner's thick hair and pressed his head close, presumably with no idea that she would be doing this many times in the future.

It became the sort of relationship that is usually labelled an 'affair'. Officially, their activities would remain as much a secret as her mother's 'affairs'. There are hyenas who claim that such tendencies are inherited.

'I want to see a photo of him,' said Henry. 'You must have a picture of him.'

'Is that really necessary?' said Maud. 'It'll just give you a complex.'

By now it was quite late on that night when Henry went to Maud's flat after the graduation party and she told him how she had gradually become Wilhelm Sterner's lover – she called him 'my lover', at any rate. And it's highly likely that the story was much less banal than my account of it. I'm telling it in Henry's dramatised form, which was no doubt distorted by his growing jealousy. At that time in the early sixties he had become fixated on his rival, whom he had never seen; he could only imagine him. Wilhelm Sterner was a corporate magnate who had trained with Wallenberg; *non videre sed esse*, to exist but not be seen – that was his slogan in life.

· 'I do have a photo album,' said Maud, giving in. 'But do we have to look at it right now? I'm tired. And I have to leave early in the morning.'

'I want to see a picture of him,' said Henry. 'I need to see it.'

Maud went into the bedroom and came back with a photo album. They started paging through it. It was a typical family album with captions that she had written herself, except for the very first ones. Her mother had given her the album for her tenth birthday with the earliest pictures showing Maud as a baby dressed in white lace, with a proud father wearing a uniform and leaning over her cradle in the tumultuous year of 1936.

Maud giggled as she read out loud her childish comments to the pictures from walks taken in New York, London and Paris. Grey-and-white pictures taken in Sweden in the early forties when her father was home on leave, wearing his uniform. Henry could see that the man had become a sergeant, and back then Maud's mother was still happy, sitting at home and listening to Ulla Billqvist with the curtains drawn.

'Here's a picture of Pappa and Wilhelm Sterner,' she said finally, showing him a photo from Jakarta in 1956. 'It was taken just before the accident . . .'

Henry was not as curious about her father as he was about Sterner. The man looked just about the way he had pictured him, wearing a double-breasted, pin-striped suit. He looked both heavy and massive in some indefinable way. He looked like a man at the height of his career, a man with ideas, initiative and creative power, easy-going when appropriate, serious and solemn when the situation called for it. He looked very fit; he had presumably thrown the javelin when young, because he had a powerful neck. That was why Henry looked so good in his shirts.

'Are you satisfied now?' asked Maud.

'He looks exactly the way I imagined him,' said Henry. 'He looked good back then.'

'And he still does.'

'Do you make him happy?'

'I think so.'

'And what about you?'

'I love both of you, as a matter of fact,' said Maud. 'You're so different, and not just in terms of age. I feel like a whole different person with you. You're so . . . inexperienced, so innocent . . . But it's different with him. He's so reserved and hard-working, although I don't really care about his work. He's actually very . . . witty, even though that sounds ridiculous. He says that I make him forget about death . . .'

'How long do you think you can keep this up?' asked Henry. 'You can't very well split yourself in half all your life.'

'Why not?' said Maud. 'But we're not going to see each other for a while, you and I. Maybe you'll have found someone else by the time I get back.'

'I wouldn't count on it,' said Henry. 'So what does he say about me?'

'He says that he understands me. And he wants to hear all the details about you.'

'Do you tell him?'

'Of course I do. Should I lie?'

'No,' said Henry, 'you shouldn't.'

Maud lit her last cigarette of the night, looking somehow relieved, as if she had cleared the air. 'Now you know everything you need to know about me,' she said. 'And maybe after this, you won't love me anymore.'

Henry took the cigarette from her and deliberately stubbed it out in the ashtray. 'Oh yes, I will,' he said, 'more than ever.'

———

Once again Willis and the Europa Athletic Club became his salvation when faced with total ruin. Henry drowned his sorrow and yearning in sweat and liniment. He devoted the summer to training for the match that Willis had nagged him into entering. It was the Swedish Championships in Stockholm, and Henry had participated in a few sparring matches and actually done quite well. After that the bitter summer had arrived with extra work for the tram system and long, ascetic training sessions down at the Europa Athletic Club. During this period of complete abstinence, Henry reached his absolute peak condition. The Swedish Championships was going to take place just as school started, and he had even arranged for an exemption so that he could train in peace and quiet, right up until the last moment. Even though the principal of Södra Latin was no great fan of pugilism, he couldn't very well begrudge such a renowned pupil as Henry Morgan a chance at success. Nor would it hurt the school to have a Swedish champion in its halls. Willis himself had rung up the school to express his thanks for the exemption. He spoke very highly of Henry and had practically guaranteed that he would be sending back a Swedish Junior Master in the welterweight division.

Only someone who has taken on the task of training himself or someone else for such an important event as the Swedish Championships can understand how this type of exertion can affect the mind. Willis had urged Henry to do road-work every single morning and evening, and Henry obeyed, dashing around all of Söder twice a day. He stuck to every detail of his training programme right down to the last moment.

But there was to be no 'last moment'. The first match was supposed to take place one evening in late August, and that very afternoon – when Henry was home to have a proper meal in plenty of time before the match – the telephone rang. Henry was home alone. Greta was at her job at the community sewing room, and Leo was in school. And as luck would have it, the phone call was from Maud. She had come home.

Henry had been on the receiving end of many punches that summer, heavy blows from dirty sparring partners, but in his indefatigable struggle he had shaken them off. But this blow was too much for him. An hour later he was lying in Maud's bed in Lärkstaden and all was forgiven.

When the gong sounded, Willis stood there swearing.

Henry Morgan's very last autumn in school took place under the sign of Indignation. The teachers brought the daily papers to class, and that alone was testimony to the fact that something historic was happening. It was not just the fact that girls were admitted to the Södra Latin school; there was something even more remarkable than that – a wall was going up in Berlin. Mile after mile of barbed wire in such huge quantities – or was it a form of extremely charged density? – that it had taken on a quality all its own: an impenetrable wall, the Berlin Wall, *Die Mauer*. Diplomacy was in high gear, agents were undoubtedly spying like never before, and the communiqués were talking about serious violations, about refugees and about tragedies. The tone became increasingly acrimonious and less diplomatic, and no one could say with certainty how powerful the Soviet Army behind the Iron Curtain might be.

All the teachers in school were discussing *Die Mauer* from their various professional perspectives. The Wall could be regarded as a mathematical problem: how many bricks could be estimated? The Wall could be viewed as a historical parallel to the Great Wall of China: what does Ulbricht have in common with Shi Huang-Ti or the older emperors' terror of the Mongols? The Wall could also be regarded from a purely philosophical viewpoint: as a symbol of the West's eternal schism between good and evil, body and soul.

The teacher who took it hardest was the philosophy instructor, Mr Lans. He saw the Wall from only one perspective: the moral one. He had completely lost all composure and was unable to see even one little crack, a single little glint of light through the Wall. He turned every class into a long and incoherent harangue based on newspaper reports from Berlin and the Wall. Apparently he had a hard time even grasping the concept of splitting an organic entity like a city into two parts, since each part presupposes the other and after the separation inevitably had to remain a mere half, incomplete. And consequently the people in a city in which the natural flow of communication is severed must run into obstructions, confronted by an artificial border, and hence become half themselves, incomplete individuals.

The pupils agreed and swore at the Russians. Henry fully agreed because he himself had felt incomplete, like half a person, all summer long. Maud had been away, down in Rio de Janeiro, where her now-remarried mother was living. Henry had been working on the trams and training at the Europa, filled with a greater longing than he had thought possible. That was why the Swedish Championships had turned out the way they had.

His longing had become transformed into a horrible jealousy. It became absolutely impossible for him to accept W.S., and Henry could still picture that image of the virile, energetic and, in his own special way, imposing man at the height of his career. He assumed that the man, in turn, saw Henry as a little shit, a mere boy who was allowed to play with the capricious Maud whenever he liked because W.S. was the one who possessed the funds and the priceless paternal power over Maud. W.S. was the one she turned to whenever she felt weak or miserable because he was an experienced man with his feet on the ground, a man with both a future and a past.

Henry got furious whenever he thought about what he had to put up with. He couldn't fathom why he didn't make greater demands than he did or why he actually seemed to accept *sharing* a woman with another man — exactly as if a Berlin Wall went right through Maud, as if she had her own east and west sections, to which the men in her life had been consigned, never allowed to look over at the other side.

Maud had sent him a few letters from the infinitely beautiful Rio de Janeiro during the summer, and she wrote that she longed for Henry, that she would be home sometime towards the end of August. She arrived home on the very day that Henry was planning to become the Swedish Junior Champion in the welterweight division, when the Berlin crisis was at its height, and the balance of terror seemed to be making Europe fall apart, yet again. And Europe did fall apart – or rather the Europa Athletic Club in Hornstull did. In a roundabout way Willis let Henry know that henceforth he could stay away from both the Europa and from boxing altogether. Willis was bitter, and Henry was too. But there were more important things in life than boxing.

Of course nothing turned out the way Henry had imagined. He felt completely weak at seeing Maud again, as if all his strength and resources ran down into his feet. Maud was tanned and looked somehow rather indistinct, almost unreal. She had suddenly become a mulatto, and he had to get to know her all over again, explore her and find out as much as he could. He didn't go rushing over with some sort of ultimatum as he had planned. He scratched at the door, was admitted and rewarded like a big, wet, faithful dog.

And that was how the whole autumn passed, under the sign of Indignation. Maud had barely returned home and got Henry into more or less top form again, and the Berlin Wall had barely penetrated into everyone's indignant consciousness as a tangible reality of bricks and barbed wire before the disaster with Hammarskjöld blared its fateful headlines.

All of Sweden was suddenly plunged into a state of national mourning, and if Dan Waern, locked out from winning the gold medal at the Rome Olympics, had up until then resembled an abused saint, it was a saint of the lowest order. When Dag Hammarskjöld crashed and lay dead in Ndola Free Church in the central African jungle, it looked as if all hope had come to an end in this world. The only Christ figure of any significance and with a sufficiently strong halo and the requisite credentials to be the United Nations' general secretary had crashed most prosaically into the African bush like some popular musician, leaving posterity with a sense of astonishment that would immediately change to the most profound sense of bitterness and loss. Where should anyone direct his hope when such a fine

165

spirit, such a genius, such an enthusiast, burning with such purity and honesty, intent on the best for humanity, could simply leave us behind without warning?

Henry's philosophy teacher at school, Mr Lans, was a sensitive soul. Like a seismograph-programmed *Weltschmerz*, he suffered all the torments of hell during the Berlin crisis, sinking deeper and deeper for every brick that was added to the Wall, as if he were forced, out of pure automatic necessity, to react, to respond, to *answer for*, as he might formulate the situation in his utter bewilderment. He was as thin-skinned as a young poet, and he hadn't become any more hardened by the Cold War. Instead he had sunk ever deeper into the wretched existence of humanity, as naïve as a good-hearted liberal. Just when he had licked the worst wounds after the erection of the 'Wailing Wall', Dag Hammarskjöld had got into a plane destined for Moise Tshombe and a possible Peace, and then the plane crashed into the jungle as if Satan himself were sitting at the controls. That was too much for Mr Lans. He could see no scrap of light in life; there was no mercy, no solace, no help within sight. As regents, heads of state, archbishops and kings mourned, as students and the entire Swedish populace began a national period of mourning, flying their flags at half mast and lining up to observe minutes of silence to honour the memory of the saint, Mr Lans had called in sick. No one knew for sure where he was. Some claimed to have seen him standing at attention at the citizens' procession to Gärdet, but that may have been just a rumour. Hammarskjöld was barely laid to rest before it was time for the school to fly the flag at half-mast again, this time to honour the memory of Mr Lans. And the stir it caused was at least as great. There was talk that he had chosen his own death, and various rumours described everything from Japanese hara-kiri – he had talked so much about Far Eastern ideas, after all – and hanging, to slit arteries and a pill overdose.

Deep down, no one really wanted to know the truth. Mr Lans would soon become canonised as a local saint, and among the students he was something of a hero, the perfect combination of courage and gentleness. He had reacted strongly to the evil in the world, admitting that he was weak, and yet he was as brave as Hemingway, who had recently put a gun in his mouth and pulled the trigger. Not that it was actually described that way, but anyone with even a shred of imagination could read between the lines. That was what he must have done. A hunter like Hemingway doesn't die from an accidental gunshot wound. The same was true of Mr Lans. He was a 'gracious

matador in the arena of life', as it said in the obituary written by the somewhat maudlin poet, Henry Morgan.

––––––––––

Young Henry mourned his teacher but didn't give a thought to suicide during
that autumn of 1961. The fact that he would never be a new Ingo or Lennart
Risberg in the boxing world didn't matter. But he did think about murder,
plain and simple. He once again found himself wrapped around Maud's little
finger; he was allowed to visit at her whim, whenever it suited her and her
arrangement with W.S. This was more than Henry *the pup* could stand, even
though Maud, both to her credit and to her ultimate detriment, could assure
her young lover that the situation was not like that at all.

Autumn passed with this strange sort of passion, and winter was knocking
at the door. By November it had already snowed, but this was just a portent.
It looked as if they wouldn't have any snow for Christmas, but back then
Henry Morgan was not the type to go around brooding over the weather.
Henry was completely blocked; he couldn't find any resolution to the question of whether he should put up with the constant shadow of W.S. He had
seen the man in a photo – sometimes he sneaked another look in Maud's
album whenever he was sure that he wouldn't get caught – and she continued
to offer him clothes and valuable items, which unerringly ended up at the
pawnshop. By now they had added up to quite a lot – everything from the
elegant cigarette cases to thick gold bracelets, cufflinks and tie tacks with
gemstones. He knew that they amounted to a sizable sum, no doubt more
than a couple of thousand kronor, and he was starting to get a bit worried.
In some sense he had sold all his honour.

Henry might go over to see Maud one evening, feeling as if he were being
guided there by an unknown power – which sometimes had nothing at all
to do with love or desire – almost as if W.S., the shadow man, were driving
him forward by constantly shoving him in the back.

But as soon as he reached Maud's flat, everything changed. He felt at home
and forgot all about his doubts. They would sit and chat in front of the TV
like a married couple. Maud said that she was happy. She desired him, she
showered him with praise and flattery and gifts, and he felt the light caress
of her favour across his chest each time he was there, like the tickle of a
peacock feather – desire and displeasure became meaningless scholasticism.

167

At first Henry felt completely inferior and uncultured – which, in a sense, he was – like the son of a servant woman who couldn't even muster enough ambition to become anything, to strive, bemoan his lot, or improve himself. All he wanted to do was dabble, play the piano in his quartet, box and live his life. Yet he shied away from any test of strength, he recoiled from the vast deeps, any possible defeat. But Maud took him in hand and over time he learned that a defeat was not the end. She took Henry *the mongrel* along to the Modern Art Museum and brought his wild brain face to face with the disciplined intoxication of the most modern art. Jazz was played at the Modern, and occasionally Henry would sit in with the Bear Quartet, which was gradually becoming a legendary group. Especially since the pianist that Henry occasionally replaced was living a life that bore witness to a deep angst, a world-weariness, and desperate creative convulsions.

It was Maud's ambition to discipline Henry, to use the pruning shears on him, as Willis would have said. Henry owed Willis a debt of gratitude, and he owed Maud a debt of gratitude too, even though she claimed that she was the one in his debt. Or rather, she said that she would be half a person without him, that she wouldn't be able to stand it. She said this so often, and showered him with so many things that he almost grew a bit weary of it all. Her generosity could so easily turn into a sort of meaningless sacrifice, a reckless extravagance.

From time to time he also had a slight inkling of the fragility that Maud talked about often yet managed to conceal so magnificently. It might happen when she discovered a pimple on her face and instantly picked up a mirror and compact to camouflage the imperfection. She did so in a frightened, distressed fashion, afraid of being caught with something shameful and degrading.

Perhaps it was this façade of perfection hiding a desperate longing for eternity that made Henry so fascinated; exactly like Scott Fitzgerald's screenplays in a Hollywood on the brink of collapse – a dream made manifest and a warning of destruction, all at the same time.

———————

Esprit d'escalier is the proper and most exact expression for what Henry experienced each time he left Maud to go to school or home or simply out somewhere because he couldn't stay at her flat. *Esprit d'escalier* means that you think of something you should have said in the hallway too late; instead, you think of it in the stairwell on your way out. As when you run into a genuine arsehole in town, someone who is really insolent, and five minutes later you come up with just the right cutting and crushing remark that would have put the lout in his place.

Whenever Henry left Maud, he most often wanted to say that he couldn't stand things any longer. Henry had never been jealous before he met Maud, nor had he thought that he ever would be. He'd never had any reason to feel that way, but now it had taken him over, remorselessly. It felt like a churning voice, a shadow, a breeze sweeping over the pavement as he walked, something that was always keeping pace with him – he could never stop and let it move past, nor was he able to run away from it.

Many people have tried to handle a love triangle, but I wonder if it's even possible. An ordinary relationship between two individuals – as hard to capture, as hopelessly unpredictable as two people can be – is difficult enough. Having to take into account another party makes the situation doubly tricky. Especially when someone like me knows only one of the people involved: Henry, *the narrator, the liar* and *the deceived deceiver.*

Thinking about W.S. was like imagining a sibling that he had never met. In some country and some city there was a person who shared his own blood, the blood he thought he was sharing with Maud. There was another person who met Maud in the same way he did, who talked about him, thought about him, maybe was even jealous of him, but he had never met the man.

Henry wore shirts on which the initials W.S. had been embroidered under the manufacturer's name inside the collar. Henry was given things that belonged to W.S., which he promptly pawned, providing him with the means to live well for a while. Maud claimed that neither Henry nor W.S. was such a complete man that either of them was sufficient on his own. She needed both of them.

During the first winter months of 1962 – when peace came to Algeria and the Swedish hockey team Tre Kronor won gold in the world championships in Colorado Springs – Maud and Henry started engaging in fierce arguments that had their origins in mere trifles. Quite often Henry would sit in with the Bear Quartet when they played at new galleries that were popping up here and there in the city. The modern artists whose work was on display insisted that the Bear Quartet should play for the opening festivities, and Henry would sit in because the regular pianist considered himself helplessly

169

locked into his own fate – which in so many ways coincided with that of other jazz stars – and his only purpose in life had become to fill in, with black accuracy, his own demise, which resembled a map with a big X on Norra Cemetery.

At these elegant openings red wine and snacks were served, and Maud glided around offering acidic comments on Art, because the only one who still counted was Pollock, and Swedish imitators could never come up with anything new, at least according to Maud. Henry *the art critic* had a certain weakness for this type of modern art, and he couldn't comprehend why Maud was in such a hurry to find something new. That's how the quarrel would start, and it could often develop into a grand drama, which was particularly appreciated by the artists but much less so by the gallery owners, who worried about their customers and providing a peaceful setting for purchases. At certain events Maud sometimes even threw glasses or china at her young lover, because when it came right down to it, jealousy was all that lay behind Henry's pleas. He was convinced that Maud was only out to show off and display her charms, a claim that had some truth to it. And that lent a certain fervour to his arguments. Yet Henry's zealously invoked affinity with modern painters was based on his desire to find equals, bohemians, chosen Creators who could love a woman in a much more serious fashion than wealthy businessmen who travelled around the world and kept their mistresses at a safe distance. Maud knew exactly what Henry's intentions were, and she could also tell that the general public – the vultures, the hydra that always came to gallery openings to spear an olive and get a little tickle – also understood what Henry meant.

After these confrontations Henry would slip and slide through the snow, and land in a snowdrift, just waiting for Mercy, for Maud to forgive him and rescue him from certain death, or at any rate from pneumonia. He waited for her to take him home, heat up some broth, and put to bed her pianist, artist and art critic. And in the early morning whisper a reconciliation.

———————

It was during that spring that Lily Beglund sang 'When it's sunny spring and you're seventeen, there's so very little that you mean.' And as much as Henry understood about Great Jazz and Great Art, he knew very little about Great Love. Like the betrayed girl in the song, he had shed his childhood cloak of innocence that had protected him from accusations and responsibilities. He now had only a few paltry years left as a teenager, and he already felt that he was a full-grown man.

One afternoon in April he went over to have a talk with the Military Enlistment Board. Since he had passed all the physical tests with such exceptional prowess and could not be classified as mentally incapable, he and the powers-that-be had agreed that his talents might be best put to use in the form of some sort of commando activity. The boxer Ingemar Johansson had been a commando in the mountains, after all. For his part, Henry would prefer to be stationed out in the archipelago, as a coastal commando. The officers in charge were delighted, and the matter was settled. They had no idea what they had done.

On that memorable afternoon he rang Maud because he wanted to have dinner with her. Spring was in the air, and he was in high spirits, naïve as Sven Dufva, the loyal and courageous soldier in Runeberg's epic work, whom he had always resembled. He and Maud had been together for a year now, and the occasion needed to be celebrated with the proper pomp and circumstance.

Maud was home from work, and she insisted that he come over. She told him on the phone that she had something important to tell him. She sounded serious, resolute and anxious. Henry was hoping that she had taken his suggestion about exchanging rings under consideration, and then taken the chance of her lifetime by deciding to agree. That would be a suitable gift for their one-year anniversary.

Maud wore a sombre expression when she opened the door. She looked as if she'd been crying. Henry hung his coat on the rack, which tilted against the wall. As a surprise, he took out a bag of salty liquorice that had cost two kronor fifty at Augusta Jansson's shop. Maud smiled and seemed touched.

'Henry,' she said. 'I'm pregnant.'

Henry felt a slightly dizzy sensation pass through his head, and he sat down on the sofa in the living room. Seriously and solemnly he lit a cigarette and said, 'I'll ask them to delay my military service right away.'

Maud couldn't help laughing. 'You're marvellous, Henry. I thought the first thing you'd ask would be who the father is.'

Henry hadn't thought that far ahead. His first and immediate thought was how he was going to make ends meet financially. 'Is that what you think about me?!' he said. 'That's not very nice.'

'A girl never knows,' said Maud. 'And you're always so jealous. But it's not going to be a problem.'

'What do you mean?'

'I've already made an appointment with a doctor. The day after tomorrow. He's a good doctor.'

Henry realised what she meant, and he collapsed like a sack, as if the air had been knocked right out of him from a sharp blow to the solar plexus.

'Are you relieved?' asked Maud.

'Don't you understand anything?!'

'Now don't get upset. It's already been decided. We've come to an agreement.'

'Who's "we"?'

'Willie and I,' said Maud, lighting a cigarette.

Henry felt sick to his stomach. He didn't want to hear that name mentioned right now, and particularly not in such a familiar form as 'Willie'.

'So you went to him first?'

'Henry, you're only eighteen . . .'

'To hell with that. I can take care of this. Don't give me that jive about my age!'

'Calm down,' said Maud patiently. 'You don't have to get so upset about this. First of all, I'm the one who's making this decision, all right? And I don't want to have a child right now. There are a lot of things I want to do first, and I want to be free for a while longer.'

'So you can keep playing around with guys like me!'

'Don't be silly! Try to be sensible.'

'Try to be sensible!' repeated Henry. 'That's cold and cynical, that's what that is.'

'You're being horribly immature by getting so upset.'

'I'm not immature at all. I want to take responsibility for this,' said Henry, trying to sound serious. 'I finish school in a month. I'll look for a good job and then there's no more to be said about it.'

'There's not going to be any discussion, Henry. I'm glad that you want to take responsibility, I really am, but . . . Not this time.'

'How can you even talk about "this time"?'

'Henry,' said Maud, putting her hand on his knee. 'You're more upset than I am. But there's nothing special about this. It happens every day, everywhere.'

'It's special for me,' said Henry. 'Very special.'

For Henry this was something enormously special, but he knew that he would never be able to persuade Maud to carry the baby to term. Once she had made up her mind, she wouldn't change it.

As he told me sixteen years later, this wasn't just about a woman who went over to some cold physician's office in the city and let a doctor remove a growing organism from her body, after which she went home, took a few pills and spent several days in a trance-like sleep. This was also about a young man who was forever denied the opportunity of growing into an ordinary, decent citizen.

Beneath the surface of bitterness and reproaches Henry felt that something much more serious was going on with him than with Maud during that spring. It didn't happen in an abortion clinic; it happened inside Henry. He said that it felt as if he would never wish for anything ever again, whatever that meant.

On that afternoon when they were supposed to be celebrating their one-year anniversary and instead Maud told him that she was planning to have an abortion, the party ended with Henry leaving. He slammed the door behind him in a show of wounded pride and drifted around the city like some feverish Dostoyevsky character. Thoughts kept swirling through his mind, and he already knew that the battle was lost, but he still refused to give up. He had to direct these seemingly invincible forces against something. He couldn't just make do with humbling himself and asking Willis to forgive him so that he could make a comeback as a boxer with double training sessions down at the Europa Athletic Club. That wasn't enough. He started really focusing on W.S. He pictured that fucking Adonis face in the middle of the sandbag, and he rearranged the features exactly as he saw fit. For Henry, W.S. had a visage full of already redeemed promise of creative power and enterprise within the business world, which was flourishing like hell. And very soon that corporate magnate would undoubtedly be one of the top executives in the kingdom of Sweden. How would Maud look then? For the foreseeable future would she be gliding around in drawing rooms, nonchalantly seeking support from a dry martini and greedily watching young men who desired her, adored her, worshipped her, as if she were some symbol of eternal youth?

If there was some evil, hidden power operating in this affair, then that power was Wilhelm Sterner. When it came right down to it, he was the one who was acting irresponsibly. When Henry finally had a chance to show that he wasn't just a buffoon, a fool who could never take responsibility for anyone other than himself, and hardly even that, he was refused that opportunity. The little embryo of a decent life was flushed away in a clinic behind closed curtains.

The initials W.S. had become an invocation, a mysterious anagram, a cryptic code, a warning signal. Henry hadn't been in contact with Maud for several days, nor had she tried to get hold of him. She had spent most of the time lying down and sleeping since the procedure. Henry was simply standing in the doorway across from her building. He discovered himself there in the dim entrance, in the stairwell, which smelled of stacks of old newspapers and the nauseating odours of fried food. Exactly the way many murderers and other criminals were said to wake up to a new kind of consciousness after committing the deed, Henry in some sense became acquainted with himself as he stood there, pressed into the doorway. He couldn't explain how he had ended up there, or why. He became aware of his own breathing, the beating of his heart, as if recognising an old childhood friend, or a sibling that he'd had all his life but had never met.

A few solitary people came out of her building, but they weren't worth any further attention. Around nine that night – it had been a lengthy spring-time dusk and now it was very dark – W.S. came out of the door. Henry recognised him at once, even though he'd only seen his face in a photograph. As soon as W.S. started down the street, Henry stepped out and proceeded to follow the man. Henry wanted to get close to him, watch the way he moved, and find out what he was going to do after spending a couple of hours up in Maud's flat that night.

W.S. had quite a springy gait. He was wearing a dark-blue overcoat, a hat with a very wide brim, and thin shoes, presumably Italian. He was very elegant and hopped lightly over the snowdrifts that hadn't yet managed to melt. Down near Birger Jarlsgatan he took out a cigarette and lit it. Henry watched as the lighter illuminated his face, and he tried to recall how many silver lighters with the initials W.S. he had pawned. He couldn't even count them all. Doesn't the man ever get tired of buying new paraphernalia? he wondered.

The man walked across Engelbrektsplan down to Stureplan, and went into the Sturehof bar, or pub as it was called in the English manner. Henry waited outside in the cold for a long time, then grew tired and went home. He had neither the money nor a sufficient amount of courage to go inside the pub himself.

By the third evening the whole process had become routine. Henry *the shadow* had the pattern down pat, just like a real detective. He would slide out of the entrance opposite Maud's building to follow in the tracks of W.S. He even dared whistle softly 'Putti Putti', sauntering along with his hands in his trouser pockets and his collar turned up. Once he was even about to dart forward to light a cigarette for W.S. with the man's own lighter. But he stopped himself.

On this particular evening he gathered up his courage and went inside the Sturehof right behind his prey. He even found a place at the bar next to the man he was shadowing. Only then did the excitement set in, the dazzling stimulus of the hunting dog. It was only by summoning all his strength that Henry could control himself; he was that close to throwing himself on the man, putting his hands around his neck, and squeezing so tight that the cartilage would snap under his fingers. But Henry fixed his eyes on the bottles behind the bar and took deep breaths. He tried to figure out what sort of smell W.S. had. Did he smell of Maud? Had he used the aftershave lotion that stood in Maud's bathroom? But Henry couldn't smell anything.

W.S. took out a cigarette and Henry was careful to do the same.

'Light?' he asked, turning towards W.S. and holding out the man's very own lighter.

'Thanks,' said W.S. 'A Guinness', he went on, speaking to the bartender.

'Sure thing,' said the bartender. 'And you?'

'The same,' said Henry, even though he didn't know what a Guinness was.

Henry watched W.S. in the mirror behind the bar. The man looked exactly the way he should, which meant very good. Even though he moved in a light and springy manner, there was something heavy and massive about him. Henry assumed that this was what Maud called 'the weight of experience'.

W.S. took the evening paper out of his coat pocket and started leafing through it absentmindedly. He laughed over a report about the Swedish twist championships, which were being held at Nalen. 'I suppose I should learn to do the twist, just to keep up with things,' he said to no one in particular.

'I wouldn't give an öre for the twist,' muttered Henry.

'I thought all young people were dancing the twist lately,' said W.S.

'I detest dancing,' said Henry.

W.S. laughed again and gave Henry a long, lingering look, as if something had suddenly dawned on him. Henry got a bit jittery and tried to figure out whether Maud might have a picture of *him* too, but he doubted it. He couldn't be identified. W.S. simply had a steely glance, and it would take a sledge-hammer to break through it. But there was nothing malicious about it; instead, his eyes held a certain curiosity, a sympathetic interest. Maybe it was this very look that was behind all his success with both women and businessmen.

Under his antagonist's gaze, Henry felt a bit weak and less spiteful. Or it might have been the strong, dark Irish brew that was making him good-natured and weak. In any case, he felt quite calm and composed sitting there at the bar. He was no longer afraid of what he might suddenly do. Well into his second Guinness, Henry started talking with W.S. about the spring and the weather, and then they introduced themselves.

'Wilhelm Sterner,' said W.S. very correctly.

'Peter Moren,' said Henry, holding out his hand.

Not a blink betrayed the least suspicion or any sort of reaction that a liar such as Henry – in this situation – always tries to trace in his quarry. The slightest little scent of suspicion would have made Henry retreat, but W.S. scrupulously played his part, schooled in diplomacy and business under Wallenberg as he was. Henry would later – when he thought back on that meeting and told me the story – never understand how someone as ice-cold and calculating as that man was, sitting there on the bar stool and playing along, could have any sort of fear or dread of death, as Maud had claimed. W.S. seemed to be the steadiest man in the whole business world.

'I can offer you another beer, if you'd like,' said W.S.

'That'd be great,' said Henry. 'I'm really broke.'

'I'm not,' said W.S. and ordered another round of Guinness. They drank a toast and W.S. asked Henry what kind of work he did. Henry came up with carpenter because he'd filled in doing some construction work for a couple of summers and knew more or less what the job involved. W.S. seemed very interested, and of course he was familiar with that type of work. He knew how the construction business operated, and they both agreed whole-heartedly that contractors could be confidently optimistic since so much demolition was going on downtown.

Henry and W.S. went through one topic after another, and Henry wasn't sober enough to realise how he was being drawn into a dead-end where an experienced and accomplished businessman wearing an overcoat stood waiting with a Luger drawn.

'I've got to run now, Henry,' said W.S. all of a sudden, slipping down from the bar stool. 'But I suggest that we meet up at Maud's flat tomorrow evening. There's a lot we need to talk about, don't you think?'

Henry didn't even manage to think up a reply before W.S. was gone, leaving him sitting there with his shame, surprise and bottomless fear. There was no longer any talk of *esprit d'escalier*. Now it was just plain panic.

The celebrated count and soldier Moltke supposedly laughed twice in his lifetime. The first time was when his mother-in-law died; the second time was during a ceremonial visit when he caught sight of Waxholm's fortress, Oscar Fredriksborg.

This was one of Henry's favourite stories, and in his version it was given somewhat greater dimensions than the way I've presented it. Listening to Henry's memories of his military service could be quite tedious, and I don't intend to spend much time on this period.

On the other hand, Henry could have a good laugh at himself when, in August 1962, he stood in the sunshine that came pouring down over the courtyard, burning the back of his neck and making him sweat copiously. The standard bearers were marching to attention, the dust was swirling in the sunlight, the pounding of the drums reverberated like shock waves and ricocheted off the fort's walls. The command sounded and the entire company of commandos and coastal artillerymen stood at attention.

The colonel read the Soldier's Creed, and it felt solemn and serious and incredibly important. The archaic endings on the words resonated of Karl XII, progress, honour, honesty and responsibility. These young men, including Henry Morgan, wearing their khakis and drilled in standing at attention through long days of rigorous exercises at Rindön, bore a heavy responsibility as they were now about to begin their military instruction, to be trained as elite soldiers, be assigned wartime stations, code names and, for at least the next twenty-five years, would be prepared to turn out if things started heating up – *when* things started heating up.

The colonel handed the Soldier's Creed – in a splendid burgundy leather-bound folder – to his adjutant and began inspecting his troops along with the company commander, a sun-tanned major. The soldiers saluted. The colonel may have paused for a couple of seconds in front of Henry Morgan to give the private's salute closer scrutiny.

It's possible to imagine that even then the colonel could see that this particular individual – who actually presented a decent salute – was completely hopeless, that this lad was already too burned, that no authority would be able to scare him because he had already been too far down, so deep down that confinement, orders for punishment, or a denial of leave would never stick, bite or take hold of him. It's possible that the knowledge of human nature occasionally displayed by a military officer of the colonel's rank would have unequivocally indicated that Private Morgan was going to present problems.

We can only guess what the others, the soldiers, saw. Perhaps they saw an odd comrade who was always the last man in the canteen and who beat everyone at poker; a man who was the last one to get up in the morning but the first to complete every order; the one who never flinched when a furious major with bad breath started shouting in his face so that the saliva flew; and the one who could always defend a sinner so that even an officer relented. In any case, that was the image Henry wanted to project, as well as the image that he presented to me.

After dinner on that day when they had heard the Soldier's Creed and been given a few hours' free time before dinner, they were lying as usual on the shore at sunset, savouring the taste of coffee and a cigarette. Henry had acquired some compatriots who were going to try to preserve their integrity in the face of the System. There was a religious, top-class athlete who was thinking of refusing to be armed when they were supposed to receive their sub-machine guns; a terrible but powerful drummer whom Henry knew from the Gazell in Gamla Stan; as well as a couple of other guys who didn't make much of a fuss about themselves.

There could be quiet nights, at any rate, in this uniformed celibacy. Henry had suffered. He had graduated from school, gone out drinking and carousing and tried to get over the affair with Maud. But he now knew that it was all a lie. He would never get over it. She would have him in her power forever, and the only chance he had was never to see her again, to get as far away from the city as possible.

They were now lying on the shore, as usual, looking out across the bay. The sunset was inexpressibly beautiful, and they were talking quietly about serious matters such as whether to carry a gun or not. A soldier came rushing up to them, shouting.

'Henry, you've got a visitor, a broad, over by the gate,' the soldier panted.

178

'A visitor?' said Henry rather absentmindedly.

'Hurry it up! She's already been waiting half an hour.'

Henry shambled over to the big gate and saw Maud leaning against the shiny radiator of a Volvo. He tried hard not to feel anything, not to be concerned.

'It's been a while,' said Maud, and Henry noticed that this was the first time he'd ever seen her really nervous or anxious.

Henry persuaded the guard to let him go out to the car and sit inside, just for a few minutes. The guard asked them to drive off a ways so that they wouldn't be seen, in case an officer turned up.

Henry was wearing comfortable baggy fatigues with a belt and marching boots. Maud gave him a long look without speaking, her expression distressed. She looked tired. He climbed into the front seat next to her and stared out of the window. He wanted to cool the whole situation down because otherwise he was afraid of completely falling apart. He lit a cigarette and remained silent.

'Whose car is this?' he asked after a while.

'What does that have to do . . .' said Maud and then stopped herself. 'It was a present, actually,' she admitted.

Maud took hold of Henry's head and turned his face towards her. Her eyes were no longer distressed and frightened but calm and tearful. She pressed her lips together, making them turn pale, and burst into tears. Henry couldn't touch her.

'How's W.S.?' he asked, swallowing a lump in his throat.

'Fine,' Maud sobbed.

'Tell him hello and thank him for not bringing charges.'

Maud nodded and sobbed.

'How did it go with his teeth?'

'Two,' sobbed Maud. 'He had to have two of them replaced . . .'

'I've got this scar,' said Henry, holding up his right fist and pointing at a deep scar left by two sharp teeth on one of his knuckles.

'But . . .' murmured Maud. 'I need a . . . a handkerchief.' She fumbled to open her purse and then pulled out a handkerchief. 'How are you doing here?'

'How do you think?' said Henry. 'But I'm not complaining. I get to look at the water all day long, and the grub is free. It could be worse – in prison.'

'Why haven't you called me? You're a cruel man, Henry. Cruel and selfish!'

'I just wanted to be left alone,' he said. 'Let's not talk about selfishness right now, Maud.'

'Are you scared of me? You have to forgive me . . . I've tried to forget all this, but I can't.'

'Me?! Forgive?!' yelled Henry. 'Surely you're the ones, you and W.S., who should forgive *me*?!'

Maud shook her head, ignoring the fact that her make-up was running down her cheeks, making her look unattractive and tragic. Henry actually thought that she looked more beautiful than ever.

'That's all over now,' she said. 'You know that. Willie realised that he behaved badly. He should have known better.'

'Call him whatever you like, just not "Willie",' said Henry. 'And it's never going to be over for me.'

'Do you have to keep harping on the past?'

'I'm not harping on the past. But something happened. I need to stay away from you two. I need to have time . . .'

'How much time? You're being so harsh, Henry. Harsh and cold.'

There was a pack of cigarettes in the open glove compartment, and Henry took out another cigarette, lit it with the car lighter, and inhaled deeply.

'That's only your opinion,' he said. 'I'm just like everybody else after they've been out here. Soon I'll know how to butcher anybody I want to. Maybe that's the point.'

'Don't you ever long for me?' pleaded Maud. 'I can't stand this anymore.'

'No, I never long for you,' said Henry. 'It's something bigger than that, much bigger . . .'

———————

As soon as they were granted leave, there was celebrating on the boat to Stockholm. Henry, just like all young recruits – and also from a sort of provincial instinct for self-preservation – had adopted the vulgar and insolent jargon that can seem so repugnant to outsiders. They went on and on about the calibre of this and the bore of that, and to a listener at a distance it might all sound quite ridiculous. But Henry was right in the thick of it.

Back home in the city, he went over to see Greta and Leo to show them his khaki uniform. Greta's eyes filled with tears as soon as Henry appeared. She thought he looked so stylish, and she hoped that this was the acid test that would once and for all make a sensible, mature and responsible citizen out of Henry. He was a commando, after all, and was going through special training. He was the only one from the neighbourhood chosen for that.

That autumn Leo Morgan was fourteen years old and about to make his debut as the sensational young poet with the collection *Herbarium*. The book hadn't yet arrived in the bookshops, but the boy had received his free copies, and when Henry showed up one weekend, his younger brother handed him a copy. Henry was deeply moved, and for a change he was quite speechless. He realised that he had totally lost touch with his little brother and that somehow he needed to repair the damage, though he didn't know how. He felt awkward and managed only to accept the book in silence, maybe giving his brother a gentle chuck on the chin the way he used to do. Leo would surely understand.

But it's well known that a young whippersnapper on leave does not sit at home, biding his time. Henry *the recruit* hurled himself out on the town – as soon as he took off his military clothes and threw on his old tweed jacket, a checked shirt with the initials W.S. and a suitably jazzy tie. He found Bill from the Bear Quartet in the studio of a brooding painter in the Klara district.

A sense of gloom hovered over the studio. Death had swept through the bohemian world, gathering up its victims, separating the healthy from the afflicted. Bill looked worn out. Henry went up to the studio, feeling in top form and appropriately stimulated because he was on leave and he'd had several lagers in the city. But Bill and this painter were down in the dumps. The pianist for the Bear Quartet had died after a blood transfusion, and Marilyn Monroe had voluntarily ended her life. The painter had been keen on Pollock in the past, but now he had abandoned action for a more meditative approach, including an extremely sensitive portrait of M.M. It was praise of the highest order, and now they were sitting there, Bill and Henry, listening to Coltrane next to a couple of lit candles which sent a flickering glow over Marilyn, forever and ever, as if she were in marble.

They drank a couple of bottles of wine and got over the worst of their grief. Bill had grown accustomed to the idea of losing his pianist, and he wanted Henry to join the Bear Quartet, but Henry was in the midst of completing his military service; he couldn't hang around. All he had to do was go AWOL, according to Bill. But that thought had never even occurred to Henry. To go AWOL was the same thing as deserting. It was practically the same thing as death.

Bill had made plans for himself and the Bear Quartet. That winter they were going to practise hard for guest appearances in Copenhagen, at the Montmartre club and at the Louisiana art museum, which had already been booked for April. It would be a sort of international breakthrough for them, and Henry could come along if he liked. Henry wanted to but he couldn't. He wouldn't be discharged until late summer. He couldn't do it.

After a couple of bottles of wine, when Henry – somewhat insensitively and thoughtlessly – started in on a military story, they got into a fight. Bill and the painter thought Henry was an idiot, a nobody who might as well stay in the military forever. He was lost. And that was the last he would see of Bill from the Bear Quartet for the next five years.

It's true that Henry's memories of the military seem to suggest heroism and bravado in which he, to the astonishment of the officers, distinguished himself as a paragon of courage and strength. He claims to have rescued a canoe and two comrades during a long paddling trip that took place in November. He carried half of an exhausted buddy's gear during a march without breathing a word of it. But these are mythic anecdotes that are of no further interest for this story.

In any case, the year passed and we have to assume that Henry was simultaneously worried and very comfortable in the role of a special commando. In fact, Henry must have been worried sick at the thought of what had happened.

That difficult winter of 1963 was coming to a close. Springtime freed the ice from the coves and bays with desolate, shrieking cries. It had been a long winter, the most bitterly cold in living memory. The ice had crept far up onto shore, breaking loose piers and boathouses, ruining things for the fishermen, who now had to repair what the sea had reclaimed.

The commanding officers were apparently very pleased with their commandos. They had drilled their soldiers, subjecting them to hardships that to an outsider might seem unbearable, but the lads had pulled through, driven by a strange sort of pride. As I've said, it was a hard winter, and now that spring had arrived it was time for some gratification. The higher-ups turned a blind eye if the soldiers relaxed a bit after all their exertions. That was only human.

A week after the long march, in early April, a couple of ruffians had gone to Vaxholm and bought some smuggled vodka for the whole platoon. They had sneaked the shipment into the barracks, and after dinner the unofficially sanctioned festivities began.

After only a couple of hours the entire platoon had nearly passed out. Henry tried to hold back, but then joined in as best he could. After the first drink, he could tell that it was no good, that it didn't give him any relief — on the contrary, the convulsive grip on his stomach got worse and worse with each drink he took. Around ten that night, several desperate athletes started breaking up the toilets in the west wing. They stamped and roared in there, smashing the whole latrine to smithereens. After that they came out and started on the barracks, breaking every single thing as thoroughly as they had just been trained to do.

At an early stage Henry could tell where this was all headed, and it was at this point that something took shape inside him. He had been out there for nearly ten months, and he felt done with it all. He had grown more and more agitated and restless, but he still had four months left, four long hot summer months. When he heard his buddies roaring and hollering like wild men, going berserk in one barracks after another, he realised that powerful forces were at work that night. There was no holding back.

In Henry's barracks two commandos were vomiting into their helmets. Otherwise he was alone. He took action exactly as if he had been planning this for a long time, but he hadn't. It had just popped into his head, and then half a bottle of smuggled alcohol had stripped away his inhibitions. Instead of participating in the vandalism, he gathered up his things, made a little package of his personal belongings and wrapped it up in his big, waterproof coat. He put on longjohns, a woollen sweater and fatigues. In the very bottom of his metal foot-locker he put a small package with a letter, saying that no one needed to worry – he hadn't killed himself, but it was pointless for them to search for him. He knew these waters better than anyone else.

Shortly after midnight he slipped out. It was now dark enough, and he went down to a boathouse where they kept the smaller Canadian canoes, a lighter type that he could paddle alone without difficulty.

A party was going on in the mess hall that spring night, and the whole camp was crazy. Not a single person noticed that a commando had stolen a Canadian canoe and paddled off like an Indian to disappear and never return.

Henry had half a bottle of vodka left, and as he paddled for an hour without stopping, he occasionally took a sip to calm himself down. The canoe moved well and the sea was obliging. He had a slight night-time breeze at his back, and he headed in a north-easterly direction, straight for Storm Island. He estimated that he'd have to paddle for at least three hours to reach his destination. The search for him wouldn't start in earnest until seven, at the earliest. That was an adequate margin of safety.

His estimate proved to be accurate. Henry had stayed on course as precisely as he could, and just as the sun came up over the horizon in the east, he saw the black silhouette of Storm Island appear like a low cloud, a heavy black cloud.

Storm Island had been Henry's second home when he was a boy; he knew every rock, every small spit of land sticking out in the sea, every little wind-blown shrub. The people who still lived there – his mother's relatives – would recognise him from miles away. He was known as a *gale*, partly because of the weather that presumably was raging when he came into the world, partly because of his temperament.

It was important to keep out of sight. The inhabitants on Storm Island might seem stupid, but they could still put two and two together. If they saw Henry paddling into Storviken in a Canadian canoe with camouflage paint, the talk would instantly start up, and even though there wasn't a single telephone on the whole island, the wind or the waves or the fish would carry the gossip to the mainland faster than a telegraph.

Henry slipped into a cove on the north side at daybreak. He was tired and felt sick from the vodka. He wanted to sleep, to stretch out his legs and sleep, to go numb. He knew that the dozen or so people who lived on the island kept to their own territory and seldom went to the north side. So he pulled the canoe into a crevice in the rocks, and from a distance of a few yards the camouflage paint did its trick; the vessel was no longer visible.

Several hundred yards from the little cove stood the lighthouse, casting its red and white lights out into the boundless sea. The lighthouse was unmanned, and Henry seized the opportunity.

———————

Everything he tried went well. Several adventurous days later he entered the flat late at night. He was back home on Brännkyrkagatan, in the middle of Stockholm. Greta and Leo were asleep. Henry hung up his heavy coat in the hallway, put his package in a wardrobe and went into the kitchen.

'Is that you?!' stammered Greta, dazed with sleep as she tied the sash of her bathrobe. 'Are you crazy, boy?' she went on, giving her son a bitter hug. 'You'd better believe that I was worried. Your commanding officer rang to tell me that you'd taken off . . . I knew that you weren't in any danger . . . But are you crazy? You're going to end up in prison!'

'There's no chance of that, Mum,' said Henry. 'They'll never get hold of me again.'

'You really *are* crazy, Henry,' said Greta with a groan. She was soon busy heating up some food for the deserter.

'I've come here to say goodbye,' Henry said solemnly.

Greta gave all her attention to the food and refused to comprehend what her son was actually trying to say.

'Say goodbye?' she repeated bitterly. 'Are you going to give me nothing but trouble?'

'I'm leaving the country,' said Henry. 'Going over to Copenhagen. I can play in a quartet there if I like. You know how things have been . . . It's been hell for me.'

'I know that,' said Greta as she stopped preparing the food. 'But why haven't you said anything before now?'

'I've tried to take care of things on my own. This is my solution.'

'Running away? That's your solution?' said Greta. 'Yes, well, I suppose that's always been your solution. You're just like your father. But you're absolutely crazy. You're going to bring the police down on me . . .'

'I'm not going to bring the police down on you. I'm going to leave the country and stay there until . . . until . . .'

'Leave the country!' Greta sank down at the kitchen table, and it occurred to Henry that he was always making sure that women would cry for his sake, although he didn't know why.

———————

'These seven years will go fast, said the boy who was given a beating the first day of his apprenticeship.' Those were supposedly the last words that Greta said to her son.

Henry stood in the hallway, dressed for travelling, holding a suitcase and his coat. He didn't want to prolong the process, because then he would just start having doubts. He cracked open the door to Leo's room and looked at his little brother for what would be the last time in a long while. Henry was going to miss his brother, but he doubted that the prodigy would miss him.

Greta came up with an old proverb as a means of encouraging both herself and Henry, and then he was off. He walked down to Hornsgatan and rang the bell of his grandfather's flat. He needed money.

Henry's grandfather stayed up late at night now that his wife was dead. He had started living life again with his odd gentleman's club, the WWW, and other secret projects that he never wanted to talk about.

'Henry, my boy,' said his grandfather. 'You're absolutely crazy, but I've always had a weakness for crazy men. Come in!'

Henry went into the flat; the whole place smelled of cigars. His grandfather had been sitting in front of the smouldering fire, reading. He was just thinking of going to bed.

'Copenhagen, you say,' said old Morgonstjärna. 'Very pleasant city, but you should try Paris, of course. That's where I was last, let's see now . . .' And then the old man began telling anecdotes from his dissipated days on the Continent, and Henry felt compelled to listen.

Two hours later he was back out on the street. Old Morgonstjärna had given his grandson a thousand kronor in cash, along with his blessing and a hint that the boy would eventually be needed back home. Only later would he find out the reason.

Henry said goodbye to Stockholm, to Greta and Leo, to his grandfather and Maud and W.S. and to everything that had so far held him there. He hurried off so as not to change his mind or succumb to doubt.

IF WAR COMES

(Leo Morgan, 1960–62)

The evening was dark and dreary; it was drizzling outside. Everyone was staying indoors. It was now a new decade, and people stayed inside at first, until they realised that it would soon be a world-famous decade and it was uncool to stay inside.

Leo Morgan was in the sixth grade and had plenty of homework, assignments that he always completed flawlessly in the evenings after dinner. On this particular evening he was supposed to be studying for a maths test. It was a dark night, very appropriate for difficult equations. He'd gone down to Verner Hansson's flat to get help with several problems, but Verner's mother refused to let Leo in. She told him that Verner was sick. Leo could hear Verner moving around in his room, and that made him curious, even though his friend's mother had made up her mind and there was nothing to be done about it. Verner had the strictest mother in the whole building. She was on her own – just like Greta – but she'd been that way all along. Verner's father had disappeared years and years ago, and Verner claimed that he was a seaman living on an island in the South Pacific. He would be going there to join him as soon as he finished school. Verner liked 'Hansson', as he called his father, even though he'd never met him. Verner liked anybody who simply disappeared, as in those cases that were occasionally reported in the newspapers, about a boy who was supposed to go out to get wood one evening, just as he'd done on every other evening, and then simply disappeared and never turned up again. And it was always at least sixty miles to the nearest town, and there wasn't a single trace left behind . . .

Verner Hansson loved to brood over these mysterious cases. He already had a whole collection of them – a kind of archive of missing persons in which he had filled in all the information he could find from the newspapers.

They were horribly exciting. Verner had no lack of appreciation for the effects.

But on this particular evening in October 1960, Leo was not allowed to visit Verner because his mother had made up her mind, and so there was nothing to discuss. That's why Leo's maths homework took a little longer, and he had a hard time getting started on his Swedish assignment. He had been asked to write a little 'treatise', as the teacher (who had a penchant for the Old Testament) called the essays, about his herbarium. He had chosen the topic himself even though the assignment was mandatory. Now he was sitting in the glow of the lamp, leafing back and forth through his herbarium, trying to say something about how he collected plants, or tell a few anecdotes about the Storm bluebell, the most glorious of all flowers.

He described the damp June mornings when he got up as early as he could to go out into the meadows and look for plants. The dew was still cold and fresh, he wrote. But it was hard to write about the herbarium from Storm Island, because no matter how he started off, it always ended with that terrible Midsummer when the red accordion gleamed in the morning sun and the wails of the people blended with the ravenous cries of the gulls, and Gus Morgan lay on the beach, drowned. Leo would grow frightened and feel sick at the mere thought of all that, and he had no desire to write about it. But he had to come up with something, and that was how he happened to slip into poetry. Leo wrote a few brief verses about his herbarium, even though he knew that it was absolutely ridiculous to write poetry. But Leo's poems were in a class by themselves; they were in some ways quite old-fashioned and formal. There was no love in them, and that was good.

He felt quite pleased. At least now he had something to show the teacher with the penchant for the Old Testament, who would undoubtedly express his approval of a lad who happened to write in verse. Leo went to the kitchen to pour himself a glass of milk. Greta was sitting out there, mending stockings and listening to the radio. They were broadcasting a tribute to Jussi Björling, and Greta looked tearful. She thought it was so sad when he died. Jussi had the kind of voice they would never hear again.

The world-famous tenor was known as 'Jussi' to every Swede. And Greta, just like every other woman, grieved for him with genuine love. She was sniffling over her mending basket filled with an endless number of worn stockings as well as socks with holes in the heel and toe. She was filled with the golden voice of Jussi, and it gave her eyes a remote and dreamy look that

Leo had never seen before. He wondered what she was dreaming about. She couldn't very well know that on that evening a new poet was born in the North, a skald whose poems would be set to music and recorded on vinyl by a well-known opera singer. If Jussi had still been alive, he might have recorded them too – that's something we'll never know.

The radio programme with Jussi Björling ended and the news came on. It was most unpleasant. Greta said that she was glad Leo did his homework and stayed inside in the evenings. Everyone seemed to have gone crazy. Young children were sniffing paint thinner and running amok, dangerous both to themselves and to others around them.

Leo knew what she was talking about. It was that murder at the Hammarby Athletic Field. They had found a ten-year-old boy lying behind a shed that morning, and there was talk of a sexual killing. The boy's father had found the body. Leo got the shivers at the mere thought of it.

Greta carried on mending her stockings, slightly absentmindedly, while Leo went back to his desk, the herbarium and his secret poems. Perhaps he was sitting there polishing his draft of 'So Many Flowers', when he was suddenly interrupted as a pebble struck the windowpane. He flinched with alarm and looked out. Down on the street that was wet with rain stood Henry, waving. He had forgotten his keys, of course. He often forgot his set. Leo opened the window and tossed down his own keys. Henry caught the keyring in his soft cap. He was whistling 'La Cucaracha', and he took several elegant cha-cha steps on his way to the front entrance. Leo was still sitting on the windowsill, looking out at the street, when he heard Henry rush into the kitchen to raid the refrigerator. Henry was still whistling 'La Cucaracha', tapping out the beat on the cupboard doors in the kitchen so it echoed through the whole building.

The next moment a police car drove up to the front door. The vehicle came zooming around the corner and slammed on the brakes in front of *their* doorway on Brännkyrkagatan. Two solemn-looking officers leapt out of the car and somehow managed to get inside without keys. It may have taken all of a minute – Leo sat there brooding over what could have happened, who might be fighting today, who might be drunk or sick or something like that – until the policemen came back out. They had Verner between them.

Utterly silent and composed, Verner Hansson walked between the two broad-shouldered cops, who yanked open the car door and quite brutally shoved their quarry inside. Leo started sweating all over; his face was flushed, the blood was roaring in his head, his legs started to shake. He couldn't fathom what was going on. What had Verner Hansson done to be arrested by the police like a murderer?

Leo slapped his hand to his feverish forehead. He pressed his head against the cool windowpane and tried to think rationally, to reason his way to what sort of serious crime Verner might have committed. Then Leo happened to think about the keys. They collected keys. They had been doing it for a long time, and by now they no doubt had more than two hundred different keys altogether. They were very useful.

There was something magical and exciting about keys. To find the right key on the ring and discover that it fit a lock, and to feel the tumblers' solid graphite clacking when the key turned was always a sensual experience. The height of excitement came from opening a door that had been closed for an eternity, a door which they had no right or authority to open. There was some sort of indelible affinity between the lock and the key that could never be disturbed, no matter where they were, or how many oceans separated them. The two parts, stationary and mobile, belonged together, the one presupposing the other. Much later, in the collection *Façade Climbing and Other Hobbies*, (1970) Leo would return to this blood kinship of metals in an homage to Gösta Oswald when he made use of his words about 'the patented solitude of the key'.

But all this had taken place a good ten years earlier, and Leo was now thinking in bewilderment about the keys that he and Verner Hansson had acquired, a considerable collection, just like Verner's stamp collection and Leo's herbarium. The boys had found the keys on the street, they had stolen keys from secret drawers and they had traded keys with other collectors. Verner and Leo had no trouble opening most of the attic storage rooms in the neighbourhood, and once a building supervisor had actually come to them for help. That was much cheaper than sending for a locksmith, since this firm worked for free, provided they were henceforth given carte blanche to the old man's attic.

But not all supervisors were so liberal-minded. Many were afraid of break-ins and vandals. And there were plenty of hooligans who sat up in the attics, smoking or sniffing paint thinner or messing about with their girlfriends. Maybe the supervisors thought that Verner and Leo were behind all the attic break-ins that had been happening over the past few years, when vandals had been killing cats in the spin-dryers and starting fires to keep warm.

Leo couldn't make head or tail of any of this. He sat down at his desk and heard Henry whistling like an idiot out in the kitchen. It was still 'La Cucaracha'. Henry had been working on his boxing, and he was probably shoving down at least fifteen sandwiches with soft cheese, Kalles caviar and three bottles of milk, all the while dancing the cha-cha-cha. He didn't know a thing about what was happening with Verner. Nor was he going to find out anything, because he couldn't keep his mouth shut.

In the bottom drawer of Leo's desk there was a metal cash box with a combination lock. He took out the heavy box, opened it and pulled out a keyring with seventy-five keys on it. Verner had one just like it. The police had probably confiscated it, as evidence. So there was no escaping it. It was too late. But they still hadn't found Leo's keys. He took the keyring and climbed up onto a stool in a corner of the room. With sweaty hands he unscrewed the cover on the vent and cast one last loving glance at the heavy keyring, which had allowed him free access to so much. Then he threw the keys into the air shaft. They fell more than ten yards, landing in a spot where no one would ever look.

Leo had done away with one of his most prized possessions. He felt a trembling pass through his body – it was the fierce sensual pleasure that comes from an act of sacrifice and repudiation. There was no going back. There was no longer any reason to be such a fusspot; something told him that it was pointless to be a fusspot.

The business with Verner Hansson and the police remained a mystery until Verner's mother came up to see Greta a few days later. She was having trouble with Verner, and she needed to get things off her chest. Both women were alone with their boys, after all; they were in the same boat, so to speak.

Sobbing hard, Mrs Hansson told Greta that Verner had rung the police himself and confessed that he was the one who had murdered that ten-year-old boy at the Hammarby Athletic Field. The police had come right over to pick up the murderer – that was what Leo had witnessed from his window – but they had brought him back after only an hour. He wasn't telling the truth. Verner had just rung the police in order to go to the station and 'see what it was like', as he put it. The real murderer was a nineteen-year-old who had been sniffing paint thinner. The police told Mrs Hansson that these 'types' always turned up, confessing to murders they hadn't committed; it was actually quite common. The police also said that they were extremely impressed with Verner's knowledge of people who had gone missing, people the police were looking for, all those unsolved mysteries that no investigator could explain. The police told Verner's mother that she should be on the alert because Verner might 'be harmed' by spending too much time on these things – it wasn't really normal.

Mrs Hansson sobbed and was in utter despair because she thought that her beloved son was such an idiot. She didn't know what she was going to do. Greta didn't have any advice to give either; all she could think of was that Verner should be allowed out of his house arrest. It was doing the boy no good to be locked up in his room. Mrs Hansson hesitated for a long time before she went downstairs and let out her little Dr Mabuse.

One of the poems in *Herbarium* (1962) is called 'Excursion'. It was presumably written some time in the spring or summer of 1961. The poem has a sort of refrain – once again the magic of repetition constantly used by Leo Morgan – which goes like this: 'We dress for war / prepare ourselves carefully / the soldiers are sleeping in the woods.' At first glance it might look as if a little boy is asking his mother to help him prepare for a hike, some sort of outing in the woods. The refrain is preceded by elegant flower depictions, a salute to all that grows – just like most of the poems in *Herbarium* – but these particular lines take on a charged meaning when we read: 'we're going down into a vault / where nothing grows / not even the flowers of evil'.

The poem is basically about a mother and son who are going down to a shelter during an air raid. The mother is desperately trying to hurry, while the child wants to calm the woman. This emerges as a shock at the end, when the dressing of the child, done so lovingly, suddenly appears clearly as something done in panic, amidst sirens wailing above the rooftops and crying and screaming and moaning. Perhaps Leo had help with the sophisticated arrangement of the material, the explanation that is withheld and then suddenly turns everything upside down. At any rate, it's a very strange poem, with allusions to Baudelaire, with whom the poet had apparently become acquainted through his teacher in school. Leo Morgan had become literary.

The idea of the air-raid siren had its origin in the evacuation exercise that was carried out in Stockholm in 1961. It was the very same exercise that Henry, completely unawares, had got caught up in on that Sunday when he slipped out early in the morning to visit his beloved Maud and have breakfast tête-à-tête.

At the very moment that the air-raid siren started wailing up on the roof, Verner rang the doorbell of the Morgan family flat. Verner Hansson had been up early to pack his gear, exactly as it said you should do in the booklet *If War Comes*. He had an enormous grey backpack waiting in the hallway. Leo was ill-prepared and had to put up with a good many comments from Verner, who was hastily squeezing a pimple in front of the hall mirror.

A little while later the boys went down to the underground and headed out towards Hässelby, all according to plan. They too heard that the king was supposed to be travelling along somewhere, although no one knew exactly where. That didn't make it any less exciting. Verner had read a lot of books about the Second World War. He could tell gripping stories about the French Resistance, and he said that he too was thinking of joining the Resistance when the war came. It was that word 'when' with regard to war that made Leo a little uneasy. He didn't like the fact that Verner should so coldly assume that there would be a war. Verner never said 'if' war comes; he said 'when' war comes.

Of course Verner had brought along the booklet *If War Comes*, and they sat and leafed through it during the trip. It had been distributed to every household in the spring, and the new version was illustrated with drawings that showed exactly what to do in various emergency situations.

In the preface it said that no one was predicting that war *would* come, but Verner paid no attention to that. In his morbid imagination he had already decided that war was definitely on its way. *If War Comes* was absolutely essential reading, in other words. Verner read aloud from the war catechism and demonstrated various alarm signals. He whistled the emergency siren with repeated short blasts, a thirty-second pause followed by another long, continuous signal. He whistled the air-raid siren's suggestive low tone with its rising and falling pitch, and he whistled the 'all clear'.

The lecture continued with the section on the spirit of resistance and vigilance. Under the heading 'Vigilance', there was a picture of a scumbag wearing a hat and trench coat and looking typically sly and crafty. He was listening to the conversation of a couple of military types; he may have been from

193

Russia. Leo could think of at least five men he knew from the neighbourhood who might be spies. There were also a lot of paragraphs containing appeals to keep quiet about things that might be secret, to be extremely vigilant during times of unrest, and to alert the police as soon as possible if any suspicions should arise regarding espionage or sabotage. We'll keep that in mind, thought the two bookworms. They wouldn't fail to report even their own fathers – if they'd had fathers that is.

After these important appeals came a couple of horrid sections on seeking shelter during an attack, protecting yourself from radioactivity, and protecting yourself against biological warfare and nerve gas. The pictures showed various types of shelters, men wearing hoods and turned-up collars that were supposed to protect them against radioactivity, and men wearing gas masks with their heads covered, making them look like draped badgers.

The last section of *If War Comes* dealt with the resistance movement, and that was where Verner envisioned a place for himself *when* war came. 'Active participation in the resistance movement requires courage and nerves of steel', it said. Verner was positive that he possessed both courage and nerves of steel. Above all, he was extremely meticulous with his gear. Just like a real officer, Verner enumerated what should be included in the pack: a blanket or sleeping bag, underwear, socks, bed linen, towels, wash things, toilet paper, handkerchiefs, a woollen sweater, shoes, a plate, a cup, cutlery, a sheath knife, a pocket torch and matches, as well as food for at least two days.

Leo had actually managed to put together most of these things, and Greta had also packed enough food for at least a week. Verner sounded pleased. Although he was a real pro, of course, and on top of everything else, he had stuffed in a pair of rubber boots, a change of clothes, a thermos, some writing paper, a battery-operated radio and a plastic tarpaulin in case of a downpour. Verner was convinced that he was acting like a true hero, and he got along well with the other, middle-aged heroes who were also taking this whole thing about the war deadly seriously. It was just such a boor of a hero that Henry ended up running into, a man who forced the young lover to go all the way out to Hässelby even though he had planned to get off at Odenplan and wanted no part in the whole operation.

Henry also met up with Leo and Verner. He ran into the two distinguished soldiers at the underground station just as he was about to catch the first train back to the city, where he would finally see Maud again. Verner and

Leo thought that Henry was a quitter. They reminded him that every message urging surrender was false.

Every message urging surrender was false, but there wasn't much resistance offered on that sunny Sunday. The boys were back home by evening, and they felt a bit disappointed, or at least Verner did. It hadn't really gone the way he had imagined. He had hoped for some cannons, smoke, bombs and grenades, exactly the way it would be in military service. But they hadn't even seen any cannon smoke. People had played football and grilled sausages, exactly as if it were a sports day at school.

Leo had quite a different perspective. He never imagined himself being as brave as Verner, who planned to join the resistance movement. That required courage and nerves of steel, neither of which Leo possessed.

On the night after the evacuation exercise, he came down with a fever. He felt dizzy and lay in bed moaning for a long time. Greta put cold, wet washcloths on his ankles and wrists – she had decided that this would help, just as it had helped the backward boys on Storm Island. Leo raved, keeping her awake until morning. Henry stayed away, just as he always did when he was needed. Greta cursed the war and Henry and the whole world for everything that she was forced to endure.

That night was presumably also a turning point for Leo Morgan. The war had never been a serious threat until this unbearable night when, in the hallucinations of delirium, it appeared with all its loathsome evil. Suddenly the war had become a reality.

He went looking for the little booklet *If War Comes* – it was next to the phone books in the hallway – and read it in secret when he returned from school and was home alone. In the booklet war was something that might happen at any moment; it was not merely something that involved the heroic kings of five hundred years ago. On the first Monday of every month the sirens on the roofs were tested, and he realised that the war would no doubt begin on the first Monday of some month, because no one in the whole city took the sirens seriously. What a terrifying realisation! Leo felt so inexorably alone with his unfathomable fear.

Eventually he memorised all of *If War Comes*, and he undoubtedly knew it better even than Verner. Some of the pictures, in all their simplicity, had a particular hold on him. Among them was the picture of the mother helping her children dress as the siren sounds. The mother is putting shoes on one child as the other child, fully dressed, waits next to the luggage. They are on their way down to the air-raid shelter. Leo had no idea where he was supposed to go when war came; he didn't know where the air-raid shelter was, or even if one existed. This dilemma taught him the most profound brand of terror.

Fear and terror established themselves very quickly in Leo Morgan's early poetry. The Swedish teacher with the penchant for the Old Testament had created a relationship of trust between himself and Leo the prodigy. Leo was constantly giving him samples of new poems. The teacher told his favourite pupil about things that the boy didn't know – certain points in poems that only an experienced interpreter would notice. When he was allowed to see the poem 'Excursion', he realised at once what Leo was actually talking about: that beneath the ethereal membrane of Nature Romanticism lay a nearly panic-stricken terror about the defenceless fragility of human beings. People had arranged things so badly for themselves that they had to dig bunkers and deep caves in the mountains in order to have even a small chance of surviving. Human beings were their own worst enemy.

The teacher – an infinitely grey man who spread a sweetish scent of sweat all around him – eventually came up with an idea. By now he had seen so many excellent poems that he thought Leo ought to send them to a publisher. He should put together a proper manuscript. The teacher himself would give him a letter of recommendation, vouching for Leo's familiarity with both biology and botany, as well as his knowledge of great literature, from the *Edda* to Ekelöf. His claim that Leo was particularly well-versed in classic literature was a complete lie. The remarkable thing about his poetic vein was that it never had to make its way across foreign regions to attain strength and auspicious heights. Leo Morgan wrote in accordance with his own mind; he didn't need mentors. He would never become an epigone. That was something he had decided long before he learned how that word was actually pronounced. But to steal a phrase or two from the old masters was a different story. That was something every writer had to do.

THE SECRET AGENT

(Henry Morgan, 1963–64)

Here begins an adventure, as we might have good reason to promise. It's going to be a real adventure, a terrible and beautiful dream that would last for five long years and would not be lacking in elements of the most singular kind.

Henry Morgan was on his way to Paris, but to reach Paris he had to travel by way of Copenhagen, and from Copenhagen it was not at all certain that he would ever make it to Paris. In reality, Henry was on his way to Paris for what seemed an eternity.

People would latch onto this strange boy who was in the process of becoming a man, this twenty-year-old youth in the odd clothing, an anachronistic gentleman, all alone in the wide world. People would try to hold on to him, use him for everything imaginable; yet to their everlasting disappointment, they would see him disappear and flee, always on his way to Paris.

Henry *the goliard*, the student of the Art of Life, always had a clear vision of Paris before him. He was fleeing for his life, escaping something vague that resembled a judgement, a destiny. During his long flight, he started to compose something that, fifteen years later, was like nothing else, a suite of music written by a wild man whom no academy or school had ever managed to discipline properly. He would call his magnum opus 'Europa, Disintegrating Fragments'. And I assume that it was the greatest realisation he would ever have when, with sudden and merciless insight, he envisioned the entire work in his mind's eye. Perhaps it was also the dream of this work that kept him on his feet during those long years in exile that were by turns perilous and extremely dreary. He was both a Gesualdo and a Chopin, as someone once said – possibly he said it himself.

The silence of the Quakers was absolute, massive, like the echo left behind by a monumental whispering. Their breathing rippled as rhythmically as the sea. A dozen people were lost in their own breath, meditating in an ocean of silence and stillness.

Henry realised that he too had to meditate, although he didn't fully understand what that entailed. He couldn't help noticing how the features of Tove's face seemed to be erased as she closed her eyes and became lost in this strange cogitation. He couldn't help looking at Fredrik and Dine, who shared the same last name and similar clothing, who could be either spouses or twins. But he was having a hard time concentrating. The light, the warm sun of early summer that came flooding through the windows, was changing little dust motes into indolent fireflies that were not dancing but floating through the cold, sacred room on the top floor of the building facing Ørsted Park.

But soon calm descended on him. His own breathing filled him with peace, and he could meditate in the sense that he was able to put his thoughts in order; they began following a sensible chronology, a searching and straightforward order. The silence became a piece of innocent, white stationery.

Henry Morgan had now been in Copenhagen for a couple of weeks. Everything had gone well for him. He had hitchhiked down to Helsingborg and left Sweden as a deserter and someone who had previously been reported to the police for assault and battery by a man with the initials W.S. But he wasn't feeling guilty; he felt justified because he had acted without hesitation, in accordance with his own inner voice. He was psychic and believed in his visions.

He arrived in Copenhagen and didn't know where to go. He wanted to find Bill from the Bear Quartet; they were supposed to be playing at the Montmartre jazz club. With only a thousand kronor, he wouldn't be able to last long on his own. But Bill disappointed him; the Bear Quartet's gig at the Montmartre had been cancelled. Yet Henry was blessed with what is often called luck, though it mostly has to do with seizing the opportunities that are offered to all mortals, although few take advantage of them.

Henry had heard a great deal about Copenhagen, of course. The Jazz Baron had talked about the city, about the jazz clubs, about the pubs, about the Nyhavn district and about Tivoli. Bill had told him about Montmartre and Louisiana, and he'd read aloud from *Angels Blow Hard* by Sture Dahl-ström.

Henry took lodgings in a small hotel near Østerport and found his way to the Montmartre, the Scandinavian Mecca for jazz fanatics. He heard Dexter Gordon play bebop the way few dared to play after Parker. There Henry ended up sitting next to Tove. It was crowded and smoky and noisy, and everyone was sitting close together. No one could help noticing him: a young, vigorous Swede wearing a tweed jacket and tie, holding two bottles of beer in one hand.

Henry took a cigarette out of the case with the initials W.S. engraved on the lid.

'You seem very well-to-do,' said the girl sitting next to him. 'Wouldn't you like to offer me a cigarette?'

'Of course,' said Henry magnanimously. 'Although you're mistaken if you think I'm rich.'

The girl gave him a big smile, revealing wine-stained teeth. She was the girl named Tove, and later that night she stated with great certainty that they needed Henry – *they* needed him. 'We need you,' she said. 'You're the right person,' she said over and over in various contexts. 'I've never been wrong before. You're the right man for us.'

Hearing that you're exactly the right man in the right place is not a bad thing when you're actually a deserter.

Tove talked to Henry about Dexter Gordon. She had listened closely to the great saxophonist, and she knew a lot about music. She was a couple of years older than Henry, and she told him that she lived with several others in a big flat near Ørsted Park. Tove was a Quaker. Henry had only vague notions about what Quakers were, but when Tove started talking about Fox with his hat and the silent meetings, he remembered that Mr Lans had spoken warmly about Quakers, about the saint who performed miracles with the wounded in the Great War, and so on. To Henry's ears, everything to do with Quakers sounded very positive, and he liked Tove at once. He tried to sense whether he felt anything more for her but came to the realisation that he probably ought to leave those kinds of emotions alone for a while.

'You're exactly the right person,' Tove went on, and Henry began to feel more and more as if that were true. But for the time being he didn't care about what being the right person might mean. He had already proclaimed himself an impossible subject for conversion to anything. But Tove was not interested in proselytising.

The music whipped into a frenzy. Henry drank a good many strong Danish beers and smoked far too many cigarettes. By the time it was well past midnight, he had forgotten all his good intentions and decided that he was head over heels in love with Tove. By this time he had learned a tremendous amount about the Quakers' contributions to world history and he was talking a mile a minute. He was in his element.

Tove had become even more convinced, if that were possible, that Henry Morgan was a true find. And in the small hours of the morning, when he confessed that he had actually deserted from the Swedish army, the only thing she could do was burst into tears of joy. Henry *the deserter* received a kiss on the lips.

They strolled home, arm in arm, through that early summer morning in Copenhagen. They laughed at the incredible story of his escape from the military, and Tove said that she was deeply impressed by his courage and his cunning. Henry was also quite taken by the solemn joy of the moment. He had made a find, and she had made a find, and everyone was content. That was exactly the way things should be in Copenhagen.

As she had said, Tove lived in a large flat in an old dilapidated building near Ørsted Park. She shushed Henry as they went inside and tiptoed down a long hallway to her room. She lived very spartanly: a bed, a chest of drawers and a bookcase. That was all she owned. That was all she needed.

He got no further with his meditative ruminations about his life on that day in the sunny, sacred room in the Quakers' building. He had now been Tove's accepted lover for the past couple of weeks; he was the right man for her. He was the right one for all of them. So said Fredrik and Dine with the same last name, and so said the entire Quaker family.

———————

Why Henry Morgan should be exactly the right person was not something he fully understood. But he had a hunch that something big was in the works. The Quakers in that house didn't just sit around meditating. They were very active. Some were teachers or social workers, while others had completely conventional types of jobs, and yet they were Quakers.

In early June Fredrik and Dine went out to the country, to a summer place at their disposal in Jutland, right outside of Esbjerg. A week later Henry and Tove joined them. Henry thought it sounded promising. He could stay out there on the farm for free, all summer long if he liked. They also had plans for what he would be doing a little later in the autumn, but that was on ice for the time being.

The farm in Jutland was very beautiful. It had a big, white brick house right on the coast. There were a hundred sheep, half a dozen cows and a few pigs. Fredrik, the Quaker father with the Rasputin beard, was a very practical man with a head for agriculture. The farm brought in a good income, and it was here that they were planning to settle permanently because Fredrik, being the prophet that he was, could already tell that the tremendous boom of prosperity that had swept over Europe would one day ebb away into a crisis.

Henry was happy and grateful that they had taken him in even though the police were after him. He laboured and toiled day in and day out on the farm to show them his gratitude. His gratitude was evidently so deep and so great that over time all the work he did would, in principle, settle his debt. Before long he had repaired the fences, re-plastered the barn, laid a new floor, mucked out after the livestock and fixed so many things that the Quakers actually told him to take it easy.

Henry took them at their word and tried to unwind. He took long walks out on the heath or along the coast, staring out at the sea. He swam and sunbathed but his body could find no real sense of peace until he started composing on a harmonium that stood in one of the rooms in the house. He decided he would write something sacred, something meditative and calm into which the others could sink, using it for their meetings. The harmonium was very old and cracked. The pumping motion made the phrases issue like breaths from a respirator. Henry wasn't really accustomed to sitting and pumping like that, but perseverance pays off.

He gave the composition the simple title of 'Psalm 1963', and I had a chance to hear it myself, played on the piano more than fifteen years later. It was a very beautiful piece. The Quakers seemed to like it. I understood why.

The months passed. Henry *the Dane* composed music on the old harmonium while the others pottered around the farm and held meetings. Now and then people would come to visit. They were very stern and reserved gentlemen, some from Sweden, who talked mostly to Fredrik in the office

201

in one of the wings of the farm. Their conversations were of a confidential nature, and Henry didn't get involved. At least he tried to stay out of things, but in the long run it didn't work.

Tove looked as if she were happy most of the time. Sometimes she would say something ambiguous, like the fact that she was so happy that she 'regretted everything'. Henry wanted her to explain, but she preferred not to. Sometimes she would cry in the night when she thought he was asleep. Towards the end of the summer Henry wanted to know what was going on, what was the matter with Tove. He couldn't stand all this monkey-business going on around him anymore.

'You'll find out soon enough,' said Tove one evening. 'It's almost time.'

They'd had a substantial dinner with all the food for which the Danes are so famous: a plump and magnificent ham, liver pâté, eel with scrambled eggs, and a good deal of Aalborg aquavit. Henry was in good spirits because of the alcohol, but after they'd made love and Tove started to cry again, he wanted to know what was going on. He said that he'd noticed quite a few things.

'Can't you just be patient a little while longer?' said Tove.

'I want to know now. Tonight,' said Henry. 'I can't stand seeing you cry.'

'I can't tell you anything,' said Tove. 'I'm not allowed to.'

'I thought you Quakers were so forthright.'

'Go to sleep,' said Tove. 'And be patient for a little while longer.'

Henry didn't feel like sleeping. He had got himself all worked up about the situation, and he was also pissed off about all the suit-clad spies wandering around the farm. He was paranoid because he was a deserter and the police were after him. He threw on his clothes and went out to smoke a cigarette and calm down, but as soon as he stepped outside, it started to rain. A quiet, cool drizzle began falling over the coast, and the sea was rolling indolently, as if heralding the autumn, a departure and freedom.

Henry wondered what the hell he was mixed up in. What was he doing out here in this flat, Danish wasteland? He had simply allowed himself to be deported out here, like some sort of prisoner. The rain and his thoughts made Henry furious, and he saw that there were lights on in Fredrik's office in one wing of the farm. He sneaked over there to peer inside.

Fredrik was sitting at his desk with his Rasputin beard, working. He was hunched down beneath a lamp, reading documents. He had a big map open before him, and now and then he would write a note in a black book.

Henry tapped on the windowpane and Fredrik flinched as if at a gunshot. He regained his composure as soon as he saw that it was Henry. He opened the window and asked him what in the name of peace he was doing out in the rain.

'I saw that your light was on,' said Henry. 'There's one thing I need to know . . .'

'Don't talk so loud,' said Fredrik. 'You'll wake up the whole countryside. Why don't you come inside, instead.'

Henry stepped into the office and sat down next to the desk.

'I know,' said Fredrik. 'I know that Tove is unhappy. She's feeling rather desperate. She loves you, Henry. That really wasn't the intention . . .'

Fredrik looked deeply concerned and he was frowning hard.

'What do you mean? What *intention*?' asked Henry.

Fredrik chewed thoughtfully on the end of his pencil. His damp sweater smelled faintly of sheep.

'What's going on?' asked Henry. 'There *is* something, isn't there? I want to know right now, because it has something to do with me.'

'All right,' sighed Fredrik, twisting a tuft of his Rasputin beard. 'I suppose it's just as well . . . Do you know about the Kjell Nilsson case?'

'The guy from Lund?'

'Precisely! Maybe you also know that he and another Swede have been indicted?'

'I can imagine.'

'Would you dare do what they did?'

'Go to Berlin?!'

'We know that you're the right man, Henry. You have the right attitude about things, and you're brave.'

'How can you know what I think about things?'

'A person just knows. I'm a good judge of character. Tove is too. And we've done a good deal of checking up on you.'

Henry sank back in his chair and started biting his fingernails. 'Let's not have any more pussyfooting around,' he said, annoyed. 'What is it you're after?'

'The police are looking for you, Henry,' said Fredrik calmly.

'So what? I plan to go back to Sweden, when the right time presents itself.'

'But it might be good to have a new passport, don't you think?'

'Is this some sort of blackmail?'

'Not at all,' said Fredrik without losing his composure. 'Not at all. It's just a question of services rendered and favours returned . . .'

'So what is this plan of yours? Let's hear it!'

'It's simple,' said Fredrik. 'You're really not risking very much.'

The Quaker demanded that Henry take a vow of secrecy, swearing on his honour and conscience, and then he explained the plan, or at least the part of the plan in which Henry Morgan would play a role, and it was undeniably very simple. In possession of a counterfeit passport, he had to take the ferry to Sassnitz, then the train to Berlin. There he was supposed to check in at a hotel and wait for a message, the go-ahead for the next stage. That would be a short trip via Checkpoint Charlie to East Berlin to hand over a whole slew of counterfeit passports. The documents would then be used later by people travelling to the West.

'There's not much that can go wrong,' said Fredrik. 'You'll have with you a perfect-looking suitcase with a false bottom. You hand it over to a man in East Berlin and then you leave.'

'How banal,' said Henry. 'Just like some sleazy thriller.'

'There are so many things that are banal in life,' said Fredrik.

'I doubt that,' said Henry.

'Of course I've forgotten to say that you'll be given a great deal of money.'

'Where?' asked Henry, immediately a bit more interested.

'In West Berlin.'

'What if I get caught?'

'That's highly unlikely. But if you *do* get caught, you'll be handed over to the Swedish authorities. There are certain guarantees. But that's not going to happen. We have good contacts with many influential Swedes. The Girrman League operates in the same way, and they'll back us up if anything goes wrong.'

'What about Tove?' said Henry. 'When do I get to see Tove again?'

'As soon as you get back, of course.'

Henry thought the whole thing smelled fishy. He had never believed that these kinds of things actually went on in real life. Yet he didn't doubt for a second that Fredrik was dead serious. A man with a beard like that was no joker. These Quakers were mixed up in something – he'd realised that right from the beginning – but he would never have dreamt that it was a shady business of this calibre. After this, he would always feel a certain kinship with James Bond.

'I think this whole thing stinks a bit of the Wennerström affair,' said Henry.

'Wennerström was on the opposite side. He was military.'

'That's beside the point.'

'This isn't a matter of political loyalties,' said Fredrik, still confident and calm. 'This is an ethical matter, a question of freedom and morality, families that have been split up . . .'

'If you say the word *responsibility* I'm going to throw up,' said Henry.

'But why? It *is* a question of responsibility. You'll take the risk, Henry. I know you will. We know a good deal about you. You took the chance of paddling a canoe to get away from the military. So of course you'll dare do something as airtight as this.'

'I'm not a *coward*,' said Henry proudly. 'Of course I dare. No one is going to call me a *coward*!'

'Then think it over,' said Fredrik. 'We can't force you to do this. Give me your answer tomorrow. I know that Tove would appreciate a *yes* from you.'

The story of Henry *the secret agent* is perhaps the most remarkable of all. It has to do with Bill Yard, who comes to Berlin, pretending to be a musician, but in actual fact, he deals in the smuggling of people from the East to the West.

It started on the ferry. The bar on the ferry was unusually dreary – silent and depressing. Henry was feeling dejected. The young deserter, now travelling under the false identity of Bill Yard, who was both a boxer and a pianist, was extremely melancholy. He had killed a couple of hours on correspondence. A letter home to his mother, telling her that everything was fine, that he was being well looked after by very nice people, Quakers as they were called, and that he had been given a unique opportunity to go to Berlin to listen to the great American jazz that was being played there for the Yanks stationed in the American zone.

He had killed another hour by writing a letter to Maud in which he included what he thought were some very sophisticated hints that he had found someone else, a Dane, whom he loved passionately. But he didn't really believe it himself.

Now he was sitting on the ferry to Sassnitz, and he couldn't help looking for other girls. It was as if he'd already forgotten Tove. She had talked about sacrifice as being the truest form of love, sacrificing your own interests for a great cause, as she and Henry were doing; that was the highest form of love. She claimed to be happy that he was going. When they parted at the door to the building near Ørsted Park in Copenhagen, she gave Henry an amulet to wear on a chain around his neck. Henry now fished out the amulet from inside his shirt and read the Latin on the little silver disk: HODIE MIHI, CRAS TIBI – today for me, tomorrow for you. He dunked the amulet in his glass of whisky and then popped it in his mouth, sucking off the drops of British spirit and wondering whether he was going to keep on collecting trophies from women all his life. He had a cigarette case with the initials W.S. engraved on the lid, and now he also had a medallion that said HODIE MIHI, CRAS TIBI.

Henry was starting to feel sentimental and lethargic, and he longed to get away from this bar, which could hardly be called a bar at all. At first he longed to be back with Tove, and he ordered another whisky, but then he started longing to be back home with Maud. This was not easy.

Henry, *the secret agent*, meaning Bill Yard, didn't want to talk to anyone, because if you were an agent, it was important to keep your mouth shut and not spill the beans. Anyone at all, some seductively beautiful woman or some insignificant busybody, might be a counter-spy. His great strength here in life was being able to judge people more or less accurately; that was why he had managed rather well during his exile. Henry claimed that he was psychic and could tell exactly which people were evil and which ones were good. But that sort of thing didn't apply in the secret-agent business; there a person had to be vigilant, suspicious and sceptical. This didn't sit very well with Henry. It didn't suit his temperament at all.

He was in a smoky, damp, greasy bar on Fasanenstrasse. Henry had been playing billiards with a guy from Kreuzberg. The German was remarkably skilful in spite of the fact that he had only one arm and had been forced to adopt a very peculiar style of playing. He was too young to have been wounded in the war, and Henry had already heard his story several times. They had been drinking hard.

He was called Franz after Döblin's hero because he had lost his right arm. Franz enjoyed games, and in the past he'd once been part of a successful bowling team. In the autumn of 1957 the team had gone on tour to compete against a couple of clubs in Amsterdam. One evening Franz and his team-mates were practising in a bowling alley when all of a sudden a confused desperado turned up, pursued by the police. The man was a paranoid type, and he shot down the whole bowling team, one after the other. When it was Franz's turn, he was lucky enough to have the bullet lodge in his arm. Then the revolver clicked. Franz seized the opportunity and killed the man with an ornamental bowling pin.

'I still have the bowling pin, Bill,' he said. 'You can come over and see it.'

'No, thanks,' said Henry. 'I have no desire to see your fucking bowling pin.'

In any case, Franz had beaten Henry by a good margin in that smoky, damp, greasy bar on Fasanenstrasse, and the price was a round of beer and schnapps. Henry had paid for a second round as well as the first. Then Franz said that he wanted more, and they started quarrelling. This one-armed devil isn't so tough, thought Henry. Besides, Franz spoke very poor English, so they were having a hard time swearing at each other.

It started raining again, and this was no meagre autumn shower. It came pouring down on Fasanenstrasse, and rubbish sailed along the gutters in a fierce torrent, disappearing into the sewers.

Suddenly and without warming, Henry got very angry and started arguing with Franz. They nearly came to blows, and Henry didn't notice that a very beautiful woman of about twenty-five had come into the bar, apparently to seek shelter from the rain. At least I assume that's how it must have been.

'Dammit, you're nothing but a fucking cheat!' shouted Henry in bad German, and that proved to be too much for Franz.

Franz dumped a whole glass of beer on Henry's head and then took off, well aware of his guilt – he actually was to blame for all the commotion.

Some of the beer splashed onto the young woman who had just come into the bar. Henry was both drunk and upset, and he hated Berlin more than ever. Yet in spite of this, he was able to pull himself together enough to apologise.

'It doesn't matter,' said the woman.

'You speak English?!'

'I *am* English,' the woman said.

That changed things considerably, and that was how Henry became acquainted with Verena, because that was her name, Verena Musgrave. Henry thought it was all a coincidence.

Henry climbed back onto the bar stool and offered her a Roth-Händle cigarette. The match exploded with a delayed little pop as he struck it.

'There are plenty of idiots in this city,' said Henry. 'A bowling pin . . .'

'A bowling pin?' said Verena Musgrave.

Henry babbled on about the desperado in Amsterdam, the bowling pin and Franz with the arm that had been shot off.

'I don't think I really understand,' said Verena.

'It's not important,' said Henry. 'I don't understand any of it myself. He was probably just a fucking liar.'

'It's cold today,' said Verena.

'Have a schnapps. That usually helps. You can borrow my coat if you like.'

'No, thanks,' said Verena. 'I think I'd rather have a schnapps.'

The rain started coming down hard, and a sullen Alsatian slipped inside the bar to rest and dry off in a corner. He was a stray, like so many other creatures in that city.

'What sort of business brings you to town?' asked Henry, because he had now opened his bloodshot eyes and taken a proper look at this young woman.

'I'm doing research,' said Verena. 'At the Geheimes Staatsarkiv in Dahlem.'

'And what does someone like yourself do there?'

'I search for people,' she said. 'People who have disappeared but can't really be called dead.'

'I see,' said Henry. 'That doesn't sound especially festive.'

'It isn't.'

'Then why are you doing it?'

'It's research,' said Verena curtly, coughing from the strong cigarette.

Henry *the secret agent* was trying to pull himself together, to concentrate and think for a moment. And naturally he happened to think of Verner Hansson, the chess genius. 'I have a neighbour back home in Sweden, in Stockholm. He's a bit nuts, but he just loves people who have disappeared. He was a chess genius as a kid, and he started a club for young inventors . . .'

Verena laughed in an odd way.

'Go ahead and laugh!' said Henry. 'But it's true. He got a little strange and started developing an interest in mysterious cases in which people vanished without a trace – young boys who went out to get wood on a cold evening in January. It was only twenty-five steps to the woodshed, but on that particular night . . .'

'They disappear?' said Verena, coughing again.

'For good,' said Henry, lighting another Roth-Händle. 'My pal Verner has an entire archive of missing persons. The police envy him. You'd love him.'

They each ordered another beer, and Henry, alias Bill Yard, babbled on, as well-mannered as he could be when he was in top form, and he didn't notice how loose-lipped he was becoming. Verena told him – as he managed, with great difficulty, to remember later – that she lived in a boarding house run by an old woman, and the whole building consisted of old flats whose owners had disappeared, in most cases during the war, although they were never declared dead. The boarding house was supposedly located on Bleibtreustrasse, not far from Savignyplatz.

The secret agent liked Verena. She seemed so earnest, in a vague sort of way. He was drunk but still aware enough to want to make a respectable impression. He wanted to turn on the charm here at the bar. So he excused himself and went out to the men's room to wash off the lager that had stuck to his hair. His face was flushed but he was freezing.

When he came back to the bar, Verena was gone. She had paid for his last beer and left. Henry collapsed like an empty sack; he was crestfallen. He left the smoky, greasy bar on Fasanenstrasse, thinking that all of a sudden a lot of people seemed to be disappearing from his life.

———

He had now been in Berlin for more than two weeks without receiving a single sign, not one indication that he was supposed to make his big contribution in the name of Freedom. He had checked into the hotel where he was supposed to stay. Everything had gone without a hitch, and as far as he knew, he hadn't aroused any suspicions. Henry *the secret agent* had played the role of the tourist and by now he had walked up and down the streets in every part of town. Kreuzberg, Schöneberg, Tempelhof, Steglitz, Wedding and Charlottenburg – he knew them all by heart, as the English say. And he had seen the Wall, *Die Mauer*. He had seen the wet, dripping, heavy Wall, which ran right through town, like some sort of architectonic terror. It went right through buildings, right across streets and squares: the bricks were mute, with the tears of totalitarian silence dripping down each side.

But he didn't receive the slightest signal. Henry was starting to suspect that something was wrong, that something had happened. Yet he was just a little cog in a large-scale machine. The Girrman League was not the only group occupied with this sort of self-sacrificing 'charity' of people-smuggling.

As time passed, Berlin too became a dreary place. Henry had heard a great deal of marvellous jazz, going to every club in town since he was officially there to study the music scene. But even music can start to pall if you're feeling properly depressed.

On the day when he left the bar on Fasanenstrasse, quite intoxicated after

211

his argument with Franz and quite disappointed after Verena had disappeared, Henry staggered through the rain towards his hotel to go to bed. He felt drunk and a bit sick, feverish and sluggish at the same time, and all he wanted to do was go to sleep.

'Goot eftning, misterr Yard,' said the hotel clerk in lousy English. 'Zere iss ah letter forr yo,' he continued, handing over an envelope.

Henry was thrilled, and he sobered up on his way to his room. He went in, sat down on the bed, still wearing his drenched coat, and slit open the envelope.

'You play part very well, Bill. Trust in you. Hear from us in two days. Money in advance. Franz.'

Henry read the words backwards and forwards at least fifteen times. Then he riffled through the crisp dollar bills, which were the equivalent of five thousand kronor. He couldn't believe his eyes. Everything started spinning around, and he fell asleep.

———————

The next day he had a hard time remembering anything. He had slept heavily and dreamlessly all night, fully dressed, and he couldn't even recall what Verena Musgrave looked like. She had red hair and freckles and a rather large, Jewish nose. But that was all. There was something pale and hazy about her. She interested him much more than that fucking Franz, with his money and his armless exploits.

After lunch Henry went down to Bleibtreustrasse to look for the boarding house near Savignyplatz. The ground shook and rumbled beneath his feet as the U-Bahn, the underground, passed through its tunnels. He had a hard time finding the way, since he never used maps. Henry usually took his bearings from the sun, but there was no sun right now. Berlin is an undermined city, a flat city with few monuments to use as landmarks. There was no use even dreaming of the sun.

He walked through the streets, reading signs and wondering who had been able to remember the names of all the bombed streets after the war. Some avenues had been renamed after new heroes. Others had been restored, and perhaps the names were actually the only indication of the streets' existence when there was nothing but ruins and burning rubble, with no street signs or building numbers. The reality was ruins and burning rubble, but the names lived on as ideas, as concepts. In the collective subconscious of Berlin's citizens there was a picture of a city with addresses and squares, and presumably they sat down with the outline of a map to rechristen everything when peace was declared. Not even the Stalinists could blast away a language.

It turned out to be true that there were many dilapidated boarding houses along Bleibtreustrasse. There were also many landladies, including a talkative old Polish woman who ran her business with Polish zeal. But she didn't have any Verena living in her building, although she let it be known that she could provide girls with plenty of other names.

Henry thanked her for her thoughtfulness and gave up. He was disappointed and dispirited, slightly hungover and out of sorts, so he went into a pub. He ordered a beer and a schnapps as a pick-me-up. On the walls hung old name plates made of dark wood that had been fastened to hallways before the war. Henry read all the names on one sign: Schultze, Hammerstein, Pintzki, Lange and Wilmers. Maybe they too had just disappeared, not yet declared dead. Unknown soldiers who would remain unknown.

Several days passed during which Henry did nothing in particular. The days flowed by in exactly the way he often allowed his days to flow. He would lie motionless on his bed with his hands clasped behind his head as he whistled monotonous tunes, his eyes fixed vacantly on the ceiling. That's how he and Leo used to lie in bed when they were little, competing to see who could whistle most off-key. Leo usually won with the piercing and unbearable sound he made when he inhaled.

Henry lay there, longing to be somewhere else. He suddenly had five thousand kronor in crisp dollar bills, but nothing was happening. No one contacted him, no one wanted to have him cross the border. He felt superfluous.

On a rainy, gloomy day — it was the greyest day he had ever experienced, and he told me that it seemed as if there were no sky at all over Berlin on that day — he made his way back to Bleibtreustrasse. He was determined to look for Verena again. He had nothing else to do. Maybe he just wanted to buy her a beer in return, or maybe he was actually in love with her.

There are moments in a person's life when he goes looking for something; it might just as well be in a bureau drawer as in a world metropolis, but he blindly seems to head straight for his goal. This was just such a moment for

Henry *the secret agent*. He stepped out into the foggy street and went inside a boarding house that he had missed the first time. The woman in charge of the place was, appropriately, an old, magisterial woman wearing a black dress with her grey hair in a French twist. Henry asked her if she had a lodger by the name of Verena Musgrave.

'You mean the English lady?' she said, her face lighting up.

'Exactly,' said Henry.

'Top floor,' said the woman. 'Room 46.'

Henry climbed the stairs, feeling a little nervous. The whole place reeked of a deeply-rooted mixture of paraffin and clothing that had been hanging in a wardrobe for two winters. It was dark, and every step creaked. Here and there he could heard murmuring and fragments of conversation. Someone was cooking.

On the sixth floor a big, heavy door opened onto a corridor. Henry walked straight over to room 46. The door was ajar and opened even further when he knocked. The room was empty. He went in. It looked as if the lodger had left in great haste.

Henry immediately assumed that the old woman had been mistaken, and he raced back down the five floors of stairs to ask her if she had really meant room 46.

'The room is empty?' said the old woman in alarm. 'That's not possible!'

'Yes, it's empty,' said Henry.

'You must be mistaken, my young man,' said the woman. She checked the hotel register herself to make sure.

'Maybe I made a mistake up there in the dark,' admitted Henry. 'It's so dark today.'

'It really is dark today,' said the woman. 'You must have made a mistake.'

Henry climbed up to the sixth floor again, convinced that he had made a mistake. But he hadn't. Room 46 really was empty, abandoned in haste. Maybe she had simply run off without paying the bill.

Henry went into the room. The curtains were drawn. He pulled one aside but it made no difference. The wardrobe was empty, except for a few swaying clothes-hangers. It smelled of mothballs.

There was a mirror above the sink next to the wardrobe. A little picture was stuck into the frame. He pulled it out. It was a silhouette, the kind that old men cut out in one fell motion in places where tourists gather. This one had presumably been cut out by the man who had staked out a place near the abandoned U-Bahn cars at Nollendorfplatz. He charged five marks, which was considered cheap.

Verena had actually stayed in this room. Henry recognised her profile at once in the little silhouette of black paper on a white background. Her hair falling over her forehead, her nose with that cute bump, and her full lower lip. That's exactly how she looks, thought Henry. The portrait had been cut with skill and sensitivity.

He put the silhouette in his pocket and left the room. The old woman was waiting on tenterhooks in the foyer.

'Well? Were you mistaken?' she asked with satisfaction.

'That's right,' said Henry. 'I made a mistake in the dark.'

'I thought so,' said the woman. 'She seems so respectable, that girl.'

He cut across the street, went into a bar and ordered a beer. He lit a Roth-Händle and started to brood on things. There was something very wrong about this situation, but he couldn't figure out what it was. He went over every word he had said to all the people he had met, especially Franz and Verena. The talk about people who had disappeared, the archive in Dahlem and that silhouette. He put the piece of paper in his wallet, thinking he would keep it as a souvenir. Maybe he wasn't really in love. He was just a lonely secret agent in Berlin.

After a good month of rain and fog, grease and smoke and soot and damp in Berlin, Henry was well on his way to falling apart. Nothing had happened, and he no longer even thought it was fun to go out drinking. But then another letter arrived, this time postmarked Stockholm. Henry was very surprised. No one in Sweden was supposed to know who Bill Yard was.

He eagerly slit open the envelope and read the letter in astonishment. 'Get out of there, Bill. The game is up. Go to see Miss Verena Musgrave at 'Pensionat Belleke', Bleibtreustrasse 15. If you find her picture in the display case at Kurfürstendamm 108, it's all right to take off. You're very brave. Burn this letter. W.S.'

When a sense of unreality closes in around someone, he either becomes totally paranoid with shock, or he mobilises all his intellectual and physical resources to accomplish whatever is best in the given situation. For a long time Henry vacillated between pure paranoia and the greatest clarity. After he had read the letter over and over again, he burned it in an ashtray, smoked five cigarettes in a row and started haphazardly packing his clothes in the suitcase with the false bottom and the dozen counterfeit passports. He couldn't see any reason to suspect anyone in particular. The most confusing part was how in hell Wilhelm Sterner had got mixed up in all this. The only thing he could think of was that W.S. might have been one of the Quakers' important contacts in Sweden, a man who had previously been a member of the diplomatic corps. But Henry didn't understand a thing. All he knew was that he had to go out and find Kurfürstendamm 108.

There was, as predicted, a display case in the middle of the wide pavement. It contained advertisements for nearby shops as well as a series of photographs of women, Before and After. They were ads for the plastic surgery procedures at a beauty institute – just like some ads for body-builders show how a thin clerk from Before can become a beach boy with bulging muscles After.

Except that in this instance, it was just the opposite. Here something was cut away in order to make improvements. The photos showed a couple of women with noses that were unmistakably hooked which, step by step, took on an Aryan shape. According to the text, the beauty institute was famous all over the world.

One of the women in the display-case photos was Verena Musgrave.

HAIR

(Leo Morgan, 1963–64)

It could be said that 1963 was the year when the hairdressing business was struck by a worldwide crisis, from which it has never truly recovered. On the other hand, it was a big year for Leo Morgan and many others who liked their own hair. The world was changing radically. Leo was known as the legendary Jazz Baron's son, a poet and child star, remembered from *Hyland's Corner* and considered a desirable interview subject by the weekly papers. The precocious and very shy adolescent would state his opinion only on rare occasions, but then he did so with great thoroughness, speaking about everything from Arne Imsen and the Maranata movement to the new members of the Swedish Academy. On those infrequent days when he was in a good mood, even a mediocre reporter might be able to find a gold nugget of considerable value if he panned for it.

Leo's fame made an impression at school, of course. He became a model for the other pupils and every teacher's pet. He could expect high marks in every subject, although not in gym class, where a stressed and dejected teacher had to inform his colleagues of the mere passing grade he was able to give – an insignificant blot on young Morgan's otherwise impeccable report card.

That was the spring when Henry Morgan created a scandal by becoming a deserter; he ran off, escaped across the Swedish border and went into exile in Copenhagen. Yet the scandal made very little impact because it was hushed up most effectively. Everyone was talking about it, although not publicly. Henry became a sort of secret hero. But he had never spent a great deal of time at home anyway, and Leo couldn't feel any insuperable sense of loss when Henry was gone. Greta, of course, went around in a permanent state of worry, but the younger boy could see right through her concern. It wasn't the usual sort of moaning and groaning. In her heart Greta knew that Henry

217

always turned up sooner or later, and it was absolutely pointless to wring her hands over him. Henry had always come back.

And he seemed to be doing quite well. Soon letters started arriving from Copenhagen, saying that he was being well taken care of by a group of people called Quakers. Greta and Leo looked up the word in the encyclopaedia and thought it sounded very hopeful. There were plenty of others who were worse off.

Things were undoubtedly worse off downstairs in the Hansson flat. Verner hadn't become any less strange over the years. He was now in high school, and Leo would soon follow, but they had grown apart somewhat. Their games had come to an end, as had the stamp collecting, the Key Club and other activities. Verner had founded the Association for Young Inventors – without success, since at that age boys were clearly more interested in discovering the female body – and he had become more and more obsessed with his research into all those people who had disappeared. Verner's missing persons archive had kept on growing and growing as he brooded and pondered, making charts and coming up with hypotheses about various individual cases as well as about matters in general. One such general theory was that all the people who had disappeared were sitting together somewhere on the globe, idling away the time and entertaining themselves by following the vain attempts of all the detectives trying to track them down. They had all left through some sort of crack in our reality, an opening to another world known only to those who were select co-conspirators.

Mrs Hansson thought the boy had lost his mind because he didn't have a father to look up to and respect. She had never really tried to correct his delusion that his father was waiting for him on some island in the South Pacific. Things didn't get any better when the TV series 'Hubbub in the South Seas' had its premiere that spring and became a big hit. Verner sat right up close to the TV, and of course it was himself and 'Hansson' – as he called his absent father – that he saw on the screen. His mother continued to refuse to tell him what she knew about his father, and perhaps that was what rankled most. She had something to hide that might harm the young man, and she wanted to protect him from reality, but like all attempts to protect someone from reality, it was doomed to failure.

After consulting several teachers at school, she sent her son to England that summer, to a language course in Bournemouth. Mrs Hansson really had to dig deep to scrape up enough money for the trip, but she managed, thanks to a scholarship from the school. Verner himself had no real desire to go; his mother had to persuade him. It was something that she would end up bitterly regretting.

———————

It was only by his fingerprints that anyone could identify Verner Hansson when he returned home from that language course in Bournemouth, England, in the autumn of 1963. The intent had been that it would do him good to have a change, to get some fresh sea air and meet new friends who could divert his attention from his thoughts, which were far from pleasant.

The language course was an undeniable success. The old Verner was dead. In one and a half months – the course consisted of six weeks of intensive language instruction in a cheerful, youthful environment, as it said in the ad – the boy had been transformed from a pimply bookworm with dandruff into something that indicated the start of a new era in Western history. The grey, foul-smelling, nail-biting, information-grubbing chess whiz, who was also the chairman of the Association for Young Inventors, had left Sweden at Midsummer and now returned at the end of August as a totally different person. His greasy, dandruff-ridden hair was suddenly clean and bleached by long afternoons spent on the rocky English beaches; worst of all, it was combed forward into a fringe, a *Beatle fringe*. He had also rid himself of all his old clothes – the thick, prickly, grey rags with mended patches and sweat marks – and bought new, modern gear during a visit to London.

Verner Hansson showed up at school two days after classes started, and this tardiness alone bore witness to the fact that something had changed. The lad seemed to bounce along in a pair of high-heeled shoes that he called 'boots', using the English word, and his astonishing fringe hung in his eyes, his shampooed hair fluttered in the breeze. A miracle had occurred.

Basically this miracle also had its explanation. Verner Hansson had ended up staying with a family with two teenage daughters, who nearly laughed themselves silly at the sight of the square, pimply Swede who seemed as if he were a hundred years old. Soon they were evidently seized by a hysterical creative zeal, which they directed at poor Verner. Over a period of several hectic days, he underwent a Dr Jekyll and Mr Hyde treatment like no other. The girls threw the boy into a bathtub and burned his disgusting clothes in a barrel out in the yard. In passing they also saw to it that he lost his virginity.

And that did it. Verner Hansson found a new crack in our reality, an opening to another world, known only to those who were select co-conspirators. And there is reason to believe that he devoted an intense amount of attention to this opportunity during his six weeks in Bournemouth, and that the girls got good value for their efforts.

Of course this Viking Verner brought back a number of records from his conquests in the West. First and foremost, he had *Please Please Me* by the Beatles, and when that record started playing at full volume down in Verner's flat, nothing was ever the same again. Mrs Hansson just about had a stroke, of course, and she couldn't get over the fact that it had cost a small fortune to transform a rather odd but at least conscientious boy into an even odder and not at all conscientious young man. It was in every sense a poor trade.

But the transformation was both inevitable and contagious. Soon Leo and a good number of other lads from school were also listening to the Beatles, and Verner had even started to smoke – that seemed to go along with his new style of haircut and the 'boots' on his feet.

Naturally Verner's metamorphosis made a deep impression on Leo, as it did on everyone else who knew him. The young Morgan suddenly started spending entire weekends going back and forth between the radio – he kept trying to tune in to the Top Forty – and the bathroom – where he secretly combed his fringe over his forehead, curving his locks along his eyebrows, and studying himself in the mirror from all directions. One day, completely without warning, he left the bathroom with his fringe combed down. The hair hung over his forehead, and it felt a bit strange but absolutely essential. He would never capitulate. Elvis and Tommy were nothing to Leo. He was of the new school. Pop was now in. The loose stones that would soon become an entire landslide had started to roll.

––––––––––

'Let's hand out wings / at every street corner / there is never anyone who dares / to touch the innermost sky', wrote the poet Leo Morgan, and that was precisely what happened. There was actually an endless number of young souls who dared to touch the innermost air that filled everyone's lungs with the power to scream. The finely tuned phrases are in fact an expression of a tremendous ecstasy that demanded its tribute in a fringe hanging over their eyes, a black polo-neck, jeans and basketball shoes on which it said

'BEATLES'. The names 'BEATLES' and 'STONES' were almost everywhere now, and in the spring of '64 Leo Morgan placed his herbarium in double plastic bags inside a wardrobe because he no longer wanted to look at it. All that belonged to his childhood, and the former child-star had now become a teenager.

Henry *the clerk* found himself in the middle of the hornets' nest in London, England. He had a job at Smiths & Hamilton Ltd, doing work that Greta and Leo never fully understood. It had something to do with some sort of correspondence. He had also been to Berlin; there he had listened to jazz, seen the dreaded Wall, and God only knew what else the boy had been doing during his year in exile. Greta wondered whether he would be coming home soon, and after several weeks Henry wrote that he was living with a 'girl' named Lana, and that he was very fond of the creature. In reality, this Lana was almost as old as Greta and could hardly pass for a 'girl', but Henry very deliberately told a lie, just as he had always done in order to reassure those closest to him.

But, as mentioned, London was the heart from which the new blood was spreading to all the repressed youths in the world who were in the possession of a good-sized weekly allowance. A whole industry had arisen to produce articles that in one way or another could be associated with pop music, the Beatles, and the new way of being. There were shirts, scarves, socks, underwear, posters, books, records and albums intended for worshipping their idols, and Henry sent home a cartload to cheer up his little brother.

That was how Leo happened to become the proud owner of a Beatles shirt made of orange velvet several months before the craze spread to Sweden. This meant that with one stroke he became something of a desirable quarry for a number of girls with good hunting instincts. And besides, Leo was so sensitive; he wasn't as tough and cruel as most boys were. Leo wrote poetry, after all, and he never seemed out to *get inside*. He and Verner started getting invitations to parties, and they went to them. Previously this had never even come under discussion; they preferred to keep to themselves with their clubs and their experiments. But now times had changed. Girls invited them to parties with beer and popcorn and dancing in dark rooms. That was where most of the boys tried to *get inside*, which meant sticking their hands under the girls' jumpers, squeezing their breasts, and panting '*491*' in their ears — everyone was thinking about that scandalous book.

But Leo wasn't like that. There was something a bit George Harrison about him. John was the toughest, Paul was the sweetest, George the most romantic, and Ringo was just plain ugly. Leo was most like George, and when he danced a slow dance, such as 'Love Me Do', he never tried anything – nor was he a particularly good dancer, and no one had ever seen him do the twist – but he seemed a little more sensitive than all the other boys. And it was this sensitivity that made the girls fight over him. Otherwise a certain delicacy of feeling or modesty can be a disadvantage for a boy, a real impediment, but it wasn't that way at all, because the very point of the Beatles was that they weren't as rough as the old rock and roll bands. The Beatles may have looked unkempt and intense on the outside, but inside they were soft and romantic, just like Leo.

One of Leo's devoted admirers was named Eva Eld, and that was a name that a poet had to fall for because 'eld' means 'fire' in Swedish. Eva Eld often gave parties at her house, and since her parents were very well-to-do, they were always quite proper affairs. A number of snobbish guys wore ties, and some of the girls wore long dresses. They danced the foxtrot to the sweetest tunes by the Beatles, and Eva's mother provided plenty of roast beef and potato salad and lagers and sodas. Leo knew how to wrap this devoted female around his little finger, and he also knew that her father had a well-stocked bar. It didn't matter if he dragged along Verner and five other young louts; Eva would forgive anything, since she thought she could see through that harsh shell that Leo tried in vain to create for himself. She thought she could tell that he loved her, and in an unguarded moment when she tried to kiss him on the lips, he looked so surprised, as if he hadn't believed that anyone would ever want to kiss him on the lips. He once asked for her photo, which he put in his wallet, where he had previously kept the autographs of the TV stars Lill-Babs, Lasse Lönndahl and Gunnar Wiklund. These graphological monstrosities had long since disappeared. Eva Eld was better; she reminded him a little of a film-star photo that he had once had. He just couldn't remember which one.

He'd had lots of filmstar photos, and Henry had also let him take hundreds from his collection, since he had grown tired of such childish things. They were now all in a box in the attic. Some time during that cruel spring he must have sneaked up to the attic all alone, taken out that particular box, and begun searching for the filmstar who looked so much like Eva Eld. He swiftly and systematically went through the neat stacks of twenty-five photos each, held together by two elastic bands that crossed in the middle. Doris

Day, Esther Williams, Ulla Jacobsson, Tyrone Power, Tony Curtis, Robert Taylor, Clark Gable, Catarina Valente, Alan Ladd, Brigitte Bardot, Humphrey Bogart, Scott Brady, Sophia Loren, James Dean, Burt Lancaster, Kim Novak, Gregory Peck, Pat Boone, Tommy & Elvis, Ingo & Floyd – all those extraordinary names fluttered past, reminding him of the first spring days when the snow had melted from the pavements, leaving behind a slew of sand that steamed and smelled in a very special way. And in the midst of that steam stood all the kids, trading filmstar photos, skipping rope, playing hopscotch and twirling hula-hoops that they'd bought at Epa. That was all so outmoded and uninteresting now. This spring smelled very different. It smelled of cigarette smoke and perfume. And her name was Rosemary Clooney, by the way, that filmstar who looked so much like Eva Eld.

THE CLERK

(Henry Morgan, 1964–65)

'**B**e my Boswell!' was a standing exhortation from Henry Morgan, and a writer isn't about to say no to a couple of good yarns handed to him totally free. As anyone can see, Henry's path to Paris presented various obstacles and obscure delays, in some cases just beyond the outermost limits of reason. But it was also obvious that sooner or later he would end up in London, Dr Johnson's own city, where every master of the art of conversation ought to quench his thirst and wet his whistle. The story about Henry *the clerk* starts some time near the end of 1963.

Mrs Dolan never knocked on the door – she kicked at it with her shoe because she was always carrying two or three breakfast trays on top of each other, and she didn't have a free hand. But then she never had any hands free, because Mr Dolan was an unusually lazy boarding-house manager. He had adopted Andy Capp as his household god, and even though he did get up early in the morning, it was only to sink into an easy chair in front of the TV in the lounge.

'Good morning, Mr Morgan,' said Mrs Dolan. 'What kind of a world is it that you young people are taking over from us?' she asked with a sigh. 'Now they've murdered the murderer too. But I suppose it's just as well. He didn't look very bright, that young Oswald.'

'Oh dear,' said Henry, sleepily.

'Have a nice breakfast, Mr Morgan.'

Mrs Dolan vanished as quickly as she had appeared. She was the talkative type, but she never intruded unnecessarily. Henry liked the woman, and the favourable feeling was mutual. By now she had allowed him to move upstairs to one of the best rooms. It was on the top floor of the building with a view over the rooftops, and you could just catch a glimpse of some of the trees in Hyde Park if you stood on the windowsill and craned your neck. Henry had tried it.

He'd been in London for a couple of weeks now. He'd started looking for a job but hadn't found anything yet. He had quite a bit of the money left that the one-armed Franz had given him in Berlin. Although it felt rather like blood money that he hadn't earned. It was dirty goods.

His stay in Berlin as Henry *the secret agent*, alias Bill Yard, as well as his departure had been chaotic, to say the least. He had followed the astonishing advice from W.S. and run off, high-tailing it out of there. He didn't understand any of it, nor did he want to. He had even tossed Verena Musgrave's silhouette into the canal. It was one of those rare times when Henry admitted to fearing for his life. He couldn't imagine going back to Copenhagen, returning as a huge failure and fool because he wouldn't be able to explain something that was inexplicable. Occultism and rhinoplasty were not Bill Yard's strong suit.

So he took the first train he could get out of town, which happened to be the London express. He had exchanged his money for British currency and ended up with a good five hundred pounds, which would last him quite a while. But Mr Morgan was an enterprising young man of twenty-one, and he had no desire to rest on his laurels. He wanted to find a job, to do something. He had grown restless; he was tired of being a tourist or lying around with his hands clasped behind his head and whistling monotonous tunes with his eyes fixed on the hotel ceiling.

On this particular morning he gobbled down his breakfast and then put on the roomy white coat he had bought in a second-hand shop in Kensington. He carried the breakfast tray downstairs to Mrs Dolan in the kitchen. She thanked him for his help. She said that Mr Morgan was the most courteous guest she'd ever had since the Norwegian, who had arrived just after the war. In her eyes all Scandinavians were Dag Hammarskjöld heroes to a greater or lesser degree. She felt sorry for all the Scandinavians. The Danes and the Norwegians had been occupied by Hitler, and the Finns had the Russians at their backs, while the Swedes still looked so woeful.

'Someone must have done harm to your people some time in the past,' said Mrs Dolan. 'That's why you all look so melancholy. But not you, of course, Mr Morgan. You don't look a bit woeful. You have a glint in your eye, and soon you'll find a job too. It will work out, it will all work out.'

An unreal city. The yellow smoke crept through the alleyways, rubbing its back against the windowpanes, and under the brown fog of a winter dawn, a crowd flowed over London Bridge . . .

He spent over a year there, and I have no intention of recounting all the football matches Bobby Charlton played that he saw, or all the solitary walks he took along the Thames as the fog swept its barges across the water and the rain quietly sighed above the pavements and he slipped into pubs to warm up with a Guinness and a whisky, which was precisely what someone absolutely should be doing if he's a hero in London and also in a novel at the same time.

And of course there's time for all that yellow smoke that crept along the alleyways, and of course there's room for the right man at the right time to walk into a pub and talk about life and death and all that yellow smoke. Henry entered a pub long after Kennedy was shot and missed the broadcast on TV – that alone was some feat – and it went just as badly with Oswald. But Henry picked up everything in a matter of seconds, and he was instantly engaged in a discussion about the CIA and Kennedy and Cuba and Khrushchev. And the lads in the pub might very well have taken this tie-wearing Swede for a cabinet minister or at the very least a dry academic with political science as his speciality.

Henry's unique ability to talk the shirt right off anyone he happened to speak to meant that he obtained permission to work in London and that he was hired for a great job in an office where he was supposed to handle the correspondence with Scandinavia. The Englishmen came and went as they pleased at the offices of Smiths & Hamilton Ltd, which was in the paper business, primarily from Finland and Sweden. And that suited Henry just fine. On top of everything, there were at least half a dozen girls that were easy on the eyes at S&H Ltd.

And there wasn't really much to do each day. The correspondence flowed as quietly as the Don, and Henry would do a little here or there, depending on how the spirit moved him. The bosses thought he was a real find who had learned the business very quickly. They slapped him on the back, promising gold and riches, provided he did his best to learn a bit more. But Henry didn't have all those ambitions that bosses in general are looking for. This was merely a way station, a stop on the road to Paris.

———————

But London was Swinging London, and during the spring of 1964, when Cassius Clay became the world champion in boxing, the Beatles became world champions in their own right. All of London, Great Britain, and the entire world went Beatles-crazy. 'She Loves You' was spinning in every jukebox, and *A Hard Day's Night* was playing at the cinema, a film that Henry *the clerk* found rather superficial. The whole pop scene was rather superficial. Although he couldn't resist sending home a couple of records and some accessories that Leo ought to like. There were T-shirts and posters with pictures of John, Paul, George and Ringo. And Henry wondered how tall Leo was now, whether he had grown at all. Sometimes he longed for home so damned much. It was especially hard on various holidays, but that was never any reason for him to fail to observe the Sabbath. Henry always observed the Sabbath and even the most minor of holidays marked on the calendar by resting, eating and longing.

He didn't have much time for pop. Henry was a jazz pianist and, like a number of other jazz fans who were a bit frightened and desperate, he would sit in the cellars, listening and following wherever the avant-garde led. The crowds in the jazz clubs were getting smaller and smaller, and Henry could already see that in a strange way he was out of step with the times. Henry Morgan had been passed by; he was actually the least modern person imaginable. When people of his age began heading for Carnaby Street to clothe themselves in the garments of pop, Henry Morgan was still walking around wearing his old tweed jacket – well, he did buy himself a new one in London – and his pullover and tie. The girls at the office nagged him about loosening up a bit, telling him it was definitely old hat to go around looking the way he did, but they had no effect on him.

Henry was and would always be a cheerful outsider. Through the efforts of Colin Wilson, an outsider had become a type that was 'in' among intellectuals and jazz musicians, and an outsider could definitely not be cheerful. He was someone who brooded and never really managed to fit in; he was shoved aside, he kept his distance, and if things got really bad, he might end up so far on the periphery that he would take his own life, just like the former pianist in the Bear Quartet had done. He was a true outsider.

But this whole European odyssey that Henry was on had nothing to do with searching for something or trying to find out the true meaning of life and existence, as the deep-thinkers with Sartre would have said. Henry wasn't looking for anything; he was fleeing from something. But even his flight soon came to an end. In London he had practically forgotten that he was a deserter and Maud's eternal lover. In short, he had taught himself how to live, and he was so damn curious about everything that he kept on going. He wanted to see more, to see so much that he couldn't take in another thing. He wanted to see, hear, smell, taste and burn up everything in his path. That was why so many perceived him to be a uniquely bold young man who at any time might become a hero, given the proper situation. They were wrong. Henry was merely like Runeberg's Sven Dufva character, endowed with an unquenchable thirst and appetite for life.

And so he listened to a great deal of jazz, but he also found his way into the music-hall tradition. It was a blissful combination of old songs from the days of the Great War and completely modern revue tunes with lyrics that were brazen, silly and absurd. Henry became totally nuts about a tall, gaunt man who looked like a transvestite and sang falsetto. His name was Tiny Tim, and he played the ukulele at one of Henry's favourite clubs. Henry started writing songs too. He borrowed whatever piano he could find and wrote down his tunes, which he would then sell for a pint of Guinness.

Henry also claimed – and no one was ever able either to refute or confirm his claim – that the original version of 'Mrs Brown You Got a Lovely Daughter' with Herman's Hermits had been penned by Henry Morgan. One day he was sitting in his office at Smiths & Hamilton Ltd, gazing at an incredibly sweet girl who was a secretary; he was always teasing her because she had a photo of the Beatles on her desk. She teased him back, and she thought that Henry was a funny old man. Her last name was O'Keen, and she was from the north. She was the one Henry had in mind when he wrote 'Miss O'Keen You Are a Naughty Daughter', using exactly the same refrain that Herman's Hermits later nicked. He played the tune with great success at the company party. Later he submitted the song to a record company that paid him fifty pounds and said the time might not yet be ripe for it.

Several years later it showed up, nicely reworked, but by then Henry was gone. Nor did he want to cause a fuss, for that matter. He had a generous nature. In his opinion, the English had treated him well.

The nicest of them all was Lana Highbottom. Henry couldn't make much headway with the young girls at Smiths & Hamilton Ltd because they were all so gone on the Beatles. Any lad who didn't look like the Beatles would find himself scrapped.

But Lana Highbottom was different. She was already a mature woman, almost too mature. Recently she even sent Henry *the clerk* in Stockholm some photographs of herself and her two pale, typically English children. The photos didn't really explain Henry's enthusiasm for Lana. He didn't think the pictures showed her at her best. And besides, her qualities weren't visible on the surface, and in the long run that was the only thing that mattered.

At the office Lana Highbottom was regarded as quite trying. She talked almost as much as Henry did. She was a forty-year-old widow whose husband had been a motorcyclist who drove too fast. She lived in Paddington with her old mother, who had also moved south from Liverpool, and that was no doubt her only redeeming feature, according to the younger girls in the office. 'Liddypool . . .' they would say, their eyes sparkling with delight.

When it came to working late for a number of evenings at the office, Lana was always the one to volunteer, and she did so without complaint. And since Henry was considered new at the game, he also had to stay late to do some sort of inventory in the file room, and that was how it happened.

He hadn't managed to leaf through the folders in the file room for more than a couple of minutes after hours before Lana came in and kissed him right on the mouth. She pulled the folders out of his hands and put his arms around her buxom body as she stuck her thigh between his legs.

In that sort of situation Henry wasn't much of a stickler for etiquette, but it could be that he still didn't think that was the most romantic place in the world. It smelled of file-room dust, erasers, ink, blotting paper and carbons. So when Lana started running her fingers through his hair and nibbling on his ear, he tried to stop her.

'No, Lana,' he managed to say amid the hot kisses. 'Not here. We . . . can't . . . do it here . . .'

'Oh yes we . . . can,' panted Lana. 'There's no one else here in the whole . . . building,' she went on, pressing the young Swede up against the metal cabinets, which rumbled like thunder.

Lana Highbottom had her arms wrapped passionately around Henry's neck, and yet she was as practised as an actress and able to undo his tie so that she could press hot kisses on his throat. That was it for Henry. He couldn't stop; he didn't want to stop. He hadn't had a woman in who knows how long, and Lana knew all the tricks. She was lecherous, to say the least, and Henry was depraved, and that was why things went the way they did.

'Ohhhh . . . Henry . . . ,' breathed Lana. 'You're my *bull*, my *miner* . . .' she snorted right into an annual report from 1957.

The fact was that Lana thought Henry looked exactly like Tom Jones, the Bull, the mine-worker from Wales. Henry felt flattered.

There followed a brief period of happiness for Henry *the clerk*. Lana would come over a couple of evenings each week. He savoured the treatment, and the part about Tom Jones was just something that he had to put up with. Lana would throw herself at him like some sort of starving Amazon, and afterwards, when she left him to go home to her two pale kids and her elderly mother from Liverpool, Henry would lie in bed for a long time, smoking. Then he would dash out to a pub to have a drink and enjoy his solitude.

It was just about now, towards the end of 1964, in the midst of pop's budding youth, that Henry started working on his magnum opus 'Europa, Disintegrating Fragments'. He didn't yet know that this would be the title of the piece; he wouldn't know that until he returned home to Sweden in the late sixties. But he had been struck by a vision of a lengthy, cohesive composition that would follow his route through Europe. The idea appealed to him; it would keep him company like a truly reliable travelling companion.

As mentioned, there followed a brief period of happiness for Henry *the clerk*. Over time the saga with Lana Highbottom became extremely vexing because she had a hard time handling her passion. She had a hard time separating one thing from another; she couldn't understand that everything had its place. Henry Morgan simply became too much for her. She saw him at the office every day, and the young Swede would walk around whistling hit songs and take no notice of her while she would cast long, languishing, teary-eyed glances at her virile lover, her Tom Jones. She literally swallowed her *miner*, hook, line and sinker.

As soon as Henry approached the office, his stomach would start to hurt. When he serviced his Lana Highbottom at home, everything went splendidly. But at the office things began to get awkward. Henry cared what people said about him, and he was always anxious to follow convention. If word suddenly went out all over Smiths & Hamilton Ltd that he was screwing Lana Highbottom, he would become a laughing-stock.

The brief period of happiness came to a disastrous end. Lana Highbottom had come over to visit Henry in his room at Mrs Dolan's to partake of her cure. As usual, when she left she descended the stairs twittering and giggling with delight. Henry stayed behind, lying on his bed naked and dazed, smoking. It wasn't especially late. Lana normally left early because of her kids and elderly mother in Paddington.

The evening was still young, and Henry threw on his clothes and went down to the pub. He was a regular at the place, and he was in the habit of banging out several hit tunes on the piano if it was available. In return he would get a couple of free beers. On that particular night, he sat down at the battered piano and started playing a jazz version of 'A Hard Day's Night'. That was what folks wanted to hear.

Everyone was clearly enjoying Henry's rendition of 'A Hard Day's Night' except for a big pockmarked thug who looked as if he'd been lying too long under a double-decker bus. His forehead was dented, his eyebrows shredded and it was anyone's guess what had become of his nose. The thug had hairy fists that dragged on the ground, and his whole physiognomy was straight out of textbook pictures about the dawn of humankind.

The pub pianist Henry Morgan probably hadn't studied this prehistoric Cro-Magnon type very carefully, and he'd started giving his fingers a real warm-up when he was suddenly interrupted. The thug set his privy-lid mitts right down on the keyboard, which meant that he nearly covered four octaves. He reeked of cheap whisky, and Henry only had to cast a quick glance at the monster's blotchy, injured face to realise that it was ripe for a slugging. If the thug didn't land one first, that is. But a proper gentleman doesn't go for a punch without very good reasons.

It didn't take long for those reasons to appear. Without any sort of palavering or superficial pronouncements, the thug abruptly raised one of his sledgehammer fists and aimed a blow as deliberately as if he were going to drive a wedge into a chunk of wood. Henry had plenty of time to reflect on his life and fend off the projectile, which swished past his jaw. Then the thug's left fist came down at an angle and clipped his shoulder. That did not leave Henry wishing for more.

The bartender was standing behind the bar, and he shouted to Henry to take off. Several drunk fellows slowly stepped to the side, murmuring quietly. No one made a move to intervene.

Henry ducked out from under the heavy artillery of serious, albeit totally

232

misdirected projectiles the thug was firing off, using the worst possible street style. Henry *the pianist and boxer* by turns slipped out and ducked and backed away; no doubt it looked as if he were playing with the huge guy, as if he thought it was all in fun.

When Henry had backed along the full length of the bar and everyone had stepped aside, he ended up pressed against a table. Several startled customers fled out to the street, only to peer through the window. Henry made short work of things. He clenched his teeth and charged. He threw a powerful left jab and hit the thug in the forehead and the cheek. The dunce merely looked surprised but he lost his focus. He shook his head and in confusion tried to aim another punch, but he never got that far. Henry charged with a new powerful left to the chin, followed nicely by an explosive series of right hooks just above the thug's ear. And that was the end of it.

The thug fell to the floor with a deafening crash, taking a table down with him as he moaned. He tried to fumble his way to his feet again, but without success. Several old guys came over to shake hands with Henry and to thank him for the show. Then they dragged the thug out to some convenient and suitable back alley.

Henry climbed onto a bar stool, finding himself in that unreal haze that all heroes experience after a battle. The bartender poured him an enormous whisky for his nerves and brought out some ice cubes and gauze for his knuckles, which were tender and bleeding.

'A piano player should be careful about his hands,' said the bartender. 'But you're a great fighter, Henry.'

'Who the hell was that?!' Henry understandably wanted to know.

'Not sure,' said the bartender. 'Doesn't come here often. I just know that he used to ride a motorcycle. Ended up underneath a semi. His name is Highbottom, or something like that.'

'Highbottom?!' cried Henry. 'That can't be true! He's supposed to be *dead*!'

'Don't worry, Henry,' said the bartender. 'He's been beaten before.'

'Lana's Left in London' was the title of a song that Henry put together as an homage to his middle-aged lover. I've heard that tune too, a nice little ballad about a lying woman who only stopped talking when she was kissed.

I don't think the song had anything to do with contempt for women; it was more likely just the opposite. Henry really did like Lana, but she deceived him, and he was on his way to Paris.

He'd been in Swinging London for more than a year; he now knew the city and he'd learned a lesson. Lana would quickly forgive him, because he never told her about the fight with her deceased husband. She would forever after and very punctually each year send him a glittery greetings card, wishing him a Merry Christmas and asking him whether he planned to return. But he never did go back.

One day Henry stood there in Victoria Station with his suitcase while the newspaper boys shouted at the top of their lungs that Sir Winston Churchill was dead. The breathless waiting of the entire nation had suddenly ended with the great man's last gasp. A whole era swept like a gust of wind through the station, taking along a whole generation of dutiful and patriotic disabled soldiers permeated with tonic water across the filthy floor of Victoria Station, where the handbills were whirling around in the draught. HE IS DEAD.

It was early on a Sunday morning in January 1965, and Henry lit up a Player's, blowing the smoke up towards the grimy glass roof of the station where the rain was making dismal streaks in the soot. An old woman sitting on a bench burst into tears, several distinguished gentlemen in city suits removed their hats in respect for the most English of all Englishmen, and even the trains seemed to heave a deep sigh of despair. The mourners began to line up in tight queues along the Thames. Even Henry felt deeply gripped by sadness; he had always liked Churchill. He didn't know why, since his knowledge of history regarding Churchill's role was quite limited. It was more likely a question of style, and of sentimentality.

Henry felt a sadness, a sense of indecision, and hope. He didn't know where to go, but he no longer needed to have any qualms about leaving Lana in the lurch because she would be sad about his treachery. Right now all of Great Britain was in mourning, and Lana didn't have to feel alone. Sorrow was sorrow.

SANCTIMONIOUS COWS

(Leo Morgan, 1965–67)

Leo Morgan's second volume of poetry was given the title *Sanctimonious Cows* and appeared on the booksellers' shelves at about the same time that we switched to driving on the right-hand side of the road in Sweden, which was in September 1967.

Sanctimonious Cows displayed an entirely different face. The reviewers could conclude that something fundamental had happened to the poet. His five-year silence – there is always talk of a 'silence' when it comes to poets who don't put out a steady stream of poetry books; those poets who have never been the object of this special 'silence' probably ought to give it a try; it usually does the poet good – this silence had been like the quiet before a storm. The corps of critics was almost unanimous in viewing Leo Morgan as the spokesman for the new generation, like the Bob Dylan of the Swedish Parnassus, an eccentric who united a modern idiom with classic modernism, whatever that might mean.

Presumably the poet countered this opinion with scornful silence. He had never acknowledged any gods. Those idols that he did acquire he set on a pedestal only in order to hear the exquisite crash when they fell. Blasphemy was Leo Morgan's trademark.

But it was a long road to that point, to the autumn of '67, and you could list a well-nigh infinite cataloguing and count up all the formidable stock-exchange quotations, all the literary trends from Baudelaire to Ekelöf to Norén, and all the records from the Beatles to Zappa that had battered the poet and shoved him this way or that. In the mid-sixties Leo Morgan, just like everyone else of his generation, was the object of an inexhaustible stream of impressions, whose aim it was to devour ideas, clothing, drugs, and people like one-eyed cyclopses.

Sanctimonious Cows was thus a poetic volcanic eruption, in its way heralding the political volcanic eruption that would culminate in the spring of '68. From a literary standpoint, the seismographs also showed a real impact. Many critics confessed to being tremendously impressed by the furious power, the liberated poetic *energy* that blazed in every syllable. There must have been some sort of Rilke-angel murmuring in Morgan's ears.

In this case the poetic method has to do with feeding a whole volcano full of all the cult figures of the West – like a sort of minor *Cantos* – only to have the entire decoction later detonate in an annihilating eruption of invectives that make Dante look like the most cowardly of panegyrists.

In contrast to a 'traditional' presentation of the Good – personified by Dag Hammarskjöld, Winston Churchill, John F. Kennedy and Albert Schweitzer from the twentieth century; all of them dead – the poet offers a fertile and growing Chaos. He scrutinises and castigates his victims, making them seem nothing more than naïve figures striving for the Good. Behind the façades are concealed the lowest of motives and the most vulgar of perversities – Hammarskjöld was a deviant in his own way, Churchill painted naked models, Kennedy exploited his secretaries and Schweitzer spread syphilis among the native tribes – which vacillated between general gossip and sheer figments of the imagination. But the worst thing about these ambassadors of the Good was their corrupt *Loyalty*.

In opposition to this notion of seemingly good loyalty, Leo presents altruistic ecstasy, the spontaneously combustible fire, which is anything but loyal. For the first time in his life Leo allows disloyalty into the system. The order that he strove to achieve in *Herbarium* appears to be an illusion, a false sort of order. This is a realisation that is as bitter as it is vexing and painful.

In fact, it's astonishing that a respectable publisher, and a Swedish one at that, would dare publish such an unrestrainedly blasphemous book as *Sanctimonious Cows*. Perhaps it was out of sheer thoughtlessness or carelessness. Or else the publisher was counting on a minimal print run and a negligible readership. The poet was no longer some sort of Wunderkind; he was eighteen years old and rather past his prime. He was the former child star from *Hyland's Corner* and hardly worth even a small mention in the tabloids, which reported 'now the sweet poet has acquired fuzz on his chin and written some angry poems . . .' and so on.

As I sit up here at this much-abused desk in this ever-so-dismal flat, leafing through *Sanctimonious Cows* ten years later – it's his paternal grandfather's copy, well thumbed and with exclamation marks here and there in the margins – I can only conclude that the power and the *energy* in Leo's lava still endures. By all rights, the title poem should have been included in some school anthology, but as far as I know, that hasn't yet happened. It's a testimony to the gross negligence on the part of those responsible, or possibly to the much-too-powerful impact of the material.

The perspective is brilliant. In the title poem Leo scrutinises his sanctimonious cows through the telescopic sight on a Mauser rifle. The poem is a sort of monologue, spoken by a hired killer whose assignment it is to shoot the sanctimonious cows. To be able to kill, he has stoked himself up with pills and the limited perspective that the telescopic sight allows, guaranteeing that the victims will never be people in a specific milieu, individuals in any sort of context. The people in the telescopic sight become screened off dolls, encircled figures, almost abstract. These are, of course, the conditions for killing – in order to kill, the victim must be something abstract that is called the enemy, perhaps clad in a uniform so that he can't be distinguished from other victims. The murderer and executioner is not allowed to see a human being, he has to see an abstract organism which he – with all his professionalism, his skill, and his precision – will inject with a certain amount of lead, ensuring that death inevitably ensues.

The philosophy of the murderer provides the prologue and prelude to *Sanctimonious Cows*. In my opinion that piece is among the most ferocious, the most raw, and the most nakedly brutal writing ever composed in this country.

After inserting the philosophy of the killer, the victims begin to appear in the telescopic sight: 'Hammarskjöld sleeps in his hotel room / Genesis 38 bears the dog's ears / shame has eyes . . .' thinks the murderer, aiming at Onan, who is spilling his seed on the ground. 'Churchill, who is the girl in Funchal / clinging tight to the raft of the cigar . . .' thinks the murderer, aiming at the minister's painting on Madeira. That is how the poem continues until the executioner has finally completed his assignment and cleansed the world of these saints, our sanctimonious cows. The people are indignant and feel forsaken; the messengers of the gods have left the earth and anything at all might now appear: the Messiah, Zarathustra, or a new Hitler. Not a single verse betrays who has commissioned the killer. It could just as well be a despised God, indignant at the idol-worshipping carried out by humans, or it could be Satan himself, furious for the very same reason.

In contrast to this fallen cult of sanctimonious cows, and as solace for the utter confusion, the poet presents his heavy artillery of ecstasy, rock and roll's all-embracing intoxication in which the new will be born, in which the new has already been born – the all-encompassing hope can only be manifested in this blazing ecstasy, *Unio mystica* with the Universe.

So it is the total collapse of order that appears as the world's only hope, a cataclysm, a catharsis for the besmirched. In an ironic verse targeting himself, Leo bids a final farewell to this order, the system for which he showed such eager fervour in *Herbarium*. 'My plants were the dry / burning bushes of the desert / shrieking, like every fire in the sun . . .' The lines have a threefold meaning. It's an ironic joke aimed at himself, a biblical allusion, and a paraphrase of Dylan. The dried plants in *Herbarium* stand in bright flames; the system, the order, will soon be only ashes. Yet it was in this guise – in the burning bush – that the Almighty once revealed Himself to Moses and exhorted him to lead his people out of oppression to a land that flowed with milk and honey. The image itself, the insight itself, is painful and jarring.

In general, *Sanctimonious Cows* is brimming over with metaphors, allusions, travesties, and quotations; it requires the ciphers of a special consciousness to penetrate it fully. It's a book for outsiders who were part of the in in-crowd.

Sanctimonious Cows might have been a critical success, but it did not sell particularly well. The book also became desirable quarry for intellectual Mods and Provies, who went around stealing books from shops. Leo Morgan may not have become an outright cult figure, but in certain circles he did enjoy a good reputation as a tortured conscience.

He had introduced *disloyalty* into the system, which was to his credit according to some people. Loyalty was a class weapon, something that the powers-that-be, the Social Democrats, and the SAF talked about during their negotiations. Workers were supposed to be loyal to their companies, loyal to Sweden. Loyalty was a poison, a divisive, treacherously poisoned cup. The ecstasy of rock music preached *solidarity*, and that was something quite different.

This included solidarity with the people in Indochina who were being increasingly subjected to American terror, whose resistance testified to an admirable strength. A consciousness of global phenomena such as imperialism began to penetrate into Swedish poetry in general, and into Leo Morgan's poems specifically. *Bonniers Literary Magazine* caused a minor scandal and lost a good many subscribers after publishing Sonnevi's Vietnam poem, and Leo clearly took a stand, even though he could never be mistaken for any sort of banner-waving or protest poet.

Leo Morgan *was* genuinely and sincerely indignant – I'd be willing to swear to that. The child inside the aged labyrinths of his brain knew precisely how panic sets in, how terror wriggles its way out of the body in dizziness, cold sweats and howls when the ground shakes with bombs. Leo had walked through that Inferno, and perhaps that was why he wrote a very savage and cutting poem entitled 'Blanket Angel'. This might actually sound just like any of a dozen modernist titles – signed 'Breton '22' or by one of his epigones in Sweden fifty-five years later – but it has nothing to do with striving for an effect. The ballad is actually what is usually called 'a blistering attack' on real-live blanket angels – meaning those Red Cross nurses who are constantly and persistently sending blankets to regions in the Third World struck by some catastrophe.

> The pilot casts his aeroplane shadow
> drops the snub-nosed angel of death from the sky
> soon every hut will be burning.

> The pilot casts his aeroplane shadow
> delivers the blanket-wrapped angel of mercy to the village
> from the good lady of the Red Cross.

Biggles haunts every verse and serves – exactly like the hired killer in the title poem – both Good and Evil. He is merely a professional who is doing his job. He is, in fact, the most dangerous of us all, according to Leo Morgan, because whoever allows blind duty to barter with his conscience will be lost in the jungle where he will no longer be seen – by God!? – nor is he able to see.

The 'anti-vivisectionist ladies' in the Red Cross turn out to be the wives of generals, the feminine superego of the military, penitent madonnas whose good deeds have only the effect of an echo, in the service of a returned favour instead of in the service of God. They were merely meant to assuage the Western conscience. As anyone might realise, it's no easy matter to describe Leo Morgan's path from the starry-eyed, doomed visionary who wrote *Herbarium* to the hardened shaman who produced *Sanctimonious Cows*. That

239

era, the golden sixties, has become so cloaked in bewildering and misleading legends and mystique that reaching its core seems hopeless. What is required, as mentioned, is an infinite number of stock-exchange quotations to confirm all the hunches. The monument of May '68 stands there like some over-advertised carnival that makes tourists on the horizon feel disappointed, or it's like some over-insured painting that gives an undeserved fortune to the victim of a burglary – he becomes whiny and pathetic.

But he would never howl with the wolves or go prowling around during the seventies, saying that he was disappointed that the revolt of '68 never hit home. Leo was neither a commonplace poet nor a commonplace rebel – he was much too headstrong for that. His road was not shared by anyone else. It could hardly be called a road at all – it was nothing more than a deadly dangerous path through a rancorous landscape, full of pitfalls and landmines.

This Janus-headed *skald* never felt himself to be a fully committed partic-ipant. There was always some sort of veil or an unreal aura about his life. Words never managed to penetrate that veil. Words were keys, magic pass-words, that would be forever misappropriated. When the Garden of Eden came crashing down, human beings were not only estranged from God, but words – especially the word 'love' – began their long and bloody journey towards meaninglessness. Words were fragile keys that were conveyed through cultural history without ever finding the right lock in the right door. The quantity of meanings compressed in words – just like the various notches on a key – promised something which human beings, ever since the mis-appropriation, have never managed to live up to. There are words for love, but there is no love. There is evil, but no words that can capture that evil. 'The keys promise a door / somewhere on this earth / Baptism promises a peace / although no one can find words . . .'

So language has to be broken apart, the metal of the keys has to be melted down, poured into new forms, into free forms. The only thing Leo could do was to remain free, completely free of all obligations, of all bonds and commitments. No one could demand anything of him. The responsibility he took upon his shoulders was the responsibility of freedom, which weighs more than any other yoke ever placed on the shoulders of slaves. The moment when a person realises that he is free – that is a ghastly moment when the abyss yawns like a black pit of matter compressed to nothingness. There is no longer anything to hold on to, no rituals, ceremonies, or processions.

There are no concepts that mean anything but precisely what we decide they should mean at the moment. It does no good to read old books, because books can burn, and burn well.

If the sixties can be said to have been imbued with a certain steadiness of belief, then Leo was the exception that proved the rule. He had his sympathies – as far away from his high-born heritage as possible – but his poetry celebrated its greatest triumphs when free from any creed.

'It was so dark that there was no proof / she was stateless and the sofa was clad in goosebumps / No one believes in a murderer if no bodies are found . . .' as it says in *Sanctimonious Cows*. You would have to look for a long time to find a darker picture of a love tryst. This is as far from classic love poetry as you can get.

Her name was Nina, and she had been to all the concerts that were worth going to. She had seen the Beatles in Sweden at Kungliga in '64, she had heard Bob Dylan tune his guitar at Konserthuset, and she had seen the Rolling Stones. Some people called her Nina Negg because she was so negative. She talked like no one else, and she swore so fiercely that she made everything smoulder.

Nina Negg was in some sense the hub for a gang that used to hang out down by Hötorget. She was a Mod and helped to start several riots because she hated everything that had to do with law and order. To hell with everything. No one could say this more convincingly than Nina Negg. She always carried a spray-can of red paint with her so that if she felt like it she could instantly write something on a wall or the pavement, wherever she happened to be standing. That was how Leo and Nina met – and it's well known that two negative charges that come together will result in a positive.

They were probably sitting in Nina's flat – her parents were always away – listening to the year's big smash hit, 'Satisfaction' by the Stones, a single that had knocked out everything else in the business. The gang was most likely in high spirits and decided to go downtown to see what was going on. Out on the street Nina Negg claimed to have forgotten her spray-can of red paint back home. She told Leo to wait but the others should go on ahead. When Nina came back they walked a couple of streets and then stopped to write something on the wall of a building. Nina shook the spray-can but

241

couldn't think of what to write. She asked the fucking poet to come up with something. He couldn't think of anything good, other than 'Satisfaction'. 'OK,' said Nina and started writing in big letters on the wall: SATISFACT. She was just about to add an 'I' when a cop car on patrol turned up the street. Two longhaired Mods in US army jackets, jeans and basketball shoes made rewarding booty – two hoodlums caught in the act of vandalism. Leo smelled the cops and grabbed Nina; they started running. They ran like crazed dogs. An officer tried to catch them, but he didn't have a chance. Their trainers were too fast. Leo knew the area and without thinking he pulled Nina inside an entryway and slammed the door behind them. There they tried to catch their breath.

It was all a bloody hell and a fucking pisser because Nina Negg had dropped her red paint. Leo could not console her. He stood there staring at her as she tried to pull herself together after their flight. He couldn't figure out what he really felt about her. Nina Negg looked much older than she was. She had deep circles etched under her eyes, little folds that she'd had since birth, or so she claimed. And her intense way of life had not made them any less distinct. They gave her eyes a special, appealing look, which disappeared completely as soon as she opened her mouth. It's impossible to appeal to someone if you're cursing and swearing. But in the midst of this flood of epithets she could sometimes, for just a moment, look so desperately serious, as if she really were very old.

Only then did Leo recognise where they were. They were huffing and puffing inside a building that he and Verner had used as a favourite hiding place when they were kids. They knew every door up in the attic. They had opened every lock to every little nook and cranny, and they had been allowed to operate in peace and quiet up there. He suggested to Nina that they go up to the attic to have a look at the view. He didn't say a word about suffering from vertigo; that would have just made her curse him even more vehemently.

Nina Negg thought the idea sounded fucking great, and she was clearly impressed that Leo, with a few elementary tricks, was able to open the door to that magnificent attic. A ladder led up through the dark to the hatch in the roof. Leo went first, not saying a word. No doubt he swallowed a big lump in his throat as he helped Nina over to the edge, where they could look out over the whole city. Stockholm by Night. Nina swore slightly cautiously at the overwhelming view of that shithole called Stockholm. Her billowing curses carried her across the seas, far away to Amsterdam, to London, to cities that were much more pleasant than Stockholm. As soon as she'd saved up some dough she was going to take off, and that fucking big poet could go ahead and write that down.

Nina Negg was freezing up there on that roof, so she climbed back down the ladder and disappeared somewhere in the dark. It was utterly silent and pitch dark when Leo followed. He tried in vain to listen for any sound, but he couldn't hear a thing that might give Nina away. He groped his way along the crumbling wall, pausing next to the chimney to hold his breath. He tried to recall the layout of the attic and then took up position at a sort of inter-section that every visitor would have to pass, sooner or later. He stood there, breathing, hearing only his own heart beating; Nina didn't give herself away. For a moment he suspected that she might have slipped downstairs and left him all alone up there. Nina Negg was not to be trusted, and that was undoubtedly what he liked about her.

Suddenly a match was struck only a couple of yards away from Leo. It was Nina. She had grown tired of her game; it was so damned dull. She would never have admitted to being afraid. She lit a cigarette and handed it to Leo. She asked him if they were going to stay in that damned attic all night. Stay and stay, thought Leo. They could sit down on a sofa if they liked because there was an old attic storeroom nearby that had a sofa, a table and two armchairs. Nina didn't believe him until she saw the room for herself. She sat down on the sofa and Leo lit a candle that had been stuck onto the old table.

It was this sofa that was 'clad in goosebumps', as it said in the world of his poem. It was a dark image for a love tryst, but there's nothing particu-larly romantic about making your debut as a lover on a moth-eaten old sofa in a cold and draughty attic on Timmermansgatan. Especially if the most tender words you hear are that you're an unusually nice bastard – for a poet.

———————

Presumably there is a partially denied but nevertheless deep disappointment in those words about the sofa that was clad in goosebumps. Nina and Leo had a monopoly on personal freedom, and after their premiere in the attic, neither one of them wanted to acknowledge the other, so to speak. Neither of them believed in lasting relationships. In spite of the fact that Leo, at least, had never had any experience with this sort of thing, he repudiated with high-minded arrogance anything that bore the least resemblance to marriage. And they had agreed to put up with the consequences.

At any rate, there seemed to be a certain bitterness and despair in those verses about the sofa. 'It was so dark that there was no proof' – as if love itself needed something more tangible than the memory. 'She is stateless' – she was no ordinary citizen. Nina Negg was a counter-citizen upon whom no one could make any claims, and perhaps Leo actually did want to make claims on her. He loved that sudden solemnity in her weary eyes; he wanted to share it with her.

But there were also those who wanted to make claims on Leo Morgan. His mother Greta, of course, had not sat by in silence, watching the changes over the past few years – or, as she viewed it, the going astray. Henry might be accused of many things – he was a good-for-nothing and a deserter – but at least he was neat and dapper. Leo, on the other hand, formerly a model young boy, had suddenly begun to cultivate a very deliberate slovenliness, which consisted of neglecting both his room and his appearance. Greta didn't understand him anymore.

From time to time photographs would arrive from the Continent, where Henry *the adventurer* had his picture taken at famous monuments. He was constantly running into the kind of photographer who roamed through the streets of Copenhagen, Berlin, London and other big cities taking terrible pictures that were both blurry and poorly composed. But a mother is willing to make do with very little, and there was never any doubt that it truly was Henry, always elegant, standing there and preening himself at Rådhuspladsen, Kurfürstendamm, Picadilly Circus, by the Danube and in the Tuileries.

Greta pinned one picture after another to the pinboard in the kitchen as she sighed and wondered how long Henry was really planning to stay away. The authorities seemed to have dropped his case long ago, and he would undoubtedly not have to go to prison if he returned from his lengthy exile. But he didn't come back; he kept moving on to new places. She never had to worry, though. Those photos bore witness to the fact that he was doing well and taking good care of himself.

Things were much worse with her former child prodigy. She had never imagined that she would have any trouble with that boy, although over the past several years he had changed beyond recognition. She could no longer get a sensible word out of Leo. She tried everything she could think of to coax a few words from him, to try to understand him, but nothing worked. And she didn't want to fuss over him too much, seeing as the fate of the Jazz Baron was still fresh in her mind.

A mother who disowns a son has to atone for her crime. That's what had happened to old Mrs Morgonstjärna. After the Jazz Baron departed this life without reconciling with his mother, the woman had slowly but surely fretted herself to death. The family physician Dr Helmers had made weekly house calls and prescribed everything from mysterious diets at distant health spas to port wine. Nothing did the old lady any good. On the night the Beatles performed in Sweden for the first time, she drew her last breath, barely audible even to her own husband. A month after her death and funeral, the billiard table was restored to its former position, in her room. The old dandy, libertine and permanent secretary of the WWW Club could not look back without a certain bitterness at the period of his life spent as a married pater-familias, which nevertheless seemed like a forty-year hiatus between two games of billiards. The WWW Club offered condolences and soon resumed its games, as if nothing had happened.

Greta didn't want to leave such a bitter image of herself behind. She had to keep on good terms with Leo. And besides, things could have been worse.

There were also others besides Greta who wanted to make claims on Leo Morgan. Eva Eld seemed to be consumed with love for her poet, her bohemian, her George Harrison, and everything else that she imagined him to be. She knew full well that Leo was hanging out with the Mod crowd surrounding Nina Negg, but she didn't care.

Wearing a skirt, checked kneesocks and a freshly ironed blouse, she bore a damned close resemblance to the filmstar Rosemary Clooney, and it was in her very neatness that Leo found his incentive. He now carried the photo of Rosemary Clooney around in his wallet, because it reminded him of Eva. She was full of blood and passion, and she possessed everything that Nina Negg did not.

Without a murmur of protest, Eva Eld allowed all the Mods that Leo knew to come to her parties. Someone would pick the lock on her father's bar cabinet to get at the high-class alcohol. The more snobbish bounders in the dark blue suits and ties were in some way charmed by the rowdy Mods, who had no respect for anything. Their girlfriends were especially interested; there was always so much in the newspapers about riots and disturbances and it was all very exciting.

After one party at Eva Eld's house, Leo fell asleep in her bed, and he was still there when her parents returned home, without warning. Of course they couldn't be allowed to find a Mod in their daughter's room, so Eva had shoved her poet under the bed and later joined him there on the floor. She made love to him with such passion that once again he found reason to doubt the evidence of his own senses.

Early in the autumn of 1967 a dignified procession passed through Stockholm. A number of subversive elements carried a coffin out to Kungsträdgården, the King's Garden. There they picked up a rag with a special emblem on it, drenched it in petrol, burnt it and then let the ashes slowly drift down into the coffin while a couple of quiet hymns were sung. That was how the Provie movement, barely a year old, buried itself. It's highly likely that Leo Morgan participated in the procession. Perhaps in a way he was also burying his own youth there in the King's Garden.

Just before the traditional graduation exams were officially abolished, he managed to earn quite decent final grades, presumably as a result of his teachers' favourable disposition, which by now had become a force of habit. He was definitely no longer the class genius, and it's possible that there were certain differences of opinion that arose when Leo Morgan, *the pupil*, was discussed by the teachers and principal at their last meeting. Leo had been listless, apathetic and indifferent over the past few years. The teachers thought that the life seemed to have gone out of the child prodigy. As usual, they didn't have a clue about what was really going on.

Like two demons, Verner and Nina Negg had come down to the school and whisked away their fuzz-faced bard, rescuing him from the steamroller of the conformist lessons that smoothed out every little divergent element to produce a general mediocrity. Verner had started hanging around the university – he was the department's laziest mathematician – and Nina worked if she felt like it. They devoured all sorts of things during the day, sitting in her place and smoking hash as they listened to Jimi Hendrix before they went over to the school to pick up Leo, who right up until the very end persisted in attending classes. Verner smoked up one stamp after another. He would go down to Hornsgatan to see the Philatelist – one of the men who was involved in the digging crew – and sell one rare stamp

246

after another. His mother had no idea, because he would replace the valuable stamps with worthless ones, which she could never identify. Verner thought the very idea was exhilarating: old, extremely old, tiny pieces of paper could get him as high as he wanted – it was all a matter of which one he sold.

Sometimes Nina would worry about Leo as they sat there, puffing on their peace pipes. There was something rigid about his expression, something dark and utterly inscrutable. He would never get muddled the way most people did when they smoked. In fact, it seemed as if nothing really affected Leo, nothing took hold. He just became more and more introverted and reserved, even less approachable, and that worried Nina. She thought that he hated her because she knew that he spent time with that damn hag, that slutty bourgeois broad, Eva Bitch-Eld. One time Nina tore open Leo's wallet and found those pictures that were supposed to depict her rival. She ripped them to shreds right before his eyes, then set the pieces on fire and stamped on them, just to make him react. But he didn't. She could pretend to be furious and start punching him with her fists and scratching his face with her fingernails, which were bitten to the quick. But he didn't react. She could have set him on fire, like a monk from the Far East, and he wouldn't have tried to get away. Leo always wanted an explanation, he was always trying to twist and turn every idea until there was nothing left of it. Everything became empty, meaningless rhetoric. His whole life was like a game of chess in which the pieces disappeared, one by one, until only Leo's remained – he would win, no matter how much hash he smoked.

But Nina Negg's sole preoccupation was not officially declaring everything and everyone dead; she actually was able to participate in the fight for life. She was friends with one of the prominent figures in the Provies, if it was even possible to talk about those who were in the forefront or in the background in terms of this phenomenon. If so, Leo definitely ended up in what was the background.

This person Nina knew had hitchhiked all over Europe. His name was Stene Forman, and he was the son of a newspaper baron, though it was a minor enterprise compared with the big daily papers. Stene had a laugh that could drown out almost any other. When he laughed, people in the vicinity would be ready to call for an ambulance or the fire department or the like, because his laugh sounded so dangerous. There was something possessed about his laugh; perhaps it was filled with a natural power, a wild and untamed desire. Stene Forman was basically a very positive person, and that could be why the movement in Sweden was given the name 'Pro Vie'.

In Holland it was called 'Provo' – for provocation – and there the participants had set off a minor civil war in Amsterdam when they allied themselves with striking workers. The Swedish version was somewhat nicer, more modest, more positive and not nearly as desperate or disillusioned as on the Continent.

Stene Forman was presumably the one who managed to persuade Nina Negg that it was fucking crucial to stage 'happenings', and Leo soon suspected that she had fallen in love with the guy – that was the only explanation. He wasn't exactly jealous; he refused to acknowledge jealousy, because in his world it had been eradicated, like some sort of Black Death of ownership.

The Provies staged a series of happenings and demonstrations. They emptied an entire bus full of non-returnable bottles right in front of the parliament building; they sang in the Brunkeberg tunnel; and they performed street theatre. It was all very innocent, and yet it was brutally received by the police. The Provies were stretching the boundaries of what was allowed, and that was one of the things that attracted Leo.

A lot of people were needed for a planned anti-atom-bomb action at Hötorget, and it was in this connection that Leo was summoned as a temporary Provie. It was a Saturday afternoon, in the middle of the weekend shopping rush downtown, and two processions that had started in opposite directions met down at the square, each showing up with an atom bomb made of tin foil. People from all around started getting curious, and the crowds grew. The two armies were urged towards each other by aggressive commanders. Innocent people who were out doing their shopping got dragged into the battle, and finally the bombs exploded, causing both armies to die.

Leo had been assigned the role of a soldier who wore a gas mask. As he lay on the ground and the police were trying in vain to figure out what was going on, he peered into the throng of people that was staring down in astonishment at the sea of bodies left by the huge explosion, and he caught sight of Eva Eld. She was standing there holding a shopping bag and staring at all the Provies. She didn't recognise Leo, of course, since he was wearing a gas mask, but he imagined that her affections for him would not be diminished even if she did recognise him. For once he was a participant in something. He was seen. Somewhere in the swarm of bodies was Nina Negg, who was swearing energetically because it was too damn cold to be lying dead on the ground that day.

So if it's possible to claim that *Herbarium* was the poet's farewell to his childhood, it could be said with equal justice that *Sanctimonious Cows* – which was introduced to the public during that autumn when Sweden switched to driving on the right side of the road and the Provies staged their own funeral in the King's Gardens – represents the final balance sheet of his youth. That volcanic eruption, that explosion may have acquired its monumental force in the same way the atom bomb does – a force field, a shock wave is created through fission, a Big Bang that establishes a new Universe in accordance with entirely new laws, a whole different moral codex.

Without a doubt, it had to do with the urge to create some form of unity, balance and – paradoxically enough – order in this chaos. Perhaps poetry was Leo's only refuge where inconsistency was the rule. His brother Henry *the adventurer*, went abroad, while Leo began his own internal exile. The world was on the verge of tearing him apart, yet he could not leave. This was where Eva Eld was, with her suffocating, maternal adoration, and this was where Nina Negg was, with her seductively lovely catastrophe. Here was pacifism's uncompromising hatred of evil, and here was the liberation movement's righteous love of armed struggle. Here was his own cultivation of the printed word and his desperate longing for sensual grace.

It was a world thirsting for the truth. Leo would stay in it for a while longer, at least in order to make an attempt to hunt down the evil. But he would lose his way.

LE BOULEVARDIER

(Henry Morgan, 1966–68)

When the truly big elephants danced, only the best of venues would do. Paris would do, even for a *citoyen du monde* such as Henry Morgan. It was the merry sixties, and there were still big elephants who wanted to dance. *Henri le boulevardier* turned up wherever anything was happening. At a large demonstration, for instance, on Boulevard Michel he stood very close to Jean-Paul Sartre, and he asked the philosopher a question that was never answered. Even today no one knows what that question might have been. Henry was not trained in rhetoric. He was a man of action and physicality.

Sartre, for his part, was a very short man. Anyone who has ever seen him will attest to that. Minou was also short, appallingly short, though without being either a dwarf or a cretin. He was just very little, that was all. Minou worked as a waiter at the Café Au Coin, down by Rue Garreau where Henry spent his days. Henry could often be found at Au Coin, sitting there with a *pastis* as he stared at the throngs of people on the street. This was in Montmartre, and there was always something to stare at, especially for a namedropper like Henry.

One day in the autumn of '67 a black Lincoln Continental came gliding down the street. It was raining and slippery. The huge Yank vehicle was moving much too fast, and it rammed right into a rusty little Citroën 2CV which, with a small bang, was transformed from one miserable shape into another, more compressed one.

The Frenchman in the Citroën leapt unscathed out of the wreckage and started shouting and screaming, as was to be expected. He attacked the gleaming, sneering Lincoln Continental, apparently prepared to rip the 50,000-dollar vehicle to shreds with his bare hands. But he stopped when he caught sight of the two figures climbing out of the car – a fat, knock-kneed man wearing a wide-brimmed cowboy hat in the company of the world-famous painter, Salvador Dalí.

A moment of massive silence and monumental stillness followed. A big elephant was about to dance, and the world seemed to pause for an instant. The Frenchman, so enraged only a moment ago, began scratching his head. The world-famous painter had, of course, been recognised. He twirled his celebrated moustache and absentmindedly poked at the Citroën with his cane.

Suddenly the bewildered Frenchman had an idea, something that Frenchmen often have. Quick as lightning he dashed inside the Café Au Coin where Henry Morgan was sitting with his *pastis* and where Minou worked. The victim asked for a bucket, some paint and a paintbrush, all of which fortunately could be found in the café. He then went back out to his demolished Citroën. The whole business was resolved amicably, without any gendarmes. The immensely marketable surrealist willingly signed the wreck with his distinctive signature, and the victim instantly became the proud owner of a *Citroën détruit par monsieur Salvador Dalí*, an original. Later the car was undoubtedly sold for a high price to some crazy American collector.

But that wasn't the end of the story. At that point all was well and morale was high. The fat American in the wide-brimmed cowboy hat was clearly elated by the whole affair. With his friend Dalí and the Victim, he went into the café where Henry Morgan was sitting and Minou was working. The American insolently clapped his hands and shouted for champagne. The occasion had to be celebrated as if they were dedicating a new sculpture in a public place.

Minou bowed very politely, showed the party to a table, and ran off to get a bottle of chilled, dry champagne. As the cork flew off, the Yank finally noticed the extremely short Minou. He shoved back his cowboy hat and announced to the attentively listening crowd in the bar that he had just bought a fantastic castle 'down in Lorraine', which happened to be totally inaccurate, since Lorraine lies to the east. He was thinking of having it transported home all the way across the Atlantic to his property in Texas where it would be reconstructed. He was one of those crazy American collectors.

'*Merveilleusementable* . . .' said Dalí with a sigh, twirling his moustache.

And it was here that Minou entered the picture.

'You'd suit the place perfectly!' bellowed the cowboy, giving Minou an appraising look. 'How much are you, monsieur?'

Minou didn't reply and tried to slip away. He was shy and didn't welcome attention.

'I mean . . .' the cowboy persisted, his voice just as loud. '*Combien êtes-vous?*'

Minou had evidently heard this question before and perhaps he thought that he could afford to be a bit amiable – that usually resulted in a nice tip and restored tranquillity, if nothing else.

'One twenty-five,' said Minou, because that was his height in centimetres.

'No, monsieur,' grunted the American. 'I mean in dollars!'

That was clearly the last straw for Henry, that blue-eyed, loyal Sven Dufva. He jumped into the situation, striding over to the cowboy and landing a well-aimed right hook right between the eyes of that swine.

A tumult ensued. Dalí was on his guard and gave Henry a thrashing with his cane that was worthy of an old-fashioned schoolmaster. Minou tried his best to separate the combatants, but without success. He was, in fact, too small for the task. Gendarmes were required to restore peace to Au Coin, and Henry was taken in for questioning.

The boxer and bohemian Morgan was never again welcome at Au Coin after his heroic intervention. Life, Jean-Paul Sartre and Minou were all very short; art, on the other hand, was very long. That was what he learned.

––––––––––

There are people who go to museums, and there are those who go to cafés. Some people go to museums, while others never do. That might be a good subject for a historian, to investigate *when* and under what circumstances humans started collecting and preserving things from history and what importance this had for humanity's self-awareness. Perhaps this is even something that is particularly Western; I'm not sure. Museums are our bloodless past, exposing traces of our lives; they're a type of conscience, captured in display cases and equipped with seals and burglar alarms. All art is actually museum-like, with the exception of music. Henry Morgan was a musician, and as far as I can tell, he lacked any notion of time or space.

The Paris in which Henry spent his last springtime in exile was at the heart of the world revolution, a city on the brink of ferment, exactly like in the days of the Commune ninety-seven years earlier, and exactly like in Blum's days, approximately thirty years earlier. This was no time to be going to museums, at any rate not for a man like Henry. He belonged to those who went to cafés.

Henri le boulevardier read all the newspapers he could find, laboriously making his way through *Le Monde*'s weighty columns, spelling his way through all the leaflets and communiqués from the revolutionary forces. He saw all the soon-to-be legendary heroes in full action on the street: the short physicist Geismar, the red-faced Cohn-Bendit and even Sartre. He listened to all the talk on the street and was, of course, drawn into all the skirmishes wherever he showed up. People willingly allowed themselves to be duped – they thought that he was some sort of hero.

He lapped up *Froth on the Daydream*, and I have no difficulty at all in picturing *Henri le boulevardier* waking up in a narrow bed, rubbing his eyes and casting a weary glance out across the galvanised roof where the cooing from the dovecote was enough to wake the dead. He gets up, washes himself in cold water and then sets the table with a Continental breakfast.

The man was truly in his element. He had finally found his way. Here was Paris, waiting for him with its chestnut trees, boulevards, allées, cafés and clubs; its beautiful women, plain women, rich plutocrats and poor clochards, its fumbling bohemians, opportunists and newly launched shooting stars – everything that Bill in the Bear Quartet, Maud and Hemingway had spoken of with such enthusiasm. Henry could swim around like a fish in water; Paris was the place for inquisitive explorers. Henry very quickly became *Henri le boulevardier*, the man who walked more than two thousand miles in less than a year, who wore out four pairs of shoes, who traipsed up one street and down the next wearing a long white coat – the one he had bought in a second-hand shop in Kensington, London, in 1964 – and his old worn cap, with his pockets full of magazines and tabloids.

He would sit drinking his chicory coffee dissolved in hot milk until late in the morning, gazing out across the galvanised roofs and properly taking in the day before he undertook anything more sensible. He rented a small room on Rue Garreau, in that hodgepodge of buildings between Montmartre Cemetery and Sacré Coeur, not far from Place Clichy, where Henry could dash around for hours pretending to be Henry Miller if he liked. He lacked for nothing. Sometimes he would pick up girls on the street. There were Arabs with peculiar card games, there were people from all parts of the globe who could teach him their tricks and the best gimmicks for staying alive. And he did stay alive.

After breakfast he would shave, and he did so with great care. He studied his face in the mirror above the cracked washbasin, and perhaps he saw that he was getting older. The years can have such a varied effect on different people – some get spare tyres and pot-bellies, others develop big bags under their eyes, wrinkles and nodules, scars or vacant eyes empty of all dreams.

Henry was getting older. Four years in exile had left their mark. His hair was still short, neatly cut and parted. He actually looked like a strong boy who had dug in his heels to resist, who didn't really want to grow up. His eyes were an ageless blue. Yet he had grown older, in a very particular way. His body had acquired a weight and solidity. He had seen so much, been involved in so much, yet strangely enough he had escaped mostly unscathed, although not always with his honour intact.

At one time or another everyone who has been out in the wide world has to ask himself the question: where am I? You wake up in a strange room somewhere, having stumbled into bed the night before, and for all the world you can't remember where you are. Town after town and room after room pass through your mind until you finally catch up with your own drowsy and worn-out body in that particular bed. By this time Henry Morgan had slept just about everywhere. In train stations, in Copenhagen, on a farm in Jutland, crashing with chance acquaintances or with friends who suddenly became enemies, in cheap boarding houses in Germany and in whorehouses in Rome. Yet he was seldom plagued by the feeling that he was a step behind, that he had missed the train and watched his own body ride off, with his soul left behind on the platform. He had rarely asked himself the question where am *I*? – because he never brooded over that subject. Henry Morgan was a kind of soldier in flight, on excellent terms with his own name and the body that other people – primarily women – admired. Or that some – primarily men – attacked with canes and clenched fists. Now his worn suitcase was standing on the floor in that cheap room on Rue Garreau, covered with labels that shouted: Copenhagen! Esbjerg! Berlin! London! Munich! Rome! Paris! And the list would get even longer. It would have made his grandfather Morgonstjärna, the globetrotter and permanent secretary of the Well-travelled, Well-read and Well-heeled Club, very proud.

Henry made shaving into a great art, using a cake of soap, a brush and a straight razor, just like a real barber. He had plenty of time to devote to this; he had time to develop every little daily ritual into great artistry. His movements were precise and meticulously planned. Every little gesture meant something, as in Japanese Noh dramas – which are equally incomprehensible to the uninitiated. The movement, the gesture, had become his language. He had learned to describe increasingly subtle things through pure movement; it was his way of expressing himself. A gesture in and of itself can be a form of music; it moves through the air like a wave, like spoken words and tones. He had worked at a billiards hall right near Ponte Umberto in Rome, as well as in countless bars in Munich, and he had acquired a unique control over his hands. He had taught himself to master every tap, bottle, glass, rag and brush – how they felt and where they were to be found – and he could do any sort of hand manoeuvre blindfolded. Anyone who watches a master bartender – and I mean a true master who takes his work seriously – will know what I'm talking about. He can make great art out of even the most insignificant cocktail.

Henry, the Marcel Marceau of booze, was incredibly proud of his dexterity, his 'supple hands', which also benefited his piano playing. There was something grand about the whole thing, and it began to seem more and more as if he were taking great pains to acquire a fundamental view of the art of living, a profound everyday ethic. Henry believed wholeheartedly in all these rituals; he put his entire, fiery soul into whatever was commonplace, trivial and banal, trying to turn it into great art. Henry had come to a realisation: his exile was not wasted time. Perhaps he was doing everything simply in order to endure his melancholy. It can be boundlessly dreary to be in exile. Hamlet knew that long ago, as did Odysseus.

Those who know how to look out for themselves, as Henry Morgan did, have never needed to starve. A mendacious tongue like his could get him far. He supported himself with odd jobs here and there, in bars and hotels, on the street and in lounges, and now and then he would put his 'supple hands' to use – they were quick and could snatch up a valuable or two if the situation presented itself. But they never took advantage of anyone who was poor.

Henri le boulevardier was a bohemian, and there were swarms of bohemians beneath the medieval vault of Bop Sec. That was one of the genuine jazz clubs on the Left Bank, and the owners operated under a very specific objective, to carry on the traditions and to ennoble bop. Dixieland and happy jazz were banned from Bop Sec. That was the place for the more advanced and introspective audiences who wanted to sit and nod their heads behind dark glasses as they smoked cigarettes, sipped at a demi and perhaps, in an abrupt show of ecstasy, snapped their fingers to the beat. Bop Sec was the last outpost of real jazz.

Now and then this insularity might be disrupted by some poet who acted like an alarm-clock and scanned his verses, like a kind of thermometer: communiqués from the revolts in Berkeley, in Berlin, Tokyo, Madrid, Warsaw, Stockholm . . . The poets liked to end their lyric sermons with slogans from the walls of Paris, such as: 'Be realists, demand the impossible' or 'The dream is reality' and other phrases. The poets would always leave the stage to standing ovations.

Henry had become friends with the owners – a big fat man and his very thin Algerian wife – and he would sit there night after night, listening. He wanted to show off his talents. At the end of May during that fermenting spring when all of France was paralysed by a general strike and when everyone was waiting for de Gaulle's departure, Bop Sec was one of the few places that remained untouched. The police were constantly raiding other places, but in some mysterious way the owner of Bop Sec had been given carte blanche and was ignored.

Henry showed off his talents and was invited to sit in with a group during the following month. At that time there were frequent guest performers, and on that particular evening in late May, he sat down on his usual bar stool, ordered a demi, lit a cigarette and listened to a saxophone from the room next to the bar. It sounded strangely familiar.

He took a long drag on his cigarette and listened to that horn. It sounded as if the tenor saxophonist had practised with a pillow in his throat; he had an unusual, explosive force that erupted right down the medulla oblongata, where it became firmly riveted and sat there, vibrating. The drums fell in with the sax, the bass came gliding after and the guitar moved alongside with its terse, staccato accompaniment.

It was the big city, with all its roaring and bellowing, that could be heard between the beats as the drummer literally pounded on the bass drum. It was the big city with its bricks, its dilapidated buildings with some commotion going on at every corner and suicide candidates in every window; it was the hot, trembling, undermined streets with all the dustbins, cigarette butts and lit-up signs, the cars and faces gleaming in the red neon; it was all that

257

wailing in the riffs that piled up on top of each other, getting closer and closer until the rhythm intensified to the unbearable, approaching the pain threshold where everything broke out into the lyric coolness of mercy, which not only asked for beauty but *demanded* beauty and made the audience tremble like the Shakers, as if confirming that the divine existed right there, at that very moment, fully within reach and yet so elusive and transitory. It demanded the impossible; the dream was reality.

That tenor saxophonist had listened to Coltrane on a wintry night in front of a woodstove near Odenplan in Stockholm. The audience burst into rapturous applause. Henry had finished smoking his Gitane and was in a cold sweat. He sat there shaking. The dream was reality, life a dream.

'Are you feeling OK tonight?' asked the hefty proprietor of the club.

Henry stared at him as he stood there, polishing glasses.

'Is there something wrong?'

'No . . . no . . . ,' stammered Henry. 'That's not it . . .'

Henry was done in. He had listened to every single note from that saxophone, recognised every trill, every little attack of the terse and so typically spontaneously combustible riffs. It sounded as if the tenor saxophonist were playing for the very last time, as if he had to draw out every little note lengthwise and crosswise until they were about to burst. But it sounded so much better now. Bill had really become a fucking good musician. Bill was starting to sound like the truly great, constantly pursued and sometimes wounded elephants. The ones who danced in Paris.

———————

Perhaps the hunted hero now realised that time was catching up with him, that he could no longer flee, because there was nowhere to flee to, that the monogram – and everything it entailed of desire and impotence – engraved on his cigarette case was not his own, and yet it pursued and haunted him like some fateful anagram all over Europe. The initials were etched like a Kilroy into every new central train station. He never dared obliterate them out of a respect for destiny.

It's possible that both men felt threatened, as if in Maud they had invested a great deal of capital which now, via this encounter with fate, had suddenly become associated with certain incalculable risks. Love and passion can have just as much in common, in terms of risk calculations, as strict economics.

Bill, at any rate, was aggressive, like someone on drugs. Henry felt someone slap him on the back. He calmly stubbed out his Gitane in the ashtray on the bar and turned round to meet Bill's ravaged, weary visage. Bill was not the same; he had let his hair grow down over his shoulders, his cheeks were hollow and his skin was pale and rather rough-looking. He would never learn to appreciate daylight, and he still wore his dark glasses, even though they were deep underground in the medieval vault.

'Hey, old pal!' exclaimed Henry, embracing his friend. 'I could hear it was you. I couldn't see you and I didn't dare look to make sure, but I *heard* you playing. You're really great, Bill. You're fucking *great!*'

Bill put a damper on his laughter. He was aggressive, but in that cool kind of way. Yet he still couldn't help laughing, just like a kid who tries to repress his laughter, pretending to be displeased. 'This is too much!' said Bill. 'I recognised you right away. You haven't changed a fucking bit. How many years has it been?'

'Almost five,' said Henry.

'*Five years!* This is too much,' said Bill. 'I'm really cooking tonight. Everything's clicking!'

'You've really got damn good. I haven't heard anything about you in a long time. Maud wrote to me a couple of months ago . . .' said Henry.

'Maud is here, Henry. Maud is *here!*'

'At the Sec?'

'Here in Paris,' shouted Bill.

'So are the two of you a couple right now?' Henry asked.

Bill was high, and to him everything seemed right on that evening at the Bop Sec, but his gestures didn't seem as expansive as before, when back in Stockholm he had walked around bragging about Paris and the great jazz. Perhaps he'd become chastened and hard by the long path of his career, becoming one with his harsh, ruthless, yet beautiful music. Or maybe he simply felt upset when Henry got a remote expression on his face when he mentioned that Maud was in town. Henry's eyes looked so sad. Bill talked about everything that had happened to the Bear Quartet, about their gigs in Denmark and Germany, and he talked about all those things a person wants to talk about when he meets an old friend. But he noticed that Henry wasn't listening, Henry was far away. There was something sombre about his eyes.

'So are the two of you a couple right now?' Henry repeated. 'You and Maud . . .'

'Sigh!' said Bill. 'Well, we have been, off and on.'

'What do you mean by off and on?' repeated Henry.

'Until today, for instance.'

'Did you have a fight?'

'You know how it is when you've got a gig,' said Bill. 'You get a little touchy . . . She was going out to a dinner tonight, with some fucking ambassador. She always has to put in an appearance wherever something is happening. If Paris is burning, she has to see the fire; that's how it is with that woman. She's thirty now, by the way.'

'Time flies,' said Henry.

'But she's probably back at the hotel by now,' said Bill. 'The Hotel Ivry, on Rue de Richelieu. Go over and see her, Henry. You *have* to go.'

Henry still had a totally vacant look in his eyes, and he took a big gulp of beer. 'Why should I?' he said.

'Because she's the most beautiful woman in the world, and you know it.'

'Whatever happened to Eva?'

'Married with children, hitched to a tie-wearing devil like yourself.'

'Get down off your high horse,' said Henry morosely. 'It doesn't suit you.'

'Shit,' said Bill. 'I'm no fucking martyr . . . Have you got a smoke?'

Henry handed over his cigarette case, on which the initials W.S. were engraved in script. Bill read the monogram and laughed.

'Have you met him?' asked Henry.

'Sterner is a real gangster,' said Bill. 'He's one of the world's best *mafiosi*. Maud is his chick. I'm his pimp.' Bill gave a loud, shrill laugh. His teeth were brown and presumably hollow, just like the rest of him. 'But she's the world's best whore, and you know that. It's only popes and real bums that are any good. Popes like Sterner and bums like us.' Bill laughed again, that shrill, hollow laugh, and Henry felt as if he was going to pass out. The dream was reality, and reality was a nightmare.

'You have to go there, Henry,' said Bill. 'The Hotel Ivry, on Rue de Richelieu. It's fate. You were bound to come back some time; it just happened to be tonight. There's nothing stopping you.'

Henry practically passed out, and he muttered something about phoning. 'I should . . . I should ring first,' he said.

Bill looked like a perverse film director. 'What do you mean "ring"?' he said.

'I should ring first,' said Henry.

'Then go ahead!'

'I'm asking you,' said Henry. 'Ring and make sure.'

Bill blew smoke up towards the ceiling, took a couple of swallows of beer from the glass that the corpulent owner had placed in front of him and gave Henry a slap on the back. 'OK, buddy. I'll ring her.'

Still weak in the knees, dazed and aching all over, Henry ordered another beer. The idea that Maud was sitting all alone in a hotel room on Rue de Richelieu and waiting for him was almost a horrible thought; it was too upsetting to be appealing. All of Paris, all of France as a nation was on its way to being overthrown, revolutionised by the striking masses of workers and students who at any moment might seize power and force de Gaulle out. All this ferment was making Paris tremble like a jittery teletype machine, and there sat Henry Morgan in the middle of the whole mess, *Henri le boulevardier*, in a medieval cellar with a vaulted ceiling, and he too was shaking, but for strictly personal reasons. The world in which the big elephants danced no longer had anything to do with him.

Bill came back from the phone booth, smiling, calm and collected. 'It's a go, buddy,' he said, hanging over Henry's shoulder. 'All she could say was "yes, yes, YES". It's all OK. You've got the night to yourselves.'

'So are you just going to hang there on the cross all night long?'

'That's none of your business,' said Bill.

'If that's the way you want it . . .' said Henry. He stuck out his hand and Bill slapped it with the palm of his hand, the way some blacks greet each other. He was having a fucking great evening at the Bop Sec. And if you were having a fucking great evening at the Bop Sec, then a thirty-year-old *hot number* from Stockholm didn't mean a thing. Henry Morgan, on the other hand, was not having a particularly good evening at the Bop Sec.

On that night in late May of '68, Maud and the entire French nation were gripped with breathless suspense. De Gaulle had gone underground – people suspected that for tactical reasons he was hiding in Colombey in order to devise his last, brilliant plan and stage a counter-offensive, to wrest the weapons from the hands of his enemies – and Henry Morgan had likewise gone underground.

Maud was in a room at the Hotel Ivry on Rue de Richelieu, alone and filled with anticipation. She was waiting for a man who never arrived. When Bill rang from the Bop Sec, he had indeed said that Henry was down there at the pub, and the lad looked just like himself, he hadn't changed a bit. He would soon be on his way over to see her, and Maud told Bill to go to hell. No doubt it was fate.

The audience at the Bop Sec was in high spirits as Henry left the place. A poet was reading de Gaulle's obituary to loud cheering, and Bill was having a great night. Maybe he was on his way to making a real breakthrough. A producer had already contacted him. There was talk of cutting a record. Henry wasn't envious, though he felt a bit cheated. He wondered where he might have ended up if he'd stayed home and continued playing with the Bear Quartet. Perhaps he too might have made his international breakthrough that night at the Bop Sec. Perhaps he too might have been offered a record contract, a tour, interviews in *Jazz Hot* and *Jazz Journal*, maybe even in *Down Beat*. What good were these five years on the Continent, this long exile? He had a few pitiful drafts of 'Europa, Disintegrating Fragments'. Maybe it was something new, unique and original, but he had spent so many days and nights merely drifting around with the crowds in London, in Munich, in Rome and in Paris!

He felt dejected and pensive. Meeting Bill again, at the height of his career, talking about Maud and hearing that he hadn't changed a bit in five years – it felt as if he had simply squandered his time, as if he could just as well have been asleep, although the dream was reality. Life was totally meaningless, and down there the Seine flowed past, with its black, cold water. There were no empty bottles, sandwich wrappers, no cardboard boxes or cigarette ends to be seen. The Spree, the Thames, the Isar, the Tiber, the Seine – the rivers were all alike, and they had taken many people with them. So many anonymous lives had sought out these waters, and perhaps death was the only thing at which they had really succeeded.

The May night was warm and vibrant. Henry roamed aimlessly along the Seine staring at the black water – he couldn't just set out for Rue de Richelieu. He lit a cigarette and leaned against the stone wall. He stood still for a long time, trying to reflect on his life, which had never seemed so meaningless as it did at that moment. He felt like some tragic character in an opera, like the musician Schaunard just as he discovers that Mimi isn't in fact merely asleep; she's dead. Curtain. When Henry was feeling out of sorts, he did a proper job of it.

He tried to console himself with the improbable thought that he could be received by Maud at the Hotel Ivry on Rue de Richelieu. She would be standing in the doorway wearing her black kimono with the peacock on the back. Perhaps she had already poured a couple of drinks in order to wipe out the past five years. She would say that he hadn't changed a bit, although perhaps he looked a little thinner. Then they would make love, calm and collected, like two grown-ups, without illusions. Everything would be exactly, precisely like before. His exile like a dream, a totally impossible flight, because there was nowhere to hide on this earth.

The police riot-squad van gently slid to a stop at the pavement, and Henry didn't even have time to react before four cops jumped out and pressed him against the stone wall. He had to stand there with his hands against the wall while they searched him, as if they thought he were carrying cannons in his trousers. They asked for ID, and fortunately Henry had his papers in order, because he knew the methods of the police.

'Where do you live?' one of them asked.

'Live?'

'Don't play dumb!'

This lonely, tragic opera character was completely preoccupied with his brooding and didn't manage to wriggle his way out of the situation, was incapable of wriggling out. The cops cuffed Henry's hands behind his back and led their victim to the van, which was already occupied by five other men about the same age. They all wore baggy white coats, which also looked as if they'd been bought in second-hand shops in Kensington, London. Henry realised that he matched the latest description of the evening.

The interrogation took all night, and Monsieur Morgan managed to control himself quite well. He was allowed to smoke in the waiting room, under the malice-filled eyes of the Law. He bit his fingernails and ran through all the swear-words that he knew in German, English, Italian and Swedish. In spite of everything, there was a certain sweetness about his defeat, a special sort of pleasure in his failure. He had been freed from the Hotel Ivry on Rue de Richelieu. He had been freed from the decision and the anxiety. He claimed that never had Sartre made so much sense to him as on that night.

But the French forces of law and order had now taken charge of Henry, freeing him from all decisions and displaying just the right amount of hostility on the street. He couldn't answer the question: who are you, monsieur? Because on that very evening, after the meeting with Bill at the Bop Sec,

Henry was for once beset by doubt. He had wrestled with the big issues, questioning himself. And just at that moment he was unlucky enough to end up in a police interrogation which, on some other day when he was in the proper frame of mind, he would have managed splendidly, prompting even the most experienced interrogator to question his *own* existence, as well as that of the French police, the EEC, the United Nations, de Gaulle and the entire Cosmos.

But Monsieur Morgan was not at all in top form on that night. He gave answers that were vague, evasive and fumbling to all the intricate questions that were levelled at him about his life and habits. The French police didn't like bohemians or tragic opera characters. But Henry had a bit of luck in the midst of all this misfortune. A zealous rat of an archivist managed to find a folder containing a document stating that this Swede had played a role in connection with a riot at a certain Café Au Coin in Montmartre, during which the world-famous painter Salvador Dalí had been subjected to an attempted assault six months earlier. Monsieur Morgan had been taken in for questioning back then too, but he was later released when the world-famous surrealist explained that the whole commotion was actually a happening that had been planned far in advance. Naturally *Henri le boulevardier* hadn't the faintest idea about all this. Although he wasn't about to tell the police that.

Upon hearing this report, the chief interrogator raised both his eyebrows and his moustache and deferentially offered his apologies, since he now realised that Monsieur Morgan was actually a prominent musician, bohemian and close friend of Salvador Dalí, an artist whom he had always respected. Salvador Dalí praised the Spanish system and Franco, and that was splendid.

Without understanding a thing, Henry was released, departing the arduous interrogation under a shower of apologies, like an honoured guest. It almost came to the point where he was asked for his autograph, although the chief interrogator didn't dare go quite that far. Henry was offered a lift in a patrol car right to his door, but he politely declined. He was no longer especially tired or surprised. In the big world where the elephants dance, anything could happen, although he had exhausted all his possibilities. He felt empty and done with this odyssey. A power struggle had taken place in the umost ethereal strata of society, while a real soul-searching had taken place inside both de Gaulle and Henry Morgan. The latter was now strolling calmly towards Rue Garreau in Montmartre, where he would make himself a Continental breakfast and cast furtive glances at his suitcase. There was no room for any more labels. Kilroy had been everywhere.

His homesickness had left its mark. On the day when a country's postal service is put out of commission, the crisis can be called serious. The post office is supported by duty and devotion; it represents an end in itself, a categorical imperative, nourished by symbolic postage and stamps.

On the day when de Gaulle made his awful comeback and gave his speech about War, Order and Revenge without actually being seen, on that chaotic day a letter dropped through the letterbox addressed to Henry Morgan, 31 Rue Garreau, Paris IXème, France.

It was from Sweden, from Greta Morgan of Brännkyrkagatan in Stockholm. She was worried but didn't really know how to express herself. She enclosed a clipping with a photo from an evening paper, from the student occupation of Kårhus on Holländargatan which had been called off. It actually depicted the foremost revolutionaries, and there with the crowd of leaders was none other than Leo Morgan, standing slightly off to one side.

But that was not what worried Greta most. In fact, she was rather proud that her son was in the newspaper. But Henry's paternal grandfather had died. She couldn't think of any less blunt way to say it. The old dandy Morgonstjärna had never been ill, nor had he exhibited any serious symptoms of weakness other than what was a natural result of old age. He was made of first-class stuff that should have lasted for ninety years, at least. But during this turbulent spring he had stubbornly insisted on walking up the stairs to his flat on the sixth floor, and one day he simply collapsed in the hallway, with blood trickling out of his mouth. Pulmonary oedema, said the family physician, Dr Helmers. Heart attack, wrote Greta. He would be buried in about a week.

Old Morgonstjärna left no living children. His only heirs were his daughter-in-law Greta and his grandsons Henry and Leo. Like the clear-sighted man that he was, he had thought the matter through, and in a desk in his library there was a folder with the blunt heading 'After I am dead'. It contained envelopes addressed to a lawyer's office, to Greta and to Henry and Leo. Henry's envelope was still unopened.

But the most surprising envelope in old Morgonstjärna's folder was the one labelled 'The Crew', written in ink, and 'To Henry Morgan' written in pencil underneath. Greta swore that, in spite of great curiosity, she could not bring herself to open anyone else's letters. Nor did she have either the courage or the desire to send them by post to Henry in Paris. You couldn't trust anyone anymore. The postal workers might go on strike during these turbulent times.

That was enough for Henry. He took care of all his affairs in Paris and made it back to Sweden in time for the funeral. A deserter made his comeback after five long years in exile. He was done with playing around; he had sowed his wild oats, become a grown man, and he would now start on something serious.

THE HOGARTH AFFAIR

(Leo Morgan, 1968–75)

In America hundreds of thousands of people gathered at Woodstock as a manifestation of what was still some sort of counter-culture, an antidote to everything in Western society that involved aggressive imperialism and intellectual colonialism. Sweden wasn't much better, and in 1970 the first celebration was held at Gärdet. Those who lay there in the grass, on their blankets, in their makeshift tents and hammocks, having fun and listening to the music, may recall a very strange man who walked around selling a poetry book. He was dressed as a pirate, with a scarf tied over his long hair, a patch over one eye and a soiled striped shirt that reached to his knees. He was both drunk and high, but he could still recite all his poems by heart, flawlessly.

The poetry collection was called *Façade Climbing and Other Hobbies*, and it was written by John Silver. That old pirate name was, of course, a pseudonym for Leo Morgan. He never explained why he produced that collection on a duplicating machine and self-published it under a pseudonym. Perhaps it was because the poems weren't sufficiently high-class, or because he wanted the book to seem more dangerous and insidious than a book published by the establishment.

Façade Climbing and Other Hobbies is not a very good book, nor is it what is rather naïvely called 'straight protest poems'. Instead, it's a collection of texts characterised more by the difficulty of writing political or so-called 'placard verse' than examples of successful attempts.

The title poem 'Façade Climbing' is a tribute to Harold Lloyd and to all the men who have dared take risks, who were forced by various circumstances to take those very risks while their heroism was constantly being tested. And it was not entirely unexpected that the tallest of all American skyscrapers ends up being in Bolivia, where a hero is forced to race higher and higher, at an ever-increasing pace, until only the sky remains. The allusion is to Che Guevara, and it could be that the idea of comparing him to a comic like Harold Lloyd isn't quite successful, but there is a certain force, a special power of suggestion in the poem that holds the lines together. You read it all in one breath. It's rather nicely done.

The most successful piece in *Façade Climbing and Other Hobbies* is named after the pirate and hence the poet as well: John Silver, pirate, poet, cigarette.

> Smoke your cigarettes slowly, comrade
> They may be our last
> Sing your songs quietly, comrade
> They can never silence us
> For this march there is no map
> The terrain lacks a commander
> No one speaks so purely that we obey
> The points of the compass are always militant
> The points of the compass are never vertical
> We can reach both God and Satan
> Without knowing where we are

Here Leo Morgan, alias John Silver, is making use of the magic of secret codes. The stanzas are occasionally of the type that resistance movements and rebels have used as passwords at important checkpoints – the questions, replies, and statements are to be answered in a certain manner, known only to the initiated. The whole poem is really one long incantation, and this part of the rhythmic phrases quickly became a sort of recited popular song in a number of circles. It was also frequently quoted in pubs and cafés. For much of the early seventies 'The points of the compass are never vertical' could be read in countless men's rooms.

John Silver actually managed to preserve his secret identity and was categorised in various ways as both a 'muddled anarchist' and a 'militant pacifist'. People spoke in the same breath about both D'Annunzio and Ginsberg, and all these traits that were attributed to the poet are indicative of how difficult it is in general to define anything about Leo Morgan.

I myself believe that he – perhaps in a process of self-examination – took his bearings in that gap between his official actions and his private persona, which had always afflicted him, ever since he was a kid and saw that red accordion lying on a rock near the shore. It's so obvious that he starts by trying to write a straight poem with comrades of indefatigable fighting spirit and using a confidently calm tone. But after only a couple of verses he reaches a staccato pitch and gets himself entangled in heavy symbolism that doesn't belong at all in 'placard verse'. It's more Dylan–Cohen than Hill–Brecht. John Silver could applaud Che Guevara and the struggle's character of self-effacing sacrifice, and yet be accused – and perhaps rightly so – of being a selfish and conceited individualist who absolutely refused to submit to anything.

––––––––––

Those who took part in that first Gärdet festival in the summer of 1970, and who don't recall the disreputable pirate who was peddling poetry, might on the other hand be moved to remember the group Harry Lime, which performed very late in the evening and which some people called Sweden's *real* underground band. That first celebration at Gärdet was a successful show insofar as the quality of the music was subordinate to the joy of playing. It was the politics of the will that counted. In other words, no one was going to prevent the Harry Lime Group from playing. Harry Lime existed only for that one evening. The group consisted of Verner Hansson and Stene Forman on guitar, Nina Negg doing the vocals and tambourine, Leo Morgan as solo poet and a rhythm section that I haven't been able to identify. So many people have disappeared from the scene. The group was formed at Stene's initiative when he heard about the planned festival. Harry Lime was created for a single performance, like a truly exclusive supergroup made up of irreconcilable stars, rather as if the Beatles were resurrected for one night.

It was probably some time in the spring that Stene – the former Provie with the amazing laugh – contacted Leo to check out the situation, as he said. Stene sounded like Lazarus rising up from his grave. They hadn't spoken to or seen each other in years. Leo was now living with Henry because their paternal grandfather had passed away two years earlier, and Henry had taken over the whole show at Hornsgatan. Leo was studying philosophy, and for a brief and intense period of time he'd been living a somewhat regular life.

In any case, Stene told him about the planned festival at Gärdet and said that he was thinking of putting together a band, a real underground band that is. Stene was working for one of the three weekly magazines owned by his father. It was called *Blixt*, but it's no longer in operation. He also kept up with the American magazines, which discussed the new crop of underground bands. Stene wanted Leo to put together some good lyrics, because this called for something that was a bit intellectual. And Leo couldn't deny that he had quite a few things lying around.

But there was only one hitch: they had to find Verner Hansson and Nina Negg. Leo thought they might still be living in Stene's enormous building on Karlbergsvägen, but they had actually both disappeared. Things had gone to hell for both Verner and Nina.

Two years earlier, Nina had told Leo to get lost – he was free to choose how. It was the spring of '68, that legendary spring when the whole world was in uproar and mighty statesmen, kings, presidents and ministers lay awake praying that God would punish those disobedient students. Leo had enrolled at the university to study philosophy. Verner was in a different department, and mysteriously, they had both passed their preliminary exams even though they never put much effort into studying. Yet this prompted all the more frequent theorising at the cafés. They questioned the university reforms of U-68 and the system and the means of production and everything else that could be called into question. This pleased Nina Negg. Out of pure instinct she had always questioned everything and everyone. She had never needed to be an intellectual, nor did she plan to become one.

They all lived in a huge flat in Stockholm that Stene Forman had arranged on Karlbergsvägen, right near Corso, Noras and Kårhuset, where the notorious occupations would soon take place. This was actually the golden age of the neighbourhood. Stene Forman had just started as a hack writer for *Blixt*, and he was making good money. Nina Negg took odd jobs here and there, and Verner and Leo were in charge of everything that was 'deep'. For the most part, this depth of thought was expressed in lengthy bacchanals that could go on for several days.

Nina was actually the only one of them who did anything pragmatic, who undertook any practical work in the struggle that the students and workers supposedly shared. When the agitated reports from Tokyo, Berlin, San Francisco and Paris started filling the newspapers, she tore out big pictures and taped them to all the walls in that huge flat. She went to all the demonstrations, toiled over duplicating machines, helped distribute leaflets and attended conferences when new manifestos were drawn up. In spite of the fact that she wasn't especially affected by whether the UKAS reform was implemented or not, she sympathised with those who were rebelling, because Power was Power, after all. She had almost stopped swearing; her vocabulary now included numerous revolutionary slogans that she enjoyed pounding into Leo's head with great proficiency.

But he was faithful to his disloyalty. That was what had brought them together on a mangy sofa in a draughty attic room long ago. Leo never felt at home in the organised struggle. He *did his thing*, as he said, preferring to sit and drink or read Hegel rather than take the German dialectic's successors at their word. Disloyalty as a beautiful art – that was Leo Morgan's motto.

When the actual occupation took place, neither Leo nor Verner was present. They had been out roaming among the crypto-fascists in Spök Park a couple of times, and as luck would have it, Stene Forman, Verner and Leo all ended up in a photo on the front page of an evening paper as background for one of the chief ideologues of the occupation. But during the occupation itself they were going through a period of utterly pointless drinking. Leo was doing his best to run through the small inheritance from his grandfather quickly. Verner's stamp collection had long since lost all value. He had drunk and smoked away every little philatelic rarity, one after the other, secretively and with exactly the sort of precision that an old chess player ought to display. No one ever dared get to the bottom of what the two men were actually doing during those periods. They would retreat from everyone, either together or separately, with a substantial battery of bottles and drink them in profound silence, as if in some sort of desperate devotion, a demonic requiem mass for the innermost circle.

They were not ashamed of themselves, they *did their thing* and observed the world *von oben*, from above, or at least that was how Nina viewed it. She thought they were fucking quitters, both of them. They got out of serving in the military and were granted exemptions; they got out of everything. They inherited money and ate their meals at home with their mothers whenever they were short of cash. They were spoilt little brats, especially Leo. All his fucking poems, as well as his lovely talk about underdeveloped countries, imperialism and the global conscience were just empty words. All his talk about alternative Christmas Eve celebrations and cosmic love was nothing but putrid piss. He cared about only one thing in life, and that was himself. The little child prodigy loved only himself, yet he didn't realise that the child prodigy had died years ago and that the myth was no longer valid. It was time to wake up, now that the whole world was awake and on its feet. But that wasn't quite right; even Nina Negg could see that. It was too late to wake up. The party was already over.

The big blow-up occurred at the end of May in '68 when the occupation was called off, the revolt in France ended with de Gaulle's unbelievable victory, and everyone was immensely tired. Nina Negg had fallen in love with Stene Forman, and when he kept on bringing home a steady stream of women, it got to be too much for her. Nina struck back and literally tossed Leo out onto the street. He would have to move in with Henry on Hornsgatan. Verner sided with Nina, and Leo turned his back on both of them. He was planning to *do his thing*.

The result of this dramatic confrontation, recounted here in an extremely fragmented version, was that Nina went abroad that summer, to Amsterdam, the Mecca of the drug culture. She had been heading in that direction for years, and finally she set off. It was the beginning of her wandering towards Hades. Verner underwent various cataclysms, and rumour had it that during one confusing period he tried to get accepted by a commune of rebels – this was back when the Rebel Movement was running rampant – but the group quickly threw out this individualist. And that was no doubt the definitive end to Verner's very obscure political career. Soon he too – some time after the big mining strike in '69 – would come to a realisation that his studies were going nowhere. He needed to venture out onto the paths of life. A hard rain was going to fall.

———————

Those who were still there, late on the night of the first Gärdet Festival in 1970, got to see a true underground band called the Harry Lime Group, named after Graham Greene's sewer hero no. 1 from the forties.

Late that night Stene Forman – that tireless producer of unforgettable happenings – lined up a few guys as back-up musicians, with Verner on guitar, Leo as the solo poet, and the feverish Nina as vocalist. A miracle had occurred. In the best Baden-Powell style, Stene, with Leo right on his heels, had combed the ungodly dense jungle known as The Old Swamp and fished out both Nina Negg and Verner Hansson from a disgusting shithole on Tunnelgatan – the place was stinking of sewage from a broken toilet, mouldy food and rotting mattresses. He transported the two wrecks home, fattened them up and got them off drugs with the help of some private experts. As a newspaperman he knew all sorts of markets inside and out. It became a sort of reconciliation at Stene's place over on Karlbergsvägen. Nina's weary eyes became a little less weary, and after a couple of days her marvellous epithets slowly began to come to life. Verner's delirium was transformed into a period of intense creativity – he had never in his life held a guitar, but he could play three gnarly chords like no one else had ever done. It started to seem like old times again, and Leo churned out one hit song after another. Stene took care of the administrative tasks.

I was present that night at Gärdet, and I remember the Harry Lime Group very well, especially the singer with the weary eyes. She moved in a special way, jerky and disjointed like a marionette with tangled strings. The back-up musicians sounded heavy and harsh, false and awful, but that didn't matter. Several of the songs actually enjoyed a certain success. 'Military Service Mind' was a protest song à la Country Joe & The Fish. The refrain went like this: 'The generals can always buy / Some big and strong and bloody guy / But we will make it hard to find / A Military Service Mind . . .' And here and there the audience could actually be heard singing along with the words.

The song 'Vinyl Figureheads' had a hallucinogenic tune and a special background that was indicative of Leo's life during the period between *Sanctimonious Cows* and *Façade Climbing and Other Hobbies*. It was probably late in the autumn of '67, and Leo had just started studying philosophy at the university. That was a completely understandable choice, since philosophy was Leo's proper element. The positivism of the natural sciences seemed more and more like an offshoot of a Power, and Leo wanted to be subversive. Poetry and philosophy are in many ways the same thing. Great, true poetry is a subcontractor for philosophy: the poets deliver the raw material, a sort of theoretical cement for the builders of philosophical systems, who then lock in and fix the concepts' bricks in their cathedrals and their ladders to heaven. Leo Morgan felt like an architect without a blueprint – he had to become a philosopher.

But on a cold and nasty day during that autumn he felt tired of everything that had to do with books. He put on his flea-bitten Afghan waistcoat and went down to sit on Stockholmsterrassen above Sergels Torg, where it was amusing to watch the cars. Cautiously, seeming a bit clumsy and fumbling, they would keep to the right in the roundabout and then occasionally lose

273

their heads and crash into each other. That was, of course, excellent entertainment. Leo was not feeling at all well that day because he was weighed
down by hash, and he felt burned out from booze; nothing gave him any
peace. He and Nina had *meditated* together and read the *Bhagavad Gita* and
Hesse and other serene things that you could read about the East, but none
of it had stuck with Leo. Nina was smoking a lot, and she thought that Leo
was too cold. He wasn't even any different when he got drunk. She couldn't
stand to see his eyes grow dark and rigid, disappearing into some inaccessible realm. It was driving her crazy. They were locked in a horrible, vicious
circle.

On this cold and nasty day he was now sitting on Stockholmsterrassen,
shivering and feeling completely done in. When Nina turned up she saw at
once that he was thoroughly depressed. She tried to entice him with tea and
coffee and aspirin and all sorts of other things. But nothing did any good.
Finally she took out a tiny green pill, which she ordered him to take. She
didn't tell him what it was, but she insisted that it would help. He would be
cool if he took this pill, which was reliable goods.

For once Leo gave in and swallowed the pill. He slouched in his chair,
closed his eyes, and began waiting for the drug to take effect. It took a long
time. He watched the traffic driving on the right, and gradually the cars started
moving slower and slower, as if they were circling inside a sunny aquarium.
The headlights looked the way they did on the postcards that Henry had
sent of London and Paris 'by night' – photographs taken at night using a
time-exposure that made the lights turn into long streaks, neon-like strands
winding through dark and slippery streets. Stockholm fell silent, and the
traffic was soon flowing so slowly that all movement became imperceptible.
The whole city seemed to pulsate in time with his own heart, the asphalt
and cement were warm and mute and utterly still. Leo blinked his eyes but
couldn't keep them open. He disappeared into a warm and beautiful trance.

He may have shuffled out to the street on his own, or else someone called
the police and hauled him out to the street. People may have been annoyed
with him because he looked so typical with his long, greasy hair, his thin
droopy moustache, and his ratty Afghan waistcoat. The only thing he clearly
remembered was that a couple of police officers put him on a bench inside
a van, and he apparently resisted because a cop twisted one of his arms
behind his back to make him lie still and stay calm. And he did stay calm;
he didn't feel a thing. He didn't hurt, but he was feeling extremely hot. He

began to regain his sense of smell, and the van smelled of vinyl, a disgusting, sticky, sweaty, and filthy vinyl. Disgusting vinyl can have a singularly revolting smell, and Leo drank in that smell and then returned to his delightful trance.

The next time he awoke he smelled the vinyl again, but this time even stronger. He was lying motionless, taking in that vinyl odour, and with infinite caution he opened his eyelids. He was staring at a wall, lying practically naked under a blanket. Gradually he realised that he had been placed in the drunk tank over in Klara.

Using his impressions from this experience when the police took him into temporary custody – they had treated him much better than he thought they would treat people of his ilk – he composed the song 'Vinyl Figureheads' a couple of years later.

> You are the vinyl figureheads of the SS *Sweden*
> You try to force me into your social incubator
> Your raised batons are an inverted command
> A white inclamation point
> But I will never come back in
> But we will never come back in

That was the incorrigibly individualistic credo that was presumably received with both praise and criticism at Gärdet. At any rate, the words made a certain impression on me, and I recall that Nina joined in to sing the phrase 'But we will never come back in' with a fierce, agitated voice that left very little room for doubt. There was also a deep sense of tragedy behind that voice, so proudly decadent, because she never did come back in. For the brief future that remained to her, Nina was a total outcast, at the mercy of the demonic interests that would profit from her cravings.

Anyway, the Harry Lime Group completed its performance with its honour intact. The group would never perform again. Not even an enthusiast like Stene Forman could keep Nina and Verner on their feet.

––––––––––

In 1974 another music festival was held, a little Woodstock, at Gärdet in Stockholm. The event was accused of being 'too establishment'. The pioneering appetite for experimentation was supposedly gone; this time it was standardised lyrics and dry professionalism that counted. What was initially an enthusiastic counter-culture had been bought out by the establishment and become stereotyped, conformist and dull. The movement had dispersed in various directions; some had gone institutional, while others had dared to 'come back in' to use the words of Harry Lime. The group was not revived for that festival, and no one knew whether there would even have been a slot for it. Four awful years had passed, and time had quite simply made a revival of the Harry Lime Group impossible.

A couple of years earlier, in '71, Leo had run into Nina downtown. They were both demonstrating to save the elm trees in the King's Garden, and they saw each other on Fregatten on a few nights, but then she disappeared once again. Leo immersed himself in his studies and didn't know what happened to her. In the spring of '73 he learned that she had been found dead of an overdose over in Söder. On that very day Leo was supposed to take part in a big poetry festival in Gamla Riksdagshuset – dozens of more or less well-known poets were going to read from their work, and he had been looking forward to being remembered – but he ended up not going. No one knew where he went. He was gone for several days and came back in a deplorable state. That was his way of saying goodbye to Nina Negg.

At about the same time, in the spring of '73, Verner was committed to a detox centre for alcoholics. There he was cleaned up and dried out, fattened up and processed, only to end up under house arrest a few months later. His stern mother met him at the door and told him that she'd damn well had enough of all this nonsense. Then she dragged home her twenty-eight-year-old wreck of a son and locked him in his childhood room, which was filled with worthless stamps. Rumour has it that he's still sitting there today.

People were dropping like flies, right and left; many were gone by the summer of Gärdet '74. The only reason even to mention the festival was that it fundamentally changed Leo Morgan's life. No one can say with certainty what he was actually doing during this period. He was still enrolled at the university to study philosophy, but the curriculum and pace were all his own. Leo Morgan *did his thing*, no matter what he was involved in. He had polemicised about both Marxists and Wittgenstein adherents, and no one knew where he stood. At one point – when he was taken under the wings of an eccentric

professor – he became preoccupied with trying to establish a kind of nomen-
clature for the one hundred most important concepts in Western philosophy,
from Thale's '*archê*' to Sartre's '*être*'. This Jacob-style wrestling match was said
to have ended in total confusion, prompting Leo to retreat and disappear
again, moving out to or into a periphery known only to himself, not to anyone
else. At least half of the six years that Leo spent at the university could be
categorised as squandered time. He spent days, weeks and months in a state
of utter passivity, merely lying on his bed, staring at the ceiling, whistling
monotonous melodies, and living on next to nothing. Maybe he had adopted
some type of Eastern meditation and entered another world in which time
and space no longer had any meaning.

He had set up for his own use part of his grandfather's enormous flat on
Hornsgatan – which in practical terms meant getting rid of most of the
furnishings. He shared the hallway and kitchen with his brother. Leo's section
consisted of two small but pleasant rooms with windows facing the street.
Even so, Henry felt that his privacy was being disturbed. At that time he was
just completing his 'Europa, Disintegrating Fragments' and needed all the
quiet in the world to finish the piece. It was the fruit of five long years in
exile – Henry Morgan's magnum opus.

Yet Henry was at his most friendly and considerate when Leo lay on his
bed, whistling. Presumably this show of consideration was not entirely altruistic. Henry was a man of action, an enterprising man in his prime, and he
couldn't stand people who simply drifted. Perhaps he was frightened by Leo's
inaccessible state, the same way he would be scared of a child with mysteriously piercing eyes. Henry went around babbling to himself all day long,
and every morning he pinned up his list, describing everything he had to do,
point by point, on that particular day. He could just as well have made carbon
copies, because the lists were exactly the same, down to the very last detail.
Henry's life was filled with singularly uniform kinds of work – which in Leo's
eyes were meaningless – and it would have sufficed to use one list starting
on the first of January and continuing for the remaining 364 days of the
year.

Henry had come back to Sweden and to Stockholm as a man who was
totally unrecognisable and yet more grown up. His desertion from the Swedish
army had unofficially fallen outside the statute of limitations. He had returned
to Stockholm, where everything seemed to slip out of his hands. He wanted
to believe that everything had stood still, impatiently waiting for Henry

277

Morgan's comeback, but that was not at all what had happened. The city he remembered as his home town had changed drastically. Whole neighbourhoods, whole sections of the city had been torn down and levelled; the Klara district resembled a ruin, motorways cut through downtown and a year earlier the last tram had been taken out of service. All his friends had settled down. Some of them had already completed their education and were now married with children; they had a good salary and a regulated life with brilliant prospects for the future. Jazz was practically dead, and no one even talked about Dixieland anymore, except with a slightly ironic, nostalgic smile on their lips. Even the Bear Quartet was no more than a faded memory. One member had died, another had become a studio musician for top Swedish bands, and Bill himself was still on the Continent, in the midst of what was called an international breakthrough.

Stockholm had been betrayed and misappropriated; it was trying to live up to something that *Henri le citoyen du monde* didn't fully understand. He had seen the real metropolises, after all, the real cities in Germany, England and France. Stockholm could never be their equal; even trying seemed ridiculous. But he would never be part of life there again. He was passé, an anachronism. Whenever he ran into old friends, he couldn't accept them as they were; he always wanted to view them as they had once been. This made everyone furious, and they pushed him away. Only Willis down at the Europa Athletic Club was the same as ever.

Henry simply could not accept change or renewal, and he grew more and more isolated in that old flat on Hornsgatan where the cigar smoke of his paternal grandfather still clung to the heavy curtains. He tried to tell stories about the big world to his brother, but Leo just got bored. He thought that Henry was living in a fantasy world, a pseudo-existence. Henry could never convince him otherwise.

They got on each other's nerves, those Morgan brothers. Leo *did his thing*, and Henry fulfilled his obligations. He was trying to finish 'Europa, Disintegrating Fragments' – music that left his brother cold – while he continued the digging down in the cellar. Leo thought the whole endeavour so naïve that it made him feel like crying. Yet Henry was forced to keep on, since it was a requirement for receiving his allowance. Leo probably felt bitter because he had squandered every öre of his own inheritance in a matter of months. He couldn't comprehend why Henry had to pretend, at any cost, that there actually was something to dig up. Leo tried to open Henry's dreamy blue eyes and get him to realise that the whole thing was nothing but play-acting, that he was really as much a fool as the Philatelist, Wolf-Larsson, the Flask and the other lads down at the Fence Queen's shop. But Henry would fly into a rage; he refused to tolerate such low blows, nor would he discuss the subject. There were rules and certain things that a person simply had to accept. End of discussion.

Quarrels ensued. Henry nagged at Leo like a crotchety old landlady, pointing out every mistake and every failure on his part to keep things neat and clean. He would like nothing better than for Leo to pack up and clear out. They yelled at each other . . . shouted and screamed, and then Henry would inevitably start to bawl. He felt so lonely. He didn't want to live alone. He was an artist, after all.

Yet when Henry saw his little child-prodigy brother lying there, seemingly paralysed by his talents, he would do an about-face and suddenly behave as nicely and considerately as he could. He brought tea to Leo in bed and asked him what he wanted for lunch and dinner; he took care of his brother as if he were an ailing and beloved spouse. He would go into Leo's room and sit down on the edge of the bed and tell him stories, wearing out the Brahman with endless tales and adventures from the Big World. He was thinking of venturing out into the world again because it was so hard for an artist to breathe in Sweden. But Leo knew that Henry was home to stay. Henry would never leave Sweden again.

These periods of utter passivity were always followed by the exact opposite – long frenetic spells of working, reading, drinking and copulating. During Leo's extroverted periods, Henry's attitude would change completely. He tried to be moralistic, stern and admonishing. And he was deeply bitter whenever he saw that none of his ploys had any effect on Leo. Not even dastardly tricks or threats of eviction did any good.

During that summer of '74, Leo Morgan was apparently in a bright period of productivity and somewhat extroverted socialising. He had completed a work that was printed as a booklet by a small press specialising in philosophy. It was called *Curiosity, Inquisitiveness and Knowledge*, which was clearly a moderately inflammatory title. We will have occasion to return to this modest work a little later, since it would presumably end up being his last achievement in book form. On a couple of occasions he had seen Eva Eld again – his devoted admirer from his school days – and it's quite likely that they also had sexual intercourse. Leo Morgan sowed his wild oats as often as opportunities presented themselves, which was quite frequently since he managed to arouse in women a peculiar protective instinct – that is, until they realised that he really had no need of their protection. Rather, they were the ones who needed to be protected from him.

But to get back to the festival at Gärdet. Leo was presumably feeling a bit lonely. The old gang from the past had split up – they had either died or vanished. Time had taken a harsh toll, and people had been dropping out right and left. But no one could defeat Stene Forman. He circulated among the crowds of people, lofty as an eagle, weary and haggard, feeling the pressure of bad business deals, high overheads and constant arguments at the weekly magazine *Blixt*, which was being forced into more and more salacious territory just to keep its readers.

So Leo happened to run into Stene Forman among all the festival booths and guitars, the bongo drums and peace pipes, and Stene practically fell upon Leo with joy. The famous laugh was gone – it now sounded more like a heavy wheeze – but he was glad to see Leo still alive, as he said. Leo couldn't hide his own delight, and they tried not to talk about the past. They had grown so much older, more mature and wiser.

————

The weekly magazine *Blixt* – which was shut down in the autumn of '75 – was a typical men's publication that existed in the shadow of the publications put out by the major newspapers. Nicely enough, it lacked any hint of sex or pornography. That was why things went wrong. The paper was the life work of Stene Forman's father, and it would have celebrated its thirtieth anniversary if only it had survived one more year. But Stene's father – who, against all odds, had founded three publications – was a lone wolf who went against the current and refused to surrender to the demands of a new era as long as he was in charge. Yet by the early seventies he was old and worn out, so in '73 his son took full control. Stene had grown up in the industry, chasing down news stories while he was still in short trousers, and he had shown a natural talent for the business. He continued in his father's footsteps during what was a very propitious time. The year 1973 was a remarkably good one for the weekly magazines. They didn't even have to go looking for news; it just came pouring in. Stene enjoyed major coups with the death of the old king, the Norrmalmstorg drama, and a series of articles following in the wake of the IB Affair. He himself wrote a huge 'I was there' report from Norrmalmstorg, which evoked a certain acclaim even far beyond the less respected journalist cadres of the weeklies. An excerpt was translated for readers of the American magazine *Esquire*, which was not something that happened to many Swedish reporters, fashionable as it was to encourage investigative journalism, new journalism and whatever else people liked to call the age-old muck-raking from the nineteenth century. At any rate, the size of *Blixt*'s circulation rose appreciably during that year, reaching an all-time record of 147,000 in November '73. The magazine's success was, of course, celebrated with appropriate tributes at well-known restaurants, and Stene Forman – like every father's son – did not skimp on the food. He had become part of the system.

He had been a Provie and a hippie; he had tried just about everything. But the long and the short of it was that he'd had a large number of children with a somewhat smaller number of women, and he'd put a damper on his laughter. That tremendous, wild, almost absurd laugh from his youth in the sixties had now become a heavy rasping that bore witness to complications. His difficult position was widely known and shamelessly exploited by the forces of the free market which, for a certain compensation, were allowed to plant 'news' in *Blixt*. This news had to do with reporting that competitors' products – such as exercise equipment, charter trips and new car models – were deadly dangerous or of inferior quality. It was an old gimmick – maligning other products by manipulating the facts. In other words, Stene Forman had become corrupted, albeit no more corrupted than other editors-in-chief, as he was always eager to point out. If you wanted to play the game, you had to accept the consequences. Eat or be eaten. Among all the accountants, corporate trouble-shooters and publication experts who were called in to rescue the small magazine company, the editor-in-chief was considered a hothead and crazy man. The magazine's success – exactly as the experts had predicted in their highly scientific prognoses and calculations – was only temporary. A duckpond like Sweden couldn't provide dead kings, bank dramas and espionage affairs more than once a decade. As soon as the champagne bubbles evaporated the circulation figures were back down to disastrous levels. The threat of closure cast a shadow over the editorial offices on Norr Mälarstrand, and the magazine's printing bills began rising towards amounts that augured bankruptcy. Stene Forman was thinking of scuttling the ship. The two other trade publications – also the work of his father –

were devoted to electronics and antiques and could be saved through various efforts. But *Blixt* was a defenceless little animal without claws, vulnerable in a jungle of dragons and behemoths. Forman persistently refused to capitulate – which would have meant focusing on pornography – because he didn't want to betray his father's ideals. At least not as long as the old man was alive. It was a question of honour and conscience, he claimed.

This made Stene Forman into a sort of ethical model for a number of radical groups who supported all private enterprise that didn't try to be a monopoly. Stene became the subject of a major interview in *FiB/Kulturfront*, in which he complained long and loud about the shallowness and moral decline of the magazine world. He himself had clean, absolutely lily-white hands, which he held up as if he were being robbed in the photo accompanying the interview, apparently without any sense of irony. His heart was with the left, as it always had been. But in business the law of the jungle ruled, along with trial and error. It was a matter of fighting your way through by constantly using new equipment, as well as coming up with fresh new ideas. During the continual, chaotic brainstorming sessions in the *Blixt* editorial offices on Norr Mälarstrand – with creative and improvisational forces specially summoned from various other professions – Stene Forman tried to be dynamic and formulate a new image, a new drive that would save the publication from death by suffocation. But everyone was tired. The life had gone out of the magazine. Forman was not lacking in a dash of charisma, but that was not enough. At any rate, it was during just such a brainstorming session that Stene – all on his own – came up with an idea that might have ended up in the wastebasket among all the other hackneyed ideas if it hadn't included two old obsessions of his from the past, namely Leo Morgan and Verner Hansson.

———

Restaurant Salzers was located on John Ericssonsgatan, between Hantverkargatan and Norr Mälarstrand, not far from the editorial offices of *Blixt*. Leo Morgan turned up there one day in the new year of '75, and the maître d' very politely showed him to a table that had been reserved under editor Forman's name. It was a secluded table intended for confidential conversations, and Stene was sitting there waiting, the ashtray in front of him already half full. He stood up at once and greeted Leo with enthusiasm.

This was meant to be a proper lunch, and Leo was urged to select whatever he wanted from the menu. When their orders were taken, Leo leafed absent-mindedly through the latest issue of *Blixt*, in which a new model car was reported to have a countless number of defects. The headline said: SAFETY KILLS THE POOR. Stene had presumably made a real pile on that story.

Stene seemed to be in high spirits, and Leo was naturally curious since the editor had rung him up to say this was urgent. He had an idea that he wanted Leo to hear. Leo was the only one whose advice he trusted, the only one who had not already been compromised with a clutch of fiascos in the business.

This was actually true of Verner too, but they hadn't seen Verner for several years now. He was still under strict house arrest at his old mother's flat; he was not allowed to go out, nor did he wish to. She couldn't stop him from boozing, but apparently she preferred him to do it under her supervision. It was the strangest relationship imaginable. Pure Ingmar Bergman, in Stene's opinion.

But the most peculiar thing of all was that Verner had been ringing Stene nearly every day lately, dead drunk on the phone, to babble away about his dad 'Hansson', as he called him. He had never stopped fantasising about his father, even though he'd disappeared in 1944, before Verner was even born, and maybe that was why he had turned out the way he did. His mother refused to say a word; she was as silent as the grave. All she would say was that the man had left, and that was the end of it. When Verner was a kid, he had imagined that his father owned an island in the South Pacific and that he would go there someday when he grew up. By now Verner had been grown up for a good ten years, but he still hadn't gone there. Instead he had perpetually cultivated an interest in similar disappearances, and in his present situation he had apparently taken up this research again. Or maybe his mother had disclosed something that she had been keeping secret, accidentally letting something slip that prompted Verner to return to those same old, worn-out paths.

So he had been ringing Stene Forman every day, because Stene had plenty of contacts, after all, and he had babbled on about some old journalist supposedly named Hogarth, who apparently had information about the case. Stene had tried to calm Verner – who was always very drunk – assuring him that he would check it out, thanking him for the tip, and promising to be in touch. Stene Forman hadn't really paid much attention to these phone calls until he was suddenly struck by a brilliant idea.

He happened to know who this Hogarth was – the old journalist actually did exist in the real world – and he realised that there might be something to what Verner was saying. Old Edvard Hogarth was even something of a legend among serious journalists. He had been a bright star in the thirties and forties, but he had displayed such good foresight that he cut short his career long before the business became sullied by the depraved filth of the times.

Leo couldn't really see how he came into the picture or what the idea was behind this meeting. He had known for a long time that Verner was under house arrest and that he spent his days drinking and leafing through albums of worthless stamps and trying to solve classic chess problems. Nor was it a surprise that Verner was also attempting to formulate theories about missing persons. If he thought he had found some trace of his father at this late date, that was not something Leo was going to get into.

Stene Forman wheezed and stubbed out his fifteenth cigarette as an exquisite salmon trout was served after a good-sized prawn cocktail. They tasted the fish, drank a toast with a light white wine and then Forman explained that his idea had to do with starting a series of articles about these missing persons. All the unsolved cases and mysteries that the most experienced detectives on the police force, the inspectors and investigators, had failed to solve. Of course this was not an original idea; this type of material could always be found in any weekly magazine. Readers loved mysteries, enigmas and unsolved crimes. People wanted a bit of speculation, that's just how it was. But the difference was that *Blixt* would not simply speculate – *Blixt* would be so bold as to present the truth, the whole truth and nothing but the truth. Furthermore – and this was the humanitarian core of the whole matter – they would really find out whatever they could about Verner Hansson's father, they would redress the wrongs of the innocent, restore contacts that had seemingly been lost for good, release those who were wrongfully committed and so on, *ad infinitum*.

And this was where Leo came into the picture – he was the one who would do the writing! Leo swallowed a piece of salmon trout the wrong way and had a classic coughing fit. He took a gulp of white wine and watched with tear-filled eyes as Forman lit a cigarette – he didn't much feel like eating – his expression both proud and entreating at the same time. He waited nervously, full of anticipation, for Leo's response.

The year 1975 had started off very well for Leo Morgan, especially for the poet. The philosopher had been forced to retreat indefinitely in favour of the poet, who had a premonition of a new lyrical 'ejaculation'. He began a rough draft in a black workbook – it's still there among the rubbish in the flat – for a long suite called *Autopsy, First Suite, Jan. '75*. The word 'autopsy' is derived from the Greek, meaning 'a seeing for oneself', or 'post-mortem', which prepares the way for certain associations. The draft is interspersed with quotes and literary gems from ancient philosophical documents and from Robert Musil's *The Man Without Qualities*. As far as I can judge – it's well known that peeking at other people's workbooks is a dubious pleasure, and you never allow yourself the proper tranquillity to do a thorough study of the material – *Autopsy* could definitely have been Leo Morgan's break-through and led to recognition even from the most stringent arbiters of taste. One recurring theme is the subject–object relationship, the insistence of human beings to regard, for instance, a dead body as a 'person', a creature with certain characteristics, which in fact involves a persistent inability to regard oneself as an object. A human being becomes a corpse: a semantic distinction that Leo elevated to an all-embracing perspective. 'Life's forms, an infinity of combinations, / predestined revolutions, / glide silently into the rock / with the water foaming all around as pain. / Death is one and the same crystal / deep inside the highest mountain . . .' This is a passage that I couldn't resist stealing.

Perhaps *Autopsy* would have been completed during that winter in early 1975 if the demiurge Stene Forman hadn't stepped in and presented the idea about Verner Hansson and the mysterious disappearance of his father. The flat on Hornsgatan provided plenty of peace and quiet for Leo's work, and Henry had even encouraged him to write by providing various inducements such as an answering machine and flexible hours for mealtimes. But *Autopsy* was never completed; it remains today only a fragment in a workbook, which Leo would soon abandon in favour of something entirely different.

Stene Forman undoubtedly had a touch of charisma that did not leave Leo unaffected during that lunch at Salzers. Leo had not given any specific sort of answer; he remained basically sceptical and had a hard time imagining himself as a co-worker at *Blixt*. He would forever consider it a disgrace, and he wanted to remain unsullied.

Nevertheless, he was impressed by the idea itself. Stene jabbered on about what a *scoop* they could produce together if everything worked out. There might be big journalism prizes for investigative reporting in the service of humanity, sky-high circulation figures, fat salaries and so on. But for the time being they had to keep the lid on it; this could be *hot stuff* and it was absolutely *off the record*, as they said in the White House. Leo was not a professional, and he'd have to learn that things that were discovered in this business could be *off the record*, and then it was important to keep your trap shut. Everything that Stene had told him would stay between the two of them. Leo couldn't leak a word or that would be the end of the entire matter.

In spite of his exhaustion, Stene was still a great producer and stage-setter of various events that were more or less scandalous. He could undeniably blow things up to impressive and grotesque proportions, all with that charming con-artist glint in his eye. It didn't take long before the editor-in-chief received a phone call from Leo in which the poet expressed his willingness to give it a try. He would make contact with that old guy Hogarth, *off the record*, not for the sake of the money or the glory but for the sake of Verner Hansson. Maybe Verner would be OK again if he found out what had become of his father. Who knew? Maybe that was all he needed.

So it was Leo Morgan in the guise of Jesus who picked up the phone one day in March 1975 and dialled the unlisted number that Stene Forman had provided for the old journalist Edvard Hogarth. Leo did it solely for Verner's sake; the Prodigal Son had to be saved.

But the voice that rattled off his telephone number, one digit after the other, in response – like a nervous thief in the process of memorising a code in a bank vault – sounded more as if the battle were already over. Edvard Hogarth was obviously a very old man, and – when Leo introduced himself and explained what he wanted – he seemed only moderately interested, if not totally uninterested, in meeting anyone for a chat.

Leo made a real effort, trying to sound extremely polite on the phone. He said that Stene Forman spoke very highly of Mr Hogarth's work over the years. Oh yes, Hogarth knew Stene Forman all right, and in particular his brilliant father. The old man thought the boy seemed quite promising, but he hadn't kept up with their activities for a very long time. The name *Blixt* was no guarantee of any journalistic ethical revolt of tremendous proportions, but it offered an important counterweight to the monopoly.

The old man was just on the verge of saying goodbye and hanging up when Leo mentioned something about the 'Hansson case', which was the real reason for his call.

Then all hell broke loose. At first the old man was silent on the other end of the line. This is clearly a sore subject, Leo probably thought. Staying calm and collected, he said that he knew Verner Hansson, the son of the missing man, and for all these years he'd been interested in finding out what had really happened in 1944 when the man so ignominiously vanished from sight. Leo went on, laying out the text and displaying a rare eloquence until the old man interrupted him.

Edvard Hogarth had evidently been sitting there, getting all worked up, because now he suddenly launched into a sulphurous speech about the fact that he'd been working on that 'affair' for over ten years, and that 'you' or 'they' were damn well not going to shut him up. This was 'blackmail', and it would be over his dead body that 'you' or 'they' would keep him quiet.

Then the man slammed down the phone.

―――――――――

'Death is a precious stone, a frogfish / a hardening, with a seductive promise of peace . . .' That was a poetic note in Leo's workbook from his *Autopsy* period. This story is filled with strange things, and the note about the frogfish is just one of them.

Stene Forman had tossed out a hook, and Leo Morgan had taken the bait. He, in turn, had tossed out a hook, and Edvard Hogarth had taken the bait. Staying with these purely marine metaphors: it was probably more a question of a net than a fishing line. Leo wasn't merely fastened to a hook; he had already been caught in a huge net with incalculable offshoots throughout all of society, and he didn't even know it. That's what makes the note about the frogfish so strange.

A frogfish is called *Antennarius commersoni* in Latin and is said to have 'a protuberance on its face which functions as bait for small fish, enabling this ungainly, slow-swimming fish to hunt actively while still remaining well-nourished'. The frogfish − as anyone can tell from its name alone − is a tremendously ugly fish, perhaps the ugliest fish in Swedish waters. It lies on rocks and lake bottoms with its antennae − like an extension of the human nose − attracting the small fish and luring them right into its repulsive mouth. If you watch this *Antennarius commersoni* − as Leo *the scientist* had done − you will see our entire Western civilisation of bribery and persuasion by any means possible illustrated in a single image. The *Hogarth Affair* certainly

287

shared some similarities with the frogfish method of fishing. One small fry after another took the bait, only to be swallowed up by poisonous jaws a moment later. 'Commersoni' stands for the fish tanks of commerce, trade, business and capital. Of course this is not an entirely misleading impression. It did in fact have to do with money and business.

But Leo Morgan was not the one suffering from gluttony for gold – he had always dissociated himself from anything having to do with money. That was the one thing he never collected as a kid. His whole conscious attitude towards life was based on the stoicism of dissociation. It was this philosophy of dissociation that also meant dissociating himself from everything that Henry signified. Leo had never harboured any dreams of glory or riches, while Henry was toiling by the sweat of his brow in a damp, stinking, unhealthy earthen tunnel beneath Söder, with a hypothetical gold treasure as the carrot. Leo never passed up an opportunity to taunt Henry about his childish dream, and that's why things turned out the way they did.

Leo was out after the *truth*, at all costs. Puzzles existed to be solved, fog to be dispersed, rituals to be broken. Mystery was to be banished forever as a frill of oppression. A truth could be found hidden behind every stage-set, and Leo had evidently run into one of them. He had devoted his entire life to tearing down stage-sets, and now he seemed to have mobilised the full power of his spirit to tear down the stage-set concealing the old journalist Edvard Hogarth.

Leo became obsessed. He brooded for a long time and then wrote a letter. He wrote a very beautiful letter in which he explained who he was, why he had sought out the old man, and why he valued the truth so highly. After all, the concept of truth is one of the absolute cornerstones of our philosophical tradition, and it was easy for Leo to compose a lengthy, substantial and – for a layman like Edvard Hogarth – instructive letter about truth.

The no. 12 tram glided through the sleet, crossing Äppelviken, Smedslätten and Ålsten, before letting off a rather gaunt figure at Höglandstorget. This solitary man drew his scarf tighter around his neck as he looked for some street signs to take his bearings, since there was no one around to provide directions.

It was Leo Morgan. His ploy had worked – the letter had been well received.

Edvard Hogarth had thawed out, and finally he gave in and invited the letter-writer to a meeting out here in Bromma.

The silent, secluded street was just about how Leo had pictured it, with well-kept gardens, villas from the turn of the century and magnificent gates. But Mr Edvard Hogarth's front gate was worn-looking and decrepit, with the paint flaking off and a letterbox that undoubtedly leaked in a downpour. The gate was also creaky and sluggish when opened and Leo assumed that it wasn't used very often. The gravel path leading up to the house had not been raked in a good long time. Autumn leaves were piled up under the snow that was now starting to melt away, no longer hiding a virtually abandoned front garden with shrubby cinquefoil, Abbotswood roses, lilacs and a couple of apple trees – all of them overgrown and neglected. The house was a good size, a brick house with a black roof. It looked deserted, except for a little lamp that was shining in a window on the upper floor. It looked like one of those lamps that shine year-round to ward off burglars.

The visitor walked up the gravel path to the door. He rang the bell, which emitted a toneless snarl deep inside the house. He waited a long time but heard nothing. He rang the bell again and waited.

Edvard Hogarth surprised his guest by appearing from around the corner. He explained that the front door was locked; he never used it because it was so damned cumbersome. Leo walked down the stairs and shook hands. Hogarth had grey hair and a furrowed face, alert eyes and a beak of a nose. Stooping slightly, he led Leo inside the house through a kitchen door. He kept his hands shoved deep in the pockets of his cardigan, which was the same beige as his trousers. A silk scarf around his neck made him look quite elegant, almost a bit coquettish. In some vague way he resembled a resident of the Höstsol home for ageing actors. Vanity was waging an equal battle with the wisdom of age.

The guest hung up his coat in the hall, and Edvard Hogarth showed him around the unbelievably cold house. Heating oil was so expensive, and enormous crises were going to develop down there in the Arab countries – that was something that old Hogarth had realised long ago, so he had become accustomed to being cautious and frugal when it came to heat. The oil crisis two years earlier – so mendaciously presented by our mass media, according to Hogarth – was not a real 'crisis' but more of a warning to be taken very seriously.

The ground floor consisted of one large room with genuine leather furniture and excellent art on the walls. Leo recognised a number of the artists as highly sought-after by collectors. Hogarth explained that in the past he had been good friends with many painters, and he bought their work before they got expensive. His favourite was a desolate seascape by Kylberg. On the mantel of the big open fireplace stood a photo in a gold frame showing a beautiful young blonde wearing a typical suit from the forties with broad shoulders. She was his wife. She had died an untimely death in 1958, and he had lived all alone ever since. The only person he saw anymore was the housekeeper, who came every Wednesday to tidy up and look after things.

His study on the second floor was exactly like the type of room Leo and Henry had seen in museums when they were kids – the studies of great men, where great ideas were formulated and important decisions were made. The parquet floor was covered with an enormous Persian rug and the walls were lined with shelves of Hogarth's newspaper-clipping files and scrapbooks, as well as a library containing everything from the obligatory standard works to unusual literary volumes in the major languages of the world. He had read a good deal, that old man. It was amazing that he got by without wearing glasses.

Hogarth sank into a chair behind the massive desk, cautiously tapped out one of his seven pipes, and began filling it again. He smoked a special blend of cola-tobacco that produced a very thick and extraordinary smell, quite sweet and pleasant. The blue smoke whirled around the Strindberg lamp, and for a long time he didn't say a word.

Leo wasn't sure how he should start things off. He lacked the professional journalist's casual approach that could get the subject to open up. He had been offered a seat in an easy chair, as if visiting a doctor or a boss who absolutely had to have people below him so that he could look *down* on them when he spoke *to* them.

Edvard Hogarth nodded towards a cabinet in the centre of the bookcase. A whisky would taste good on such a cold and overcast day. Leo obeyed, poured two shots and handed the old man a glass. Hogarth took a swallow, smoked his pipe for a while and scrutinised his guest from head to toe. Leo lit a cigarette, but he didn't feel terribly ill at ease.

Leo had grown so big, said Hogarth. Leo had become a real man. He puffed on his pipe and smiled. Leo wondered what he could mean. Why this personal tone of voice all of a sudden?

Hogarth laughed and then he explained that when Leo had sent the letter, he'd suddenly realised that Leo was old Morgonstjärna's grandson and the Jazz Baron's son. Old Morgonstjärna had been one of Edvard Hogarth's best friends. Hogarth had even been a member of the WWW Club. He had played cards and billiards with Leo's paternal grandfather right up until the end, when Morgonstjärna passed away in the spring of '68.

Leo still didn't understand, and perhaps he tried to recall all those grey-headed gentlemen who used to visit his grandfather, smelling of cigars and pipes and whisky, but he never really could tell them apart. They'd all looked the same. Hogarth chuckled and said that it must have been fate that had brought them together on this day. He apologised a bit for being so unfriendly the first time they spoke, but he had been forced to protect himself.

It turned out that Edvard Hogarth had followed Leo's literary career from a distance, and while he may not have entirely shared the poet's reckless fury, he could fully admire the purely lyrical and philosophical sides of his work. It was important to read literature, even for journalists. It was useful from an artistic sense.

But he also liked Leo's letter. He had received many letters over the years, and he could undoubtedly donate a good many of them to the Royal Library. Leo's letter could stand comparison with correspondence he had received from ministers, professors and literati who did nothing but compose profound letters to their colleagues.

Leo had decided on truth as the object of his investigations and discourses, and that was quite in order, according to Hogarth. The person who does not brood over the concept of truth is heading in a dangerous direction. He too had studied philosophy in his youth. He had met Axel Hägerström many times, a man who was as caustic as he was lethal, but that was another story. Truth was not a question of language or sliding scales of values; nor was the truth something absolute for all ages. Truth was the shuttle, so to speak, that moved between law and practice, that wove together those human actions that we call moral. In the long run, the only thing that we as civilised people could call ourselves was 'humanists'.

Edvard Hogarth sat there in his desk chair, holding forth, speaking only long enough between each puff to ensure that his pipe would not go out. Now and then he took a sip of his whisky, and the alcohol seemed to give him a bit of energy and fervour. He never went out anymore; each day had to be devoted to his work – he placed the palm of his thin hand on top of a manuscript basket that seemed all the thicker by comparison – and the days were just getting shorter and shorter. He didn't have the strength to do much anymore. But not much more was needed. His project was a work on a grand scale, and he needed only a couple more months to finish it. Then the bomb would go off.

It was going to be his legacy. Like all journalists, he had run into cases and affairs which, for various obscure or obvious reasons, were to be kept under wraps for an unspecified length of time, sometimes permanently. Someone high up in some administrative office had felt threatened and put a lid on it. They had rung up an editor-in-chief or a publisher and, by virtue of their official position, had threatened reprisals. And so the presses were stopped. But anyone who goes digging for the truth collects piles of memories and material which some day may land in the spotlight and suddenly change the public image of the heroes of the past and the rulers of the present. That was precisely what Hogarth was intending to do. He had a collection of a dozen different affairs that had been put under wraps by people in high places. The 'Hansson case' – referring to Verner's father – was one of these affairs. There were also other, more well-known stories regarding Haijby, Enbom and Wennerström, which Hogarth could elucidate as no one had ever done before. But a person could not be timid; nor could he be thinking about his future career if he planned to drag old ghosts into the light. Edvard Hogarth was old, at the end of his life. But he wanted to go out with a real bang, and that was why he had written this sensational testament: *Fifty Years of Political Scandals in a Sweden Governed by Law*.

Hogarth's indefatigable obstinacy had made him get to the bottom of all these affairs – which now filled an entire manuscript basket all the way to the top – and bore witness to such a large measure of courage and self-sacrifice that it bordered on insanity. The fact that it might be fatal was something he had already sensed.

They had now been sitting there for several hours, talking about everything from Grandfather Morgonstjärna, the Jazz Baron, Henry's piano playing, and the press situation to vague philosophical ideas about right and wrong. The sound of the telephone ringing jolted them back to the present. Hogarth was noticeably disturbed by the sound. He grimaced and excused himself to go into the next room. He answered the phone by reciting his number, and Leo noticed how Hogarth pretended to be much older, more senile and more scatterbrained than he was.

Without really thinking, Leo picked up a sheaf of the typewritten A4 pages from the manuscript basket and started skimming through the text. He read sentences such as: ' . . . the official Swedish attitude was politically neutral, but extremely loyal from an economic point of view', and '. . . which in the thirties made the German war industry one of the mightiest in the world', and 'Zeverin's Precision Tool Company AB, at the time one of the Griffel Corporation's most profitable subsidiaries, had exactly the supplementary resources that the Third Reich needed to acquire . . .' and so on.

He skimmed haphazardly back and forth through the pages, becoming more and more confused. The only thing he understood was that it had to do with the weapons industry and deliveries to the Third Reich. He didn't manage to find out more before he heard the phone being slammed down in the next room. He instantly put the pages back in their place on the desk.

Hogarth looked distressed and low-spirited when he returned. He didn't sit down but instead leaned his arms on the back of the chair, looking out the window, as if to slowly bring his attention back to his guest.

He said that Leo would have to leave. For a change, Hogarth had to go out to an urgent meeting. But it was with his sister. She was ill, dying. Unfortunate, in every way. Leo's visit had been most pleasant, and he would like to talk to him again. His guest was welcome to come back.

They hastily said goodbye, and the old man, shaking his head and muttering morosely, went back upstairs. Quite bewildered, Leo took the no. 12 tram back into town. It had stopped snowing, and the weather was merely an all-encompassing grey.

Then it was Easter. Leo shocked those who knew him by accompanying his mother out to Storm Island in the archipelago. He hadn't been out there in Lord knows how many years, and he generally hated to travel. He had not yet been out of the country, not even across to the Åland Strait in Finland. He had even gone so far as to claim, both to himself and to everyone else, that it was *his thing* never to leave Sweden. Undoubtedly it was not so much a fear of missing out on something here at home as it was the fear of regaining his sense of curiosity.

Greta had not been this happy in a very long time; that was evident just by looking at her. She looked ten years younger. She praised Leo's good health. She was immensely proud of going out to see her relatives on Storm Island with a son who was radiant with well-being. He too was happy to be there. The old child prodigy again walked around the houses, asking how

293

everyone was. The islanders presumably remembered the skinny little boy with the vasculum and herbarium, and they were surprised to see this tall, stately man who looked old, sombre and authoritative, like a public prosecutor on a tour of inspection.

The population of Storm Island had now shrunk to the deplorable present-day total of seventeen people. Some of the oldtimers had breathed their last, a number of them having outright refused to move across the bay to the retirement home on Kolholma. And Leo's maternal grandmother and grandfather persisted in their belief that times would change, that people would come back and they themselves would be vindicated. That's how things had always been. Justice would be done. The land on Storm Island had been good enough for several hundred residents in the past, and it was no worse now than it had ever been.

As for Leo Morgan, something happened to him during that Easter on Storm Island. Utterly sober and well-groomed, he walked around his childhood island without shivering. His feelings of anxiety and the spasms of feverish hallucinations at the place where the red accordion had been placed on a rock near the shore had been deflated and silenced, dead forever. He visited the rocky caves where he had scratched stone-age runes on the walls with sharp sticks; he sought out the marshy meadows where the Storm bluebell still shot up in the summer in all of its majestic height; he peeked at the Ark in the boathouse, lying there with its naked ribs and the cobwebs spreading upward from the keel, looking just the same as it had fifteen years before – everything had stagnated; all human activity had come to a standstill. But flowers still bloomed, and the sea kept on raging as if nothing had happened, as if it had all been an annihilatingly beautiful dream, a nocturnal parenthesis that would soon be forgotten.

Leo continued to work on his notes for *Autopsy*, which he was assembling in his black workbook. One fragment is particularly interesting because it signifies a *return* which is quite obviously a rewriting of Leo's own return to his childhood. The fragment says: 'The fisherman comes back, dazzled by the immense sea, / as always the first time / – a new species crawls up onto the rock / clinging fast, constantly starting over again . . .' The frogfish, the origin of life, the fishermen, etcetera – perhaps all these marine-based metaphors evolved during this visit to Storm Island. It sounds highly plausible, since so much of the draft was written with the very same pen, with the same composed and pleasing handwriting, as if in one long breath.

In any case, it was a rested, inspired and, in most senses of the word, well-balanced Leo Morgan who came back to Hornsgatan just after Easter in 1975. He had regained the desires of his body: the desire to write, the desire to reproduce, exactly as if he had been to a very good health spa.

On his own initiative he saw Eva Eld a number of times; she is the *ingénue* of this drama. Over time she had developed into a robust and sensible schoolmistress with stringently scheduled activities in which even eroticism had a limited scope. Yet it was not so limited that her old lover Leo could not be given space, and according to later reports, she testified that Leo had seldom looked as healthy as he did at that time.

But it didn't last long. Cruel fate was about to call on him, seek him out in the middle of the night to lead him astray and make him mute.

———————

The doorbell rang in the middle of the night – Leo didn't know how long it had been ringing before he awoke. Everything was very unclear. Feeling quite muddled he went out to the hall towards the furious ringing. He was alone in his two-room quarters. Henry was away, in the midst of a film that was being shot in Skåne.

At the glass door – through which he could see the hazy silhouette of a man wearing a coat and hat – he asked what this was all about. Edvard Hogarth muttered his name with annoyance, and Leo opened the door. The old man stepped inside. He looked haggard and worn out. He placed his briefcase on a chair in the hallway and said that he was not planning to apologise – this was important and he would make it brief.

After throwing on some clothes and noting that it was just after four in the morning, Leo returned to his guest and asked the man to sit down, but he declined. Hogarth wandered through the flat, through all the rooms and corridors, and peered into the billiard room, which had once been occupied by Leo's paternal grandmother. For a time Hogarth seemed to have forgotten the purpose of his visit. With his hair standing on end, Leo followed the man around, no doubt completely uncomprehending. Hogarth murmured and chuckled at old memories, and Leo began to suspect that the man was suffering from dementia.

It was cold in the flat, and Leo was freezing. He still had the lovely warmth of the bed in his body, but he had to admit to himself that he felt a newly awakened curiosity tingling inside, which was making him shiver. Old Edvard Hogarth finally returned to the hallway where he had left his black briefcase.

He said that a taxi was waiting for him downstairs, so he had to make it quick. He then opened the briefcase and rummaged through the confusion of documents and dossiers – the whole time complaining that 'it was all such a mess' – until he found a sheaf held together with an elastic band. This was for Leo to keep; the old man wanted to leave these papers with Leo for the time being. Leo was to read the papers, which contained important information. Perhaps they would help set Leo on the right track. Something might happen. Although what that might be, he couldn't say. Perhaps it was all just illusion and a figment of his imagination. Old people often grew alarmed for no reason.

Hogarth laughed – there was a hint of insanity in that laugh – and all Leo could do was to accept the papers with a nod, unable to think of anything to say. He merely nodded and listened, and then they shook hands. There was also something strange about that handshake. It was fraught with solemnity, and it may have lasted just a second too long, a negligible little second that was still too long, as if the old man were bidding farewell to someone who was about to go away.

Finally the old man said that he trusted Leo. That was the first time in a very, very long while that Leo had heard anyone say that they trusted him. Then Edvard Hogarth disappeared out the door, back to his taxi, which was waiting down on Hornsgatan.

The same maître d' as before showed Leo Morgan to the same secluded table in the Restaurant Salzers. This time Stene Forman had managed to fill up almost the entire ashtray as he waited impatiently. He had a very hard time hiding his excitement. He kicked out a chair, reached out his cloying hand and leaned conspiratorially over the table. Leo had done a great job. It was a real pleasure to invite him to lunch again.

Over a heavy lunch with wine and then coffee with cognac, Leo calmly gave his report. With an almost exaggerated composure he matter-of-factly recounted what had happened. He repeated certain phrases, added things he had forgotten, calmed down again and at last came to the strange night just after Easter when he had received a sheaf of papers from Edvard Hogarth, almost as if it were a top-secret dossier in some clichéd thriller.

Stene said that was so typical of Hogarth. The old man was not just some nobody; he had a reputation for being a bit odd, so to speak. Whether it was a matter of an ordinary persecution complex, an over-active imagination, or something else, no one could say. Edvard Hogarth *did his thing*, which could make a person feel a little confused, but there was nothing to be done about that.

It could be that at this point we should at least give some hint as to what this whole affair actually concerned. The dossier, handwritten on typing paper, which Leo Morgan received that night contained excerpts, selected in the greatest haste by Hogarth himself, and they could do little more than provide a hint of the themes of his magnum opus.

The *Hogarth Affair*, as the matter came to be called, had its roots far back in time. Zeverin & Co. – a firm that plays a central role in this drama – became the Zeverin Precision Tool Company AB in the twenties. The company moved to a new plant, considered impressively modern at the time, in Hammarby, not far from the Sickla docks. Hogarth spent a lot of time describing the CEO Hermann Zeverin, his previous career and the status of the Swedish precision tool industry at the time. It would be much too long-winded to insert that reverential account here; the work had taken Hogarth many years and it was brimming with details and statistics.

At any rate, during the thirties the Zeverin Precision Tool Company AB seemed to be an unusually lucrative and successful business for its day. While many factories around the world had folded as ruined and obliterated wrecks, the Zeverin Precision Tool Company AB was hiring new employees and continued to grow at a calm and steady pace. The nature of the labour market was such that companies could pick and choose among hordes of skilled workers who possessed tremendous expertise. One thing that might seem curious but was based on ice-cold calculation was the fact that even back then the Zeverin Precision Tool Company AB utilised a special variant of the employment interview, a questionnaire for those seeking jobs. It was a cleverly worded form that evoked answers revealing everything from the applicant's shoe size and marital status to membership in trade unions and opinions on the political situation in the world, if the applicant had any such opinions.

In the late thirties, the Zeverin Precision Tool Company AB at Hammarby Harbour near the Sickla docks employed about a hundred workers as well as a score of office clerks reporting directly to management. Over the previous decade production had become more extensive and diversified. They were producing everything from machine parts – in addition to entire machines for specific purposes – to little stainless-steel parts for kitchenware. The firm had customers all over Scandinavia, mostly large workshops where the Zeverin Precision Tool Company AB could supply the time-consuming precision work.

Business was booming for this small company when the Second World War began. It was significant that the workers at the Zeverin Precision Tool Company AB received considerably higher wages than workers at, for instance, the newly built huge plants of the Hedlund Brothers or General Motors.

Here Hogarth interjected a comprehensive cost estimate which showed that the move to the large plant in Hammarby was made possible by generous bank loans taken out against various securities. At the same time, and perhaps for that very reason, another transaction was undertaken, which would require an entire academic dissertation to explain properly. In any case, the gist of it was that, in a brilliant manoeuvre, the Zeverin Precision Tool Company AB became linked to the already vast Griffel Corporation. This association – which still exists today – was by no means official, and it took Hogarth at least four months of dogged persistence, as he mentions in a personal passage, to find proof to support this claim. The verification lay buried under pounds of archival dust, historical 'obfuscation', and the reluctance of civil servants. This was not the least bit surprising – rather, it was entirely expected – because this fact reveals that the activities of the Zeverin Precision Tool Company AB during the Second World War were not an unfortunate coincidence, an unpredictable consequence of the avarice of some unscrupulous capitalist. It was cold-hearted business, completely in keeping with the directives of the large corporation, and that was why the affair had consequences, even today, when the Griffel Corporation has acquired the dimensions of an empire that every governmental administration must take into consideration.

The move from the small workshop near Norrtull to the large plant near the Sickla docks in Hammarby Harbour took place with much pomp and circumstance. The plant was opened by the Finance Minister of the future coalition government, and CEO Hermann Zeverin himself gave a long speech in which he thanked and praised the company's capable rank and file. The nearly 120 employees applauded and were then invited to partake of coffee and rolls.

The gigantic factories of the Hedlund Brothers, General Motors, Luma and Osram cast their shadows over the facilities which, seen in context, were actually quite modest. But everything is relative. The German boot, in turn, cast its menacing shadow over them all, though the danger was mentioned only in passing by all the speakers.

'These are uneasy times,' said the future minister, even daring to mention the deep wounds left by the Kreuger crash, but, 'we have to be grateful that things are the way they are for us.'

CEO Zeverin spoke in benevolent terms of the AK-jobs and their favourable effect on Swedish business. Not without a certain satisfaction he noted his own company's unique position, which drew a small round of applause from the fawning office clerks.

A certain spirit of agreement, mutual trust and loyalty hovered over these inaugural festivities in the best 1930s style. The manufacturer also disclosed that production would be altered to a certain extent, and that training courses would be arranged for this purpose. Some employees would soon be singled out, that much he could promise. It was easy to read between the lines: some specially chosen, co-operative, and subservient workers would be selected.

This was where Tore Hansson came into the picture. Tore Hansson, who was Verner's father, could be mentioned in Hogarth's summary only in passing, which made it all the more irritating. Tore Hansson had to disappear.

In the copy given to Leo, Hogarth had underlined the name Tore Hansson each time it appeared. But because of time constraints he had been forced to cut his account short. The intent – if there was any sensible intent behind this – may have been to point Leo in the right direction. But instead the effect was mostly annoying.

Stene Forman couldn't hide his agitation. During this second lunch at Salzers he had managed to fill the ashtray to the brim, and sweat was dripping from his forehead. Leo had done a good job, even though he had merely received a pile of papers that were largely incomplete.

But this was just the beginning, according to Forman, as he got more and more worked up. He started firing off ideas about how they were going to dig into the whole affair. The Zeverin Precision Tool Company AB still existed at the site near the Sickla docks, and the Griffel Corporation was one of the largest companies in Sweden. There was plenty to dig into – ownership relationships, customers, international transactions and so on, ad infinitum. Somewhere in the mix they would find Tore Hansson, there was no doubt about that. The job had to be done with great thoroughness, nothing could be left to chance, as Forman said, laughing in almost the same way as before. The maître d' looked worried and tallied up the bill.

Leo couldn't understand Stene Forman's excessive enthusiasm. He had merely recounted a fragmented story that ended with one big question mark.

A totally normal person would presumably have been well on his way to exploding with curiosity after having come this far in the intrigue – exactly the way Stene Forman was about to burst with something that at least appeared to be curiosity but would later turn out to be greed. But not Leo Morgan. He might have been able to admit to an uneasy tingling in his body, but that probably wasn't enough to be called curiosity. As previously mentioned, he had once written a treatise on the subject. It was called *Curiosity, Inquisitiveness and Knowledge*. Anyone who is not put off by this academically shabby and unimaginative title – how far he had come from his beautiful and sublime titles of the sixties: *Herbarium, Sanctimonious Cows* and *Façade Climbing and Other Hobbies*! – can actually read a truly exciting, instructive and entertaining put-down of curiosity which, in the author's take on the subject, is one of humanity's lowest vices.

Of course the discussion ends up in an epistemological argument that goes right over my head, but as far as I can tell, Leo rejected the type of deduction in which truth becomes the intuited manifesto of the thesis. The human being cannot guess at anything but can only examine one thing at a time, inventing categories and concepts, constantly trying to test them over and over again.

For a trained philosopher, these are naturally truisms, not to mention nonsense, but it all becomes quite ludicrous by virtue of the fact that Leo Morgan continually confronts these assertions and theories with our daily human life here on earth and shows how gossip and the reading of magazines hardly makes us wiser or our minds more inquisitive – we would rather hear perpetual confirmations and no surprises. The way out of this lowly condition – and here the author suddenly turns pragmatic and didactic – is via a stoic and exalted sense of calm. The gossip of curiosity is a vice, the calm of indifference is a virtue. Perhaps this is not exactly what he meant, but that's how I interpret it. I never managed to ask him, but one thing at least is clear – the author of *Curiosity, Inquisitiveness and Knowledge* must have scorned, not to mention detested, one of Stockholm's most celebrated and talented gossipmongers: Henry Morgan, his own flesh-and-blood brother.

300

Curiosity, Inquisitiveness and Knowledge was printed as a small booklet by a publisher with philosophy as its speciality, and it's probably impossible to find, even in an antiquarian bookshop. I would venture to state that it was to be Leo Morgan's last published work.

It may be useful to keep in mind this parenthesis about Leo's efforts within the philosophical profession. One of the doctors at Långbro Hospital referred to the patient's philosophical studies and works in order to reveal a connection between stoicism as a virtue and catatonia as a diagnosis. New findings within psychiatry assert that the symptoms of an illness can often be seen as pure extensions of the behaviour of a completely 'healthy' individual. It's totally natural for small children to be afraid to walk through a deserted square, to get into a crowded lift, to be locked inside a wardrobe, or to discover a snake in the grass. But in adults, these fears and fantasies become manifest as phobias: in a state of illness they are called agoraphobia, claustrophobia, and herpetophobia.

One of the doctors asserted that such was the case with the patient Leo Morgan. His complete passivity and resignation corresponded fully to his philosophical conclusions, developed from a purely intellectual point of view. His theories had become anchored in practice.

Involuntarily I happen to think of the copperplate engravings above the desk here in the library. They depict a number of authors of the past such as Dante, Cervantes, Rabelais, Shakespeare, and others, including the Spanish Renaissance writer Lopez y Ortega. His play *Fernando Curioso* has been called Spain's *Hamlet*, and the magnificent final monologue, just before the cloister doors close behind the hero, ends with this self-ironic insight:

> The fool in the poem
> is no invention
> he is for the most part
> merely an extension.

Keeping in mind that this was written by a blind, syphilitic, former conquistador over four hundred years ago, the arrogant and overrated doctors of today may end up in a more equitable light.

———

More than anything else Leo Morgan wanted to continue working on *Autopsy*. *Bonniers Literary Magazine* had sent out a letter to a number of poets with the question: 'Halfway through the seventies, what has happened so far?' A written response was requested, and Leo was undoubtedly pleased to be included in the group – only the heavyweights were asked. But no response would ever come from Leo Morgan.

Stene Forman had moved into high gear, always *off the record*, as they said in the White House. 'What the hell', he would moan and groan on the phone. Leo needed to get his arse moving some time. Leo had to write letters, wise and considerate letters, pepper the old man with letters. And if that did no good, he would have to go out to see the old fellow, kick down his door and ask him what the hell he was really working on. For Hogarth to carry on like that, terrorising conscientious citizens in the middle of the night and then go underground . . . No, dammit, in Forman's opinion it was just a matter of piling on the pressure. Verner Hansson would win justice, Stene would boost circulation, and Leo would get a nice chunk of change.

But Hogarth had gone underground, and no one answered the phone when Leo rang. By then he was prepared to give up on the whole thing – he had no reason to be loyal to either Stene or Verner – yet he couldn't get the affair out of his mind. There was something special about this Hogarth. He had shaken Leo's hand in a special way, as if Leo might be infected with something or chosen for something.

So he did as Stene said. He wrote a couple of wise, subservient letters, waited for a reply that never came, and then decided to pay another visit to the old man. He might as well get to the bottom of the matter, once and for all.

It was early April, a very sunny day. The no. 12 tram took its usual route, and Leo got off at Höglandstorget. The street seemed even deader than before, if that were possible. Smoke was rising from a few chimneys, a pitiful poodle could be heard barking from some distant corner inside a house – otherwise the street was utterly deserted. This time the snow had melted away completely from Hogarth's garden, which was not an encouraging sight for a man who had once been a botanist. The garden was in a deplorable state, and the gate creaked stubbornly.

Leo cast a glance up at the house. The desk lamp on the upper floor was shining just as it should. The doorbell produced a low rasping sound inside the house, but nothing happened. It seemed absolutely dead inside. He rang the bell again, and then walked around the corner to the kitchen door. Not a sound. The little glass porch looked cold and draughty when he peered through a window. He was looking right into the large room with the leather furniture and all the valuable paintings – an attractive bounty for the cultured thief.

Then Leo gave up. There was no sense in standing there pressing the bell. The neighbours would just get curious and wonder who he was. On the other hand, there didn't seem to be any inquisitive neighbours, since the street was completely dead. At any rate, he decided to give up. He was fully prepared to go home and ring up Stene Forman to tell him in no uncertain terms to take his *Hogarth Affair* and go to hell.

Leo started walking back towards Höglandstorget to catch the no. 12 to town, but he was only halfway there when he happened to think of something. He could at least check the letterbox. He walked briskly back to look at the letterbox attached to the old, creaky gate with the peeling paint. There, just as he thought, were soaked morning newspapers from the past four days, advertisements addressed to the homeowner and Leo's equally wet and disintegrating letters.

He looked around but didn't see a single soul, so he stuffed the letters in his pocket and went back to the tram. He wasn't going to give another thought to the matter – or so he imagined.

———

Henry was actually the one who intervened and started feeling uneasy, which he would later regret. He had been down south in Skåne for a film shoot. His biggest part yet. He had a real role, with several lines of dialogue. It was now April and he had returned home, tremendously pleased with his efforts.

Henry came home to a Leo who seemed very torn, worried and abnormally restless. All of this was due to the unusual circumstances, and Leo couldn't resist telling his brother the whole story from the very beginning, including Verner's talk about his missing father, Stene Forman's imminent bankruptcy and old Edvard Hogarth out in Bromma. Henry claimed to remember Hogarth from the WWW Club. His description of the old fellow was little more than 'a man with two legs, two arms and a head between his shoulders', but just to be nice, Leo agreed and said that he must be right.

But dammit all, Henry thought it was clear that Leo had to step in and offer the old man support. They had their heritage to live up to, after all. Old Morgonstjärna would never have backed down. Leo had to see to it that nothing happened to the old fellow. In Henry's opinion, if it later turned out that Verner Hansson became a little wiser as a result and Leo earned a nice chunk of change, well, what did that matter? And he whistled through his teeth. Leo shouldn't go shuffling about and brooding; he should play the detective and ferret things out. Henry knew exactly how to do it. He'd been a secret agent in Berlin, after all. It was simply a matter of not giving the game away and not letting on, in all instances. Hell, there was no denying that Henry looked both envious and proud. He had never expected this of Leo. One way or another the little child prodigy might actually become a hero.

Without giving a thought to being any sort of hero, Leo caught the no. 12 tram once again. He had no desire to be a hero, but on the other hand he wanted to have enough peace of mind to be able to continue writing his new poetry suite *Autopsy*. And that would never happen as long as all this rubbish kept swirling around in his head forever and ever. He had developed – he was forced to admit – some sort of infection; he'd been chosen for something, but he didn't know what.

And so the number twelve drove its route, Höglandstorget sighed heavily beneath its overcoat of silence, and Leo headed straight for his goal. He walked quickly, feeling a bit excited, towards Hogarth's house. The small street was not just quiet and deserted, it was also dark and gloomy at this hour of the evening. But Leo didn't allow himself time to be scared, even though there was good reason to feel that way. He went through the stubborn, creaking gate, marched up the crunching gravel path and feverishly pressed the doorbell. The bell rasped and snarled inside the entryway, but nothing happened.

The lamp was shining in the upper floor, but otherwise the house was just as lifeless as it was before. Without questioning what was right or wrong, the visitor walked around the corner to the kitchen entrance and reached for the door handle. The door was locked. He checked the handle, the lock and the hinges. It was an old panelled door made of pale pine; a simple Yale lock shouldn't be much of an obstacle for an old locksmith who in his day had forced open hundreds of attic storage rooms.

And sure enough, the lock yielded to a suitably thin piece of metal from the rubbish bin. He was still acting without taking even a brief second to consider what he was doing. He was feeling agitated now, breathing heavily, almost panting. His hands were shaking from nerves. Maybe he knew that if he allowed even a moment's hesitation or doubt, he would be boarding the no. 12 tram to go back home. This sort of behaviour required courage, and courage often had the character of stupidity, boldness or at least recklessness. The possibility that the old man was sitting upstairs as if nothing had happened or that he was lying in bed and would take Leo for a simple burglar was embarrassing. Maybe he would even fire a gun in self-defence. But Leo couldn't think about that in this situation; he couldn't think about anything at all.

It was completely dark inside the house, and he didn't dare turn on a light. Cautiously he entered the large room with the leather furniture and all the valuable works of art. He heard only his own breathing and the pounding of his heart. To cut through the silence and the terror, he shouted, 'Hello! Hello!'

No answer, no response. He headed for the stairs to the upper floor and cautiously crept up one step at a time, holding onto the banister. One thing he had already learned: he would never make a successful burglar; this was all too much for him.

Then he saw the light from the lamp on the desk upstairs. The light was casting long shadows over the stairs, and Leo began shouting again. No answer. There was no one home to answer him. The parquet floor creaked under his feet as he walked through all the rooms up there. The three bedrooms empty, nice and tidy; and the study with the files, the books and the desk. Everything looked very orderly, and Leo almost felt a bit disappointed. He didn't really know what he had expected or what he had been hoping to find – either a body or a Hogarth very much alive.

The dirty grey light of dusk fell across the desk, and the Strindberg lamp glowed with its yellow light. Leo went over to the desk where all seven pipes were lined up, one for each day of the week, in their place next to the manuscript basket. The old Remington typewriter, the tobacco tin and the pencil box stood exactly where he remembered them from his first visit.

But there was something that was different: the manuscript basket. Leo leaned over the desk and picked up a couple of pages from the thin stack, which didn't look the way it should. He read sentences like: 'Charlie was beside himself with excitement and pulled off her dress to find what he was looking for – a moist vale in which to quench his desires . . .' or ' . . . after

305

they made love for the first time, he lit a cigarette and asked her what her name was . . .'

The whole manuscript basket was filled with the pages of a terrible pornographic novel, a serialised story for the worst of the lurid tabloids. Only now was Leo truly shocked. In a rage he began digging and rummaging through all the papers on the desk, on the shelves, in the files and anywhere else he found papers in the room. The folders in the file cabinets, labelled with numbers, were either empty or filled with uninteresting duplicated copies from various Swedish civil service departments. The stacks of papers on the shelves – what had once been Hogarth's intellectual archives – turned out to contain national propositions regarding day-care investigations.

Leo was now completely soaked with sweat, and he was breathing hard when he suddenly thought he heard a sound from downstairs. He held his breath and stood motionless for several endless moments as his blood seemed to scream and roar in his skull and the whole world stood still. For one brief and dizzy moment everything turned totally white and all strength vanished from his body as if he'd been struck by lightning. His legs buckled, but he was already on his way down and in slow motion he stretched out his arms to break his fall. Lying on the floor he continued listening but heard nothing.

Several minutes later he was standing at the station on Höglandstorget, waiting impatiently for the no. 12 tram.

––––––––––

The Good Samaritan who once rang the journalist Edvard Hogarth had now gone astray deep in the wilderness. It was no longer a matter of Verner Hansson's ill health or Stene Forman's circulation figures or Henry Morgan's putative sympathy for old members of the WWW Club. Quite simply it had to do with Leo Morgan's own well-being. He wanted to have proof of the testimony of his own mind, he wanted to come back to the reality that existed before this 'affair' dragged him into some sort of hazy dreamscape in which he did not feel at all at home. Leo had always sought tangible proof of his experiences, as if he'd often had reason to doubt. Everything he wrote was presumably based on this lack of contact with life. He had been an outsider for as long as he could remember, and only when he was writing did he feel completely real, a participant instead of an observer.

Against his will he had now been dragged into a story that was not lacking

306

in elements of unreality. A red thread ran from Verner Hansson's vanished father to Leo's paternal grandfather and Edvard Hogarth to Stene Forman and himself. Whether it was called – a caprice of fate or something else – it was at any rate enough to preoccupy Leo completely. He pushed on as if in a state of shock.

Leo presumably looked like a bewildered somnambulist or a drugged zombie as he entered Salzers to have lunch with Stene Forman yet again and to report the latest news, *off the record*, as they said in the White House.

Forman didn't seem a bit surprised at the new turn of events in the story. He puffed on his cigarettes, wheezing now and then and jotting down some brief notes on a pad as Leo tried to recall all the details, smells and sounds. Forman had brooded over this matter for a long time, and he claimed to have found out a good deal. But whatever had happened to Hogarth, it would have to wait until later. He was a cunning old guy; he would surely turn up. He had presumably gone underground, plain and simple and tidied up after himself so as not to give anything away. He was probably forced to observe a certain caution – that was Forman's theory. Leo had no suspicions of his own. He merely sat there in a state of confusion, leafing through his documents about the Zeverin Precision Tool Company AB – they were all he had that in some way proved he had even met the old member of the WWW Club – and he looked utterly distracted. He had not been sleeping well lately.

But Forman wasn't born yesterday. He had come up with yet another idea, and he cursed himself for not thinking of it sooner. He didn't hesitate to call it a stroke of genius.

There was one avenue that they hadn't yet tried: the Zeverin Precision Tool Company AB.

That meeting at Salzers took place about a week before the discovery of the death which would definitively turn this story into an 'affair' in the classic sense of the word.

But my own enquiries – it was like searching for the pieces of a bomb disarmed long ago – require a number of comments regarding the Zeverin Precision Tool Company AB.

It must have been around 20 April, 1975, on a cold and hazy afternoon when Leo Morgan took the bus from Slussen via Skanstull down to Hammarby

Harbour, a filthy industrial area of asphalt, brick and soot, which on that day presumably must have looked damned dreary. Leo was tired and feeling feverish. He hadn't had a proper night's sleep for the past two weeks. He was taking sleeping pills that allowed him a couple of hours' slumber towards morning, when the nightmares were worst. He was now completely immersed in this story, which had increasingly taken on the character of an ancient fateful drama that inevitably had to end in tragedy. He took each step of his own free will, yet these were steps that he was absolutely forced to take if he didn't want to head into a life of utter uncertainty. He could have left the stage long ago and retreated, but he would have done so as a wimp, a coward and an ignorant shit. Henry would never have forgiven him. Henry kept harping on about his damned honour and pride, which made demands of anyone who was a real man; it was actually what turned a stripling into a man. Very odd words to be coming from Henry – the perpetual quitter, wretched wimp and loser. Leo himself claimed not to possess even five öres' worth of pride, but he was driven towards the truth like a moth to the flame. He thirsted for the truth like a nomad for his watering hole, even if it was an all-engulfing, consuming fire or a putrid, poisonous oasis.

At any rate, Stene Forman had now given Leo an order to go straight to the source. The editor-in-chief of *Blixt* had thought it all through, and under false pretences he had rung up the Zeverin Precision Tool Company AB to find out if there might be any employees still working there who had been with the company more than thirty years. A sharp and obliging personnel manager had cheerfully informed him that a fellow named Berka – he was listed as Bertil Fredriksson on his pay envelope, but he had always gone by the name of Berka – had worked at that very workshop all those years, ever since the Zeverin Precision Tool Company AB had moved to the Sickla docks. There was no doubt about it – Leo had to go down to Hammarby Harbour and find out what this Berka knew about Tore Hansson.

That's where he was now headed, that feverish Leo Morgan, walking past General Motors and the Hedlund Brothers, which was now part of the Grängeskon Corporation; past Luma, Osram and several other small workshops until he reached the Zeverin Precision Tool Company AB, which had been absorbed by the Griffel Corporation. It was a brown-brick building with a zigzag roof with dirty windows above four long aisles where welders, lathe operators and about fifty different machinists and precision-tool makers were producing a deafening noise with sledgehammers, files, machines, tongs, shears, grinding machines and welding equipment. Leo shrank back from the noise as he slipped through a small door and put his hands over his ears. Several younger guys in overalls with 'Zeverin' on the back didn't seem to notice him and kept hammering away at their arduous piecework. A foreman was dashing around, clad in a blue apron and holding a safety representative's clipboard with a pen stuck behind his ear. He was demonstrating a new blueprint. A state of frenzied activity prevailed. Leo instantly felt like an interloper, a bacillus, a disturbing element in this snorting organism.

Finally he mustered what courage he had and went over to an older lathe operator to ask for someone named Berka. The man sniggered, shook his head and pointed towards the locker room. That's where Berka could usually be found.

Leo kept close to the wall as he headed down an aisle, trying not to attract anyone's attention, until he came to the locker room. There he found a coffee vending machine, and in front of the vending machine was a stooped and disreputable-looking little man with a furrowed face and brown skin. He was wearing a painter's cap with the word 'Beckers' on the turned-up visor. Leo asked for Berka, and the little man nodded and shouted that it was him, he was none other than Berka. He smelled of stale alcohol.

Berka was not the least bit reticent. He was perfectly willing to submit to an interview regarding what it felt like to be nearing retirement, but the bosses didn't like anyone poking around in the workshop so it would be best if they went somewhere more secluded. Berka coughed as if he were about to heave out his lungs, spat out some yellowish green goop onto the asphalt floor, and then swept away the mess with a push broom. He pointed at a little shed towards the end of the aisle. 'More private,' Berka said, trying to look sly and wink one eye, but he couldn't manage it; he winked both his eyes at the same time.

Berka led the way, all of a sudden looking both cocky and pompous. He was going to be interviewed by the press. No photographer? Well, maybe that could be arranged later on. He was so damn photogenic, after all. He had the broom over his shoulder and was waddling like a little tyke on his way to the football field. He also attempted to whistle, but then he just started coughing up that nasty slime again. It was a cold that he had. This damned springtime, everyone was going around with a runny nose. Yes, dammit, a fucking springtime cold.

Inside the little shed he switched on a bare bulb and closed the door behind his guest. It was slightly less noisy in there, but Leo still had to shout to be heard. He offered Berka a smoke and introduced himself as Peter Erixon. Berka accepted the cigarette and introduced himself correctly as Berka.

Purely as a formality, this Peter Erixon asked a couple of questions about what it was like to work at the Zeverin Precision Tool Company AB – the type of questions he assumed that a real journalist would ask. Berka made a great effort to concentrate, and when he resolutely gave his answers, he tried to sound like a politician on TV, using words that he would otherwise never use and whose meaning he didn't know. Leo, alias Peter Erixon, kept a straight face and occasionally wrote down a few notes.

It turned out to be true. Berka had worked at the Zeverin Precision Tool Company AB way back when the plant was located on Norra Stationsgatan near Norrtull. Back then the business was called Zeverin & Co. and it manufactured a number of other things, including items made of wood. Then Berka had stayed with the company when it moved out to the Sickla docks, and he was present at the opening of the new, big, modern workshop. That was right before the war started, but business was still good. Hermann Zeverin, the CEO, had handled things well. No one was laid off. On the contrary. Berka was a lathe operator, and he had continued in that trade until the early seventies, but lately his hands were so shaky that he could no longer do the work. He was supposed to retire a year ago, but he had refused. He knew exactly what happened when a man sat at home as a pensioner – after six months he became senile, another six months and he developed cancer and then he died. All that stuff about 'retirement age' was very slyly calculated. But that was not for Berka. If a person had been getting up at five thirty every morning since he was a little fellow, he couldn't stop doing it just because some arsehole had come up with this idea of retirement. He coughed again and brought up a sizable amount of yellowish-green slime, which he spat into a half-empty coffee tin on the floor. It didn't look like very good odds that he would reach the age of eighty, not under the present circumstances.

Leo, alias the journalist Peter Erixon, offered Berka another smoke to calm the man's lungs. Berka lit a match and took a couple of deep drags as he muttered and then launched into a long harangue about the fact that his damned job at the workshop probably hadn't been very healthy. But he was an ordinary, simple fellow, and he'd had to take the first job that was offered, and he had never shirked his duties and had never been without work for over fifty years.

The interviewer listened attentively, occasionally jotting down notes. He was feeling a bit stressed and didn't know how he was going to handle this conversation. He could let the little man go on jabbering away for hours. Berka could undoubtedly keep talking for a very long time. But sooner or later Leo would have to lay his cards on the table and bring up the subject of Tore Hansson. If that didn't work, he could just thank the man for his help and take off for home and forget about the whole thing.

Berka started getting a bit glassy-eyed after an hour inside his private shed. He used the foreman as an excuse and went out to sweep, mostly for the sake of appearances. He had to pretend to be a bit worn out towards the end of the day. It was just past four, and he should at least make a show of working, because he wasn't here on charity, after all; there was no reason for them to keep him on if he did nothing for his reduced wages.

When Berka came back to his private shed a bottle stood on the table, a whole, virgin bottle of Absolut Pure Aquavit. Under the bottle were five brand-new hundred-krona notes. Berka came in, pretending not to notice anything, dug in his overall pockets for a smoke, and then accepted one from Leo. He tried to whistle, but just started coughing again.

He was almost exploding with curiosity, but he sat down without looking at Leo or the bottle or the money. Then he stood up again. Finally it was too much. Berka picked up the bottle in his fist, quickly hid it in the corner under the table, snatched up the banknotes and counted them: one, two, three, four, five . . . He stared at Leo and stuffed the dough in his pocket.

Berka wondered what this was all about. This was no ordinary interview – even he could see that. Leo nodded, blew smoke up at the ceiling, and remained silent. Berka asked if this had to do with Leffe, Leffe Gunnarsson, and that damn car. In that case, he had nothing to say, not a single word. He was innocent. Leffe Gunnarsson had simply bolted. No one knew where.

Leo shook his head. This had nothing to do with Leffe Gunnarsson. Berka sucked nervously on his cigarette. If it had to do with Stickan and if he had broken in somewhere, Berka was again totally innocent. He hadn't seen Stickan in a year, and he no longer had anything to do with him.

Leo kept on shaking his head. He said that this had to do with Tore Hansson, a fellow who had worked there a long time ago. Tore Hansson, who had disappeared back in 1944.

'Fucking hell' was Berka's response. 'Bloody fucking hell.' He asked if he might uncap the bottle, and Leo nodded. Berka took two big gulps of the aquavit and smacked his lips; a shiver passed through his whole body. 'Bloody fucking hell,' he repeated. Tore Hansson again. So Peter Erixon wasn't the Old Bill after all.

No, he wasn't the Old Bill, Leo assured him.

———

A couple of miles east of the Zeverin Precision Tool Company AB there was a ramshackle cabin on the opposite side of the Hammarby factory road. A narrow lane led down to Sickla Lake, and that's where the cabin stood, an old, abandoned work-site cabin for construction workers. It must have been blue at one time, but the paint had faded, and unless you knew the cabin was there, you would never even notice it because it seemed to blend in with the slope leading down to the water.

Berka had acquired this cabin a long time ago, and he used it as a summer cottage, rather like an allotment garden. He headed over there on the weekends and sat there fishing and solving radio quizzes.

Leo found the cabin without difficulty, since Berka had described the road in great detail. He would join Leo as soon as the whistle blew at the workshop, because they couldn't sit in his workplace talking about Tore Hansson. That just wouldn't do. Berka had been mixed up in quite a few things, and he no longer trusted anyone.

The key was exactly where Berka had said it would be, inside the hubcap of one of the abandoned tyres. Leo unlocked the door and went in. There he found a bed neatly made up with an old military blanket, a dining table, a petroleum stove, a wooden chest with a padlock and a paraffin-oil heater. The cabin was quite pleasant, and when Leo opened the curtains, he could look out across Sickla Lake and perhaps see the sun setting over the city to the north-west. But on this day it was grey and hazy, and there was no sunset to admire.

Leo waited about an hour, then poured himself a drink and made coffee. The alcohol calmed him down, because he had imagined that this might be a trap. If anyone wanted to get rid of him, this was the most perfect place in the whole realm for a murder. They could torture their victim without worrying about the noise and then sink the body in Sickla Lake and remove all traces forever after, if they liked. But he trusted Berka. The guy seemed on the up-and-up. And Leo would never get anywhere if he didn't take risks. This was actually the first time in his life that he was taking real risks for the sake of the Truth. This was actually the first time that he was doing something that had anything to do with reality, and he knew that such things always had their price. It is also highly likely that he saw deeper into this affair, saw larger connections than the ones that I'm able to find today.

In any case, Berka arrived as promised. He was slightly out of breath because he had 'run like a herring', as he put it, and then he coughed up another glop of that yellowish-green slime as soon as he set foot inside the cabin. Leo praised his fine summer cottage, and Berka proudly showed his guest several special arrangements he had made so that he could also live there in the winter if he liked. Everything was totally free. No one had ever paid any attention to him, and he had no idea who he should pay for leasing the land, if the issue should ever come up. The cabin had stood there for fifteen years and no doubt would stand there for another fifteen, if Berka lived that long. The odds, as I've said, were not good, which he had realised long ago. He had nothing to fear, not even if he recounted what he knew about Tore Hansson.

Berka lit a paraffin lamp hanging over the table, took out some soft ginger snaps and poured himself some coffee laced with aquavit. As darkness descended over the woods, the lake, and the city off to the north-west, he told Leo everything that he knew about Tore Hansson, the Zeverin Precision Tool Company AB, and 1944. It gave Leo the shivers because it ended up being quite a nasty business.

———————

Anyone who has ever in his life picked up the phone to turn in a news tip to TT Wire Service and a few hours later switched on the radio and heard the TT voice, the indisputable voice of Truth, read those very words as part of a news report, a new fact to add to the immensely rich fact-bank of human culture, anyone who has ever done that has most likely been gripped by both an urgent feeling of importance and a corresponding sense of unreality. Every news item has wandered the same difficult route to the collective consciousness. The news was created, planted by various interests and cabled out across the globe to end up at last in people's thoughts, making

313

fellow citizens either throw up their hands in deep indignation or praise God with profound joy. Anyone who participated in creating this news might feel empty, like after botched sex, empty and blurry, as if the sudden exaltation had taken place solely in a dream during the night.

Stene Forman sounded almost happy in his fervour. He was speaking absolutely *off the record*, as they said in the White House. He talked incoherently about the *Washington Post* and the Watergate scandal and *FiB/Kulturfront* and the IB affair. And actually it wasn't until now that this story was first called the *Hogarth Affair*. That day was the first time there was reason to call the affair an 'affair', and Stene Forman didn't hesitate for a moment. Of course it should be called the *Hogarth Affair*.

When Leo later saw the morning paper in the kitchen – where Henry, clad in his elegant bathrobe and completely unawares, was making coffee – he experienced that panic-stricken feeling of unreality. In an obituary with a large photo, he read that Edvard Hogarth had been found dead in his home three days earlier.

One of the newspaper's prominent, seasoned journalists, a contemporary of the deceased Edvard Hogarth, had been assigned to write the obit of his former friend and comrade-in-arms. Not unexpectedly, Hogarth was called 'a pugnacious old champion of truth' and 'one of the very last, great, encyclopaedic journalists we have had in our country'. As is customary, the obituary developed into a minor apotheosis, recounting in pithy but brilliant terms much more than what Leo knew about the old member of the WWW Club.

Edvard Hogarth was as old as the twentieth century. He was the only child of a jurist, he studied in Uppsala in the twenties, and he made something of a name for himself as an excellent stylist for the student paper, in which he published light articles in the man-about-town vein. After successfully completing his degree, he soon turned to the field of journalism, ending up during the years of the stock market crash as editor of one of Sweden's biggest dailies in Stockholm. He wrote with great insight on everything from history, art, and literature to economics and modern science. He quickly made things very awkward for those who couldn't stand to have the truth brought to light, and his exclusive interview with Kreuger, just before the Wall Street crash, served as a model for generations of future journalists. He possessed a unique ability to get people to confide in him. It was in this connection that it seemed apt to call Hogarth 'a pugnacious old champion of truth', since he would rather fight than run away. He would take up the battle, and quite often he brought home a victory. But the tragedy of Edvard Hogarth was to be found in this unwillingness to compromise.

When his wife passed away soon after the Second World War, he became even less co-operative, if that were possible. After a series of articles about the Cold War – in which he assumed a position that hardly appealed to the legendary editor-in-chief – he soon became impossible to deal with, and he left the public arena. He was dissatisfied with the development of press ethics in Sweden. By the age of fifty, he had already fallen silent, which could be described as a premature and highly regrettable retreat. On numerous occasions the writer of the obituary had appealed to Edvard Hogarth to come to his senses, swallow his pride, and come back to the newspaper, which sorely needed men of his fervour, with his passion for the truth and his monumental refinement. But Hogarth persevered and remained true to his silence – and therein lay his 'tragedy'. A fitting epitaph might be *Melius frangi quam flecti* – better to be broken than bent.

The death notice made a strong impression on Leo. All of a sudden, among all the respectful obituaries, this peculiar old man was given a profile, a past that he hadn't known before. Edvard Hogarth was suddenly more alive and more flesh and blood now, after he was dead.

Leo lay down on his bed to think. He could imagine how the scene had looked: Hogarth was lying somewhere in the house when the housekeeper arrived on Wednesday and let out a horrible scream. She called the police and, weeping, threw herself into the arms of some bewildered officer. Mr Hogarth was such a fine and noble gentleman, and no one would understand how he could write the disgusting filth that filled his whole study, because of course that pornographic novel had not slipped the housekeeper's attention. That was approximately how the scene must have unfolded, and it was with these thoughts that Leo realised that there really *was* an affair – the *Hogarth Affair*.

The iron was red-hot at both ends, and now it was time to strike. Eagerly egged on by Stene Forman at *Blixt* magazine, Leo Morgan, in a sort of creative coma, was supposed to put together all the strange information that he had gathered from various sources into a cohesive whole, to write an

315

account of the absolutely scandalous *Hogarth Affair*. In a rare state of fury, he ferreted through various libraries, archives, and collections of public records that were readily accessible to supplement the fragmentary data which Hogarth himself and the eccentric Berka had contributed.

Since Henry *the actor* was once again down south in Skåne to shoot additional footage for the feature film in which he had a role, things were extremely calm in the flat on Hornsgatan. Leo had plenty of peace and quiet to work, and he had transformed his two-room quarters into a temporary editorial office with a direct line to *Blixt* magazine. Editor-in-chief Forman rang a couple of times a day to get regular updates on the latest developments. This was no longer dynamite, as Forman said, it was now fucking nitro-glycerine. Leo was going to be world-famous after this, Verner's wrongs would be redressed, and *Blixt* would become just as renowned as the *Washington Post*.

By the end of April – Leo had presumably lost all sense of time and place – he had gathered everything together in a neat file folder containing about fifty typewritten A4 pages. Stene Forman gurgled, wheezed and burst with curiosity; he asked his sleuth to come up to the editorial offices that very evening. It would be *off the record*, and nitro-glycerine was at its best in the darkness of night.

The April evening's stubborn twilight descended over the bay and Norr Mälarstrand where, in the distance, the skyscrapers of the major newspapers could be seen, with their rotating neon signs. Leo walked as if in a fog, a trance of weariness, and in his fevered imagination he pictured the hundreds of pros up there who would be green with envy soon, when tiny, nearly bankrupt *Blixt* made its infamous move.

Leo greeted the sleepy fellow sitting in the guard's office and was allowed to enter without any problem since he was expected by Forman, the editor-in-chief himself. All the editorial offices on the fifth floor were dark and deserted, and the glass doors leading from the lift entrance were locked. Leo rang the bell, and Stene Forman instantly appeared out of the darkness to open the door. He gave Leo a welcoming slap on the back, shook his hand and then led the way to his office, a room separated off from the open office landscape where workstations and desks stood in listless silence in the dark.

Forman looked at least as tired as Morgan did. He had a big office with a marvellous view of Rålambshov Park and Riddarfjärden. Behind his desk was a narrow couch where he sometimes spent the night. Everything had become such a damned mess with all his former wives and the alimony and financial experts, so he was lying low; here he considered himself 'unreachable'. But that's how things were in life; they would always work out.

The editor-in-chief invited Leo to have a seat in a visitor's chair, held out a box to offer him a cigarette, and gave him a healthy glass of whisky. He deserved it. Leo countered by nonchalantly producing his neat folder with the documents that would soon explode with a bang that was sure to send reverberations even as far as the government.

The evening news was on the radio, pounding out the story that the last Yanks had left South Vietnam after a lightning-quick evacuation, and that the Saigon government would most likely capitulate and agree to an unconditional surrender. This was undoubtedly a day of victory and triumph for justice and truth.

Leo was shaking with fever and sleepless nights. He took a swallow of his whisky and smoked a cigarette. Absentmindedly he leafed through a couple of back issues of *Blixt*, presumably trying to transform his own sensational material into future headlines. They might be: 'GRIFFEL CORPORATION EXPOSED – SECRET WEAPONS DELIVERIES DURING WAR' and the next, follow-up headline could be: 'YESTERDAY'S CUSTOMERS NAZIS – TODAY'S IMPERIALISTS', culminating in the inevitable third part: 'BLACK-OUT', explaining the disappearance of Tore Hansson and Edvard Hogarth. But they probably weren't very good headlines. Leo was no good at composing headlines; that takes a special art within the field of journalism that he had never learned. Leo was an amateur and would remain one. He would be a knight and a gentleman to his dying day.

––––––––––

Anno Domini 1929 is known as the year when all the stock markets crashed and people went insane and killed themselves. But the stock markets were not the only things to collapse. On gloomy, shadowy Heleneborgsgatan on Södra Malmen in Stockholm, a building scaffold – which, in the subsequent investigation, clearly turned out to have been negligently assembled – collapsed with a monumental crash. One workman broke his leg, while a young assistant ended up underneath the entire load of planks, pipes and timbers. When the whole mess had been frantically moved aside – it took a good half hour – and they found the young boy alive, the entire neighbourhood of curious bystanders heaved a sigh of relief and thanked the Lord for His mercy.

The young assistant was only fourteen years old, and his name was Tore P.-V. Hansson. Although he was definitely alive when the big, strong carpenters and bricklayers dug his body out from under all those timbers, his life was not going to be an easy one. A huge beam had crushed his right foot and a rough board had dealt him a blow to the head. His foot healed surprisingly well – the boy had a limp, but after only a couple of months he was hobbling around. Things did not go as well with his head. The boy developed a stutter and spasms that made many bigoted people categorise him as 'punch-drunk', which was not true at all.

When this Tore P.-V. Hansson, a little more than ten years later, set about completing the highly original and cunningly worded application form at the Zeverin Precision Tool Company AB, he did so with great brilliance. There was obviously nothing wrong with his intelligence. Naturally, the boy had stopped working in the construction business. His limited mobility made him more suited to sedentary types of work, so he became a precision-tool maker, a lathe operator. He made a name for himself as an extraordinarily skilled worker who was meticulous to the point of being finicky, although among his co-workers he was generally known as an easy target and a buffoon. That didn't bother Tore P.-V. Hansson, because he was just glad to have any kind of steady job, considering the state of the world in the late thirties.

So Tore P.-V. Hansson was among those newly hired workers that the Zeverin Precision Tool Company AB decided to focus on when, with much pomp and circumstance, the new facilities near the Sickla docks at Hammarby Harbour were opened. Along with a lad named Berka, Tore was lucky enough to avoid conscription. Things were good for them; they were allowed to follow the war from a sufficient distance. And Tore read the reports from the war with the same exactitude that he applied to everything else in his life.

Perhaps this exaggerated sense of accuracy was another result of the injury to his head. He tormented himself by repeatedly checking and examining everything he undertook; he had a habit of always going back to double-check the gas, the lights and the lock on the door whenever he was going out somewhere, and he kept himself impeccably groomed.

The flat on Brännkyrkagatan into which his betrothed moved looked like a showroom for a model home in the year 1939. Tore P.-V. Hansson couldn't bear untidiness, dirt or clutter. He cleaned the flat like an experienced housekeeper, running his index finger over mouldings and door frames to track down any dust whenever he cleaned the house, which he did a couple of times each week.

His wife accepted his behaviour because she truly loved this lame, stammering, slightly eccentric man. He in turn loved her as meticulously as she wanted to be loved. He never forgot a single special holiday or neglected any little occasion to give her presents, and she presumably wondered whether true love wasn't mostly a question of concentration. Tore could concentrate on her like no other lad had ever done before. Ordinary boys played football, went to cafés and came up with a thousand excuses to avoid staying at home. For obvious reasons Tore could not play football, and he didn't have many interests outside his job and his extremely orderly home. In her eyes, he was the perfect husband.

Every morning Tore P.-V. Hansson would be among the first to arrive at his lathe at the Zeverin Precision Tool Company AB at the Sickla docks. He had his tools – chisels, hooks, callipers, files and keys – arranged according to a very carefully devised system. Everything was laid out so that he could reach for a tool without even looking. He had the pattern etched into his memory, with the result that he could work very efficiently, moving faster and with greater precision than most. He had come to the attention of the foremen, who regarded him as a model for the entire workshop – especially for Berka, who liked to show up rather late and smelling of stale lager.

Hansson stood at his lathe, turning out machine parts, small cylinders and rods and other components that required great precision. He was the perfect person for this type of delicate task, and he was fully aware of his own worth, without being arrogant or haughty about it. He would always hobble with blatant nervousness over to his lathe, as if to avoid his co-workers. He was only interested in work, and he never took a break. Tore P.-V. Hansson was so damned *loyal*.

On a rainy, slushy morning in March 1944, Tore came hobbling over to his lathe, as usual among the very first to arrive at the workshop. The air was damp and raw, and he was shivering a bit, presumably thinking that it would be great to get going and warm himself up by working. Once the machines had been going for a while, the temperature would begin to rise in the workshop, and by the time the whistle blew in the afternoon and all the smiths, lathe operators and welders had been working as if in a mad frenzy, the smoke would be thick overhead and the heat in the place could almost be described as tropical.

Hansson hobbled over to his lathe on that morning and was about to take up where he had left off, but he discovered that all his tools had been rearranged. Nothing looked as it should on his workbench next to the lathe. Some of the callipers and chisels had been piled up haphazardly on the bench. There was no way he would have left his tools like that the day before – it was practically a matter of honour. He shrugged his shoulders and began working, although he was undoubtedly a bit annoyed. This was his lathe, and if anyone had to work overtime, he could do it somewhere else.

Finding his tools in disarray was really not anything to dwell on; it could happen to anyone in a workshop as large as the Zeverin Precision Tool Company AB. But it turned out not to be a one-time occurrence. If it had, the status quo would probably have remained unchanged.

When Tore P.-V. Hansson arrived at the workshop at the end of winter in '44 and each and every day found his tools in a great jumble on his workbench, ruining the whole ingenious system that he had worked out for their arrangement, he started to get properly annoyed. If he had been a different sort of person, someone less meticulous, this never would have bothered him. But he was the way he was, a lad on whose head an entire scaffold had once collapsed, and that kind of person can be either nonchalant or assiduous. Hansson fell into the latter category. And with that his fate was sealed.

The pattern was repeated for several weeks in a row, and Tore decided to ask the foreman whether any work was being done in the evenings and if so, why it had to be done at his lathe. It was such trouble to set up everything each morning. The foreman merely laughed at the badly stammering Hansson, shook his head, pounded the man on the back and said that he shouldn't dwell so damn much on details and particulars. Hansson was a real asset to the Zeverin Precision Tool Company AB. There were very few lathe operators with his skills, and the company really appreciated such a talent. But at the same time, he shouldn't become so obsessed with details – Hansson should look at the big picture and not make himself blind staring at the small things. No work was being done in the evenings, and if Hansson's tools were in disarray, perhaps it was because his co-workers were pulling a prank on him.

As a matter of fact, Tore P.-V. Hansson had long ago sensed that his co-workers, perhaps out of a certain envy, often tried to pull his leg just because he kept to himself and worked hard and was so damn *loyal*. But Tore hadn't seen any expectant glances in the morning when he, to his great annoyance, discovered that someone had jumbled up his tools again. When people want to play a practical joke, they usually lurk about to watch their victim; otherwise there's no pleasure in the prank. But Tore didn't catch the slightest glimpse of any jokers as he morosely rearranged his things on the bench. That was not even a possibility.

There were very few in whom he could confide. Berka was actually the only person. Berka was largely Hansson's opposite – an obstinate carouser and absolutely not an adherent of tidiness. But he was still a good friend, a colleague who treated everyone with exactly the same amiable scepticism. Tore asked Berka whether he was aware of any night shift that might be going on among the lathe operators, but Berka wasn't the least bit interested. He hadn't noticed anything, he hadn't even considered the matter. He worked like a slob, and his bench hadn't been swept or cleaned in years. There could have been a corpse under all that mess on Berka's bench and no one would have noticed. Besides, as far as he was concerned they could do whatever they liked. He minded his own business, and that would have to do.

Presumably it was some time towards the end of March 1944 when Tore P.-V. Hansson very impatiently decided to find out once and for all what was happening to the careful arrangement of the tools on his workbench next to the lathe. He had become obsessed with the matter and couldn't get it out of his mind. Considering he was a fusspot, a control freak, a cleanliness fanatic, and the stuttering and leg spasms he suffered, perhaps it's not particularly strange that he did what he did.

When the whistle blew on that fateful day, Tore P.-V. Hansson arranged his tools as meticulously as always and then hobbled out to the locker room, sat down on a bench and began changing his clothes. He took his time about it. There were not many lads left in the locker room when Hansson pretended to leave for home, although he actually went back inside the workshop. The lights were off and it was dark in there because everyone always rushed home as fast as possible. The buses were waiting out in the yard, loudly rumbling and crowded with weary workers.

Tore P.-V. Hansson stood for a long time pressed into a corner near the entrance to the locker room until he dared slip over to the end of one of the aisles. There a ladder led up to a bridge to an overhead crane. If you walked along the bridge you came to a span between two posts, and anyone who wanted to be undisturbed could sit there for hours.

321

He hobbled as quietly and cautiously as he could along the bridge, finally reaching the post, where he climbed up and sat down. It was very dark in the workshop, and it was smoky where he was, but he did have a perfect view of all five aisles, which made him feel quite pleased. Soon the mystery would undoubtedly be solved.

Of necessity people in history become more and more fragmentary until, with a few spectacular exceptions, they are nothing more than a name and some dates on a gravestone, and even that has to be considered something of a concession these days. Hansson's descendants have all been very reticent, and perhaps there really isn't much to find out about the man. At any rate, that spring he was twenty-seven years old, married to a possibly rather naïve but good wife who by that point had developed a certain form of sternness and sense of purpose. Many years earlier an entire scaffold had collapsed on top of him, with the result that he limped, stammered and suffered from a number of obsessions. There could hardly be any other explanation for why, on a miserable evening in March 1944, he would climb up on a beam in the workshop of the Zeverin Precision Tool Company AB at the Sickla docks, just in order to find out why his tools were in disarray every morning.

So there he sat, trying to stay awake, hidden behind a post halfway up to the ceiling. Maybe he was thinking about his wife, who was at home waiting with dinner and who would start to worry if he didn't arrive at exactly 5:55 as usual. But she was going to have to wait; this was more important.

This really *was* more important. Tore P.-V. Hansson had nodded off a few times during the course of the evening, when he was awakened by sounds coming from the workshop below. Doors slammed in the locker room, keyrings jingled, and footsteps resounded from shoes with rough soles. Hansson *the spy* gave a start and was suddenly wide awake, like a hunter on the alert, listening tensely to every sound and movement down there in the dense darkness.

He could hear voices – muted, sober voices – and footsteps from a large number of feet. This went on for a couple of minutes until a hissing, shuffling sound overrode everything else. At first Tore had a hard time pinpointing the sound. It seemed to be coming from everywhere and nowhere at the same time. He twisted around, trying to see what it was, but couldn't see a thing. The hissing and shuffling sound filled the whole workshop, but as soon as it stopped, several lamps were switched on.

Hansson could now see out across the workshop, and he blinked in the light – the whole place was blacked-out behind enormous black curtains. They had been hauled down from their hiding place in niches up in the ceiling, and Tore now recalled that someone had once told him that the whole Zeverin Precision Tool Company AB would be able to operate even if all of Sweden were under a black-out. It was a very modern security measure and was thought to be a marvellous feature.

At the same moment that the lights went on, people began streaming into the workshop, and Tore P.-V. Hansson couldn't believe his eyes. He pinched himself to make sure that he was really awake. A good fifty young men came pouring into his workshop, a blacked-out workshop, where they immediately began working, as if part of a top-secret and highly classified night shift.

He tried to identify some of the men down below, to see whether he could recognise any of them, but he couldn't. He didn't have the foggiest idea who they could be, these men who had to work in the middle of the night in blacked-out facilities. Of course he watched his own lathe with particular interest. He saw a hefty fellow in his thirties adjust the lathe and attach small, knobby cylinders to it, checking their dimensions after having milled a flange at one end. It looked as if most of the men down there were working with the same sort of cylinders, about four inches long and an inch in diameter.

For obvious reasons, Tore P.-V. Hansson had never been required to do military service. He hadn't even been utilised as a desk-job recruit anywhere, and he had no complaints about the matter. But if he had done his military service and become familiar with firearms, he wouldn't have had to ponder for long about what the lathe operators were actually working on. As it was, it took him some time to figure things out, and that didn't happen until he saw some sort of chief inspector standing in the middle of the workshop. The man examined each product by sticking a cylinder into a sub-machine gun and making several jerking movements with the weapon before removing the cylinder and placing the approved item in a box filled with wood shavings.

They were manufacturing bolts for sub-machine guns, and it was with this realisation that Tore P.-V. Hansson wrote his own death warrant – or put the first nail in his coffin, to make use of a thriller-like phrase.

Tore P.-V. Hansson sat up there for many hours in the workshop of the Zeverin Precision Tool Company AB, his eyes burning as he spied on the workmen operating their lathes and milling the bolts, which were then inspected and approved and packed up. Late at night the efficient, blacked-out work was completed and the workshop was emptied out as the workers left, murmuring to each other. The lamps were turned off, and the black-out curtains were once again hoisted up on their ropes, filling the entire building with their hissing sound.

The crippled, stammering spy must have been filled with a sense of triumph. He had been thoroughly vindicated. He had proved to himself that night work actually was being done in the workshop and that the disarray of his tools really had been caused by something other than a practical joke.

But to go into all the developments that now followed would require far too much space, and the original text which Leo Morgan had furnished filled a good fifty pages. He had added long expositions on the time period in general, as well as on the industry, the Third Reich, and so on. In other words: he had tried to imitate Edvard Hogarth.

Tore P.-V. Hansson was, of course, both pleased and confused by every-thing he had witnessed that night from his perch high up on the post. He had no idea to whom he could turn, whether this was some clandestine matter for Sweden or whether there were highly criminal interests behind the activity. It was, after all, a secret business that under no circumstances should be exposed – that much he had understood. The important thing, at any rate, was for him to convey the matter further, first to his wife. She prob-ably thought that he'd been out on a binge with Berka or some other carousers that night, and she had met him with allegorical rolling pins when he later, finally, fell into bed. At first she demanded a better story than that, but her doubts were quickly laid to rest, and she realised that Tore had actually discov-ered something quite awful. Those were terrible times in the world. Europe, Africa and Asia were all in flames, and people were capable of just about anything. For understandable reasons she wanted Tore to keep quiet, to let it go, to forget what he had seen. Let other men wage war, but not him. Tore was crippled and not suited for battle – although she knew full well that he would never comply with her wishes. Tore was much too scrupulous to forget about such a night. Not even the announcement that Tore was going to be a father could make him change his mind. On the contrary, it made the matter even worse. If Tore P.-V. Hansson was going to be a father, then he could not be a coward.

So it was shortly after that night at the Zeverin Precision Tool Company

AB that Tore Hansson contacted a major newspaper. Edvard Hogarth wrote that one day in the spring of 1944 he had a very strange phone conversation as he sat in the editorial offices. A stammering and very agitated young man told him about what he had seen one night at the workshop where he was employed in the daytime. And Hogarth added: 'If he hadn't stuttered, I would have taken him for a perfectly ordinary madman.'

But Edvard Hogarth was no fool, and he asked the young worker to come up to the newspaper office the following day. The meeting never took place. Ever since 4 May 1944, the stammering, limping lathe operator Tore P.-V. Hansson has been missing without a trace. He left behind a wife on Brännkyrkagatan, and in November of that same year she gave birth to a son named Verner. The pregnancy had been a nightmare, filled with police interviews and investigations that led nowhere. It had turned Mrs Hansson into a hard and disappointed woman, and when her son Verner was born, she decided to forget all about her missing husband. She was never going to see justice done.

By now it had grown quite late, and Leo had downed one drink after another. He was celebrating a great triumph up there in Stene Forman's office. The editor-in-chief was sitting on the other side of the desk, smoking non-stop as he read through the fifty pages of Leo's document with the greatest attentiveness. Forman muttered, sighed, and groaned, but he seemed pleased. He looked immensely tired and worn out in the sharp light of the desk lamp. Now and then his weariness would be replaced by an expression of surprise as he jotted down some comments in the margin. It was utterly quiet and dead in the editorial offices. Once in a while Leo took a stroll among all the desks in the office landscape, going over to the panoramic windows to look out at the city and the park. The two of them were all alone in the whole building, except for the guard at the entrance. The *Hogarth Affair* was completely *off the record*.

With an audible snort – which actually sounded much like the laugh that had made him famous among the Provies of the sixties – Forman closed the folder and took his feet down from the desk. He was finished. He squeezed the bridge of his nose between his thumb and index finger and sat motionless and silent for a long time.

Filled with anticipation, Leo sat there with another drink, fingering his neat dossier like some errant job applicant. Finally Stene Forman broke the silence with yet another audible snort and asked Leo if he was tired. Leo was a bit surprised by the question but replied in the affirmative. He *was* tired, dead-tired and rundown. All the excitement of discovery had kept him awake for several nights in a row, but he had never really allowed himself to notice whether he was tired or not. The fatigue was mostly like a cloud of feverish heat, an up-until-now controlled pain in his forehead. But he was still too wound up to think about sleep or rest. Right now it was the battle that counted, and Leo wanted most of all to think about headlines – glaring, screaming headlines that would convey this scandal out to the entire populace in the name of truth and information. Never before had he been involved in anything to such a degree, becoming engulfed in a mission so completely that everything else seemed unimportant, mere trifles. Not even when he was in the midst of his most intense periods of creativity had he experienced anything like this. He hadn't even touched the black workbook in which his poetry collection *Autopsy* was awaiting completion. In this context it seemed to him mere therapy, introverted nonsense. The *Hogarth Affair* had, in some special way, allowed Leo to re-conquer the world that had been lost to him so long ago.

But Stene Forman was not thinking along those lines at all. He suddenly didn't look as eager or joyfully excited as Leo had hoped he would after getting his hands on this nitro-glycerine. Instead Forman looked quite dejected and depressed, as if he were trying to control something that demanded the greatest gravity, a threat of catastrophe.

Leo sipped his drink, and now the alcohol started loosening up the warm, oppressive cloud of fatigue inside his forehead, releasing a kind of anaes-thetising precipitation over his brain. He slumped in the easy chair opposite the editor-in-chief's desk, lit a fresh cigarette and took a couple of deep drags.

Stene Forman began talking about the business in general, about how difficult everything was, how hopeless it could be at times to wrestle with truth and lies, relaying information and keeping secrets, and so on. Most often it was pure hell. Leo didn't understand where he was going with this. Forman talked, by turns, a bit incoherently about himself, his enormous alimony payments and his weariness, then about *Blixt*, his wretched finan-cial advisors, the ruthless creditors and the still-imminent bankruptcy.

It was nothing but an incoherent song and dance; Leo still didn't under-stand what it was all about. He wanted Forman to speak plainly. Surely everyone realised what economic conditions were like – that was nothing to be spouting off about tonight. Instead they should be celebrating their great triumph, saluting the fact that Verner Hansson was going to see justice done, that *Blixt* would start selling like hot cakes, and that the *Hogarth Affair* would finally become public knowledge.

All right, said Stene Forman, he would speak plainly. First, he acknowledged that he appreciated Leo's efforts and the fact the everything had been done with such proficiency. The overall picture was clear, although there were details that were unknown to Leo, but not to Forman. Editor-in-chief Forman – who suddenly looked as if he had been the editor-in-chief of the *Washington Post* for the past fifty years – recapitulated the whole story of the *Hogarth Affair*. Point by point he went through Tore P.-V. Hansson's discovery that during the Second World War the Zeverin Precision Tool Company AB at the Sickla docks in Stockholm had manufactured weapons parts during secret, night-time shifts. The crippled, stammering lathe operator had vanished quite suddenly – and the police investigations came to an abrupt halt upon orders 'from on high' – but the mystery remained. The thread was then taken up by Edvard Hogarth, at the time still an active journalist, who at regular intervals over a period of thirty years had poked around in the case until he discovered that the Zeverin Precision Tool Company AB had carried on a brisk business with the Third Reich, which was in violation of Sweden's policy of neutrality. The fact that the entire operation was also kept secret from the tax authorities made the matter even more incendiary. From Edvard Hogarth and the Zeverin Precision Tool Company AB – as previously mentioned – the red thread ran to the mighty Griffel Corporation and its headquarters on Birger Jarlsgatan in the middle of Stockholm. In reality that was where the actual core of the whole matter was centred. The Griffel Corporation was today, meaning almost thirty years later, one of the most profitable trusts we had. The company continued to export spare parts for weapons that, taken individually, were of no interest, parts that armies in Africa, for example, could assemble into fully functioning firearms. Yesterday's market in Nazi Germany had today become dictatorships such as the one in Uganda. That was exactly how the Griffel Corporation functioned, although from the outside, CEO Wilhelm Sterner looked as blameless as Gyllenhammer, Wallenberg and others. No one would be able to find anything untoward about the Griffel Corporation; any discrepancies had to be stifled, at all costs. The truth required its hecatombs.

Stene Forman talked for a long time, and Leo suddenly became sober and wide awake. What had earlier looked like a great triumph had now acquired serious blemishes, although he didn't yet comprehend what Forman was saying. OK, Leo interjected, he may have left some gaps in his presentation; he wasn't a professional, after all. But that shouldn't make any difference. The important thing was the main theme, and that was utterly clear. This Wilhelm Sterner was a different story.

The editor-in-chief sighed deeply and again looked tremendously old. Speaking plainly apparently wasn't enough. He would have to resort to stronger stuff to get Leo to understand the full dimensions of the matter.

He got up from the desk and, shoulders slumped, moved over to a big safe that was built into the wall. This was the inner sanctum of *Blixt* magazine. Everything that was in any way confidential was kept inside it: lists, sources that could not be revealed, and ready cash. Very slowly Forman spun the combination on the lock and finally opened the door with a firm yank. He leafed through a couple of stacks of paper on the bottom shelf, behind other, less important piles and then took out a couple of unmarked, sealed envelopes.

Stene Forman handed one of the envelopes to Leo, told him to open it, and then went back to his chair. Leo slit open the envelope and took out a couple of photos that made him feel sick. They were pictures from an autopsy, and only one of them, a close-up, enabled him to identify the deceased. It was Edvard Hogarth. The pictures showed a pale and surprisingly fit body which, with a few cuts that were equally elegant and nonchalant, had been deformed into a shapeless mass of flesh. In one of them, the face was pulled away from the skull into a rolled up mask around the neck, organs and entrails were looped around as if in some bloody pasta dish, and the hairy skin was splotched with dried blood. The remaining photos showed a series of close-ups of the right calf, which revealed two extremely small dots about an inch apart. The marks had been circled in pen, with comments in Latin.

Accompanying the photographs was a copy of the autopsy report, in which it was apparently established that Edvard Hogarth had died of cardiac arrest brought on by an electric shock, most likely caused when a cord connected to the power grid was pressed against his calf. In other words, it was murder.

After the first wave of nausea had subsided and Leo had wiped the sweat from the palms of his hands, he started to understand what this was all about. Forman didn't have to acknowledge or comment on very much. Leo had been his errand boy. This whole thing had nothing to do with uncovering the Truth, winning justice for Verner Hansson or any other noble causes. The editor-in-chief – Leo's former friend – had been operating on his own and had in principle come up with the same material, the same explosive formula. He had the right contacts and had only drawn from Leo's account when necessary. The material would never be published, nor had that ever been the intention.

The intention was perfectly clear, and presumably Leo was much too tired to feel enraged, surprised or depressed. He calmly took in the facts, and when the next envelope was tossed towards him from the other side of the desk and turned out to contain 25,000 kronor in crisp banknotes, he didn't even have to ask why.

This was a dangerous business, according to Forman. This was nitro-glycerine and, if used properly, it could be profitable, but one misstep could spell death, which was what had happened to Edvard Hogarth. There was no use in pretending to be proud. The game had its own rules. Forman followed the rules, and Leo should too. Leo should simply forget about the whole thing; he had done a good job, and he should be pleased. He should get some sleep and spend his money on a long trip or whatever the hell he liked, as long as he relaxed and forgot about the whole affair. That was the only proper thing to do. Forman claimed that 'they' would leave him in peace. 'They' had been in contact with Forman for a long time. Wilhelm Sterner himself had promised peace as long as the lid stayed on; he knew how to handle the situation. Forman actually admired Sterner in a way; there was such an unflinching logic to that coldness. How much Forman himself had been involved in the affair he never said. There was so much that Leo didn't know. *Blixt* was going into bankruptcy the following week, the last issue had already been put to bed. Forman would soon be moving abroad with his new wife. Perhaps even in a couple of weeks. The *Hogarth Affair* would be forevermore *off the record.*

———————

It was well past midnight on that April night in 1975 when two men exited the offices of the soon-to-be-defunct *Blixt* magazine on Norr Mälarstrand. They got into editor-in-chief Stene Forman's new car, a fancy vehicle that had cost a sizable sum. It was no ordinary company car.

329

Stene Forman drove Leo Morgan home to his flat on Hornsgatan. They sat for a while in silence, each smoking a cigarette and watching the steady movement of the windscreen wipers. Several times Forman tried to hand over the small brown envelope containing 25,000 kronor in unused banknotes, but Leo made no move to take it. The editor-in-chief then started speaking. He spoke for a long time. What he said is known only to those two individuals. Perhaps he offered promises and reassurances regarding Leo's personal safety, saying that no one would touch a hair on his head as long as he kept quiet and all the documents remained locked in the magazine's safe. They would soon fall into the hands of those who were paying. Nothing was free. Even truth had a price.

Finally Leo Morgan snatched the brown envelope, jumped out of the car, and slammed the door. The black-out was complete. For the time being.

That same night, terrorist bombs exploded at the German embassy. All of Sweden was shaken.

———

Several days later Henry Morgan arrived home from the film shoot in Skåne. As soon as he stepped inside the tall glass doors of the hallway he noticed a disgusting stench of excrement. Annoyed, he made a round of the flat and then went into Leo's private quarters.

Leo was lying on the bed as if paralysed, staring at the ceiling. The whole room was filled with banknotes that had been used exclusively as toilet paper. The floor was completely covered with 25,000 kronor – an entire fortune smeared with faeces. The stink was horrendous, and Henry opened a window as he tried to avoid stepping on the money. But he was not successful, and several sticky thousand-krona bills stuck to his shoes. He started yelling, furious and in tears. He shouted at Leo that he should at least answer his questions civilly, because he knew exactly what he was up to. He had heard about it from Wilhelm Sterner himself and had been forced to cut short his filming in order to come back and look after his fucking little brother, who was always getting himself in trouble.

But Leo did not react. Leo didn't move a muscle. Henry shook him, slapped him hard on both cheeks, but without result. Leo didn't even blink. His breathing was steady and his pulse was low. In spite of this relative calm, a tremendous process of combustion seemed to be taking place within him, because he was already quite emaciated. Perhaps inestimable psychological forces were raging within Leo and demanding great quantities of energy.

Henry rang the family physician, Dr Helmers, who arrived huffing and puffing a couple of hours later. He knew how serious this could be. But Dr Helmers couldn't make contact with Leo either. He had seen all the various illnesses that the boy had suffered over almost thirty years, and he thought he knew the routine. But this time the task was too much for him. He said that he had witnessed exactly the same phenomenon in the boys' paternal grandmother. To all intents and purposes, she had fretted herself to death in the early sixties, and she had looked just like this. It seemed as if all her desire to live had suddenly poured out of her rear end, and then there was no going back. Dr Helmers realised that he was powerless to do anything; this was far beyond his area of expertise. This required professionals. Leo needed care. He promised to arrange for him to be admitted to Långbro Hospital.

Henry went around swearing and cleaning up and washing off banknotes for several days before they found it advisable to send Leo to the hospital. Ironically enough, it was 1 May 1975. The cab driver was very helpful, and without protest Leo allowed himself to be led down to the waiting cab. Unfortunately, the driver managed to get them caught up in a demonstration on Hornsgatan. It was May Day, after all, and more than 50,000 people were on their way towards Norra Bantorget to demonstrate in celebration of the victory in Vietnam. It was a historic day.

Leo Morgan, child star, poet, Provie, philosopher and failed reporter saw nothing of the demonstration. He was already deep inside his silence. It would last for over a year.

GENTLEMEN

(Stockholm, Winter 1979)

Presumably there is sunshine over Stockholm today, on this early summer day in Sweden, in the Year of the Child, the election year of 1979. It's quiet and everything seems to shimmer in that overheated sort of way. But this vast flat is as cold and gloomy as ever. The curtains have been drawn for weeks, perhaps months.

'Be my Boswell!' was a standing exhortation from Henry Morgan whenever we sat in front of the fire in the Chippendale chairs – how many fires we lit and watched die out during that winter! – and he savoured the words, enjoyed hearing his own voice, urbane as he was and a master of the art of conversation, intoxicated with his own splendid qualities and either a good wine or a cheap cognac. For my part, patient listening was required. I sat there resting my eyes on the two Parian figures from the Gustafsberg Company that flanked the fireplace. I didn't know which I should give more attention, 'Truth' or 'Falsehood'. One was beautiful, the other was amusing, if nothing else.

Fortunately I committed a good deal to memory, because I am just as notorious a listener as Henry is a notorious liar. He salted his stories with fantasies that belonged to another world, perhaps a bygone era. Both Morgan brothers were utter anachronisms. If there had existed a *Gentleman's Magazine* as in Dr Johnson's day, I would undoubtedly have been a correspondent as well. But there is no longer room for such undertakings. Nor is there a place for either Henry or Leo Morgan.

I have always harboured a certain admiration for mythomaniacs and liars, of which there are numerous kinds. There are mythomaniacs who wind themselves up and start out cautiously with some innocent little anecdote which then expands into an absolutely implausible story. And there are more modest mythomaniacs who surround themselves with completely ordinary little white lies that wouldn't impress even a small child given to fibbing. No one has any desire to refute them. Least of all me.

The mahogany desk in this magnificent, darkened library is now becoming cluttered with books, small notes, and stacks of paper that have literally rolled out of my typewriter. Only on a few small surfaces can I glimpse the dull sheen of wood under all the dust, coffee stains and cigarette ash. The wastepaper basket adorned with mysterious Tarot cards is filled with empty, crushed packs of Camels. It reeks in here; it smells of an unlikely blend of filthy animal and great literature. T.S. Eliot would have felt quite comfortable in this room.

It's been a long time since I was able to tell the days apart, or calculate the date or the amount of time I've spent in this self-imposed exile. The telephone is silent, disconnected. The front door is still barricaded. The hallway is flooded with flyers and newspapers that I have to wade through every time I need to go to the bathroom or if I merely want to park myself in front of the gilded mirror with the cherubs to study my image, which has undergone an eerie transformation.

I'm still repulsive. My hair under the ridiculous English tweed cap has started to grow out, and I've acquired a sparse, unbecoming beard that looks as if it might at any moment come loose and free itself from my haggard face. But I'm unable to control the subtle little tics under my eyes. They seem at times charming; at other times they disfigure my entire visage, which feels nerve-racking, since that's apparently the price that this whole business has cost me. It's the type of damage that a person has to learn to bear. But my twenty-five years are too few. I think I'm too young to give up or to conclude with resignation that I've done my part, I'm past my prime, washed up.

Here and there brown and white envelopes lie amid the jumble. I care as little about them as I do about the summer outside. The intended recipients are still gone, vanished without a trace, and no one is even properly searching for them. They live on only through this artificial respiration of mine, a sort of literary moth-proof sack for eternal preservation. I have to keep going as long as I can, even to the point of collapse, as long as I can still see them relatively clearly in the feverish haze before me, as long as I can hear their voices, and as long as I can feel their love and hatred sending sparks through this gloomy flat.

In one of the newspapers in the hallway I recently noticed a picture that somehow reminded me of Henry Morgan. It showed an East German shot-putter who is currently considered to be the world champion in his field. There was something about that quite repulsive gargantuan beast that reminded me of the refined gentleman, Henry Morgan. Perhaps it was the haircut and the powerful neck. The world record is supposedly twenty-four yards, by the way.

I could easily fill at least as many yards of shelf space with writings about the Morgan brothers. It would be a worthy monument. I am undoubtedly on the track of their enemy.

———————

The Advent calendar was the old-fashioned kind, dusty and faded and with pale glitter showing in the deep blue darkness of the holy night where the star showed the way to Bethlehem. Outside the manger – where an exhausted Mary and a proud Joseph tended to their as-yet-nameless baby boy – knelt the three Wise Men who had wandered on foot from the lands of the East with their gifts: gold, frankincense and myrrh. They were three good men who would soon betray the ruthless Herod for the sake of the Son of Man. The shunned king would grow angry, an outcry would be heard from the women who mourned their murdered male offspring, but the Wise Men would go free. They were inviolable in their wisdom.

The Advent calendar hung in the kitchen in the vast flat on Hornsgatan, in Södra Malmen in Stockholm in 1978, where three very wise men were still looking to the heavens above for a sign. They were the brothers Henry and Leo Morgan, along with myself, their humble and in some respects secret historian. In late November during that sombre autumn, Henry had found the Advent calendar in an old tobacco shop that sold surplus inventory from the fifties, and he had pinned it up on the pinboard in the kitchen. He said that it was a picture of us. We were three deputies, three gentlemen who had taken on the vicarious suffering that would relieve our fellow humans of their burdens. But we would not be destroyed, because we too were inviolable in our wisdom.

It was true that Henry Morgan could forecast the weather by the ache in his rheumatic joints, read his destiny in his rough hands, point out portents, find good premonitions and bad omens, although he would never be any sort of prophet – but it would soon turn out that we were not the least bit inviolable.

337

After Leo's return 'from America', Henry and I tried our best to maintain the routines that we had established for ourselves – it was our only chance of surviving, of producing anything, of pretending that we meant something in the world. Each morning Henry, true to form, would pin the page from his notebook on the pinboard in the kitchen, filling in all the hours of the coming day with various activities. The list might say: 'breakfast, practice, digging, coffee break, practice, lunch, shopping, ring up so and so, newspaper, dinner . . .' along with the times when each item was to take place. From a practical standpoint, each list offered some small spelling mistake because he was dyslexic – just like the king, he would tell himself in consolation. At any rate, the schedule lent the day a nice rhythm and a special feeling of importance, as if we actually were employed and utilised by someone, a higher power or a lower boss, it didn't make any difference.

Leo neither could nor wanted to follow such a regimen. He refused to assign the day any special schedule in advance. He took the day as it came, institutionalised as he was, and each day arrived for him like some ominous registered letter from some malicious authority. His living quarters reeked of incense – that was his gift to Jesus – and he never got out of bed in the mornings. He could lie in bed all day long with his hands clasped behind his head, whistling tunes, staring up at the ceiling and doing nothing. That was his regimen and we let him keep it. It could have been worse, much worse.

Nothing was the same now that Leo had suddenly returned. Henry tiptoed around much more cautiously, as if he were afraid of disturbing the idler, and he showed almost exaggerated respect. Perhaps he also felt a bit ridiculous because he had lied and said that Leo was in America even though he was actually in a psychiatric hospital. But I didn't give a damn about that, so we didn't discuss the matter.

One afternoon at the end of November I ascertained with satisfaction that I had produced no less than a hundred and fifty pages of my modern pastiche of *The Red Room*. The story had taken on a certain solidity, the characters were doing things that seemed entirely natural. Arvid Falk had freed himself from his schoolmistress, rented his own little flat in Söder where he could bide his time, and resumed writing without the burdensome feeling that he was neglecting anyone or anything. He had become close friends with Kalle

Montanus, Olle's lad from the country, and fresh breezes were blowing through the coterie at Berns.

It was a sultry, wet afternoon, and all of Stockholm was steaming like a witch's cauldron of smoke, soot, sulphur and curses. It was a day when you felt cold no matter how much you worked. Henry came upstairs in his dirty overalls just before dinner, and I suggested that we go down to the Europa Athletic Club for a while. It was not a scheduled activity, but Henry was not a rigid sort of person by any means. He was always open to suggestion.

We packed up our boxing trunks and walked down Hornsgatan to the Europa, which by then was starting to clear out, but Willis was always there until closing time. Henry immediately expressed his condolences. Willis was feeling blue.

It so happened that Gene Tunney had departed this life in November 1978. His life story was undoubtedly not the most romantic boxing story that history can present – a clever boy and a marine with a sophisticated interest in literature, and so on. His was not any sort of underdog story like that of Jack Johnson or Joe Louis or Rocky Marciano. But it so happened that Willis had met Tunney in person and received a photo showing himself and the brilliant technician who had made Jack Dempsey put his gloves on the shelf. The picture was taken just after the Second World War somewhere in New York, and it was on the wall in Willis's little cubbyhole at the Europa Athletic Club. Tunney looked truly handsome; for that matter, Willis did too. They were two men in their prime, and perhaps Willis felt that he was getting old now that the man of action standing beside him in the photo from New York had passed away.

'He was a damned cultivated person,' said Willis, nodding at the faded picture. 'In *that* way he wasn't like any other boxer. All great boxers have been philosophers in some way or other; they have to be philosophers. But Tunney was special. He was smart enough to know when to pack it in. We actually didn't talk much about boxing. I remember that he was interested in Jussi Björling and wondered if I knew him. And he liked politics.'

'Aren't we actually an awful lot alike?' asked Henry, taking up a position under the picture of Tunney.

'It's one thing to know when to pack it in, Henry,' said Willis. 'But you never got properly *started*.'

'It's not too late. I can spar with anyone in the country. On any day you like!'

'Watch out that Gringo doesn't hear you!'

But Gringo wasn't at the Europa that evening, so we were allowed to train in peace, without any cock-fighting. I started getting stabs of pain around my heart after half an hour and felt a bit depressed. When your heart races you always feel a bit uneasy, and it wouldn't slow down, so I decided to take it easy. Henry was going at it at the same pace as usual, and if you saw him all alone like that you would be prepared to agree: he could undoubtedly spar with anyone in the country. At least for several rounds.

The autumn had reached its optimum greyness, and there was nothing but rain and nasty weather on the day the alarm sounded. I was sitting in the library, working; Leo was lying in his bed, breathing in incense; and Henry was plinking on the piano when the doorbell suddenly rang and someone pounded on the door.

'Come . . . quick . . . Greger . . . tunnel . . .' panted an exhausted Birger. 'You have to . . . have to come down there!'

Birger had run up all the stairs, and since he was a bit pot-bellied, it had sapped him of strength. He was covered in mud and his face was black like a real miner's.

'Calm down, Birger,' said Henry. 'What's happened?'

'It . . . caved in,' panted Birger as he began trotting back down the stairs, taking small mincing steps.

'Fucking hell!' bellowed Henry and dashed after him. He tried to ask Birger a little more about what happened, but the only thing I could catch was that Greger was still inside, behind the cave-in.

It was one of the old wooden supports that had given way, right at the end of the slope down towards the passageway. Greger had slammed into the support when he made a run with the wheelbarrow to make it up the slope, and that did it. Dirt, sand and rocks had caved in on top of him, dividing the passageway into two parts in which one of them lacked both a beginning and an end. That was where Greger was now, if he was still alive.

Without any further palavering, Henry started digging with a shovel, and as soon as there was space, Birger and I joined him.

'Shouldn't we at least ring for an ambulance?' said Birger anxiously.

'Are you crazy!' shouted Henry. 'And put an end to seventeen years of toil?!'

'But it's not worth it, Henry,' said Birger. 'The damn treasure isn't worth this kind of risk!'

'Shut up and keep shovelling,' muttered Henry between spadefuls. 'We've got to hurry it up.'

We dug and shovelled for close to an hour until we could finally lift up the old support again and open up a free passage about one and a half feet high into the tunnel.

'Yoo-hoo!' shouted Henry into the darkness. 'Greger! Greggg-ggger!'

We heard only our own heavy breathing as we tensely waited for a reply, some small, pitiful, frightened sign of life from Greger. But there was nothing. Not a sound.

'Dammit!' said Henry. 'We have to dig down half a yard so I can get inside.'

'That damn Greger,' said Birger. 'This is so fucking typical of him. Everything he touches turns to disaster. And now my whole suit is ruined . . .'

After another half-hour we had removed enough sand, rocks and dirt that it was possible to wriggle into the next section of the tunnel. Henry took a heavy pocket torch with him, shining it into the black hole.

'Whoops . . . what the hell?!' they heard from down there in the dark. 'What in . . .'

'What is it, Henry?' shouted Birger. 'What do you see?'

'Quiet!' was the response, and then the beam of the torch vanished completely.

Birger was jumping up and down with curiosity, and even I had a pulse rate that was undoubtedly 150 per minute.

'Have you got a smoke, Birger?' I asked, and the charmer pulled out a badly battered pack of Pall Malls. We each lit a cigarette and smoked without saying a word. Birger was nervous and had a hard time standing still.

'He was a good guy, that Greger,' said Birger. 'He was a simple person, unpretentious but first-rate. His old man died when he was a lad, you know, but strangely enough he's always managed to get by.'

Birger sounded as if it were time to forget about Greger. But that wasn't at all the case. Greger was alive and presumably feeling better than he had in a long time. After we'd waited exactly as long as it takes to smoke two king-size Pall Malls, we heard signs of life from below in the shaft. We heard voices, laughter and clattering, as if from two delighted fishermen on their way home from a salmon stream.

Soon the torch-beam reappeared, followed by Henry Morgan's dishevelled hair. He looked like a very happy boy who had just reeled in a monster of a fish.

'What happened?' Birger and I exclaimed in unison.

'Just come with me,' said Henry. 'One at a time.'

Birger and I could hardly contain ourselves. We threw ourselves headlong down into the dark, landing on the other side of the mound that had been created by the cave-in. There stood Henry, receiving us like Virgil himself, the companion and guide to the underworld.

'Follow me,' he said tersely and led the way.

The path diverged into a cavity that was previously hidden and that must have been part of an even older passageway than the one Henry's paternal grandfather had found. The furthest part of the cave ended in a portal made of timbers the height of a man, creating an opening to a new artery heading due west.

'Be careful here!' Henry would say now and then.

The passageway continued for approximately twenty yards until it stopped at a sharp angle facing another portal that was completely covered with earth and sedimentary formations that looked like veins of coal. There at the entrance sat Greger, puffing on a cigarette and generally looking cocky. In his hand he held something that looked like a worn tin cup. He had chipped off a bit from the rim of the cup, which gleamed. Unmistakable flashes were coming from the rim of that old cup, cutting through the darkness of the ancient cave like a telegram of joy, prosperity and a bright future.

'It glitters like . . .' said Birger, swallowing a big lump in his throat.

'Gold,' said Greger.

Spiderman was the name of one of the least repulsive creatures created by the comic-book wizard Stan 'the Man' Lee. He was a poor boy with six arms and he never knew what to do with them. Henry Morgan always followed his fate very attentively down at the Cigar Seller's shop. In fact, Henry *the bartender* was rather like that Spiderman. The only difference was that Henry knew exactly what he was supposed to do with his arms: pour, measure, shake, stir, mix, sweeten, spice, crush and serve. We were witness to his full range of talents on that day when we celebrated Greger's resurrection.

Our depressed mood had been replaced with joyous exhilaration. We had not only found Greger in the best possible condition, but we had also come a good deal closer to the Treasure. Of that we were fully convinced.

'This is a gift from above, a portent, a streak of light and hope as we head into the darkness of winter,' intoned Henry, holding up the still-muddy golden cup. 'It's a sign of hope and consolation, while this is a gift from me personally,' he concluded as he served four delicious drinks. 'Down the hatch!'

'Skål, you counts and barons,' said Birger, just as we all expected him to say.

All disasters have a certain number of casualties and a certain number of heroes. Greger belonged to the latter category, and he had grown in stature down there in his newly discovered passageway. Greger had acquired a certain presence; he looked a bit like Franzén and Fälting, the first to board the *Wasa*, as he stood there balancing his Vanderbilt cocktail. What Greger had accomplished might be viewed, in the near future, as just as remarkable as the salvaging of the royal warship *Wasa*. That's what Greger had concluded himself, and no one tried to rob him of his illusion.

Henry got out the map, that strange document that had set everything in motion in 1961, and spread it on the table in the sitting room. The rest of us gathered round to look at it.

'It must be the alternative passageway that is hinted at here with this dotted line, going due west, parallel to Hornsgatan. Don't you think?'

We murmured our agreement as we stared at the collective efforts, hopes and illusions, facts and dreams of the old historian and member of the WWW Club now manifested in the equally blessed and cryptic form that a treasure map by necessity possesses when it's reconstructed after the fact. The dotted passageway led to one of four alternate treasure chambers. Until now the expedition had focused on two others, lying in a more easterly direction. We unanimously decided that the only valid alternative was the one going due west.

'I propose that we call the new find "Greger's Grotto".' said Henry.

Greger turned bright red in the face from pride, and there were no objections. We drank a toast to Greger's Grotto, and presumably we were so engrossed in the solemn mood that no one noticed Leo as he slipped into the sitting room. He was suddenly just there, and he seemed extremely uninterested in any new discoveries.

'Anyone have a cigarette?' he asked as he yawned and sat down on the windowsill.

'Sure,' said Birger ingratiatingly, handing him a Pall Mall.

'Did you almost die, Greger?' asked Leo.

Greger instantly came back down to earth.

'No, not at all,' he assured Leo. 'It just caved in a bit, but it opened up a new passageway. Here, here it is,' he went on, pointing at the map. 'It's going to be called Greger's Grotto.'

Leo made no move to look because he wasn't interested, not the least bit curious. He stayed where he was over by the window, peering out at the even grey haze settling over the rooftops, the streets and all of Stockholm.

'Well, well,' he said with a sigh. 'That's a fine name.'

'Damn, I feel good,' said Henry when Greger and Birger had left us after several hours of discussion and drinking. Leo hadn't managed to bring our spirits down, and then he had slunk back to his incense. Henry and I were in top form that evening.

'We need to make a whole night of it!' I said.

'Of course,' agreed Henry. 'But first we just need to check on our finances.'

After some rather dubious calculating we came up with enough for a minor binge that evening. Henry had a flash of genius: we could ring Kerstin, the daughter of the football-pool king, the one who drove a Picko's delivery van. A flash of genius was the right term for it, and I took it upon myself to ring Kerstin. She was actually home, and she would definitely come for dinner, and everything seemed simply too good to be true.

We ran over to Åhléns downtown to buy delicacies like crabs, eel, salami, spreadable cheeses, and various pâtés, as well as all sorts of other things that might embellish what was a grey and gloomy evening, as far as the climate was concerned, at the very end of November. Henry was still wearing his muddy overalls, and I hadn't even washed my hands after the disaster, so people may have taken us for two desperate fugitives, blowing our money on fine food in the last tense hours before the police caught up with us.

Then we headed back home to wash up and shave, take a brief rest and put on more appropriate attire. Henry was even generous enough to ask

344

whether Leo would like to join us, but he was going into town, to the cinema. We would have Kerstin all to ourselves, or so we thought.

Just before eight o'clock another glorious and artistic table was laid out by *Henri le gourmet*. It was a splendour to behold, and he hadn't neglected a thing. The table setting was crowned by a magnificent parlour palm, adorned with small pineapples, which gave the arrangement a certain touch of the Riviera, the Mediterranean and Monte Carlo.

Kerstin arrived fashionably late and was in high spirits. Henry served us each a Palm Breeze, which consists of rum, Chartreuse and crème de cacao, a drink that had won a cocktail contest in London back in 1949, at least according to the bartender.

'I probably made several hundred of these Palm Breeze cocktails when I was in . . .' Henry began and then continued to hold forth for a dumbstruck Kerstin, who gave off a strong scent of eau de cologne.

'Well, that was good, at any rate,' she said as she awoke from Henry's numbing monologue.

'But there's just one detail,' said Henry. 'You're very beautiful tonight, Kerstin, but you're not allowed to chew gum when you drink a cocktail!'

'Sorry,' she said, embarrassed, and spat the gum into her hand. 'I always chew gum.'

'And you do it very beautifully. It makes some people look ugly, but not you.'

'That's going a bit too far,' I felt forced to intervene.

'OK, Klasa,' said the host, holding up his hands as if at a robbery.

'That was rude.'

'Don't fight, boys,' said Kerstin. 'How about showing me around?'

'Klasa will show the lady around while I take care of things in the kitchen,' said Henry and disappeared.

The dinner later proceeded according to a slightly strained and yet very dignified ritual. The delicacies were excellent, and the various wines quite superb. Above all, they made the host relax the proprieties a bit.

Kerstin chewed gum even over coffee, but neither Henry nor I felt like nagging her. All three of us were quite satiated after the repast, and we each sat in an armchair in the sitting room, digesting our food with our feet up on footstools. Between the two Parian figures of Truth and Falsehood the fire hissed and crackled in a sleepy, anaesthetising concert.

Henry was undoubtedly very pleased with himself. Whenever he was

345

pleased with himself and his efforts, he would get a particularly foolish expression on his face. It looked, quite simply, as if his eyes became narrow slits. He had now conversed and served food and entertained for several hours like a fully fledged host, and he was entitled to sit and revel in front of the fire with some coffee and a cognac.

'You're a couple of strange birds,' said Kerstin with a sigh, apropos of nothing.

'Birds and birds,' Henry repeated. 'I can't agree with that. We practically live like monks up here.'

'Monks and monks,' I repeated.

'Dammit all, Klasa!' Henry suddenly exclaimed. 'You know what we should do now, don't you?!'

'Take it easy, that's what I suggest.'

'The song . . .' he whispered. '"The Girl with the Contact Lenses and Mourning Ribbon."'

'Hell yes!'

We quickly finished off our coffee and cognac and enticed Kerstin into the room with Henry's grand piano. We sat her down on the sofa with the black tassels, lit a couple of candles for the mood and got out the sheet music for the song that we had cobbled together on All Saints' Day in honour of Kerstin. By this time we had almost forgotten it, and when Henry cleared his throat and struck a couple of chords on the piano, he seemed slightly embarrassed. Kerstin, on the other hand, looked very amused.

Henry *the entertainer* made it all the way through the song without a single mistake. It may have been a bit strained but it wasn't lacking in feeling. Kerstin was deeply moved by the tribute and applauded with shining eyes. We each received a kiss and a hug, and her lips tasted of Stimorol gum.

'One more time . . . Let me hear it one more time,' begged Kerstin. 'I've never had a song dedicated to me before . . . oh, please . . .'

Henry couldn't very well resist, and so he sang 'The Girl with the Contact Lenses and Mourning Ribbon' one more time. Our muse soaked up every single word about the marvellous daughter of the football-pool king with the bad eyesight and grief. Then we went back to the sitting room to drink whisky, put more wood on the fire and talk about mutual friends and enemies. We found no mutual friends before we also discovered that we were very drunk, all three of us.

At that moment Leo came home. It turned out to be well past one in the morning, and Leo had been to the cinema. He greeted Kerstin with unusual politeness, and her eyes lingered on him for a long time. Leo poured himself a whisky and lit a cigarette over at the chess table, because all of a sudden he had decided to make the weekly move against Lennart Hagberg in Borås.

Henry was in an exuberant mood, and he started talking up his brother, boasting right and left about his poems and amazing chess skills.

'I've always wanted to learn to play chess,' said Kerstin.

'Well, there's a genius of a teacher over there,' said Henry, nodding at Leo.

Kerstin was not particularly shy, and she went over to the genius, who for once was actually feeling sociable, and he started explaining how to move the pieces. He showed her the weekly move, why and how he had chosen it, and what effect it would have on his opponent.

Henry yawned loudly, while I sat there in my armchair, nodding off now and then. It had been a demanding day, the dinner had taken its toll, and the strong whiskies had made things even better. Soon all I heard was a quiet hissing from a slumbering Henry and a slumbering fire. Kerstin and Leo, who were murmuring quietly over in the corner at the chess table, sounded like muffled voices from a neighbour far away beyond the walls. The fire cast its warm, calm light over the easy chairs, and I too fell asleep.

———————

It was extremely cold in the sitting room when I came to. Henry was standing in front of me, kicking at my foot to wake me up. Dawn was making its way through the room like a ghost, filling the flat with that special chiaroscuro that could seem so depressing. Although right now it didn't feel particularly depressing, but actually rather pleasant.

'Kerstin . . .' whispered Henry.

'Mm,' I said. 'What about her?'

'She and Leo,' he said and tsk'ed. 'It ended up being the two of them, at any rate.'

'Nice for him,' I replied sullenly.

'That's one way of looking at it,' said Henry shrugging his shoulders morosely. 'I'm going to make a fire.'

It was only seven a.m. and we thawed ourselves out properly before there was even talk of any breakfast. By that time it was completely pointless to go to bed because then the whole day would be done for. It was better just to get on with things as if nothing had happened.

Out in the kitchen the dishes were waiting from yesterday, and there was nothing for it but to take a deep breath and dig in. About an hour later we had cleaned up and set out a monumental breakfast with glasses of hair-of-the-dog. As soon as we had sat down in peace and quiet with the morning papers on our laps, we heard footsteps coming from the bathroom, and soon a rather haggard looking Kerstin turned up in the kitchen. She looked quite embarrassed but we tried to cheer her up, because there was absolutely nothing remarkable about what had happened. On the contrary. At any rate, she ate her breakfast with a ravenous appetite and then had to run off to her job. Someone might already have called her on the radio.

'You two are much too sweet,' she repeated over and over again. 'You're not angry about this, are you?!'

'*Angry?*' said Henry emphatically like a wounded actor. '*Me, angry?!*'

Kerstin smiled happily and gave each of us a combination good-morning and thanks-and-goodbye kiss before she started gathering up her things, which lay strewn over the whole flat. God only knew what they had been doing.

'But in any case, I'd like to have that song,' she said finally, from the doorway. 'On tape. Could you record it onto a cassette?'

'Sure, I can do that,' said Henry.

'Then I can listen to it in the car and think about all of you.'

Kerstin left, and Henry stared at me over the newspaper, smiling a foolish smile.

'Chicks are also birds, you know,' he said, imitating a moronic ornithologist who people had laughed at years ago.

I flung a piece of cheese at the idiot's head.

For once Leo got up before lunch and was met with quiet sighs and low whistles from the kitchen. He too looked embarrassed, but also proud and slightly annoyed. He'd had a problem with Kerstin's chewing gum. It had got stuck in a place where it absolutely should not have got stuck.

There was a lot of whispering going on outside the door to my bedroom. It was barely audible but still enough to wake me up. The fact of the matter is that from childhood on you become particularly sensitive to certain holidays and special occasions, and for the rest of your life they retain their specific magic in the calendar. This time it was the Lucia festival. Henry had opened twelve little doors on the Advent calendar with the three wise men, and I opened my bleary eyes and stared at the alarm clock. It was a few minutes past six and I'd had only a few hours of sleep because the evening before had been both long and intense.

The whispering continued out there in the corridor, and I drowsily tried to distinguish the voices. I thought I heard a woman, a Lucia, but if so, I couldn't imagine who it might be. As I said, it had been a tumultuous evening, which started with a big bash on Strandvägen in honour of the year's Nobel prize winners. To my great surprise I had been invited in my capacity as a young man-of-letters, and I felt deeply flattered, not least because of Henry Morgan's reaction. When the invitation had arrived a week earlier, the inquisitive gossipmonger had read every single word over my shoulder, the very shoulder that he later pounded with all his might to congratulate me. According to him, this was confirmation that I belonged to the most elite, the crème de la crème of Swedish cultural life, and he insisted that I was a name to be reckoned with in the future. Things would not go for me as they had for Leo. But I couldn't figure out who had sent the card, since as far as I knew, Mr Isaac Bashevis Singer and I were not yet acquainted.

In any case, it was a grand party. Lost there in the crowds and bolstered, of course, by a glass of champagne, I ran into my publisher, Torsten Franzén, and then it all became perfectly clear. He was the one who had invited me.

Franzén had brought with him his stylish wife, who absolutely *adored* what I wrote and absolutely *adored* what Mr Singer wrote.

'You haven't *talked* to him yet?!' croaked Mrs Franzén, splashing a little champagne onto my jacket sleeve. 'You really *must* see to it! He's an utterly *fantastic* person, simply marvellous!'

'I believe you,' I said.

'You have to tell me how it's going with *The Red Room*,' said Franzén the publisher. 'How far have you got?'

'I'm making good progress.'

'When can you deliver it?'

'How the hell should I know! Is this really the place to be discussing business?'

'I never hear from you except when you need an advance. I really need to know how it's going!'

'Great,' I said. 'It's going fucking great.'

'The advances have really started to add up and people are beginning to talk, you know. I have superiors to answer to.'

'That's certainly candid of you, Torsten. Damn candid,' I said, looking deep into his eyes. 'I've never heard any boss admit that he has superiors he has to answer to except if there's some sort of disaster.'

'Klas, very soon this *is* going to be a disaster. The book is supposed to be on our desks this spring, preferably in April after the big spring sales. That's four months from now.'

I was starting to feel pressured, and it was so hot in there that the sweat was trickling down my cheeks and there was no more champagne in my glass. Franzén had backed me into a sweaty corner, and I had nothing to say to him other than to offer random jabs in the form of bad promises and multiple excuses, but then my salvation arrived in the figure of a Jewish ambassador who, with Mrs Franzén's shimmering gown right behind him, stepped over to me and said in English:

'You are a young writer, yes? Then you must meet Mr Singer. All the young writers must meet Mr Singer!'

'OK,' I said. 'I *do* want to meet him.'

The ambassador guided me through the sea of people to a little, nodding old man peering out from a corner. He seemed weary and worn-out after having made his way through an ocean of handshakes from the east coast of America to the Baltic Sea in Europe.

'This is a young Swedish writer,' said the ambassador, pushing me in front of the Oracle.

'Hello, Mr Singer,' I said.

'Hello, young writer,' said the Sorcerer. 'Do you live here?' he went on, and before I could reply he added, 'I am Isaac Bashevis Singer, and I live in New York. Very, very nice to meet you.'

And that was that. Because the next second, as we were shaking hands, a vulture wearing a pearl necklace landed and sank her claws into the febrile shoulders of the little, mouselike man, completely inundating him with a cascade of flattering and admiring phrases. She stuck a pen in his hand and spelled her name, which presumably was prominently entered both in the peerage books and the tax records. She wanted at all costs to have a signed copy.

After that the rest of the party disintegrated into champagne and smoke and cocktails and Israeli snacks that tasted superb in a rather restrained way. What with one thing and another, and after making a night-time round of the city's bars, I was now lying in my bed on the morning of the Lucia festival, listening to someone whispering outside my door.

In a moment this nervous whispering finally metamorphosed into a beautifully sung Lucia song. The door opened and the room was filled with the smell of candles, freshly made coffee, freshly baked saffron buns and gingersnaps. Henry was the Star Boy, wearing the cone-shaped hat and the shift and everything, while Kerstin was Lucia. It was as impressive as it was surprising. I sat up in bed and received the attendants like a delighted schoolmaster.

'Why all this for little old me?' I naturally wondered.

'Why not?' said Henry. 'Actually, I knew nothing about all this. Not a thing.'

'I was planning to wait on all of you,' said Kerstin. 'But that didn't happen because Leo isn't here.'

'Let's go out to the kitchen,' said Henry. 'Göring's old bed isn't the appropriate place for a pyjama party.'

No sooner said than done. We went out to the kitchen to drink Lucia coffee and talk about the winter that was fast approaching. Kerstin was going away for Christmas, while Henry and I had decided to hold the fort here at home. We didn't know much about Leo's plans, but we were aware that he didn't care much for holidays or special occasions.

Henry was immensely pushy and obstinate about wanting to know whether Kerstin had fallen in love with Leo.

'I'm not sure,' said Kerstin with her mouth full of Lucia bun. 'He seems so fragile somehow. But I'm not sure.'

'And no one's asking you to be sure, either. In any case, it will do the boy good to have a girl like you. It would do anyone good.'

———————

Winter arrived all at once. It was going to be a real winter. Overnight all of Stockholm was blanketed by the first snow, and then the frost set in so that it looked as if the snow would stay. The word 'Wood' began showing up more and more often on Henry's daily schedule, and we spent several hours each week going out to search through abandoned Dumpsters and then lugging boards up to the sawhorse in the attic to saw them into manageable pieces.

There was an impressive and overwhelming consistency about that particular winter – it would linger on well into the following April, although we fortunately didn't know that at the time, since Henry's prophecies didn't reach that far ahead – and it's always pleasant to deal with consistency. A friend who is consistent becomes increasingly indispensable, and an enemy who is equally consistent becomes more and more something that consistently must be called dispensable. Winter arrived overnight, and then it was here to stay.

As mentioned, Henry was very superstitious, and he had full confidence in that famous Lapp who carves up reindeer stomachs to predict the weather. We looked through every newspaper to find that Lapp, but we never did find him, and Henry had to prophesy as best he could by relying on his sensitive joints. As a child he had been very hardy in terms of the wind and weather, but by now he went around rubbing his creaky joints. He said it was rheumatism. It ran in his family, and the five years he'd spent roaming through central Europe, waiting in draughty train stations and staying in rented rooms hadn't made things any better. That was the price he'd had to pay. But it was worth it.

'My mum has rheumatism too,' he said. 'Mum! Mum . . .'

'What about your mum?' I asked.

'When did I last ring my mother? It must have been several weeks ago!'

'No kidding!'

'We'll be going over to see her soon to have Christmas lunch, just so you know. She pops over to Storm Island for Christmas. She'd be deeply hurt if we didn't show up.'

So we were all invited to Christmas lunch with the Morgan boys' mother, but it proved to be a hell of a job trying to get hold of Leo. He'd been gone for over a week now, and no one knew where he was. Henry tried several phone numbers of various free spirits, but without success. Finally we had to go off to the Christmas lunch without Leo; he seemed to have been swallowed up by the earth.

Mrs Greta Morgan didn't really look the way I'd pictured her. She was much smaller and thinner, and she greeted me with an almost entreating handshake and said that it was very nice to meet me. She had heard such good things about me. Like any good mum, she had outdone herself with the lunch spread on that Saturday just before Christmas. She had even gone to the State off-licence and bought half a bottle of blackcurrant aquavit. She went to that shop at most once a year, when she would actually return the bottle from the previous year. Henry thought that was splendid. No one returned bottles to the State off-licence for the sake of the money; it was a matter of principle. Bottles were not to be thrown away. Bottles should be become part of the natural cycle, just like people. Mamma Greta listened and shook her head at her son. He was never going to grow up.

So this was their old boyhood home – a dark two-bedroom flat on Brännkyrkagatan, and one of the rooms was usually kept closed up. That was the boys' room, filled with things that Henry and Leo had left behind. For some inexplicable reason, Greta had kept the room untouched, deciding not to use it for anything else. The room had such a strange air about it. Attached to the wall next to the bed was a bast mat to protect the pale wallpaper. Still taped to the mat were photos of the boys when they were kids, as well as pictures of Charlie Parker, Ingemar Johansson, the Beatles and the Rolling Stones. On brown-stained wall shelves stood a large number of model aeroplanes, cars and boats along with old schoolbooks, children's books and photographs. One picture showed the happy family some time during the late fifties. There stood the Jazz Baron, just the way I'd seen him in a couple of photo cavalcades from the great era of Swedish jazz. There stood Greta, wearing a beautiful dress that she'd made herself down at the community sewing room on Mariatorget. There stood Henry with a swollen cheek that he'd no doubt acquired down at the Europa Athletic Club. And there stood Leo, so small, birdlike and enigmatic.

353

On a bench next to the bed was the cumbersome old radio from Philips in Holland, the one that Leo had received from his paternal grandfather, and next to it was an aquarium in which listless bubbles were the only sign of life or movement.

It was like some sort of museum, a monument to a brotherly harmony and concord that was nothing more than a maternal dream. It seemed to me that every little thing could be easily traced back to one of the boys. All these items were the signatures of the two brothers, their indelible fingerprints. It felt almost as if they were sitting there somewhere under the beds. They were united for all eternity through these objects left behind.

I was standing there staring at the aquarium when Henry came into his childhood room. A dull, diffuse shadow suddenly began moving in the sludge at the bottom of the aquarium, like a ghost from the past.

'That is one of the world's oldest aquarium fishes,' Henry bragged. 'In Stockholm, at any rate. There are some old bream out in Bromma that are older. But this fish is at least seventeen years old.'

'It's Leo's, isn't it?'

'Yup. He got it when he was a teenager, if I remember right.'

Henry traipsed around, occasionally poking at things in the room. He snorted once in a while and then picked up the picture of the happy family from the late fifties. He pointed at each person with his stubby index finger, one after the other, and told me exactly what I had already figured out. I listened to him patiently, because this was really important. I had never seen Henry Morgan as serious, almost resolute, as he was when he walked around and talked about the things in that room from his boyhood. Each piece of furniture bore its mark, and each mark had a story. Boys' rooms tend to get quite worn out over time. Just like the boys themselves.

———————

The Christmas lunch was as good as Christmas lunches always are, especially at the start of the holidays, before everyone grows tired of the food. Henry sang drinking songs, and the aquavit made us all merry and warm. After a while Greta managed to forget that Leo hadn't shown up, or at least she put a good face on it; this was something she was used to, after all.

Afterwards she gave us more than twenty pounds of preserves and pâtés, sausages and ham, salad and herring, and there was nothing we could do but accept it and say thanks. Greta didn't want us to starve, and the prospects were good that with all that food we wouldn't.

In the stairwell Henry decided that he wanted to look in on Verner. He always did that around Christmas time.

'He goes out a bit now and then. Verner, I mean. But he likes it if someone looks in on him once in a while.'

'It's too awful,' said Greta, looking as sorrowful as only a mother can. 'I don't understand what has become of our boys.'

'Don't worry, my dear,' said Henry. 'They just need some peace and quiet for a while. Then everything will be fine. I promise you.'

Greta smiled and smoothed down her apron without replying.

'Well, well,' she said then. 'I suppose whatever happens, happens. Thank you for coming, anyway, the two of you.' And in the midst of all that solemnity she suddenly produced yet another terse old proverb from Storm Island: 'That was a nice party, said the old woman when she buried her husband.'

We wished her a Merry Christmas and left. Downstairs on the third floor Henry rang the bell to the Hansson flat. He gave it two quick jabs, just as he'd always done. It took at least a minute before the door opened. Verner's mother was the one who opened it. She looked very tired and gave us a rather strained smile.

'Hi, Henry,' she said in a toneless voice. 'It's been a long time.'

'About this same time last year,' said Henry. 'Is Verner home?'

'Verner . . . no, Verner's not home,' said the woman, and even an innocent little child could have seen right through her.

'Does he have his own place now?' asked Henry, slightly puzzled.

'Well no, he stays here sometimes, or else with friends, his buddies.'

'All right, well, tell him hello, at least. Tell him to give me a ring.'

'I'll do that . . .' she managed to say before we heard a crash and a groan and a scratching sound coming from the room beyond the hallway.

'Merry Christmas, and thanks for stopping by,' she said and then slammed the door.

Henry didn't look the least bit surprised, but he shook his head bitterly.

'What a bloody mess,' he said with a sigh. 'Verner sits locked up in there, drinking and solving classic chess problems. He's got the sharpest mind in the whole city. But he's like a child who's been sent to sit in the corner. It's impossible to reach him anymore.'

Verner was a man who had once been a boy. As a boy he had had to be protected from the nasty world. As an adult, it was just the opposite – the world had to be protected from him. That was his awful fate.

One day Henry wrote down only one thing on the daily schedule: Christmas cleaning. Considering the size of the flat, over two thousand square feet, it looked as if the cleaning could easily go on for several days, if we were going to make a thorough job of it. Every single rug had to be taken down to the courtyard for beating, the floors had to be washed and waxed, and so on.

We got started straight after breakfast, and Henry swore furiously at the fact that Leo was so conveniently away, because that bastard was never home when anything useful had to be done. A little work would have done him good. Henry took on the job of beating the rugs, while I went around with an old Nilfisk vacuum cleaner that had definitely seen better days. That's how the morning passed. After that we focused on the cupboards, the library and the wardrobes, which all had to be cleaned of any vermin.

In the service corridor there was a long row of wardrobes that served only as storage space for old junk, the sort of abandoned things that can take several years of an archaeologist's life to evaluate. Henry claimed to have made a valiant effort, although without any real success. There were all of his grandfather Morgonstjärna's clothes, as well as his paternal grandmother's clothes and shoes, some hatboxes filled with letters and several bureaus containing odds and ends. Henry cautioned me about going through the wardrobes because once you started, you could get held up – it was so damned easy to get sidetracked.

It was in one of these wardrobes that I found the submachine-gun. The bottom drawer of one of the bureaus was locked, and I got nosy. The key ring hanging in the kitchen had keys to the attic and cellar as well as a good many keys that didn't seem to fit anywhere, like most key rings. Henry was down in the courtyard, conducting a veritable concert with the rug beater, so I swiped the key ring and eventually found a key that fit. I pulled out the drawer and was instantly struck by the way the smell of stale mothballs was mixed with the smell of grease and oil. I lifted up a rough piece of jute and saw the old gun lying there like some cold and frozen snake.

The submachine-gun was the old-fashioned type, the slightly heavier and more cumbersome model that was in use before the M-45. It was grey, and the mechanism seemed sturdy and reliable. Like most Swedes, I lacked any familiarity with guns except for what I had gleaned from national service. But I couldn't help noticing how well-kept this gun was. It was lying inside a mothproof bag, of course, but something told me that the contents of this particular drawer had not been forgotten, although the contents of all the other dusty drawers inside the wardrobes had.

When I'd satisfied my curiosity and looked my fill at the old gun, I closed the drawer, hung the keys in the kitchen and went back to cleaning. When Henry came up from the courtyard with a couple of newly beaten rugs, I felt embarrassed and nearly blushed. Of course, he didn't notice. And eventually I had plenty of other things to occupy my thoughts.

———

Soon the whole flat smelled of soap and floor polish, and we had done a great job. There were three big cardboard boxes from the forties full of decrepit Christmas decorations, and it took us almost two whole evenings to put everything in its place. We outdid each other with lively arrangements of groups of little elves, mistletoe and candle-holders. An experienced housewife couldn't have done any better.

Henry and I had made a gentlemen's agreement – we would protest against the buying frenzy by not giving each other any Christmas presents, not even symbolic ones. But there were still a million other things to purchase if we were to survive the holiday as respectable bachelors. We made extensive lists of what we ought to buy, what we wanted to buy and what we could reasonably expect to be able to buy, considering the state of our finances. Through our combined efforts – without even consulting me Henry sacrificed a world history in a dozen volumes with half-calf bindings – we managed to scrape together a nice sum to spend on food and drink and other types of supplementary solace.

On 23 December we each went on a buying expedition in separate parts of town. I was home by six in the evening and started making dinner. The door slammed and I thought it was Henry coming home. But instead it was Leo, and he looked quite wretched.

'Where the hell have you been?' I asked. 'We've been looking for you for weeks.'

357

'For weeks?' said Leo and sank down onto a chair at the kitchen table without taking off his outdoor clothes.

I was thinking of telling him at least to take off his running shoes before he tracked a load of sand and salt into our newly cleaned flat, but I decided not to complain because I didn't want to seem a fusspot, like Henry.

'I've been with a couple of buddies,' said Leo.

'You seem really tired.'

Leo didn't reply. He just glared at me as I stood there at the stove, frying pork and boiling brown beans.

'Are you hungry?'

'Is there any grub?'

'Of course there is.'

Henry still hadn't shown up, so we decided not to wait with dinner. We opened a whole bottle of Renat and several Christmas beers to have with the pork. Leo downed two shots of aquavit on an empty stomach and without uttering a word. I didn't feel like initiating any sort of interrogation, so I didn't say anything either.

'So how *are* you, anyway?' he finally asked me, using that nagging and pig-headed tone of voice that truly drunk people sometimes have.

'What do you mean, how *am* I?'

'How are things up *here*, I mean, with Henry? Can you put up with him?'

'Of course I can. Why shouldn't I?'

Leo chewed slowly, snorting and shaking his head, as if there were something very basic that I just didn't fathom.

'What exactly do you mean?'

'I don't know you,' said Leo. 'I don't know how you function. We've never really talked to each other.'

'You're never home. So that's not so strange.'

'You're scared of me because I was locked up in a loony bin.'

'I'm not the least bit scared of you. I've told you that before,' I said.

Leo muttered something into his food and poured two more shots of aquavit.

'There's something funny about the vibes in here. Have you noticed it?' said Leo. 'You're always defending yourself and Henry. Haven't you noticed that?'

'What is it I'm defending us from?'

'Hell if I know, but you are.'

'If that's the case, it damn well isn't my fault, is it?!' I said. 'You come here dead drunk, and there's nothing wrong with that, but you should bloody well make a little effort. We've been cleaning and fixing things up for several days now just to make things a little more bearable. We were actually counting on you.'

'So let's drink a toast, then,' said Leo with exaggerated heartiness.

We drank the aquavit in one gulp and I washed it down with a lager. Leo savoured the taste of the aquavit for a long time.

'I don't want you to think that I'm trying to spoil things. It's just that I can't stand all this fucking grandeur,' said Leo. 'Henry tries to be so fucking grand and clever, and you try to be so fucking grand and clever. I don't like it.'

'What do you mean by "grand"?'

'You sit here on your arse and write all day long like a good little boy. You should go out instead! Go out and have a look around this city. Go out and check out the people who are walking around on this street. Check out their faces and you'll see what's going on!'

Leo lit a cigarette and dropped the match in the butter, then he instantly picked it up and scraped off the soot with a knife. At the moment I had nothing to say.

'Don't you *see* what's going on?!' he repeated. 'What the hell it is they're doing? The newspapers write about some fucking thing called assisted dying. You're allowed to take your own life just because you're old; all you have to do is sign a paper. What's *that* all about?!'

'Calm down, Leo. You don't have to shout.'

'I am calm, dammit. You're just scared of me because I was locked up in a loony bin.'

'I'm not the least bit scared of you.'

'OK, I'm sorry. It wasn't my intention to come here and bring you down.'

'I'm not down,' I said. 'But you don't have to be so fucking aggressive all the time. It seems like you feel threatened.'

Leo snorted again, apparently trying to look superior.

'I've got to go,' he said. 'I'm just spoiling things by being here.'

'No, you're not at all. Why don't you lie down for a while and get some sleep?'

Leo snorted or sneered or just made some sort of noise. He got up from the table and left. I called after him but got no response. I was furious because he seemed to detest me.

After dinner and the argument with Leo, I went to the library to work for a couple of hours, before it was time for the Christmas show on TV. I spent a long time on how Kalle Montanus, Olle's lad from the country, lay on a bench in a kitchen in a building scheduled for demolition in the Järnet district, down by Erstagatan. Kalle had participated in the whole occupation of Mullvaden and was one of the last ones left. It was now December and very cold, and I re-read the scene in Strindberg's book in which the older Montanus lay up there in Sellén's atelier and froze and the floorboards had been used for firewood, and he was reading about food, about mayonnaise, and trying to sleep, but he couldn't sleep, and he thought about killing himself since it was so damn cold. I tried to imagine how his son would look in today's clothes, and I started describing his face, his posture, his personal charm and appearance, and I thought I had captured the character quite accurately when, to my great disappointment and horror, I discovered that it was actually Leo I was describing. I was furious again, and I crumpled up the worthless character-sketch and flung it into the wastepaper basket. At that moment the front door slammed, and I went out to the hallway to see what was going on.

Henry lay in the middle of the floor under a mountain of bags, boxes and packages, crowned by an enormous Christmas tree. I heard a heavy panting coming from somewhere under a new Christmas-tree stand, and I dug out my friend, only to find him dead drunk. I then learned, amid a copious flood of implausible excuses and pretexts, that Henry was on friendly terms with at least a dozen Christmas-tree sellers, each of whom had a thermos of *glögg*, and it was a tradition for him to go around and visit these comrades in his search for the most beautiful coniferous evergreen, otherwise known as a Christmas tree. And obviously that sort of fastidiousness takes its toll.

––––––––––

The morning glittered exactly the way it's supposed to glitter for Christmas Eve, and when I got up Henry was already awake. He had lit the candles on the tree, which we had decorated during the night amid fierce discussion. The flat was fragrant with the smell of resin from the forest and coffee from the kitchen. Henry had made breakfast and was sitting there enjoying his solitude with all the little doors on the Advent calendar now open and the candles blazing full blast.

'Merry Christmas, young man,' said Henry.

'Merry Christmas,' I said, and we shook hands.

The fire in the kitchen stove was crackling and sparking, and it was quite warm even though frost roses were clinging to the windowpanes.

'Have you seen the tree?' asked Henry after I'd poured myself some coffee and sat down at the kitchen table with the morning paper.

'Of course. It's magnificent,' I said.

Henry cleared his throat and looked a bit downhearted.

'I think you'd better have another look,' he said.

I could sense that something was up, and so as not to disappoint the Christmas elf I went back to the sitting room to admire the grandeur. There was a traditional straw goat standing under the tree, and on either side of the goat was a present. I sighed, feeling rather flattered, and kicked myself for not buying a Christmas gift for Henry. We had made a gentleman's agreement not to do so, but I should have known that he could never keep his side of the bargain.

One of the presents was for Leo, and the other was for me. There was a note on each of them with a rhymed verse, signed 'Birger's Timely Rhymes' because the wordsmith down at the Furniture Man had opened a verse workshop that was open every day up until Christmas Eve. It had turned out to be a big hit. People would bring their gifts over to Birger, and then he would slap together a verse for ten kronor, one after the other. He made a ton of money, tax-free. Henry had probably been given a discount, since the verse on my present was not particularly high-class.

> When the cold grips the poet's arm
> Something is needed to keep it warm
> But he has no girlfriend, he has to admit
> So he'll have to settle for something that's knit.
>   Birger's Timely Rhymes '78.

Even so, I was moved. And I went back to the kitchen with the present to shake hands with a wide-eyed Henry. I opened the gift. It was a dark brown Higgins cardigan made of good-quality cashmere.

'You can exchange it if it doesn't fit, but it's a good colour for your jackets,' said Henry.

'This is too much, Henry, way too much. And you know we said that . . .'

'But I wanted to buy you something. I was feeling generous yesterday.'

I put on my Higgins cardigan, and it fit perfectly.

'It's just perfect,' I said, standing in front of the mirror in the hallway. 'It's just what I needed.'

'And that kind of sweater is really warm, believe me,' said Henry. 'You can wear it when you're writing.'

'It fits like it was custom-made.'

Henry was pleased with my response, and I wore my new, warm Higgins cardigan all day long. I had a strong feeling that he had put a certain amount of calculation into that Christmas present. When I was growing up we always opened our presents in the evening on Christmas Eve, and when we were really small – so small that only our impatience was big – we used to get an 'appetiser' present in the morning that would keep us occupied until the evening. Now it was just the reverse – I had a whole day to produce something to give him in return. And that was probably exactly what Henry had counted on.

Consequently, I went out that morning 'to buy cigarettes', which is what people say in this situation. I went down to the NK department store and pushed my way through the chaos of stressed men who at the last minute were emptying their bank accounts. I had very little money left so I opened an account. After various checks and controls I was given a fifty-kronor bonus from heaven. In the men's department on the ground floor I caught sight of a very sophisticated tie with jazz patterns from Yves Saint-Laurent, Paris. It was a subdued, austere, restrained affair, burgundy with tiny beige musical notes at the tip and several bars of music above, scattered here and there.

'A very elegant tie,' said the clerk. 'Is it for your father, brother, brother-in-law . . . ?' she went on, making a cute sucking sound through her teeth as she surveyed the sea of shoppers with that type of superior expression that only truly haughty and pompous shop clerks can muster.

'It's for a good friend,' I said.

With the gestures of a conjurer – it looked as if the clerk nonchalantly tossed the noose up in the air – she produced what looked like an ordinary knot, to make the tie even more distinctive. It was undeniably stylish, and I asked the price.

'Two hundred and twenty-five,' the clerk said tersely, and again made that cute whistling sound through her teeth.

I decided on the Yves and received an elegant package, in exactly the right shape for a gentleman in his prime. Then I headed home through the city, stopping for a glass of *glögg* at Stortorget. And I was back just in time for Donald Duck's Christmas Cavalcade.

―――――――

That evening, after a snack of *glögg* and nuts while watching Donald Duck's Christmas Cavalcade, we set the table for three in the dining room. It looked very festive and the room was fragrant with hyacinths. Leo still hadn't put in an appearance, and Henry replied evasively when I asked him where his brother was.

'If he shows up, he shows up,' said Henry with a shrug.

In any case, we set the table with everything we had to offer, which turned out to be a great deal. Henry had made his own herring salad, which was better than anyone's mother could make. We were quite hungry and valiantly launched into the food. Henry sang a few silly songs, but after a couple of toasts we began casting uneasy glances at the empty plate which, in its own way, was spoiling the symmetry.

'I know what to do,' said Henry in mid-bite, nodding at the empty plate.

He went out to the kitchen, opened the window facing the courtyard, and called for Spinks. To our great surprise, we saw something black and lithe actually come slinking across the snow-covered roof. Spinks hadn't been seen for days, just like Leo. The cat rubbed happily against our legs, purring like a threshing mill. He seemed in good shape.

'God only knows how he survives, this guy,' said Henry as he carried the cat into the dining room.

The third plate was now delegated to Spinks. He sampled nearly everything and ate with good appetite. He seemed to share our opinion that the herring salad was one of the best dishes of the year. Henry *le chef de la cuisine* had doubts about the ham; it was a bit too watery for his taste. Otherwise it was a most successful dinner.

Afterwards we sat down in the armchairs in front of the fireplace with coffee and cognac to digest the food. Henry seemed a little depressed and pensive, as if something didn't quite add up. At first I surmised that it had to do with Leo, but then I happened to think about the Christmas present I had for Henry. I went to get the very subdued package from NK, and handed him the gift with a recited verse: 'Here's something for you from Paris / to hang yourself with in a crisis.'

With great curiosity, Henry eagerly tore off the paper, blushing bright red at my thoughtfulness. The tie suited him to a T. He immediately went out to change ties, making a perfect Duke of Windsor knot, and then he came back, beaming like the sun. The bars of music, the little beige musical notes at the tip, and the burgundy colour were just what he needed.

'What a little rascal you are,' he said. 'Going out to buy cigarettes! Ha! And I actually believed you!'

After that everything went much more smoothly. We lit a fire in the fireplace, drank our coffee and cognac, and of course listened to 'Silent Night', with Jussi Björling on an old, worn-out 78 from his grandfather Morgonstjärna's collection. The crackling and popping just made the music seem even more solemn. And naturally we ended up feeling quite sentimental and weepy. I talked about my childhood and realised that the Christmas tree was actually the only kind of tree that I could identify in the forest. I was a real city boy; the only time I ever went to the woods was when my sister and I went out in the country to steal a Christmas tree.

Henry sighed and groaned at the way the youth of today was going downhill, and he told me long stories about all the Christmas holidays he had celebrated in exile when he was Henry *the clerk* in London, *Heinrich der Barmeister und Schloßdiener* in the Alps, and *Henri le boulevardier* in Paris. Those were the days.

––––––––––

Celebrating the holiday was fun for about two days; after that the time started to drag. Sleeping late in the morning, eating, digesting and absentmindedly reading a few classics for more than two days is never a good idea, especially because Henry 'in his old age' had discovered *Don Quixote* and he kept insisting on reading aloud from particularly brilliant passages. We quickly began to get on each other's nerves, and by the second day we decided to put an end to the Sabbath. It was time to pin up the daily schedule again; we were going to make it through the long and demanding holiday by working.

We went downstairs to scratch around in Greger's Grotto for a couple of days, just to see if there might be more finds in the detritus and sediment near the western portal. The strange cup that turned shiny when we scraped through the layers down to the metal had lost its lustre. And without broaching the subject in so many words, both Henry and I had realised that its gold content probably wasn't very high. So he didn't dare take it to an expert to find out the true value. That's how I interpreted the situation, although Henry claimed that the reason he didn't dare do it was because it would create such a stir. People would want to know where they had found the cup, and then we'd have a bunch of nosy journalists after us. And that would be the end of the whole operation.

In any case, we didn't find any more items, so we went back to other activities. Henry was polishing up 'Europa, Disintegrating Fragments', and I was working on *The Red Room*.

Some time during the days between Christmas and New Year the Prodigal Son returned home. He had a terrible cold. He said that he had celebrated Christmas with some old pals in a cabin out on Värmdö and, aside from the cold, he seemed to have made it through just fine. Henry had a hard time hiding his delight – though for the sake of pride he did try to hide it – and he gave Leo the Christmas present that was still waiting under the tree for him. It was a Higgins cardigan identical to the one I had been given, and Leo accepted the garment amid a great deal of sniffing and coughing and put it on. He seemed very pleased. Then he decided to go to bed, and as soon as he was under the covers, Henry started plying him with hot toddies, a liquid crystal thermometer and comforts such as *Spiderman*, *Superman* and other comic books. Suddenly everything was exactly the way it had been before.

But the joy was short-lived. Soon Leo's cold had spread to everyone in the flat. And this wasn't some ordinary cold; it was undoubtedly some awful Asian or Soviet flu. Anyway, it was the worst cold I've ever had. By the end of December all three of us were in bed wearing caps, socks and long underwear, surrounded by hot-water bottles, rolls of paper towels, aspirin and jars of Nivea. Occasionally one of us would muster the energy to get up and make tea and a few sandwiches with Christmas sausage and hot mustard, which we couldn't taste at all, only to collapse back in bed, exhausted.

That was the worst New Year's Eve of my life. Just before midnight Henry mobilised all his strength to haul himself out of bed in order to mark the occasion by at least being on his feet. He had lined up three stainless steel basins containing Scholl footbath salts next to the window in the sitting room facing the street. He had lit a fire and some candles and brought out a bottle of Opera champagne. He insisted that we too should drag ourselves out of bed to keep him company.

So we lined up three chairs and sat there, each of us with his respective steaming footbath, which wasn't such a bad idea. At the stroke of twelve the corks and the rockets sketched their pyrotechnic parabolas through the muffled sphere of the winter night. The bubbly seemed absolutely tasteless. I nearly had a heart attack, Leo felt guilty for bringing the illness into the house and Henry tried to smooth over everything.

'We would have got sick anyway,' he croaked. 'This kind of flu always gets you, sooner or later.'

'It's not your fault,' I said, trying to sound chipper.

'Happy New Year, boys,' said Henry with a sneeze.

We clinked glasses and splashed our feet in the footbaths, and for a brief time it felt as if the rockets outside in the winter sky, the ringing of the bells and our own disastrous condition had brought us together like three real brothers.

Naturally Henry, at that solemn moment as the New Year was so fatefully rung in, felt obliged to hold some sort of New Year's speech. He spoke in an incoherent, slurred voice about the times, saying that we were approaching a new decade that would be a good one for all of us. Leo would become a poet again, I would reach the pinnacle of my creative ability and he himself would find success as a composer. If only there would be peace on earth, we had nothing to fear. It was a worthy wish, and we drank another toast.

The new year of 1979, an election year and the International Year of the Child, started off bitterly cold. The frost hung on, and we very slowly recovered from the terrible flu, which not even the snorting, huffing, puffing family physician, Dr Helmers, was able to treat. Henry Morgan went around grumbling about how few Christmas cards he had received. His women had all forgotten him. A glittery card arrived from Maud on Friggagatan, along with an extremely tacky family photo from Lana in London, and that was about it. The cards were displayed on the table in the sitting room next to the hyacinths. Leo and I received no cards at all.

Things did get better after order had been restored, when the newspapers began arriving as usual, and as people all around us started working as usual, and we were finally able to get out of bed, as usual.

But the newspapers were reporting the kind of stories that made us actually wish the holidays had continued. The news was not the least bit uplifting. Skåne was struck by a disastrous snowfall. The snow had literally buried houses and cars, and people had to be evacuated with the help of the military's emergency forces. This was followed by a mixed bag of tragedies and fiascos. The head of Volvo landed in hot water when the Norway deal fell through, and there was talk of a scandal because small, miserly investors in the Association of Share Investors had been able to block it. I got to thinking about how the matter would be handled by editor Struve in *The Red Room*. And Levin, that sly fox with all his insider information and his multifarious contacts within the financial world would present his own, sensational interpretation of the defeat.

The global crisis and depression acquired an all-too-obvious correlation to our own personal daily life, even though we did our best to keep out the world in order not to go under. After a few weeks all the Christmas food was gone. The pantry, the storeroom and our wallets were empty, and we could see no sign of improvement.

It was now a cold and nasty afternoon, and we actually didn't have even an öre to spend on food. And we wouldn't until Henry received his allowance – everything had been upset by the damned holidays – while I was waiting to be paid for various articles, but the money never came. Every piggy bank had been smashed in our frenzied hunger, our bankbooks were depleted, and there wasn't a single acquaintance who hadn't adopted the attitude of a more or less wounded creditor.

But neither Henry nor I – Leo wasn't to be counted on when it came to anything financial – had any desire to take on any sort of bourgeois work that was more lucrative. We were both completely engrossed in our extremely serious artistic projects, which absolutely must not suffer. The rhythm was perfect, the pages were pouring out of me in a steady stream, and from the piano room an increasingly exuberant succession of notes could be heard. Greger's Grotto was easy to dig in, and life had undoubtedly never had a more solid or appealing structure than during that time, which in an official sense offered nothing but cold and poverty, crisis and war.

Yet it did put a strain on our spirits that we didn't have decent food to cook. Henry's enormous stock of luncheon vouchers had completely run dry, and he went around casting suspicious glances at Leo, because the vouchers had disappeared rather swiftly ever since he had come home. Henry suspected that Leo had been selling luncheon vouchers in order to rustle up some cash. No one knew what else he could be living on. Leo was hopeless with money. He had once raked in 25,000 kronor all at one go, but that money was long since spent – used for booze or parties or otherwise misappropriated.

So, there we stood in the kitchen on that cold afternoon, trying at least to keep the heat going in that draughty flat. We each heaved a big sigh, and Henry massaged his hungry stomach as he inspected the pantry and fridge for the fifth time in two minutes.

'Not even a crust or a piece of crispbread. Nineteen hundred and seventy-nine. This can't be true. The fridge has never been this empty, not even when it was new.'

'We'll have to go and visit someone's mother,' I said. 'It's the only solution.'

'Things will work out. Just you wait and see,' said Henry. 'Just think if someone in this damn city rang us up and invited us to dinner. But they won't. There's nothing but disasters in this bloody country. Just think of Italy. They're always having disasters, but at least it's warm there. Ah, *una idea! Bene, bene! Sacramentito idioto! Meatsa-ball!*'

The man lit up like a gastronomic sun. He had an idea. He went into the pantry and began singing a very seductive tune: '*Niente pane / niente pasta / ma siamo tutti fratelli / per un po' di formaggio . . .*'

'Cute,' I said.

'A popular Italian song,' said Henry. 'No bread, no spaghetti, but we are still brothers because we have a little cheese. Real cute. Luco Ferrari, '64.'

'But what exactly does it have to do with us?'

'Take it easy, amigo. This is going to be a southern Italian dish. They're poorer than we've ever dreamt of becoming, being, or however you say it. *Po' di patata / pochino di formaggio / nella casa di Bocaccio . . .*' he went on in a high, shrill voice like some sort of pizza maker. And then he threw together a dinner that tasted mostly of onions and thyme, but at least it filled a couple of hungry stomachs. And that was an admirable thing.

After the meal we each retreated to our own rooms and devices. I sat in the library, casually reading passages from several volumes of *Notorious Tales of Life and Manners. Intimate Life Through the Centuries in Stories and Pictures.* The six beautifully bound books were among the highlights of old Morgonstjärna's library, and Henry claimed to have read the whole set from cover to cover. There was no reason to doubt him. De Quincey's *Confessions of an English Opium Eater* and Diderot's *The Nun* bore obvious traces of Henry's slobbering curiosity. He claimed to have hunted in vain for Brantôme's *The Lives of Fair and Gallant Ladies* because he always wanted to read books in which he could recognise himself.

Morgan *the courtesan* stuck his head in the door of the library late that night, beaming like the sun itself.

'I'm going to pop over to see Maud on Friggagatan,' he said. 'I don't know when I'll be back. Tomorrow, or maybe the day after tomorrow. You'll have to handle things here the best you can, on your own.'

'I'll be fine,' I said, engrossed in eighteenth-century eroticism.

'Look after Leo if he sees fit to show up. Cheerio, old chap!'

'Bomb Bavaria, Biggles!'

'I will,' Henry promised, and he was gone.

With admirable accuracy Henry had again made himself scarce just when the laundry was due to be delivered. Right now the delivery boy from Egon's Laundry was standing at the door with two big wooden boxes filled with linen and a dozen of Henry's white and striped cotton shirts. By this time he had managed to convince me of the pleasures of sending out the washing – it was a marvellous feeling of pure and unadulterated luxury to use my index finger to slit open the delicate paper band that kept a fragrant and properly pressed shirt neatly folded – so I couldn't avoid my own responsibility for the bill. Henry had managed to convince me of quite a few things, and consequently I shared a piece of the pie.

I was in a real bind, and the only thing I could think of to do was to invite the delivery boy in for a cup of coffee and then surreptitiously dash over to the Furniture Man and cadge a hundred kronor from their day's take.

A vigorous discussion was going on at the Furniture Man that day. It was Thursday, and they were in the process of arguing about the football pools. The Furniture Man and Henry shared a standing points system, and they had actually won close to five thousand kronor a couple of years back, which wasn't bad. Henry was usually in charge of submitting the bets, but he was gone at the moment, and I had no idea where he kept their complicated points system. I promised to try and find it.

But the heated discussion went beyond that; it had to do with purely existential matters. Over the past few days the newspapers had carried a story about the insane nineteen-year-old who worked at the East Hospital in Malmö. He had poured the cleaning agent Gevisol into the fruit juice of geriatric patients, causing many of them to die. And after horrible suffering. A matter of twenty-five to thirty individuals had allegedly been murdered in this utterly horrendous way, and Greger and Birger down at the Furniture Man couldn't understand what was happening to the country.

'Sweden is sick,' said Birger.

'It's all the fault of that bitch with the assisted dying,' said Greger. 'She's the one who started the whole thing. Without her, that kid never would have thought up such a damned evil thing to do.'

'Jesus,' said Birger. '*We* would never had thought up anything as perverse as that when *we* were kids!'

I was in full agreement with both of them, but I was a bit stressed because by now the delivery boy up in the flat was presumably starting to wonder about the laundry bill. I couldn't really throw myself into the discussion; instead I tactfully asked about borrowing a hundred-krona banknote.

Birger and Greger were amenable, and Birger wrote up a proper IOU, which I signed. Then I dashed back to the delivery boy, paid the bill and heaved a sigh of relief.

For some strange reason, everything always got so complicated and messy whenever Henry was away visiting Maud on Friggagatan. He had managed to make himself indispensable in all sorts of connections – even though that was the last thing he wanted to be – and this time he had gone off without turning in the football bets.

I went to talk to Leo. He had come back home after a brief sojourn with some pals of his, and I found him at his desk. He looked to be in fine form, sitting there scribbling in a black workbook. Leo didn't know where the prototype for the football-pool system was either, but he guessed that Henry probably had it in his wallet and would see to it that the bet was placed in time, no matter where he happened to be. We took solace in that idea and thought no more about the matter.

Leo was going through a good period at that time. Calm and composed, he sat there in his two-room quarters, which reeked of incense, and actually resumed work on his long poetry suite *Autopsy*. That made me happy. I had, of course, read through his old poetry books. There were worn copies of them in his paternal grandfather's library – old Morgonstjärna had naturally been enormously proud of Leo's success – and I wanted to ask the poet about a number of things I had observed. But Leo had no desire to discuss those books anymore. They were passé, immature, half-baked, abortive attempts. In his opinion he had had no idea what he was doing when he wrote them back in the sixties. It was only now, after several journeys, both long and short, into silence at the psychiatric hospital that he truly understood things.

From what I could understand, he had been following the debate about assisted dying. He had saved various newspaper articles and pinned them up on the wall over his desk. Otherwise he no longer read newspapers; he thought they were stupid. If I understood him correctly, he maintained that

371

death was our only truth, and that only the person who experienced his own death could truly see himself and the rest of the world. That was what his poem was about, and all poems had to be paradoxical.

But for my part, I didn't have the stamina to spend so much time thinking about death. I confess that I was cowardly; I was afraid of the subject and preferred to talk about something else, such as the daughters of football-pool kings. Leo understood me, and besides, he had nothing against that particular topic.

Only a thin and delicate membrane separates us from catastrophe. Great tragedy is always part of the calculation, and every ordinary, trivial under-taking has to be planned with consideration for the various risk factors – just as truly big and comprehensive strategic military manoeuvres as well as peaceful civilian enterprises handle the risk of a defeat with the same cautious approach as they handle the chance of success. But what makes our era a bit special is the existence of something resembling an international league that is solely preoccupied with the calculation of risk factors and risk results, in order to produce deeply depressing sums which, if transformed into real practice, could with one blow mean the end of all life on earth. And we citi-zens no longer need to look for portents in the sky, because the threat is with us at all times, legislated, regulated and fine-tuned with mathematical precision so that every individual will have his allotted share, his small dose of the punishment. Unfortunately, Adam may have been able to hide from God, but his sons and daughters today cannot escape, no matter how forsaken they may feel, they are always seen.

The thin, delicate membrane that separates us from catastrophe burst for a brief moment one evening in the middle of January, in the Year of the Child, 1979. It was a Saturday evening, and it was cold. I was sitting in front of the fire in the sitting room, reading about Cyrano de Bergerac. Leo was sitting at the chess table, stirring a wine toddy. And Henry hadn't yet come home from visiting Maud on Friggagatan.

All of a sudden everything went black. The whole flat fell silent and went black. At first, of course, we thought that a fuse had blown in the cellar, since that had become routine over the years when the tenants were over-burdening the ageing power system. But out on Hornsgatan everything was also dark and silent. The whole city seemed suddenly at a standstill. People lit candles in their windows and looked outside with curiosity, searching for an explanation, but just then there were no explanations. The cars down below were suddenly driving more slowly and cautiously because the street was dark and dangerous, as if they were in enemy territory, an occupied part of town.

'It must be war,' said Leo quite calmly as we peered out across the completely blacked-out city.

'That does seem possible,' I said, listening for the muffled droning of enemy bombers.

At that moment Henry came home, slamming the doors.

'Goddamn, what a mess,' he said. 'I took the stairs to get some exercise. If I'd taken the lift, I'd still be stuck in it. The country is in crisis, you can bet on it. Light some candles, dammit all. I can't even see my hand in front of my face.'

We rummaged around in the storeroom for candles and filled the whole flat with candlelight. We turned on the battery-powered radio to see if there were any reports about what had happened. But the music was just pouring out, the same as usual. There was no denying the fact that it all felt exciting and stimulating, like just the right sort of adventurous interruption to a daily life filled with toil and routine. The fragrant candles filled the rooms with their dramatically flickering light, infusing the flat with life and movement.

Henry smelled as if he had just bathed, and he looked exceedingly rested. He poured himself a wine toddy, then went over to stand at the window facing the street and looked out.

'I wonder if the Beagle Boys are busy right now. There can't be a single alarm functioning the way it should in this darkness. Never mind all the thieves they're probably dealing with!'

'We really ought to go out,' said Leo. 'There must be a lot of panic in some places.'

'The underground isn't running, and all the damn restaurants are blacked out . . . Ha!' said Henry. 'I'd really like to see that!'

Henry was actually right with regard to the Beagle Boys. The power was out for about half an hour, and when it later came back on, the burglar alarms all over town went off. The next day the morning newspapers reported that a high-voltage transmission line up in Norrland had gone down, and the black-out had extended all the way south as far as Copenhagen. It was like a foretaste of The Catastrophe. For a brief moment the possibility had penetrated the delicate bubble, merely as a small reminder, a faint warning.

The really serious snow arrived in February, *en masse* – it literally came pouring down for a couple of days, and then there was chaos again. The snow-removal department fell apart at the same time as it was being criticised for not having the situation under control. And the newspapers, as usual, showed a contrite city commissioner sitting on a park bench near the city hall, talking about how the budget had seen better days.

Both Greger and Birger down at the Furniture Man had worked for the snow-removal department, back in the good old days when the guys would get out a shovel and start digging for dear life. After accomplishing their mission, they could collect their wages at the nearest cigar shop. Every worker had his own territory and did an irreproachable job, but that was long ago; these days they had to get out on the street, each with his own shovel, for purely humanitarian reasons. Of course they had to clear the pavement, because Greger and Birger were both decent citizens. People shouldn't have to suffer just because the damn snow-removal department didn't show up.

It was a matter of taking responsibility, of course – the responsibility that was theirs as consummate gentlemen – and that was also what the big fight in our flat ended up being about, during the first week of February.

Leo and I were going to go to a big demonstration against Stockholm's lousy environment. A bunch of environmental groups had joined forces with a group that lived in the Järnet district down by Erstagatan, where buildings were about to be torn down by a fanatic contractor who was completely in love with demolition. Furthermore, an investigation had shown that our Hornsgatan was one of the most toxic streets in the city. The lead content of the air from car emissions exceeded the acceptable limits, even in America.

We tried to recruit Henry, but he was sulking and had no desire to come along.

'I'm bloody well not going out to demonstrate,' he kept saying over and over again. 'I think the air smells good in this town. I've always liked big cities.'

'But you can't very well go around talking about responsibility for this and responsibility for that if you won't ever take a real stand in public,' said Leo.

'Don't come here and talk to me about taking *responsibility*,' said Henry. '*You* are the last one who should be doing that. I'll be damned if *you* can come here and talk about responsibility when you're just living off us and all of society like some kind of parasite. You can't even take responsibility for yourself.'

'That has nothing to do with . . .'

'Oh, yes, it does. And let me tell you,' said Henry, sounding like an agitated school principal, 'that if a person can't take responsibility for himself, then he has no business going around babbling about taking responsibility for others!'

Surprisingly enough, Leo kept his composure. Henry was the one who seemed most upset, presumably because he was feeling attacked, and he had to defend himself at all costs. I tried to keep out of the argument as long as possible, because I could tell that it mostly concerned a personal dispute that had nothing at all to do with Stockholm's environment.

'OK, then,' said Leo. 'I'll stay home if you go out. Then *you* can take responsibility for yourself and half the world.'

'Listen here, my boy,' said Henry. 'I've taken responsibility for you, and that ought to be enough. I've written several hundred different kinds of documents on your behalf, confirming and guaranteeing that we'll take care of things. Don't you think that's enough?'

'You're always hitting below the belt,' said Leo. 'You just use me so that later you can sit there with your arms crossed, acting smug. That's how you've always been. You're a damn Philistine, Henry. What do you think? Isn't he a fucking reactionary?' he said, turning to me.

'Right at the moment, Henry, I think you're definitely behaving like a typically absurd reactionary,' I had to agree with Leo.

'R-e-a-c-t-i-o-n-a-r-y', the sinner spelled out as he ran one hand through his hair and stared down at the table. 'Just because I don't feel like going to every single demonstration? That's ridiculous, fucking ridiculous!'

'But that's not all by a long shot. It's not a question of going to every single demonstration – we're just talking about one. You talk on and on about the fact that you're a gentleman and that you can manage perfectly well even though you don't have a proper job. That's fine. You may be able to take care of yourself, but you should never pretend that the world outside your door is any sort of paradise.'

Leo had touched a sore spot and, as always when the discussion started heading in this direction, Henry flew into a rage and rushed off to his own room because he could no longer evade the question. He was backed into a corner by one big conspiracy aimed at him personally – an ungrateful, parasitic conspiracy that knew nothing about Life or the World.

Leo and I, at any rate, set off for Slussen. It was a successful demonstration, filled with music and *festivitas*, like a winter carnival. Hornsgatan hill was painted by a painter brigade over a hundred men strong as a blue city official, who tried to intervene as the lone long arm of the law against anarchy, was completely sprayed with blue paint. At that very moment, just by chance, I happened to glance up at our sitting-room window, and of course I caught sight of Henry Morgan's nosy mug sticking out. He looked as if he were itching to join us. After that the procession headed past old Mullvaden and down to the Järnet district, which was then declared to be occupied.

Leo disappeared in the crowd and found a few old buddies. I also ran into a number of other acquaintances and didn't get home until very late. By then Henry had calmed down, and we put the whole thing behind us. I had no wish to re-ignite that discussion. Henry would be a childlike conservative to his dying day.

'Rise and shine, campers! Rise and shine, campers!' was the first thing I heard on Sunday morning. 'Rise and shine, campers! Rise and shine, campers!'

Henry *the scout leader* was walking around and waking us up at the early hour of seven thirty a.m. because he'd had another great idea – we would cultivate the outdoor life by going skiing. It was a magnificent day, the winter's very best, with a blue sky, sunshine and glittering snow. Perfect for skiing.

There was actually an entire stockpile of old skis up in the attic, and after breakfast the recreation leader and his sleepy youths went up to try out the worn-out and much-oiled ski boots, the skis with their old-fashioned leather bindings and the heavy bamboo poles. We had no trouble putting together

377

three complete sets of gear and finding some old ski wax that still did an excellent job.

The recreation leader packed up a grey-green knapsack with sandwiches made of fried eggs, salami, cheese and cucumber, along with fruit and a thermos of hot chocolate, as well as some extra clothes. Reluctantly we put on some sportswear – Henry was looking good in his grandfather's plus-fours and a ski cap with a visor and ear flaps – and when all three of us were once again on good terms, we took the bus out to Hellasgården.

Henry, of course, was a real pro on skis. He took off with the knapsack bobbing up and down on his back, and we soon couldn't see a trace of him. Leo and I fell in behind, taking it much more slowly. Leo was a real whiner, and he kept complaining about his skis sliding backwards, the snot running into his mouth and the snow trickling down the back of his neck.

'Damn it to hell, this fucking skiing!' he swore so loudly that the snow melted and the jock types who came whizzing by on their modern felt-bottomed racing skis, had to turn around to catch a glimpse of the swearing monster on the cross-country trail. 'What the hell are we doing out here?!' he complained. 'And now these fucking clothes are starting to chafe!'

We shuffled along at our own tempo and kept getting knocked off the trail by snorting bloodhounds wearing tight tracksuits. After half an hour – after we had made it across the ice into the woods and had ascended the worst of the slopes – Leo got a little less cranky and could no longer deny that it was an unusually splendid day. Henry had pointed out the green trail, which covered six miles, and about halfway along we found him waiting on a slope where he had spread out some lunch things . He had also picked up a young mother who was out on the trail with her son.

'Welcome, Sixten and Nils!' he shouted as we joined the camp and said hello to the woman and her son.

Henry had scraped the snow off a log, which made an excellent bench where we sat to stuff ourselves with the sandwiches, guzzle down the hot chocolate, peel oranges, catch our breath and bask in the sun. The woman was a lively teacher from Nacka, and her nine-year-old son thought it was just as much fun to slide around on the trail as Leo did. He kept wanting to go home, and not even Henry at his most cheerful, could get him to think of anything else. We tried our best to tell the boy that this was something he would look back on with joy later in life when he could no longer go out skiing, because there was never as much snow as when you were a kid. The boy didn't think that made any sense, since he could see with his own eyes that we were grown-ups and that there was still snow, so there would undoubtedly still be snow when he was grown-up too. We were just trying to trick him, and he had no intention of being tricked. All he wanted was to go home, and when there was no more hot chocolate to offer him as a bribe, he turned surly. The young, lively, beautiful single mother decided it was time to head home. She thanked us for the lunch, got her son to give us a bow, and then they were gone.

'Shame about such nice chicks,' said Henry with a sigh.

'Can't you ever relax?'

'If you hadn't come and ruined things by making the boy think that skiing was boring, we could have gone home with her. She would have invited me to Sunday dinner, I could have read a story to the little beast, and the rest you can figure out for yourselves . . .'

'We'll just have to enjoy nature and asceticism instead,' I said. 'Henry, who's so damn charming, can lead the way and pick up girls.'

'Phooey,' said Henry. 'Somebody sounds a little jealous. Just because a guy has a little charm . . .'

'It's probably all because of those trousers you're wearing.'

———————

Presumably only very old people in Sweden still know what it means to be cold, how it feels to wake up in the dead of night wearing stockings and socks, long underwear and pyjamas and a night cap, in a bed with two blankets and extra covers and a hot-water bottle and still be shivering with cold. I awoke in Göring's old bed even though I was dead tired from the skiing expedition at Hellas, and it felt as if it were below freezing in the room. The window was completely covered with frost roses, and I imagined that I could see the vapour from my own breath when I blew on my hands. The tip of my nose was totally numb and my skin was stinging.

That night was probably one of the coldest post-war nights that Sweden have ever experienced. I got a good dose of what 'cold' really means. Even the sheets of newspaper in the bedroom felt stiff, almost frozen. I crumpled up a few pages from the sports section in the bottom of the wood stove and topped them off with pieces of masonite, which were easy to light and produced a nice glow that would ignite heavier and more recalcitrant materials.

The fire got going nicely, and I squatted down to peer into the flames, thawing out my fingers and tossing in some pieces of old moulding and chunks of wood. I was now wide awake – a person sleeps so heavily when it's cold – and I went over to the frost-covered window to see if anyone was awake in the building across the courtyard. But all the windows were dark, as if we were once again under black-out orders.

I was struck by some strange, nocturnal thoughts about the Morgan brothers, and I felt worried on their behalf. Something was wrong in that flat. Henry seemed more and more desperate in his attempts to make everything look good. He was no real master of disguise. He could take care of his own façade, but he had no control over Leo's.

Everything in general seemed terribly cold and gloomy, as if our country were undergoing some sort of crisis and depression, as if everything were falling to pieces, and all of us poor citizens had been left to our own devices and our own ingenuity in order to survive. Initiative and willpower were required along with great discipline just to haul yourself out of bed in the middle of the night to make sure the fire was still burning. I have never believed in strong men, but if the fire wasn't kept going, nothing else would survive either. The cold forces people towards the fire, and only someone who has sat up in the middle of the night, staring into the flames, understands anything about life.

You can chatter as much as you like along the boulevards and avenues of our civilisation, feeling enormously impressed by the architectonic achievements of humanity. Technology has long ago crossed the boundaries of comprehension, and everything that might be called impressive came about in the timespan between the construction of the Pyramid of Cheops around 2900 BC and the landing on the moon in AD 1969. This timespan consists of approximately five thousand years with regard to enraptured babbling about humanity's marvels. But after the moon landing, everything moved to another level, to the incomprehensible. There was so much that I had no desire to understand; I would prefer to call it evil, plain and simple.

I was not struck by any sort of banal primitivism as I squatted there, warming myself in front of the woodstove in the middle of the night. Rather, I was struck by a very fundamental insight about the fragile state of human beings. You can learn something from many things, but waking up in the middle of the night in Göring's old bed solely because of the cold taught me something major. I was probably shivering as much from terror as from the cold.

It was the time of the semla, the buns eaten during Lent, and the most intense semla frenzy was raging. Consumption per capita could reach several each day. Henry was sent out on a pilgrimage through unfamiliar parts of the city to legendary bakeries with world-famous marzipan, and even skinny Leo could sometimes be seen devouring them with a healthy appetite. All the while he would be constantly debating with his brother about such fundamental matters as whether Shrove Tuesday buns weren't actually the most deceptive bakery goods ever invented, since the hollowed-out wheat roll was originally supposed to have been a hiding place for ungodly sweets. The fact that nowadays the cream, unashamedly, almost proudly, oozes out in all directions seemed just a measure of how thoroughly secularised society had become.

Well, all right, enough of all this culinary scholasticism. It was Shrove Tuesday. Henry came home late from his expedition. He was drunk, stinking of beer and complaining about his rheumatism. His fingers no longer allowed him to play the piano. It was so damn cold that he had to take to alcohol because his joints were literally shrieking, or so he claimed. I could just listen for myself, he said, and he let me press my ear to his shoulder. It was as silent as a tomb; I didn't hear a peep. But that was probably because of my incipient ear infection.

At any rate, he had brought home a box of semla buns, and I thought it was a miracle that he'd managed to balance both himself and the box all the way home from Östermalm without destroying them. The whole city was full of people slipping and sliding and skidding around in the slushy snow, carrying bags or boxes of semla buns. Everyone looked equally determined and resolute. A semla bun should not be mistreated. A semla bun that has been squashed or tipped over, or mistreated in any other way, is a sorry sight. Even a little fingerprint on the powdered sugar can obliterate all pleasure. The semla bun must have an orthodox and unmolested freshness about it. Henry was fully aware of the ethics of semla buns, and he had skidded his way along with the box held firmly in some sort of gyroscopic suspension in his hands. He was prepared to take any sort of beating, as long as the semla buns made it home in one piece. It was like a narcotics delivery, sacrosanct and precious.

I then warmed up a litre of milk, and we each ate two of the delicate semla buns, which had just the right substantial amount of grainy marzipan and real, heavy cream. Afterwards Henry fell asleep in the sitting room in front of the fireplace, while Leo and I went to our respective rooms to work.

Dusk arrived, and I was sitting and shivering at my desk in the library, huffing hot air on my hands so that I could type at all. I had tried wearing gloves with the fingertips cut off, but they were too awkward and clumsy. The typewriter was so cold that I had needed an engine warmer to get it started that morning. I'd been having trouble with it all day long, and now in the evening, as the cold paralysed nearly all of Sweden, it was definitely time to stop. My ability to formulate my thoughts had reached absolute freezing point.

Henry couldn't do any more that evening either. When he'd sobered up after his catnap, he had tried to play the piano, but he claimed that he needed a blowtorch to thaw out the strings inside. The instrument was so frozen that it sounded like a spinet.

We ran into each other out in the kitchen and made some broth to warm ourselves up. A children's programme was being broadcast on the radio. Kids up to the age of thirteen could phone in to request a song and then answer a question. They could win an LP, and they cheated shamelessly. Henry never missed a single broadcast of that programme, he was the only person I knew who could sing all the words to the theme song. Henry would actually participate in the programme by clearly answering out loud each question about how many 'b's there were in the word 'abborre' or what was Sweden's highest mountain, and so on. If he couldn't come up with an answer off the cuff, he would feel put out and embarrassed. Then he would unfailingly defend himself by saying that he had been dyslexic all his life, just like the king. This time the programme was more entertaining than usual, since the radio announcer was talking to a twelve-year-old girl from Värmland whose only hobby was wrestling. She was upset, this girl, because she always had to spar with younger boys, and that didn't seem right to her. I don't think I've ever heard anyone laugh as hard as Henry while he listened to that wrestling girl from Värmland. He mimicked every word she said, and it seemed as if he missed having kids of his own – he undoubtedly would have been a perfect fool of a father.

'We have to go out and get some wood,' he said after we finished off the broth and the radio programme had ended with its incomprehensible theme song. 'We have to go out and get wood, or else we'll never make it through the night.'

'All right,' I said. 'I'm getting nowhere with my writing anyway.'

'It's no good trying to shut out the rest of the world,' said Henry bitterly. Without coming right out and saying it, he acknowledged that Leo was right. It no longer did any good to shut out the world, yet that was exactly what we had tried to do. We had our dreams about our great work that just needed a little fine-tuning, and we had tried to isolate ourselves, to close ourselves in during that bitterly cold winter in order to achieve the perfect creative concentration. But it wasn't working. There was always something that slipped in; right now it was the damn cold. It could only be kept at bay with fire and we had no more wood, and so we were forced to go out.

We bundled up in old, cast-off sheepskin coats and Christmas-tree-seller hats made of lamb's wool, and then we went down to Hornsgatan in search of the closest skip. There was one over on Tavastgatan that was full to the brim because they had torn down a couple of ramshackle buildings. We found some good, nail-free boards, a couple of splintery joists, and some other smaller pieces that looked as if they would burn nicely. Henry also found an old deep-frozen top hat, which he insisting on putting on over his lambswool cap.

We lugged and dragged the wood home to Hornsgatan and loaded most of it into the lift. The creaky old lift hauled itself up, one floor after another, as we held our breath. But when we reached the sixth floor we gave a shriek of fright. As soon as we were level with our landing we saw a rigid, lifeless face staring into the lift. The light reflected off the pale face like a spotlight in a horror film.

A young woman was lying right in front of the lift door. We opened the door as best we could, stepped out onto the landing and tried to shake some life into her. To no avail. We turned her over and concluded that the uncon-

383

scious girl must be in her twenties. She seemed to have an enemy here in the world, because one of her eyes was completely swollen shut from a black eye, and blood had trickled out of her nose.

'Goddammit,' groaned Henry. 'As if we didn't have enough problems. What should we do? Call the police?'

'Not on your life,' I said. 'Then we can calmly wait for her thirty pimps and pals to show up to thank us for snitching. Very funny. Do you have any other bright ideas?!'

The only thing we could agree on was to load the girl into the flat along with all the planks, joists and other lumber. Then we groaned from exhaustion and sank down onto chairs in the hallway to ponder our find.

'I wonder who she is,' said Henry.

'She's certainly sleeping soundly, at any rate.'

Henry leaned over her to see if she smelled of alcohol, but she didn't.

'Other substances,' he surmised.

'Should we drag her down to the Maria clinic?'

'I've seen this sort of thing before,' Henry claimed. 'She'll come round in a while. Although we ought to give her a bath.'

'Too bad Leo isn't home. He'd know what to do about something like this.'

I don't really know what came over us, because in reality we weren't very good gentlemen that winter, but on that Shrove Tuesday in February we were both struck with some kind of charitable insanity or good Samaritan frenzy. All of a sudden we were busy taking off the clothes of that mistreated girl while hot water was slowing filling up the bathtub. Henry really laid it on thick by contributing some scented oil and bubble-bath.

'No . . . cut it out, cut it out . . .' groaned the girl when she was naked and we carried her thin body to the bathroom. 'Not again . . . Leave me the hell . . . alone . . .' she went on.

Henry spoke to her soothingly and said that we weren't going to hurt her, but she didn't understand a thing; the words never entered her consciousness. She was in a foetal stage and could only take in purely physical sensations. As we cautiously lowered her body into the warm water her protests grew weaker and the grotesque face took on an almost peaceful expression.

We were a bit clumsy, and embarrassed at the same time, because we didn't know how scrupulous we should be. We had no experience in this area. Henry rubbed her feet as lovingly as if they were his own, although he asserted that there were professionals who could cure all sorts of ailments simply by manipulating the feet. But in this case it probably had more to do with the fact that he wanted to stick to whatever could be lifted up out of the bubble-bath. I bathed her swollen eye.

The girl didn't even wake up when we dried her off with a large bath towel and put her to bed in the guest room under starched fresh sheets.

'She's really out of it,' said Henry. 'Damn, this isn't good. It's an omen about something. Something really terrible is going to happen. I can feel it. And it's not just my usual rheumatism this time.'

I rarely took very seriously his harping about rheumatism, horoscopes and occult portents, but that night, as he sat there looking at the girl's bruised and yet largely peaceful face immersed in a deep sleep, with the swollen eye bulging like some awful medallion above her cheek, I couldn't help feeling a little uneasy. Henry sounded so damn prophetic, and in a moment of weakness I was prepared to give in, to agree that this really was a sign that something was going to happen that winter. The girl could be a dark angel, sent to us as some sort of harbinger.

'We need to keep watch over her tonight,' said Henry. 'I'll light a candle for her, a tall and beautiful candle, and keep watch.'

'I suppose that's best,' I said. 'If she wakes up she might think she's already dead.'

'I'll read to her from the Bible,' Henry went on, sounding as pathetic as a zealous army chaplain.

'The Bible?!' I said. 'Why the hell would you read from the Bible? Why don't you ring for the Pentecostals, Imsen or Målle, at the same time!'

'Don't be so superficial, Östergren. I'm going to read to the young girl about grace. She needs a little grace, as do we all. I'm going to say a mass for a nun.'

'OK,' I said. 'But now I wash my hands of this whole thing. I'll come to relieve you at two a.m.'

It was already late, and we agreed on a preliminary schedule for the night. I went to bed wearing pyjamas, socks and a night-cap because of that incipient ear infection. I read some appropriately encouraging words by Cervantes and thought about Spain for a while, but it got too cold to have my hands above the covers, so I went to sleep instead.

The alarm clock rang at two, and it took more courage than usual to get out of bed. It was still a night with frost on the inside of the window, and

I don't want to boast, but I did find the courage. After I threw on my clothes and flailed my arms about to get warm, I tiptoed over to the guest room and opened the door. Henry *the army chaplain* was dozing in his chair in the light from the tall candle and the fading glow of the woodstove. He was holding the girl's hand, exactly as if he had been trying to tell her fortune in the dark.

At his feet lay a volume of fairy tales by Hans Christian Andersen. Apparently nothing had come of reading from the Bible or holding a mass for a nun. Instead he had read a story aloud, as if for a daughter who was ill and couldn't sleep. Maybe the one about the little match girl; it seemed a likely choice, and Henry was so hopelessly sentimental. The girl herself hadn't heard a word, of course.

Henry awoke when I gave him a little pat on the shoulder, mumbled something incoherent, and then went off like a zombie to his own room. The night passed without incident. The cold dawn of Ash Wednesday slowly rose over Stockholm, and the girl still slept heavily, though her breathing became more and more regular.

———————

The cold retained its iron grip on Stockholm, and every single evening we had to go out and find wood for the stoves. Otherwise we would have died, plain and simple.

One evening when we were out on just such a mission – absurd as it sounds, officially it's a crime to take anything people throw into skips, so just to be safe, we carried out all our operations after nightfall – we were struck by a completely devastating thirst in the midst of our work. We were busy sorting through boards over at Mariaberget, but we decided to take a break and go over to Gropen to have a beer and thaw out in the warmth of the bar.

We had no sooner sat down in a booth with a lager for each of us when Henry gave me a poke with a sharp elbow and nodded significantly towards the table next to us. I glanced over there, and in the dim, sleazy light I actually saw none other than our little protégée, the dark angel whom we had nursed like our own daughter on that dreadful cold night a couple of weeks earlier.

She had recovered nicely. Her face looked quite lovely, and she seemed to have put on a few pounds, all in the right places. After our intensive treatment, she had started talking, with all the speed of an expert commentator at an ice-hockey match which never took place, so to speak. She had jabbered and rambled on and on about everything in her whole life, when a single sentence would have sufficed, since it was not exactly a pretty story. In any case, then she had left us, and without thanking us for our help, but that didn't matter because by then we were happy to get rid of her.

Yet here she now sat in Gropen with a beer in front of her. She may not have looked like someone in a ladies' magazine, but she was alive, anyway, and laughing at the jokes that a pockmarked bruiser was serving up.

'It's *him*,' muttered Henry out of the corner of his mouth.

'Who?'

'The guy who beat her up!'

'How the hell do you know that?!'

'I know how the game is played. Just *listen* to them.'

I tried to listen to what they were talking about. Their conversation was filled with promises and hopes and a whole lot of cold numbers. He was apparently going to start earning money again, and the girl said that she trusted him. He promised that everything was going to be fine. The situation was quite clear.

Henry and I didn't have much time to brood over the matter before I felt the girl's eyes fixed on me, pinning me to my seat as if she were trying to remember something. She squinted and turned her head and glared like an inquisitive kid.

'Hi,' I said to her.

'I *know* you,' she said.

'I suppose you do,' I said.

'You . . .' she said. 'Oh shit, yes . . . What's your name again? You're on TV, aren't you?! I've seen you lots of times!'

Henry doubled over, trying to stifle a laugh, while I tried to keep a straight face, thinking that ingratitude is the world's reward. On the other hand, I'm used to being taken for someone else – it's been that way all my life.

'What's the *name* of that damn programme you were on?' the girl asked. 'Check it out for yourself,' she said to the pockmarked bruiser who stuck his enormous head out of the booth and stared for a long time without being able to place the celebrity either.

'Ask him for his autograph,' he said, sniggering. 'Shit, I *sold* my TV. But I promise to buy a new one!'

Henry and I downed the rest of our drinks and went back out to the street to complete our mission. The last I heard of the girl was:

'It's a bitch that I can't remember which programme it was!'

'Fuck it,' said the bruiser. 'I'm going to buy a new TV. Tomorrow.'

Perhaps she really was a harbinger, that nameless girl whom we'd found on the landing. Perhaps she was sent to us as a foreboding dark angel whom we were supposed to nurse and then send off into the world. Because it was no easy or trouble-free time that we were about to enter.

We had opened our own private income-tax-return agency the weekend that China marched into Vietnam and the whole world seemed about to be torn apart. Henry Morgan was no financial genius, and I was even worse, so we had set up our makeshift office in the library. We swore and calculated and read aloud and quoted from the confusing tax forms that had come with the newspapers but without really bringing any sort of clarity to the whole matter. I alone had eighteen different sources of income, and Henry was not far behind. He also wanted to be discreet and secretive about his income, so he refused to give me full insight into his affairs. The most significant amount was his monthly appanage, which was paid out from a trust fund. Added to that were a host of smaller entries from various odd jobs and his wages as an extra for different film companies. In principle it was much the same sort of hodgepodge for me. Finances were not the strong point of two gentlemen like us who were so removed from the world. And besides, the idea was to cheat with a certain amount of elegance; neither of us wanted to *acknowledge* our deceit.

But on that Sunday morning when we could read that China had entered Vietnam and a Third World War would soon become fact, it seemed so superfluous to be sitting there wrestling with a hundred kronor here and fifty kronor there. No matter how slipshod we were, we still belonged to the absolute lowest income group, and that seemed very unfair.

Henry was perhaps a bit more upset than I was, because he always went to extremes, no matter what the mood in question – euphoria as well as depression. The Soviet Union had, of course, issued a sharp warning to China, urging the Chinese to withdraw their forces immediately, because the Russians had signed a defence treaty with Vietnam and were therefore obligated to intervene in some manner.

'What a hell of a Sabbath!' said Henry, sighing. 'The world is undeniably *sick*. It practically makes you want to *vomit*!'

'It does seem undeniably superfluous to be sitting here with our pitiful income, having to report every öre,' I said morosely. 'It's just like Beckett, Samuel Beckett.'

'I think I need to go to church today,' said Henry. 'Go and listen to a sermon and the whole rigmarole. That's the only thing to do in light of today's situation.'

'Just don't say that to Leo,' I told him. 'I can't face an argument today.'

'Fuck that bastard and his peace-loving friends in the East.'

'That might be a *bit* harsh. There's no need to be an ass about it!'

'What a damn mess there's going to be after all this. How the hell are they going to make sense of anything now? The Russians have been nasty for a long time, and now the Chinese are nasty and malevolent as well. Who are they going to worship now?'

'Let's hope it's not God, anyway.'

'Don't try to pull my leg. I'm a weak man,' said Henry.

'But I *wasn't* being sarcastic,' I assured him. 'I just can't understand why you suddenly want to go to church.'

'Don't give me your hatred for Luther again,' said Henry. 'I don't buy it anymore. Never mind that he threatened damnation, you can always obtain grace.'

'Don't you have to die first?'

'Not at all! They sure don't teach you much in school these days, do they?'

'As soon as you feel pressured, Henry, you have to start taking evasive action. Do you realise that? You hit below the belt. It's the same every time anyone tries to have a serious conversation with you. You can never give a serious answer. You always have to hit below the belt.'

'You've been listening to Leo too much,' said Henry bitterly. 'That's his standard argument. That's what he says every time there's something going on, that I hit below the belt. But dammit all, Klasa, we need to stay calm

390

right now. We can't start getting desperate just because the Chinese are crazy. I respect you, and you have to respect me. All right?'

'Sure, all right.'

Henry actually did go to church, and he came back home in a significantly better mood. The pastor had spoken some extremely well-chosen words. Henry was a good man at the Maria Magdalena congregation; he wasn't the least bit removed from the world, if anyone should imagine that he was. He could handle an issue in the proper manner, sum up the whole thing, and get it to flow into a calm and gentle sense of hope, which was exactly what Henry Morgan needed.

In any case, we finished our income-tax returns on that black Sunday when it looked as if a Third World War were right around the corner, and everyone was just waiting to hear the news about what was going to happen.

Henry was quite brilliant that afternoon, and I don't know whether it was because of the pastor's comforting words or because of our argument that morning. Maybe it had been gnawing at part of his brain, because he really did make an effort not to behave evasively or to dismiss things. Henry *the cineast* was a big fan of Ingmar Bergman, of course, and he drew my attention to the scene in *The Serpent's Egg* in which Inspector Bauer is interrogating Abel about his sins and Abel wonders why there's such a fuss about his lowly person when the whole world is in flames. Inspector Bauer then says that he's just doing his job, that everything around him is in chaos because people aren't tending to their jobs. He's just trying to create a little patch of order in the appalling chaos of the twentieth century, and that's the only reason that he can even manage to survive.

There was something grand in that dilemma, and Henry thought it was exactly the same thing that was preoccupying us that afternoon: we were creating order in our finances, amid our little private chaos, perhaps to maintain a little patch of order in the midst of the vast, public Chaos that had befallen us and every other vulnerable citizen of the world.

Henry felt that as a mature man he ought to do his duty, but that was no reason for him to call himself *reactionary*, as Leo and I had. I thought that I understood him, even though all that talk about duty above everything else led my thoughts back to the old days of one-krona coins and scouting expeditions.

As usual, Henry had pinned up his daily schedule on the pinboard in the kitchen since it was his intention to carry out his routines, do his duty and arrange for a little patch of order in the midst of life's chaos.

On Monday, when we were supposed to take over from Greger and Birger down in the passageway, we were met by a strange sight. Greger was lugging around some big boxes filled with tinned goods, packaged foods, clothing and blankets. He dragged these essentials into the grotto that bore his name, where he had already placed electric lights and spare lamps that ran on paraffin oil.

'What the hell are you doing?' asked Henry.

'It's Birger,' said Greger curtly.

'What do mean "Birger"?'

'This is all Birger's idea, the whole thing. He was the one who said we should do it.'

'*Do what?*'

'The war,' Greger went on, just as cryptically. '*The war!*'

What this was all about began to dawn on us as we stood there in bewilderment, watching as Greger busily created an air-raid shelter down there, underground. Just then Birger showed up to inspect Greger's efforts, and he had an air of rigid self-confidence about him. He was completely convinced that the Third World War was going to break out any day now. Once the Russians started out, the Bear could reach Sweden overnight. It was best to take precautions, and Greger's Grotto was just as good an air-raid shelter as anywhere. It had good ventilation and it was dry, discreet and private.

'I'll take responsibility for this, Henry,' said Birger a bit arrogantly. 'We'll lay in provisions for at least two weeks, enough for ten people. I'm including the three of you from upstairs.'

'OK then, boys,' stammered Henry. 'I'll leave it to you.' He tried to sound as serious as the current situation warranted. 'It looks like if you've already done a great job.'

'We won't lack for anything by the time we're finished,' said Birger.

'We reckon we'll be done by this afternoon,' said Greger solemnly.

'Around five,' Birger clarified. 'After that, any damn thing can happen in the world, but *we* are going to survive. *I'll* see to that!'

'That's fine, Birger,' said Henry. 'We'll be going back upstairs now.'

'You do that,' said Birger, and he seemed on the verge of offering us a salute, like a professional soldier.

We went back up to the flat, feeling resolute and very moved.

'A-p-o-c-a-l-y-p-s-e,' Henry spelled out in the lift.

Then he happened to remember that we hadn't seen Leo for a couple of days. Henry wanted to tell his brother not to worry, that a place had been reserved for him in a private air-raid shelter, which was a privilege granted to very few in those disorderly times.

But Leo had flown the coop. He'd gone out and hadn't slept at home for several nights now; even his bed was neatly made up. On the desk in his room lay the black workbook with the draft for the poetry suite *Autopsy*, which he had been working on for nearly four years now, though he still hadn't found the energy to complete it. He had slipped into a different period now, and it would soon turn out to be of the more serious kind.

'So you haven't heard anything from him?' asked Henry uneasily.

'Not a peep,' I said. 'He told me a while ago that he was going to ring Kerstin. So maybe he did. She likes him.'

'Yes, unfortunately,' said Henry. 'But it's nice for him, at least. If only he doesn't beat himself up again. You have no idea how he can get. No one can booze the way he can, even though he's not *supposed* to drink, and he knows that damn well. It triggers a load of processes in his brain that just make everything a lot worse.'

Henry looked around Leo's room, but there were no clues, or at least no indications that he had sat there drinking.

'I hope I wasn't too hard on him,' Henry went on, sounding worried. 'Do you think I was? Was I too hard on him?'

'No,' I said. 'I don't think you were too hard on him. If he's feeling down, it's because other people were too hard on him.'

'I sure as hell don't feel like being some sort of nanny anymore. But I have to, at least for a while. Otherwise he'll be given a disability pension, and that would be the end of him.'

In early March it looked as if the storm would subside. The Soviet Union was lying low and restricting itself to verbal threats – or that's what we were told, in any case. We read at least four daily papers, and in between them, *Henri le boulevardier* would go down to the central station to buy *Le Monde* in order to get some objective information. He would read aloud to me in

French, and he had undeniably perfect pronunciation, as well as beautiful, melodic diction. He could turn an utterly depressing article in French into a joy to the ears, and that is no doubt the dilemma of every musician.

Henry *the pianist* really got going with his work at the beginning of March, during that Year of the Child and the Swedish elections of 1979. As mentioned, there had been some unforeseen interruptions in our work pattern, but now we both got going again, and we followed to the letter the daily schedule that was pinned up in the kitchen. The appanage and honorariums came streaming in as they should, and I managed to arrange a few advance royalties as a sort of artificial respiration.

Franzén the publisher had summoned up his courage and rung me a couple of times, now that I had definitely missed the deadline. And naturally he wanted to know what the hell I was doing, since this was starting to look like a breach of contract. He had already forked out close to 15,000 kronor. The only thing I could tell him was that these were difficult times, cold and ruthless times, and that under such conditions, things could take longer. He had a rather hard time comprehending this, but I managed to get an extension of a couple more weeks, just for the sake of fine-tuning the book. The story was by no means finished, but I didn't breathe a word about that to him. He would have to be prepared for a lot of changes in the proofs.

Some time in early March the occupation of the Järnet district also came to an end – an event that was immediately incorporated into my modern pastiche of *The Red Room*. It never led to any major riots like at Mullvaden, and the whole thing received very little publicity. Henry and I were convinced that Leo had buddies in Järnet, and that he would now come back home since the police had sealed off the whole area and the demolition team had started excavating. But Leo remained missing-without-trace. We were gradually starting to feel concerned, even though he had been gone before and we hadn't worried. But this time we had a bad feeling about it.

Henry went around worrying and fretting because he thought that he'd been too hard on his younger brother.

'Do *you* think that I was too hard on him?' he asked incessantly.

I kept trying to reassure him.

'It's not our fault if he's in a bad way. There are plenty of other things that are worse, much worse.'

Henry would calm down for a while, but not for long. He could no longer concentrate, and he went around wearing his slippers, shuffling along and slamming doors; he practically drove me crazy too.

As a diversion, we tried going down to the Europa Athletic Club to work out, but it didn't help. I watched him hammering in punches more stubbornly and energetically than ever, but there was no longer even a trace of that cheerful playfulness, that quick and improvised unpredictability that made his boxing so charming, for lack of a better word. Now he reminded me more of an untalented palooka of a heavyweight who didn't give a damn about being good as long as he was big and had muscles and could throw punches precisely the way they were supposed to be thrown, neither better nor worse.

I could see that Willis had also noticed Henry's decline. Willis watched him from a distance, looking concerned, as if he could read in Henry's heavy, sighing blows that something was wrong. There was so much melancholy enmeshed in those gloves that it robbed his punches of sound. The sandbag no longer whistled or sang in that shrieking way it used to do.

After we had showered and were sitting on the benches with aching knuckles and steaming backs, Willis came out of his office and asked us how things were going.

'You seem a little locked up, Henry,' said Willis.

'Oh, it's nothing,' said Henry dismissively. 'I'm just a little stiff in the shoulders. It's so damn cold in the flat. It's my rheumatism.'

'Bullshit!' said Willis. 'Somebody with rheumatism couldn't even kill a fly. That doesn't make sense, Henry.'

Henry rummaged through his bag for clean clothes and groaned.

'I don't have a woman, Willis. That's what it's all about. I don't have a real woman.'

'Then go get one,' said Willis, giving him a wink. 'You shouldn't have any problems in that area. You're so damned *charming*, for God's sake.'

'I don't have any problem with women,' said Henry. '*They* have a problem with *me*!'

Willis shook his head. He knew Henry and realised that he wasn't going to get anything else out of him that evening. Then it was the same routine as usual: Henry combed his hair in front of the mirror, scrupulously knotted his tie, and said 'So long, girls!' just like always.

When we got back to the flat that evening, the phone was ringing for a change. It rarely rang. But in this case it was a saxophone player who had greetings from Bill of the Bear Quartet – who had actually found success with a respectable solo career south on the Continent. The guy on the phone was the leader of a quartet with an alcoholic piano player. He wanted Henry to sit in for a couple of sessions, or 'gigs', as they were called in the business, over at Fasching during the weekend. Henry thanked him for thinking of him, but said he didn't have time. He was fully occupied with his own practising.

I couldn't understand why he turned down the invitation, but he refused to discuss the matter any further. It was his business, and I should just keep out of it, although he had a hard time hiding how pleased he was. He was a sought-after pianist who was forced to turn down an offer.

A very depressed atmosphere hovered over the chiaroscuro of the flat, and I had no idea what caused it, except that Leo's lost soul seemed to be haunting us during his physical absence. In any case, it had nothing to do with our finances, which were meagre but not absolutely hopeless. It had nothing to do with the cold, since by now we had learned the trick of keeping the fires burning, wearing pyjamas in bed with hot-water bottles, and keeping our Higgins cardigans on at all times. Nor did it have anything to do with our work, because we had now surfaced in a gentle cacophony of typewriter keys and explosive chords from the grand piano.

Henry was feeling optimistic. He said that he'd been in contact with the Södra Theatre and had tentatively booked a Wednesday evening in early May when there was an available slot in the theatre's schedule. For Henry Morgan's part, it was just a matter of kicking the machinery into gear, deciding on the repertoire from 'Europa, Disintegrating Fragments', printing up the programmes, and sending out stylishly designed invitations to all the elite. I instantly took it upon myself to sell at least a score of seats in the orchestra section. Things were looking promising for the composer; he had no reason to be in despair. And yet he was, deep inside.

It even went so far that one morning in March he refused to get out of bed. I went out to the kitchen, where he normally would have laid out that monumental breakfast of his by seven o'clock, but I found only a bare oilcloth on the table. I found the chef himself in bed, wide awake but apathetic.

'I don't feel like getting up today,' he said. 'I've got a fever and I feel awful.'

I went over to the bed and felt his forehead. It was even colder than one of those lampposts that kids get their tongues stuck on when it's a very cold winter day.

'I think it's best if we ring Dr Helmers,' I said. 'This seems quite serious.'

'Does it?!' said Henry, putting his hand to his forehead to check for himself. 'It doesn't seem *that* bad, does it?'

'It's still probably a good idea to have it checked out,' I said, and with a grin I went to get the liquid crystal thermometer.

Henry eagerly pressed the strip against his forehead, and naturally it showed that his temperature was below 37°C. He was both deeply disappointed and quite reassured.

'No reason to panic,' he said. 'It's just my rheumatism.'

'Then wouldn't you feel better if you got up? You'll get so stiff lying in bed.'

'The only thing that would make me feel better right now is a woman.'

'So go over and see Maud!'

'Easier said than done. She had another man—'

'Isn't there anyone else?'

'I'm going to lie low today. There isn't a single woman in all of Europe who would want to have anything to do with me in this condition. Even Lana in London would shun me.'

I left him in peace. He wanted to lie in bed and feel sorry for himself, like a child. He had a couple of new *Spiderman* and *Superman* comics, and he ate every crumb from the breakfast tray, so at least there was nothing wrong with his appetite.

The sudden low pressure eased up a bit, and Henry got out of bed to resume his activities with all the snorting vitality, authority and energy that he had stored up under the covers. But it was like a boxer staggering to his feet from the mat in the ninth round, only to face another pounding. The altogether real, and actually anticipated, catastrophes began to happen, blow by blow, as if they were being timed by some merciless boxing demon.

At the end of March disaster struck in Harrisburg, Pennsylvania, USA. The nuclear power plant on Three Mile Island suffered an accident, and there was talk of leaks in the pipes for the coolant water. Technicians and experts, mayors and the president all appeared like some elegant cabinet decorated with golden question marks. No one really knew what had happened; they knew even less about what might happen next. Rumours quickly began circulating about an ominous cloud of gas that was expanding inside the power plant. It could explode with an effect many times greater than that of an atomic bomb. Radioactivity would spread on the winds, and people would have to be evacuated. Hundreds of thousands of citizens would soon be fleeing Armageddon. In early April several reassuring reports appeared – the cloud of gas was under control, and the risk of a meltdown had diminished. Swedish Social Democrats made a duplicitous about-face and started calling for a national referendum on nuclear power in Sweden.

The world had barely caught its breath and the hope that things were not over on this earth after all was once again just beginning to dawn, when it was time for the next sledgehammer: Russian oil was found floating in the Stockholm archipelago. The tanker *Antonio Gramsky* had caused the Baltic's worst oil-spill disaster to date. The tanker had run aground at the end of

February outside Ventspils in Latvia, and 5,600 tons of heavy crude had leaked out. Now, in early April, the oil had drifted far across the sea and into Stockholm's archipelago, where it lay in thick clumps under the ice, threatening the shores and the breeding grounds of sea birds. Twenty-five thousand islands – between the Svenska Högarna in the north and Landsort in the south – were threatened by the oil, and traces of it were beginning to show up everywhere. Reports came in from Nassa archipelago, Björkskär archipelago, Sandhamn, Langviksskär, Biskopsön, Norsten, Utö, Storm Island . . . The list went on and on.

Henry almost went completely out of his mind. That was quite evident as I watched him spell his way like someone who was near-sighted through all the newspaper reports about the oil, one statistic after another, one location after another. He shook his head, sighed, groaned and pulled at his hair in distress.

'This is too much,' he said over and over again. 'This is all just *too much!*'

I had to agree.

'I'm going to go hibernate, or hang myself, or whatever the hell else I can think of. I just don't want to be here anymore,' he moaned. 'What the hell is a person supposed to do with this world? People are out of their minds!'

'People are *not* out of their minds,' I said. 'It's the ones in charge who are greedy. Capitalism is greedy. That's why things like this happen.'

'I'm allergic to that kind of talk,' said Henry. 'You know that, for God's sake. And anyway, it's the *Russians* who did this!'

'They're no exception.'

'Bullshit! This is something else entirely. It won't work to blame everything on capitalism anymore. They're all equally bad. As soon as they get their hands on a little paragraph of Power, they all turn into piles of shit. That's the way it is, Klasa, believe me!'

'Well, OK,' I said with a sigh. 'It's possible.'

'Bloody hell,' Henry went on, still sounding bitter. 'Here I am barely on my feet again, and the disasters come pouring down on me, trying to bring me to my knees. I'll never be ready!'

'For the concert?'

'For the concert or anything else! I can't live with this . . .'

He seemed utterly desperate during those days, restlessly pacing around the flat, opening and closing doors, hanging out at Greger's Grotto – or rather, the Shelter, as the tunnel was simply called nowadays – but then he'd come right back upstairs after a little listless and restless poking about in the dirt.

This went on for a couple of days until the weekend arrived, and then Henry decided to go out to the archipelago to volunteer to help with the clean-up efforts. A headquarters had been set up on Stavnäs with radio huts, skips, and boat docks for the transport of personnel and equipment out to the disaster areas. They needed as many people as they could get, and Henry was not one to hesitate. When things really mattered, he always turned up.

Henry put on his overalls, packed up a few things that might be required, and left on Saturday morning for Stavnäs. That same day I participated in an impressive demonstration against nuclear power, starting at the King's Garden and proceeding over to Sergels Torg.

April slunk in with vexing, dirty-grey weather. It was going to be a long-drawn-out, rough spring that kept out the sun and any green foliage for as long as possible. People started feeling exhausted from the cold, the snow, the rain, the fog and the reports of various catastrophes coming in every single day. It felt as if people were collapsing all over the city, more and more with each day that passed. Greger and Birger looked worn-out down there at the Furniture Man. They were making dents in Greger's Grotto, the Shelter, but it was hard for them to keep up the enthusiasm. Especially since the strange cup that had been found in the dirt still hadn't been properly analysed, according to Morgan, the boss. The Cigar Seller looked ashen in his little shop, the Flask and Wolf-Larsson were holed up in their flats, cringing behind the drawn curtains. Everyone was equally engrossed in his own struggle to survive.

Henry was out in the archipelago for several days, cleaning up. He came home in the middle of the week, feeling both pleased with himself and in despair over the situation. He had stayed at disaster headquarters in Stavnäs, where various entrepreneurs within the clean-up industry were making money hand over fist during those days. He had been out to Storm Island and seen how every rock, every little spit of land, and every bay was completely smeared with the thick, stinking, sticky oil. It had taken a team of twelve people two days to get rid of the worst of it. The local populace would be using scrubbing brushes all summer long.

Henry's maternal grandparents had suddenly grown so old that he could hardly recognise them. It seemed as if the air had gone out of them. He went out to the Storm Island of his childhood – he hadn't been there in years – as a member of a special disaster task-force, and there he'd found his grandfather and grandmother looking like two trembling reeds, two innocent sea birds whose lives were in jeopardy. They couldn't understand a thing about what was happening. They didn't even mention the oil. They invited Henry for coffee and talked as if nothing special were going on. Henry couldn't tell whether they had suddenly grown senile or if they simply refused to accept the disaster.

Then Henry had gone over to the boat-building house to have a look at the Ark. It should have been there with its bare framework, its slender keel and the plankwork that they had only just begun putting on fifteen years earlier. But the Ark was gone. Henry found nothing but reeds on a rock. The incredible ice had crept up onto the shore and taken the entire boat-house with it. It had slowly hauled itself over Storm Island and shattered, smashed and crushed his grandfather's boathouse.

Henry couldn't believe his eyes. The only thing left of the boathouse and the Ark was a pile of reeds and boards under big sheets of ice, black with oil.

The month of April, in the election year of 1979, bore a great resemblance to a tragic Wagner opera. It was grey, unrelenting and gloomy. Everyone was waiting for the redemptive, liberating rays of light from above. But April was holding back, refusing redemption, *die Erlösung*. The month of April continued to be an endless melody of gloomy, grey tones.

With flagging hope, we kept up our search for Leo. We had several arguments – Henry blamed himself for being too hard on his brother – about whether we should ring Kerstin, the daughter of the football-pool king, since Leo had mentioned that he was thinking of looking her up. They'd had some sort of thing going, after all. And that turned out to be a good lead.

After a run-around among various telephone switchboards and busy car phones, Henry finally got hold of Kerstin. She was in a traffic jam on Strandvägen, and she could tell him that Leo had spent a couple of days at her flat several weeks earlier, but they'd had a falling out. She thought he was a bit too passive and self-destructive, the way he just lay in bed smoking all day long. Leo had ended up feeling angry, hurt and offended. She hadn't heard a peep from him since. Now she too was worried, because she had assumed that he had come home to us to lick his wounds. We all agreed to keep our eyes and ears open.

With equally flagging hope we read our four daily newspapers. In the press they were already starting to speculate about the local and national elections, barely six months away. It was in connection with this hot issue that I one day found an article, which covered an entire page, about the Griffel Corporation's CEO, Wilhelm Sterner. It was in the conservative morning paper, which was reporting on the candidates for a possible right-wing government. Included, of course, were all the old, worn-out, furrowed faces, ravaged by interminable discussions and compromises. But there was also a photo gallery of powerful men who were totally unknown to the general public – influential men who worked behind the scenes, chaps who had trained with Wallenberg and learned the importance of those words of wisdom: *non videre sed esse*.

Wilhelm Sterner, the CEO of the Griffel Corporation, was portrayed in a slightly ironic tone as 'an irreproachable sixty-five-year-old gentleman', a man who had taken a relatively long route before reaching, at last, the top of one of Sweden's largest corporations. As a young lawyer in the forties, he had started off on the diplomatic path. He had moved from one appointment to another, showing himself to be an accomplished career diplomat. Finally he ended up as counsellor at the embassy in Vienna, Austria. For a while he was also stationed in Jakarta, Indonesia, but in the late fifties, he decided to leave his quite brilliant diplomatic career behind in favour of a position in the private sector.

He soon emerged from Wallenberg's shadow and reached dizzying heights within the Griffel Corporation. He was full of ideas and possessed great stamina and knowledge. The only time he ended up in hot water was in the early sixties, when he was accused by East German authorities of helping people flee over the Wall and through the Iron Curtain. The incident very nearly cost Sterner his entire future, and it was apparently considered extremely embarrassing for Swedish authorities as well as the stockholders of the Griffel Corporation. It was not customary among VIPs to meddle so blatantly in the diplomatic affairs of other countries. Sweden had experienced enough trouble with its assistance to refugees. Via various adroitly executed manoeuvres – presumably arranged by Sterner himself – the lid was put on the matter and the incident was relegated to a few columns of small print. It was hushed up, and everything was once again peace and joy. Sterner had saved his own neck.

After that, Wilhelm Sterner had refrained from any more diplomatic escapades. He worked entirely behind the scenes, making a name for himself as a capable, hard-nosed negotiator who never underestimated an opponent. He was 'an eternal bachelor with grey-templed charm', but 'the infrequent tabloid photos confirm that the magnate does enjoy female company'.

Like all CEOs in charge of giant corporations, Wilhelm Sterner also worked at least fifteen hours a day, but he presented a good example by foregoing private jets and other extravagant luxuries. He regularly played tennis with another well-known corporate executive, and he hadn't missed a single Båstad tournament since the big ruckus in the sixties. He actively supported Swedish track and field sports, he had financed a golf course in the Stockholm area and he had won a bronze medal in shot-put in a district championship in 1935.

In spite of the fact that he had now reached retirement age, he saw no reason to slow down. Wilhelm Sterner was actually in his prime. If the right-wing forces should win the election in the autumn, it was highly likely that he would be a candidate for some ministerial post, even though he was regarded as 'conservatively apolitical'. The title of Minister of Industry seemed a natural. The job would be well suited to his impressive qualifications, his long experience in the business world and his extensive international contacts.

No one feared as yet that Sterner might turn down the offer. It was taken for granted that he would 'clean up' his past, as was expected of a respectable minister, in order to avoid any opportunities for corruption which the post of Minister of Industry might afford. It was not uncommon for dignitaries who were associated in some way with high finance to use manipulation to win a politically sensitive post.

In all likelihood, Wilhelm Sterner would accept an offer and wind up his activities with the Griffel Corporation and its fifteen subsidiaries – including Skandia Plaster, EKO Cement, Bogren Brothers Shipyard, Baltic Fisheries and Hammars Construction, as well the Zeverin Precision Tool Company AB, near the Sickla docks at Hammarby Harbour.

Someone who was being considered as the next Minister of Industry had to be clean and inviolable.

———

Quite unexpectedly, Henry showed proof of rather admirable strength in this situation. After a couple of days when I thought that he might be going straight to the dogs, he pulled himself together and confirmed his booking for that evening at the Södra Theatre in May. Now all he had to do was send over a programme and polish up his final version of 'Europa, Disintegrating Fragments'. Suddenly it looked as if his breakthrough were just around the corner.

In an eager, obstinate, hot-headed mood, he came into the library as I sat there, trying to work. For my part, I was in the midst of something that could ultimately be called the final stages of my modern pastiche of *The Red Room*. I knew exactly how the story should end, and all I needed to do was to pound out the decisive and, for Arvid Falk's part, very disheartening last fifty pages. It could be done in a couple of days, once I got going properly. But I never seemed to get going. I just stared out of the windows at the uniform grey of Hornsgatan, looking at the slushy, nasty weather down there, which sapped me of all incentive. A strenuous, virtuous task meant little in a world that was nothing but evil and greyness. No one was expecting anything of me, no one would miss me if I didn't get up in the morning, and no one expressed their profound concern for my welfare or any sort of success on my account. Apropos accounts, Franzén the publisher was the only one who was talking about 'my account'. He'd been nagging about my manuscript for months now, and evidently he was starting to have doubts and feel that he might have been cheated. It had cost him 15,000 kronor.

So Henry came dashing into the library, asking me whether he was disturbing me. That was a completely superfluous question, since he was always disturbing me.

'I wanted to ask you a favour, Klasa,' he said with feigned humility. 'Since you're such a man of letters . . . It has to do with the programme. I've got hold of a cheap printer.'

'What's this about?' I asked, annoyed.

'Södra Theatre . . .' said Henry, staring at me with his innocent blue eyes.

'Yes, that much I know!'

'I'd like to have something written . . . something lyrical and rather elegant.'

'Something lyrical and elegant about what?'

'About me, and about my music, of course,' said Henry, sounding offended.

'And you think that *I* could write something like that? But I don't know anything about music!'

'That doesn't matter. It's the feeling that's important. It has to be a text that captures the music. You don't have to say much about Henry Morgan or musical keys or that sort of thing. It's better if you try to capture the *spirit* of the whole thing.'

'Are you finished yet?'

'For the most part,' he said. 'Well? Will you do it?'

'Of course I'll do it,' I said. 'But I'll need to listen to the whole piece through a couple of times.'

'Whenever you like,' Henry offered magnanimously and bowed.

'How about right now? I'm stuck anyway.'

Henry pensively rubbed his swollen hands – we had been over to the Europa the night before, and he had gone a couple of rounds with Gringo and was still feeling a bit tender. He played a few bars in the air.

'All right, I'm sure it will be fine!'

We were just on our way to the piano room for a concert of 'Europa, Disintegrating Fragments' when we heard a few shrill rings from the telephone. It was Kerstin. She was sitting in Picko's delivery van number 17 and ringing from Kungsholmstorg. There was a howling and shrieking in the receiver, and the fact that the daughter of the football-pool king was so agitated didn't make things any better. She had received several calls from Leo over the past twenty-four hours. His speech was slurred, and he sounded completely out of it. He absolutely refused to say where he was or what he was doing. She couldn't get a sensible word out of him, and then he had just slammed down the phone.

Kerstin was naturally very worried, and Henry tried to reassure her. He said that Leo was sometimes like that, he went through phases but he usually snapped out of it. In any case, Henry urged Kerstin to try tracing the call the next time Leo rang. We'd had it with coddling him.

'He's been playing this game long enough,' said Henry.

'So this is some kind of *game*?'

'It's the most dangerous game of all,' said Henry.

There was no private concert that day. Henry lost all inspiration after that conversation with Kerstin. He excused himself by saying that his hands were still too tender; it wouldn't have sounded very good, anyway. We would just have to wait until some later time.

But there never was any 'later time'. The next day it was my turn to stay in bed. I refused to get up to eat breakfast just to read a depressing morning paper and then sit at a desk that was becoming more and more of a witness to some sort of defeat. *The Red Room* was starting to seem more and more like a failure, and Arvid Falk's tragic end was becoming reflected in my own destruction. I was stuck. I knew exactly what I wanted to write, but I couldn't put the shit into writing; something inside me was resisting, and of course I decided to blame the weather. It was possible to dump all sorts of blame on the weather during those days. The weather was affecting everyone, and there wasn't a soul who wouldn't understand that a writer was especially susceptible to the low pressure and that damn sirocco which had found its way to our latitudes, or that it was completely natural for any sensitive fellow to feel like coughing himself to death in the Lido or escaping from the world across the mountains and into the clouds, like a Hans Castorp, the most melancholy character in any novel ever.

———————

My dream of a liberating death in the Lido ended when Henry came in and sat down on the edge of Göring's old bed to wake me up. Kerstin had called, and she knew where Leo was. He had rung her in the middle of the night, and she had put down the receiver and dashed over to use her neighbour's phone to trace the call. It turned out to be from a summer house out in the Värmdö area.

'Hell if I know where that is,' said Henry. 'Löknäs is what it's supposedly called. Not far from a military training ground. But wasn't that where he hid out with some pals over Christmas?'

'I assume so,' I said.

'I suppose we'll have to go out there and take a look, anyway,' said Henry. 'Could you go tonight?'

'Of course.'

'Kerstin offered to drive.'

'That's nice. Just as long as there isn't any trouble, or else I'll completely fall apart!'

'No chance of that,' said Henry firmly. 'Leo's not the type.'

That day was like so many other of those thoroughly grey days. The only bright piece of news was that the bureau drawer in the hallway was suddenly full of booklets of luncheon vouchers again. Naturally I didn't ask where they had come from – I had been ordered not to ask – but I had my suspicions. I had my suspicions about a lot of things at this point, but we tiptoed around each other like cats on hot bricks, perpetually trying not to let on.

At any rate, we had a fortifying lunch down at Costa's on St Paulsgatan with a Greek salad and souvlaki, those deliciously spiced kebabs, with first-class beef, onions and paprika. The Flask and Wolf-Larsson had turned up again, looking relatively fresh. They had spent a long time behind drawn curtains in the company of a real stockpile of bottles, but now that period was over. Now they were on the wagon for a while and were going to work in Greger's Grotto, the Shelter, and collect empty bottles and plod their way through the approaching springtime like two proper gentlemen. They both wanted to know what had been going on lately, and Henry gave them a rough summary. True to form, he promised them each a ticket to the Södra Theatre when the time came. The lads thanked him in advance and wished him luck, in which order no one was quite sure.

Kerstin showed up as promised to collect us after she'd finished work. She was still driving Picko's delivery van number 17, and she was all wound up. She angrily and ruthlessly chomped on a small piece of chewing gum as she hissed terse, rapid-fire remarks out of the corner of her mouth, just like some sort of American gangster.

'Can you find it, Henry?' she asked.

'I hope so,' he said, taking from the inner pocket of his trench coat a map that he had drawn. 'This is how it looks, approximately.'

'Oh, that's really a big help,' said Kerstin.

'You're sure in a hell of a mood today!'

'It's all been so fucking difficult today. Everything's so screwed up.'

'I want you at least to know that you'll get a reward for this,' said Henry.

Kerstin muttered something inaudible and turned on the radio. It was one of those formidable and terribly uninteresting DJs from Värmland, and he was warning listeners about the slick conditions and hydroplaning on large sections of the main roads. It had rained hard in the morning and the temperature was going to drop to below freezing in the evening. Then followed a long tune from Elton John's latest LP, a tough, moving, very magical tune.

'Turn it up a bit,' said Henry.

Kerstin turned up the radio so loud that the entire vehicle was filled with that sunny Elton John tune, and it went on almost all the way from Danvikstull along the new motorway and out to Gustavsberg. We hardly said a word the

whole time. I don't know who deserved the blame or the credit for that –
Leo Morgan or Elton John.

Henry carefully guided the driver up towards northern Värmdö, along a
number of slushy side-roads until none of us knew where we were. Henry's
map was looking more and more like a scientific chart of the way an earth-
worm moves during twenty-four hours of rain, and it was no longer of any
particular use to us. He had to get out of the van and ask some locals how
to find the road to Löknäs and the military training ground.

Gradually it grew dark, and by then we had wound our way through all
sorts of little villages and cultivated fields until we slipped onto a forest road
heading east, which seemed to be the right one because it was completely
empty and deserted. Deep in the woods there was still snow, and the road
was covered with black ice so that Kerstin had to drive very cautiously, making
use of everything she knew about driving in lousy terrain.

'Pat Moss,' said Henry. 'All I'm saying is Pat Moss, the racing-car driver.'

'Shut up!' snapped Kerstin, turning off the radio. She needed to concentrate.

Henry rolled down the side window, but it instantly got horribly cold, and
he could tell that the temperature really was dropping below freezing. Not a
single person was out on the road.

'It seems desolate as hell,' I said, shivering.

'There must be some old summer cabin that they've taken over,' said
Henry.

'What do you mean by *they*?'

'You don't think my brother is sitting out here all alone, drinking, do you?'
said Henry, though he didn't sound very convincing. Or maybe he knew a
lot more than the rest of us.

'It sounded like he was alone,' said Kerstin. 'But he did sound fucking out
of it, actually.'

'Leo gets really stupid when he's drinking.'

'Then why does he do it? It can't be much fun to sit out here in the wild,
drinking.'

'Kerstin, my dear,' Henry began, 'you may be a fantastic driver, but you're
not especially smart.'

'What do you mean?' said Kerstin, sounding surly as she slammed on the
brakes in the middle of a slushy curve.

'Nothing. I apologise,' said Henry. 'But what the hell do you think?! Do
you think Leo is acting this way because it's *entertaining*?!'

'Of course, I realise . . .' said Kerstin, a little embarrassed. 'But sometimes I wonder what kind of wet blankets the lot of you are.'

'Don't go lumping *me* in with them!' I said. 'The Morgan brothers are famous, and famous brothers always get a little screwy.'

'*C'est la vie*,' said Henry.

Kerstin parked the van, switched off the headlights, and set the handbrake. Then we climbed out into the darkness.

'It looks completely deserted,' I said.

'I thought I saw a glimmer of light from one of the windows,' said Henry. 'Are you sure this is the right house?'

'How the hell should I know? I'm just trusting my intuition. It's led me in the right direction before.'

'It looks like a darling little place,' said Kerstin in a whisper, as if we were doing something that was strictly prohibited.

The little summer cabin stood on a bare hill with a view of Löknäs Bay, where the ice hadn't yet thawed. On the opposite shore another hill rose up, forming a magnificent inlet to the bay. Presumably this was sheer paradise in the summer, with swaying reeds and water lilies and sunshine all day long.

Henry took a few steps ahead of us, seeming both eager and hesitant at the same time. He was probably very unsure about what he was actually doing at the moment, but there was no longer any turning back. Right now it was purely a matter of going through with it and finding out what was inside that house.

We slipped and slid our way to the door. Someone had recently shovelled the snow away from the porch, so the place couldn't be totally deserted. Henry went up to the door and knocked. A faint light was visible in the window facing the bay, but it didn't look like an ordinary electric light; it seemed like a tiny flickering flame.

We heard a sound from inside the house, and Henry again knocked on the door. Not a sign of life. We waited for a good couple of minutes in utter, reverential silence but heard only the cold wind blowing through the tops of the fir trees. Then Henry grabbed the door handle and opened the door.

'Hello!' he shouted into the house.

'Let's go in and check,' I said to give Henry courage.

He went first, and we noticed the stench at once. The rank smell of sweat, paraffin, leftover food and excrement. After passing through an ice-cold, draughty room, we found, at last, the missing Leo. He was lying on a bed asleep under three heavy blankets. The floor all around was covered with empty bottles, all of them the same brand of whisky: Johnny Walker, elegant in a red frock-coat, with pince-nez, a cane and a top hat. Next to the bed was a box with more unopened bottles. The liquor in that house would easily have cost 10,000 kronor.

'I'm going outside,' Kerstin whispered in my ear, her eyes brimming with tears. Whether it was from sympathy or because of the nauseating stench of ammonia, I couldn't tell.

Henry went over to the bed and started shaking Leo. He had suddenly lost all his fear and was now as bold and cocky as a Boy Scout. Things needed to be cleaned up here, and so there was no use standing around in bewilderment, letting ourselves get disgusted because Leo had suffered a minor collapse. With a little bad luck it could happen to anyone. Henry shook Leo's head and called his name but got no response. Something moved, and Henry gave a start of surprise when another head emerged from under the jumble of filthy blankets.

It was a terribly emaciated girl who couldn't have been more than twenty or so, although drugs had given her an appearance worthy of a worn-out pensioner.

'What the hell . . .' groaned the girl as she listlessly rubbed her eyes. 'What the hell are *you* doing here?' she said, as if she knew at once who we were.

And it turned out that she actually *did* know who we were.

'I was just about to ask you the same question,' said Henry, sounding annoyed. 'Who *are* you?'

'Fuck off,' said the girl.

Henry grabbed her and lifted her skinny body out of the bed, but nearly dropped her in astonishment.

'Do you see what *I* see?' he asked me.

'It's a small world,' I said.

'At least this world is!'

'Cut it out . . . cut it out,' said the girl just as she had on that evening when we'd found her beaten up on our landing and given her a hot bath and watched over her all night long.

'Cut it out,' said the dark angel again in her toneless, raspy, worn-out voice.

'OK, OK,' said Henry. 'I'm Leo's *brother*, and we're here to take him back home to the city.'

The thin little creature sat down on the edge of the bed and rubbed her eyes. She didn't seem to comprehend much of what was going on. She sat there and rolled her eyes, rocking back and forth as if the whole world were spinning round.

'Fuck off,' she said again. 'Not *now*!'

'What do you mean, not *now*?' asked Henry. 'It looks like the two of you are trying to drink yourselves to death!'

The girl groaned and toppled onto the floor. I propped her up against the bed, shoving aside empty bottles and mouldy tins of baked beans and ravioli that smelled of puke, to be quite blunt.

Henry went back to trying to shake some life into Leo. He lifted his eyelids and slapped him hard on the cheeks, but without response.

'You were just drinking, weren't you?!' said Henry, turning to look at the girl on the floor. 'You didn't take anything else, did you, *goddammit*?!'

The girl was still sitting on the floor looking dazed. She rolled her eyes and obviously didn't comprehend a thing.

'Do you have any *syringes* here?' Henry shouted right in her ear.

'Do *I*?' she said, slurring her words. '*I* have my *own*,' she went on, sounding almost proud.

'What about Leo? Is *he* on drugs?'

'*That* guy?' she slurred. 'He just *drinks* . . .'

Henry went outside to get some snow. He came back with the snow and with Kerstin, who wasn't looking too good. Her face was streaked because she had been standing out there bawling.

We rubbed snow in Leo's face, and only then did he begin to show any sign of life. He grimaced at the cold snow, started spitting and suddenly pulled his head out of my grasp and laboriously opened his eyelids a little. He muttered something completely incoherent, moaned and then tried to turn over to face the wall, but he couldn't manage it.

Without warning the girl on the floor gave a start, leapt to her feet and began jabbering just the way she had done when she came to in our flat, like an auctioneer, in a loud, shrill, strained voice. She didn't seem in a bad mood at all – quite the contrary.

'You have to see! You have to see what we've done!' she shouted. 'You have to come with me and look, look, look at what we *defied* . . .'

Henry and Kerstin and I glanced at each other and then looked in surprise at the girl, who with jerking, spasmodic movements was trying to interest us in something they had *dared*.

'Take it easy,' I said. 'We're not here to hurt either of you. We're going to drive back to town soon.'

'You have to . . . it's nothing but shit, the whole thing!' the girl went on and then literally careered out the open door.

'Klasa,' said Henry. 'Go out there with the girl and keep on eye on what she's doing. We'll try to get Leo down to the van.'

'OK,' I said and dashed after the girl into the dark.

I could hear her furious chatter from the slope leading down to the ice, and I could make out a well-worn path with a snow-covered railing that probably functioned fine in the summer. But right now, in the deep snow, it reached about as high as my ankles. The path led down to the water and was icy and slippery. I had to make a special effort not to fall and really hurt myself, but the drugged girl flew down the slope with all the force and superhuman power that certain insane individuals can sometimes possess temporarily.

But down at the ice I managed to catch up with her and grab her emaciated arm, although she then tore herself free and ran right out to the middle of Löknäs Bay. I've always had a great respect for ice, and I'm not experienced in deciphering where it will hold or break, but this was no time to stand around arguing with my fear. Right now it was a matter of catching that girl, and she had dashed out to stand in the middle of the bay. That's where she stopped, not even out of breath.

'What the hell is this all about?' I asked.

'You have to see . . . You have to see,' she said, and then I noticed a hole in the ice that someone had made in the middle of the bay. It was just enough for a winter dip, and the skinny girl could have easily jumped into the water at any moment. I stood poised to stop her if that was what I was supposed to witness.

But the girl seemed crazier than ever. Without warning she started jumping on the ice next to the hole. She jumped with both feet, stamping as hard as she could, up and down in an incredible frenzy.

'Jump . . . Jump . . .' she urged me, panting.

I was cold and shivering, and my shoes were soaking wet. I had no intention of jumping around like an idiot in the middle of ice that might give way at any time. I refused to do as she said, which made her furious, and then she slapped me across the face.

'All right,' I said, and started jumping. I thought it was best to play along.

We jumped and stamped on the ice with all our might, and I saw a look of delight gradually appear on her face. The bitter cold of the evening made the cracks in the ice shriek. There was a whistling and screeching around the ice, a slapping and snapping like broken strings, and the echo ricocheted far away over the hills and bays. The moon cast its blue light across the ice, which shrieked and howled in its plaintive misery, and when it echoed best into the infinity beneath the deep blue sky, the howling would pass from the metallic pain of the ice into flesh and blood, the fur and pulse of animal throats: the foxes were answering the howl of the ice! Each time the ice shrieked in torment and cast its elegiac echo over the area, a fox would answer with a long howl. And each time the fox replied, the wild girl would find more strength to jump and stamp, making the ice shriek anew, and then the foxes would answer again in this furious dialogue between the moon, the tortured ice, the crazy girl and the frightened foxes.

I felt as though I'd found myself right at the edge of the outermost boundary of what was possible.

J ust like any tragic opera, every story of respectable rank ought to have
some sort of *clou*, that is to say a zenith or *peripeteia*, a turning point,
although nowadays people prefer to call it by the more popular term:
climax. Without either boasting or taking great pains to sort out and chart
the reality we were struggling with up in that flat on Hornsgatan, I can say
that the *clou* of our story occurred during several hectic and feverish days at
the end of April, in the election year and Year of the Child, 1979.

'What time is it?' was the first sentence that Leo Morgan said after returning
from the valley of the shadow of death where he had spent the past month.
Henry took this as a definite sign that his brother was on the road to recovery.

We both stood there watching Leo as he lay on his bed and gradually
came out of the fog. Occasionally he would squint his eyes at the trouble-
some light from some chance ray of sunshine, then he would fall back into
a trance, exhausted from the effort, cleansed of all strength and vitality, his
awareness at nil, far beyond anyone's reach.

'What time is it?' he asked one day as we stood there, keeping watch over
him. Ignoring the metaphysical aspects – perhaps he had drunk himself
beyond all sense of time and space – Henry replied very concisely:

'Twelve-thirty in the afternoon on the twentieth of April, 1979.'

Leo seemed to comprehend the answer and groaned. He rooted around
in bed until he ended up on his side in a restful position and opened his eyes
to look round the room.

'You're home, now, Leo,' said Henry in a loud, clear voice. 'We've brought
you home.'

'Mm,' murmured Leo. He didn't seem to have any objections.

'You haven't been feeling very well,' said Henry. 'But that's over now.

415

Klasa and I are going to see to it that you get back on your feet. Aren't we, Klasa?'

'Of course,' I said, a bit annoyed at the way Henry was talking. It sounded as if he were speaking to a dying man in a hospital.

The patient immediately fell asleep again, and Henry and I very quietly returned to our own activities, calmly and cautiously, so as not to disturb the restorative slumber of our ward. In any case, he was on the road to recovery, and the worst of the withdrawal had passed with surprising ease. I had expected delirium and climbing the walls and horrible roars in the middle of the night and so on, but nothing like that happened.

We had driven back to Stockholm with the two rescued wrecks from the summer cabin in Löknäs on Värmdö. The girl reluctantly allowed us to put her in the car, where Leo lay like a big sack on the back seat, sleeping the whole way home. We drove the dark angel over to the Maria outpatient clinic, and we hadn't heard a thing from her since. We assumed that she was being well taken care of.

Henry then immediately contacted the family physician, Dr Helmers, who showed up at once with a large array of injections – B vitamins and other special treatments for withdrawal – that would make life a bit more tolerable for us and for the patient. Huffing, puffing Dr Helmers was the only family physician I've ever seen who looked exactly the way an old family doctor should look. He had bifocals, grey hair and perfect teeth. There was an air of weighty authority in the way he held his shoulders, and he had a quite vigorous stride for his age. Naturally he knew everything there was to know about the Morgonstjärna family – he was intimately familiar with all the childhood illnesses the boys had been through, and he was the one who had sat by their paternal grandmother's bed when she died in the bedroom that would soon become the WWW Club's most distinguished billiard room. Dr Helmers claimed that the old woman had raved about light, just like Goethe himself, when death stood at the door – but then he was also a very well-travelled, well-read and well-heeled gentleman, who was once a member of the Club, of course.

Dr Helmers was in full agreement that Leo, too, should be nursed and treated at home if at all possible. He had very little use for new forms of therapy or penetrating experiments with the human psyche. Leo would do best if he received the excellent, thorough care that a good home could offer. But the fact of the matter was that Henry Morgan's home was perhaps not a particularly good home for a mutist or a catatonic. That's why things had turned out the way they had, with a couple of sojourns in Långbro Hospital. But this time – when it was 'only' a matter of alcohol – there was no discussion of the matter. Leo would get back on his feet, and if the situation turned critical, we should just ring Dr Helmers, day or night.

But everything proceeded relatively pain-free. Leo lay in his trance, sweating heavily and raving a bit. He had convulsions, possibly some type of vascular spasms, but they never got out of hand, and the attacks would be followed by peace and calm and the deepest Sleeping Beauty slumber. After four days he asked us what time it was, and then Henry considered the situation resolved – Leo had come safely into harbour, the storm had subsided, and the two assiduous nurses could shake hands and feel satisfied with their efforts.

'Not bad for two amateurs,' said Henry.

'We're not out of the woods yet,' I said, being the born sceptic that I am.

'Don't bring me down!' muttered Henry. 'Don't bring me down as soon as there's some hope!'

'OK, I'm sorry I said that,' I admitted. 'We've done a great job, and we should be pleased.'

That was followed by a couple of days of intense care for Leo, intense work for us, and equally intense longing for the spring that would not come. Dr Henry & Co. took turns bustling about in the long and lugubrious servant corridors between the kitchen and Leo's two-room quarters, with herbal tea for Leo, special porridge for Leo, health-food nectar for Leo and all the magic brews and medicines and world-famous preparations that would get his sabotaged organism to start functioning again. We made steady progress and noted down everything from his appetite to the smell and shape of his bowel movements on a temperature chart pinned up on the pinboard in the kitchen.

Nor did our Art seem to suffer any harm from what had happened. I turned out approximately five pages a day and seemed to be homing in on Arvid Falk's downfall and defeat with great precision. Behind the piles of notebooks, the notes on scraps of paper, the phrases and dialogues, the gloomy descriptions from a depressing winter, I could discern an end – a massive coda, an overwhelming final chord that would take the sting out of the satire and pass beyond the pathetic into a deep, profound and genuine tragedy.

The same was true for Henry, according to his own testimony. 'Europa,

417

Disintegrating Fragments' emerged from fifteen years of playing jazz clubs in Stockholm, a hissing harmonium with the Quakers in Denmark, a pub piano in London, a piano in a Munich bar, a grand piano at the Mossberg estate in the Alps and at Bop Sec in Paris. It resembled a magnificent synthesis of one person's entire experience of the history of European suffering. In any case, that was how the composer himself expressed it. I had not yet been allowed to hear the piece.

─────────

The annual World Championship games in ice hockey began, and we decided to let up on our work schedule a bit for the sake of our mental health and the coverage of the Tre Kronor Swedish team. Nasty rumours were circulating about a particularly weak young team that hadn't trained properly before the annual tournament. Before the opening game, we very nervously laid out a spread of peanuts, crisps, popcorn and Ramlösa mineral water – in a show of solidarity with Leo – in front of the enormous TV set in the sitting room. The armchairs were drawn forward to front-row seats, and Henry had convinced Leo that he absolutely had to get out of bed to watch ice hockey. Leo had acquiesced and now sat in an armchair, wrapped in a blanket with his feet on a footstool. He had his weary, gloomy eyes fixed on the Soviet test pattern.

The Tre Kronor team wasn't nearly as weak as the nasty rumours had made out. As usual, every little success crowned new heroes, and the young goalkeeper was praised by all of Sweden. But Henry screamed himself hoarse when the Russian Bear crushed our heroes, making them look like crippled teenagers.

As usual, this sort of intense interest stayed high for the first few games, but about midway through the championship matches, it felt more like an obligation to load up on peanuts, crisps, popcorn and Ramlösa mineral water to watch some tired, worn-out, injured national teams that just wanted to go home to their wives and girlfriends. But Henry completely refused to acknowledge that every ice-hockey championship got a bit tiresome – until the interest was suddenly re-ignited for the final games – because he was just as childishly delighted every time he heard the Swedish national anthem resound across the ice and wash over our sweaty knights. Sometimes he was even on the verge of bursting into tears out of gentle euphoria.

After the third game, Leo was definitely worn out, and he no longer bothered to get out of bed. Instead, he stayed in his section of the flat, breathing in the incense. For him it was all a totally meaningless exercise, and he was no doubt right, although that seemed a bit lacking in imagination. It was a game with make-believe rules, but there is so much in life that is based on make-believe.

It was during these less colourful and intense matches midway through the tournament that Henry actually touched on an enormous abyss when he began lecturing about what he called Leo's 'hockey nihilism'. According to Henry, Leo viewed all of life as a game. He'd always been like that. The game was exciting and fascinating and generally worthwhile as long as you accepted the rules, the instructions to which you agreed as soon as you entered the game. As long as you stayed within the rules, you could develop your own expertise and stretch the boundaries of what was permitted, learning to control what was possible, and making what was impossible resemble the possible to a very high degree. But as soon as some small boy in welly-boots jumps into a hockey rink, he breaks the magic of the conditions, he sabotages the performance, and the game becomes ridiculous, childish and meaningless. Leo always wore wellies on the ice because he had never made an effort to master skates. And it was exactly the same thing with chess. The only lasting friendship that Leo had retained over the years was with that accountant Lennart Hagberg in Borås, because their friendship was based entirely on brief, concise, cryptic codes that almost no one other than the two of them could decipher. Their loyalty was completely abstract, and if they accepted the game, they could continue until death finally separated them, or maybe even longer. Leo was a 'hockey nihilist' as well as a 'chess fascist'.

This was so typical of Henry. He sat there, seemingly totally engrossed in a boring ice-hockey game, and with half an ear he was listening to the cutting remarks that Leo and I were making about how fucking worthless everything happening on the ice was. He pretended not to hear a word we said, just so that he wouldn't be brought down again. But later everything he had heard re-formed inside him until he managed to construct what was in his eyes an airtight defence of ice hockey or whatever else was in question, even bad ice hockey. Then it would suddenly all come pouring out in one brief outburst in which he could actually be quite brilliant, only to vanish into oblivion once again.

Spring lived inside us as nothing more than a notion, a longing and a dream. Each morning we were forced to conclude that there was a clear discrepancy between metaphysical dream and meteorological reality, which in turn caused a frustrated tension that never found any natural release. This disheartening weather situation, known as low pressure, combined with the world politics and ecological intermezzos, known as disasters, laid the groundwork for a suicidal spring that would demand its tributes, its *hecatombs*, just like the Truth.

With a sudden breeze behind me I started speeding along again and reached the very last chapter of *The Red Room*, but then hit a dead calm. Yet that is the predicament of a prose writer – to swing incessantly between a fierce creative euphoria and a paralysing double-sided uncertainty. But, being quite young, I lacked the practice, experience and strength to handle setbacks. I suddenly found myself drifting backwards, down into the listless depression of winter and heaving big sighs.

This resulted in an excess of libido, to be quite candid. I began devoting more and more attention to Greger's Grotto, the Shelter and to Leo's monumental hangover. The Flask and Wolf-Larsson had started in on the digging again, and in April we had all joined forces in a six-man team working three shifts down there. We were proceeding at a rate of approximately three yards a day, heading due west, and each day we set a new record. The earth was loose, dry and easy to shovel. And we were absolutely positive that we were on the right track to find the Treasure.

It took a long time for Leo to get back on his feet. People had called from the hospital to hear how things were going, and Henry had lied and told them that it was mostly a question of finding him a good job and that should be the end of the matter.

But it turned out that the hospital was not the only one keeping an eye on Leo Morgan, the poet Leo Morgan. In a literary magazine to which I subscribed, a young literary hotshot had launched a vigorous attack on all of contemporary literature, especially poetry. It was high time to start evaluating the literature of the seventies, and according to the author of the essay, it could be compared to a street-sweeper who here and there finds some dog shit among all the empty beer bottles and discarded condoms – whatever wasn't empty or used up was downright disgusting. The result was what might be called a general assault on both the politically 'engaged' literature and the newly awakened 'surrealistic' genre, whatever that meant. The most prevalent method was the oppressive mechanism of ignorance, sloppiness and indolence, which was keeping brilliant young talents from daring to test their wings – not from a fear of heights but because they were scared they would be refused permission to land.

That angry young literary hotshot from Uppsala saw very little chance of improvement – thanks a lot, I thought to myself – but did offer a reprieve to several authors who tragically enough were no longer on the scene, so to speak. He listed a few names and enquired about Leo Morgan, 'who was actually ten years ahead of his time in his solitary march with a bomb and Artaud, Genet and an eternal Eliot in his knapsack as he went on his botanical expeditions through the swamps of anxiety in the post-war period.'

Naturally I rushed elatedly into Leo's incense-filled rooms, waving the literary magazine, in order to cheer up the poet a bit. He was in demand, and if he would just go back to that black workbook with the draft for *Autopsy*, I would take on the job of marketing it. Any publisher would be eager to publish it.

'Have you got a smoke?' asked Leo apathetically.

'You shouldn't smoke in bed,' I admonished him.

Leo was no longer interested in any literary discussions. He scanned through the praise of the young literary hotshot and then dropped the magazine to the floor with a yawn. He hauled himself out of bed and put on his bathrobe. We went out to the sitting room to have a smoke and look at the impressive grey outside the windows. We each lit a cigarette while Leo shivered. I was completely at a loss.

'Why the hell do you stay in this madhouse?' he asked.

'I suppose I'm just as much an idiot myself,' I said.

'That might . . .' said Leo, 'that might actually happen if you don't watch out.'

He gave me one of those long, dark, lingering stares of his that could make anyone feel uncertain and puzzled.

'You'd better watch yourself, my boy,' he said, slapping me on the shoulder. 'You're undoubtedly going to be somebody important, and you need to be careful. There's so much that you don't know about.'

'There's so much that I don't *want* to know about.'

'But you can't avoid it.'

'What do you mean?' I asked. 'What can't I avoid?'

Leo took a drag on his cigarette and blew the smoke out through his nose.

'I don't know,' he said evasively. 'Insanity, maybe. It's taking hold all around.'

'I'll just have to try to protect myself.'

'That won't help. It can slip through concrete.'

'I still have quite a few dreams left,' I said. 'There are also glimmers of light. It'll soon be spring, and good things do happen.'

Leo snorted, but it didn't sound *totally* patronising.

'What kind of glimmers of light?'

'Resistance,' I said. 'Some sort of counter-citizens who refuse to accept evil – punks who defend Kurds, youths who defy Nazis at upper-class schools in Östermalm, action groups . . . There's always *something*, dammit!'

Leo stared for a long time at the Persian rug that had a long path worn thin between the tables and armchairs in the sitting room over to the chess table.

'Hmm,' he said, nodding his head. 'I suppose there always is something. But there's so much that you don't see. A person sees only what he *wants* to see.'

'So what do *you* want to see?'

'It's always easy to define what's negative. I don't need any utopias to survive. I can afford to be a pessimist.'

'I don't believe that. I think that utopias are indelible.'

'You've been listening to Henry too much. He's like one big, blue-eyed utopia.'

'But he's perfectly harmless.'

'Don't be so sure about that. You have no idea how many lies and myths he's created around himself.'

'And I don't want to know. I've always liked mythomaniacs.'

'One day you'll find out,' said Leo. 'It's best to be prepared.'

———————

Now the big, gloomy flat was filled with all the scents of Easter: from newly budding branches and lilies, and from the garlic and thyme of the Easter lamb. We went around suffering from the cold in our Higgins cardigans, and we suffered through the interminable Good Friday. We suffered with Jesus and we suffered with Leo. We watched all the feature films on TV about the Crucifixion and the Resurrection, and on one of the most sombre evenings during Easter there was a programme about Henry's colleague, Allan Pettersson.

'Dammit, Allan has had a hell of a time,' said Henry.

'Do you know him?' I asked.

'Know and *know*,' said Henry. 'No one really knows Allan, but I've gone over to visit him a couple of times. He looked through a number of things that I'd written. That was *long* before he became *popular*.'

'So what did he think?'

'Oh, Allan is rather difficult. He didn't say anything special.'

The programme clearly gave Henry pause, and he couldn't stop whistling that whimpering theme from the Seventh Symphony. He said that he was thinking of writing a letter to Allan to tell him that it was a damn good programme. But then he decided not to, saying that it wouldn't sound right, not genuine enough. It was so hard to be positive without sounding ingratiating.

And anyway, positive signs were few and far between. We went around outdoing each other with sighs that got deeper and deeper. The evenings were never sufficiently enticing to lure us out, and no work seemed sufficiently interesting to hide us from the world.

Henry suggested a drink in secret – somewhere that Leo wouldn't notice the fumes – and dug out half a bottle of whisky from his wardrobe. We locked ourselves in the billiard room and played a listless game in almost total silence. Henry just hummed now and then to draw attention to a few of his best shots. I still didn't have a chance, and I blamed the chalk. In spite of his depression, Henry had not lost his sense of discipline, and whoever saw him might have thought he was a man in his prime. His tie was meticulously knotted, he was impeccably shaved, the parting in his hair was perfect, and his jacket had classically casual wrinkles.

Defeated, I sank down on a chair in the billiard room and stared listlessly out the window, sucking on a cigarette. I coughed and then asked Henry how much he *really* thought he could handle.

'What do you mean?' he replied at once. 'What you mean by "handle"?'

'Don't play dumb,' I said as I replaced my cue in the rack on the wall.

Henry realised that I was serious, and he leaned against the windowsill and looked out across the rooftops. Maybe he was looking for some little star, a streak of light, something to wish on.

'We all have our limits,' he said. 'Perhaps I'm able to stretch mine rather far. A little *too* far. At least that's how it seems sometimes.'

'Have you talked to Leo? I mean really *talked* to him?'

'About what? Of course! I talk to Leo every single day!'

'There's so much that is . . . unexplained. Where did he get all that whisky out at the cabin? What sort of pals does he have who want him to drink himself to death?'

'Pals . . .' said Henry, throwing out his arms and shrugging his shoulders to show that he had no idea.

'We can't just go around as if nothing is happening and keep quiet about all this, can we? I've tried to talk to him without seeming overly nosy. But it does no good. He's closed up like a clam, and he turns everything against himself like a boomerang.'

'That's how he's always been. Leo is a pro at defending all sorts of impossibilities. He was on his way to getting a doctorate in philosophy, for God's sake!'

'But you can be just as impossible, Henry.'

'I know, I know. I've heard that all before, ad nauseam. You don't have to repeat what Leo says like you're some kind of parrot.'

'The two of you talk exactly the same way. You always just shift the blame to someone else.'

Henry was still standing at the window with his back to me, and he kept shrugging his shoulders like some defiant child who can't defend his actions.

'Don't you see,' I said, 'that I just want to know what you're thinking, how you manage to endure this fucking mess. I personally don't know how I'm going to stand it.'

'Then move somewhere else!' said Henry sullenly.

'I don't mean to bring you down,' I said. 'I assure you, it's just that I take this whole thing very seriously.'

'Don't you think that *I* do too?!'

'Sometimes I wonder.'

'Well, let me tell you,' said Henry, and now he was getting really worked up. 'Let me tell you *this*: if I didn't take this whole thing seriously, Leo would be in some loony bin on a fucking disability pension, holed up somewhere without a friend left on this earth, and I'll be damned if anyone can claim that I'm taking this matter too casually. And let me tell you something *else*,' he went on, jabbing his index finger at me, 'if I *really* gave in to all these depressions, we would have starved to death this winter.'

And then, without warning, Henry dashed out of the billiard room and disappeared into the kitchen regions, only to return with a loudly purring Spinks in his arms.

'There's one thing you should know, Klasa,' he said. 'I'm not some damn intellectual, and I can't fill my speech with lovely phrases the way the two of you can. I like things like this,' he said, and he dumped Spinks onto the middle of the billiard table.

Spinks instantly stopped purring and crouched down in a pose that was both playfully curious and tense, with his bushy tail slowly moving back and forth, sweeping over the green felt.

Henry *the animal trainer* pointed out a corner of the billiard table to Spinks and picked up a couple of balls. He rolled the spheres cautiously towards Spinks, who stopped them with his paw, shoved them straight into a pocket and then waited for the next ones. The trick was repeated over and over again, and I didn't really get the point, at least not at the time. It's only now, much later, that I can grasp what was so grand about that scene: the harried and always slightly affected Henry Morgan in the role of the animal trainer, and his ever-devoted friend Spinks who does what he's been taught to do because he knows that it will pay off. How many hours had it taken to get that trick down pat! An absolutely meaningless trick which had, of course, fascinated Henry for days and nights on end, and which still made him equally surprised, almost happy.

I would like to remember him that way – as a man with inexhaustible resources and talents that he squandered on pure nonsense, purely symbolic feats undertaken for their own sake.

'Let's try one last gasp, Klasa,' said Henry. 'Let's take a break and go into town. We *might* get a little sunshine today.'

We'd had a midday thaw for a couple of days. The snow and icicles were briskly dropping from the roofs, and the streets had dried out and were filled with dusty gravel. Occasionally, above the grey cloud cover, it was possible to see that the sun actually did exist and that it might peep out at any time.

'Let's pop downtown, just to check things out,' said Henry. 'Surely there has to be a little spring in the air.'

So we strolled towards town, walked across Slussen, along Skeppsbron in a cutting wind, and stopped for a while in the middle of Ström Bridge to look down at the wild current.

It was an afternoon at the very end of April, and there were scores of people out walking. Presumably everyone was looking for signs of spring, but, except for an occasional crocus, we all had to make do with the fact that the women had left their fur coats at home. It was as good a sign as any that things were about to change. The skating rink in the King's Garden was deserted, worn out, uneven and now of no further interest.

'I didn't go skating even once this year,' said Henry.

'Me neither,' I said. 'What did we actually do this winter?'

'That's a good question,' said Henry. 'But *dammit all*! We have irons in the fire, my boy. Things are going to start happening now.'

'Maybe for you, but not for me.'

'Pish posh. Let's go over to Wimpy.'

'*Wimpy*?' I said. 'Why the hell should we go there?'

'We can have an espresso and feel right at home, as if we were in London.'

I gave in, and we crossed Kungsträdgårdsgatan and slipped into the bar just as that Elton John tune was playing, the one we'd listened to on our way out to Värmdö. We climbed onto bar stools, unbuttoned our coats, stuffed our caps in our pockets and looked around.

'I feel right at home here,' said Henry. 'You can't imagine how many hours I spent in Wimpy in London. They've got exactly the same vinyl everywhere.'

He carefully pulled out a handkerchief and blew his nose with a loud blast. Then he just as carefully folded up the cloth and put it away in his jacket pocket. I hadn't thought about it before, but he was the first person I'd seen in years who still blew his nose on old-fashioned handkerchiefs.

We each ordered a double espresso, and Henry whistled along with the catchy Elton John tune as he took out the little penknife in the burgundy leather case. Absentmindedly he began cleaning his nails, interrupting his manicure now and then to glance at the customers coming in. I thought it was a damned bad habit.

When we got our double espressos, he took out the silver cigarette case with the initials W.S. on the lid and offered me a Pall Mall. He lit it with an old Ronson lighter and went back to whistling along with Elton John.

The coffee felt nice and warm in my stomach. That marvellous combination of caffeine and nicotine tastes of the big city, of slow periods in cafés spent quietly leafing through a foreign newspaper and empty dialogues while waiting for something that never happens – it's the possibility alone that makes the blood tremble.

A very pimply teenager on roller skates came wobbling in and rolled up to the bar to order a hamburger. Henry was delighted by the roller skates and asked the boy everything there was to know about roller skates today: the manufacturer, price, technology, weather and rinks. The boy politely answered all his questions, stuffed the hamburger in his mouth and left. That was how Henry always behaved in order to gather information; he could actually have become a remarkably proficient detective if he'd wanted.

The wobbling, pimply boy on roller skates was replaced by a chic woman about Henry's own age. She lithely slipped onto the bar stool next to him, unbuttoned her trench coat and dropped a silk scarf on the floor.

'Allow me!' Henry promptly said, and he bent down to pick up the scarf.

'Thank you very much,' said the woman in the purest American English.

Henry immediately frowned and tried to look irresistible. His eyes suddenly took on that absurd narrowed look. I'd seen that expression before and was intimately familiar with the full routine.

He hummed along with that monotonous Elton John tune, lit another cigarette from that splendid case of his and cast a furtive glance at the American woman. She ordered a hamburger and a Coke, then took a map of Stockholm out of her handbag and unfolded it over Henry's coffee cup. He had absolutely nothing against such an encroachment, and he followed with interest as the woman's index finger strolled from Stadshuset across Gustaf Adolf's Square and through the King's Garden to the corner of Hamngatan and Kungsträdgårdsgatan, which was undoubtedly the location of this particular Wimpy.

'Nice promenade!' he ventured, in English

'Uh-huh,' said the American with a smile.

'Are you searching for something in particular?'

'Aren't we *all* searching for something in particular?'

'Very profound,' said Henry *the charmer*. 'Very profound indeed. I am a very simple kind of fellow but I meant a house, an address . . .'

'Well, where do *you* live?' asked the American, her mouth full of hamburger, though that didn't make her look any less chic. She had probably tried that trick before.

'I live here,' said Henry. 'Here on Söder,' he said, putting his stubby index finger in the middle of Hornsgatan. 'Where do you live?'

'In New York,' she said.

'Nice, nice,' said Henry.

427

'No, it's *not* nice in New York. It may be a lot of things, but it sure isn't *nice*.'

'Oh, I see,' said Henry, looking tremendously interested.

'Would you like to show me around the Old Town? I haven't been there yet.'

'Of course, you must see the Old Town. With pleasure,' said Henry. 'You know what?' he went on, turning to me and reverting to Swedish. 'I think I'll go out for a little sightseeing. I'll see you tonight. Or maybe tomorrow morning.'

I couldn't very well object. Instead I wished him luck with all my heart. We parted with a handshake and a wink. Like two English ace pilots on our way to a raid over the German front.

'Cheerio, old chap!'

———————

It started drizzling again. Out on the street Henry Morgan, pianist, boxer and charmer turned up the collar of his coat, put on his cap and helped the American woman over a puddle of water on the pavement, all the while chattering away. It was exactly as it should be. I stayed in Wimpy's for a while, listening to that never-ending song by Elton John, with my eyes fixed on Henry until he disappeared into the King's Garden, gesticulating non-stop. I could only wish that incorrigible gentleman luck with all my heart.

That was the last I would ever see of Henry Morgan.

Now everything started happening very fast. I headed home around dinner-time – after taking a long walk through downtown in the drizzling rain without meeting a soul that I knew – but I wasn't feeling very well. I bought a little food for dinner and had plans to work. It was high time to go for the final sprint on that damn *Red Room* and finish up all my commitments before summer.

When I arrived home around five o'clock, I found Leo sitting at the kitchen table. His upper body was stretched out over the oilcloth on the table, and he was sleeping heavily. He had downed half a bottle of Renat whisky, all in one sitting presumably. I couldn't shake any life into him. I was furious and my eyes filled with tears as I swore my head off. Suddenly all our work was in vain. As soon as we left him without supervision he had to defy us, just like a child.

428

With all the strength of my fury, I grabbed him under the arms and dragged his body into his room. Only then did he come to, muttering, slurring his words, giggling, sulking and thanking me for my help as he told me that he loved me. Then he fell into a deep slumber in his bed.

I threw together a light meal of frozen meatballs and spinach, made a thermos of coffee and withdrew. I locked the door to the library and sat down at the desk to start sorting through all my papers. Soon I was engrossed in *The Red Room*, which looked to be quite nicely arranged, in its new incarnation.

I had no idea that I had seen the Morgan brothers for what is starting to seem more and more like the very last time.

Approximately twenty-four hours later I tried to open my eyes to fix my gaze on something specific so that I could figure out where I was, but without any luck. I couldn't do it. I couldn't keep my eyes open because they hurt so much from the light in the ceiling, which was a glaring and vitriolic fluorescent light. Instead I had to listen to the testimony of my ears, and that was slightly more comfortable. I heard the sound of wooden clogs on a linoleum floor, brisk, officious footsteps going back and forth in the corridors; doors slamming, the clattering of metal instruments on steel trays and voices, both male and female, talking about surname, social security number and other data.

Approximately twenty-four hours later again I awoke in what I assumed was a hospital, the intensive-care ward of a hospital, and I had a hell of a headache. My skull was filled with roaring, exploding, rushing sounds, and I found it was a good idea to keep my eyes closed.

But someone, presumably an assistant nurse on night duty who had been assigned to my delicate case, had at least noticed my diligent efforts and said, 'Hello, Klas. Can you hear me?'

'So I suppose I'm not fucking deaf either,' I said, slurring my words.

'No, you're not dead,' said the nurse quickly.

'I said *deaf*,' I told her, annoyed. 'Would you please hold my hand?' I went on and instantly felt a warm little hand take hold of mine. 'Tell me what happened.'

'I don't know anything,' she said. 'I just got here. The others said that you fell and hit your head hard.'

'*Fell!*' I shouted and tried to sit up, which just prompted more explosions inside my skull. 'Ay-y-y-y!' I shrieked, and sank back against the pillow. 'I'll be damned if I fell!'

It sounded as if the nurse suppressed a laugh.

'That's what your friend said, at any rate.'

'Who? Who was it? What friend?'

'The one you live with.'

'Henry? Henry Morgan?'

'I don't know his name, but he . . .'

' . . . he wears a tie and he lies and talks a mile a minute and his hair is parted on the left and he's clean-shaven, right?'

'Yes, that must be him,' said the nurse. 'He was up here a little while ago with flowers. He left a letter for you. It's right here . . .'

'A letter?!'

That was as far as we got, the nurse and I, because I was suddenly overwhelmed by a strong attack of nausea, making me heave and puke, which she countered very routinely with a kidney-shaped cardboard bowl, which I filled with an embarrassing fluid. Then she wiped the cold sweat from my brow until I once more sank into a deep torpor.

I awoke again from my trance on the following morning. It must have been the morning of 29 April, and the weather actually wasn't half bad because strong sunlight was coming through the blinds of one of the many windows in Söder Hospital. This time I was able to take in the splendour with my own, wide-open eyes. The headache had eased up slightly, and I managed to slide up a bit towards the head of the hospital bed. I even had the presence of mind to start fumbling for the lever to raise and lower one end, but I couldn't find it.

Only then did I notice the cold air whirling around my ears. It felt as if a moderately brisk breeze were blowing through the room, but of course it wasn't. With a shiver, and without actually confirming the matter by touching my head with my hand, I realised that I no longer had any hair – I, Klas Östergren, was suddenly bald, or at the very least my head had been shaved. I went through a terrible internal battle until I could no longer contain myself, and I reached up and discovered that I was right – some nasty bastard had shaved all the hair off my head. My thick, in fact admirably thick, and oh-so-beautiful, naturally flowing hair was gone! Hell, I thought, I've really landed in bad company now. Furthermore, using my hand I discovered that part of my scalp, which had been completely liberated of any hair, was terribly swollen

432

and covered with a compress. It started aching as soon as I even thought about it. That must have been where the impact of the blow landed.

Just as I came to this conclusion, a new assistant nurse came into the room. She was pushing a trolley in front of her with a telephone on it.

'Phone call for Mr Östergren,' she said.

'Great service,' I said and waited to hear if that idiot Henry Morgan would start offering excuses, but he wasn't the one on the phone.

It was my mother, who was both worried and very angry all at the same time. The assistant nurse was laughing, apparently at my humiliating hairstyle, as I made a great effort to use reassuring words to try – in the sacred name of calm – to reconstruct exactly how I had so unfortunately stumbled over the threshold in the doorway and knocked myself unconscious against the fine marble with orthoceratites and other exciting relics from a bygone era. But I didn't get very far. My mother was of course absolutely convinced that her dear son had been on a binge, and there was no one around who could certify that it wasn't true. She could believe whatever she liked. We agreed, at any rate, that I was on the road to recovery, and that large parts of my mind were intact, and then I thanked her for the phone call. I was completely worn out from talking. The last thing my mother managed to say was that I ought to move back home with her for a while, and that was only to be expected. That was also the conclusion that I would have preferred to draw.

Later that day I had the pleasure of meeting the good doctor, who shook my hand and told me that I was suffering from a bad concussion. At first they had posited a hypothetical diagnosis of something called a 'subdural haematoma', which meant bleeding just below the membrane of the brain, something that commonly happens to drunks, and it often requires emergency neurosurgery. That was the reason for the assault on my hair, just in case.

But my hair would soon grow back, and I could thank my lucky stars that my mind was intact. I was getting off with a concussion, which required peace and quiet for at least a couple of weeks, and I was advised to walk up the stairs a bit more carefully in the future.

That last comment was what really annoyed me. I was ready to punch that doctor and any other damn fool who came in the room with insinuations about how fucking easy it was to take a fall these days when I definitely had not taken a fall, damn it to hell!

Over and over again I tried to ring Henry and Leo at home to get some kind of explanation, but no one answered. I rang at least thirty times, and the assistant nurse who had to bring me the phone trolley at last got so cranky about it that she let me know that she had other things to do with her time. After the thirty-first attempt, I gave up. The boys were gone.

This is what must have happened. I came home from Wimpy and found Leo dead drunk, sprawled over the kitchen table. I dragged the wreck into his bedroom, where he, alternately sobbing and pathetically giggling, passed out.

Then I cooked myself a dinner of frozen meatballs and spinach, made a thermos of strong coffee, and locked myself in the library. Suddenly *The Red Room* – after a serious going-over of the material – had started looking really good, and all that was needed was some polishing and a certain modulation of the consummate, final chord of the tragedy. The work was flowing along nicely, and I thought that everything might finally be in place and looking good by daybreak, if only I didn't get carried away. I had to keep a cool head and not rush things, while I smoked fewer cigarettes and drank strong coffee. And I had to be left in peace.

But that was exactly what didn't happen. It must have been around eleven p.m. – I had just taken a break and was listening to the late-night news on the radio – when the doorbell rang. I heard a few muted rings through several closed doors, and I knew that Leo was certainly not going to wake up and go out to the hallway. And Henry was still out with that beautiful American woman who was searching for something, just like all the rest of us.

I switched on the lamp in the hallway and saw through the glass doors the silhouettes of a couple of men out on the landing. Quite unsuspecting, I opened the door.

Approximately twenty-four hours later, with a thundering headache, I tried to open my eyes in the intensive-care ward of Söder Hospital. I tried to remember what I had seen, but I hadn't managed to make out much before everything went totally black and starry. Maybe I did recall a crunching sound and a strange kind of hissing and whining inside my skull. It was like something that I once heard in my childhood when I fell off my first 22-inch bicycle and hit my head on the kerb.

But this time I definitely didn't fall.

I was undoubtedly both very tired and very confused, because my thoughts were not particularly lucid. I kept doing checks on the status of my brain, formulating difficult math problems that I solved faster than ever. I also recited the succession of Swedish kings without stumbling once, not even on some shaggy Viking. It seemed to me that my brain had actually become more agile after being treated so roughly. Now, long afterwards, I realise that I still wasn't quite right in the head, because the letter that Henry had brought remained unopened for several days before I finally decided to read it.

Henry's letter was delivered on the day after the bang on my head occurred. He had come home after having 'partaken of a fortifying aphrodisiac in a bar', and later that beautiful American woman had administered her cure in her suite at the Sheraton Hotel. Henry learned that Greger, of all people, had found me lying unconscious on the landing, and he had then taken me to the emergency room of Söder Hospital. Greger, being the naïve and trusting individual that he was, had assumed that I had fallen in the stairwell and hit my head.

But Henry was smart enough to see that there might be a connection between my deplorable condition and Leo's conspicuous absence. To top it off, Wolf-Larsson, during his usual nightly rounds, had seen two dapper gentlemen dragging a woozy Leo between them out to a waiting car. They had driven off, quite cool and calm, as if it were a matter of a completely legal and welcome transport back to the protective paradise of a locked ward.

That was the official version, at any rate. Citizen Östergren had for some reason fallen flat on his face out on the landing, and citizen Leo Morgan could no longer be allowed to go free because he was a danger both to himself and the rest of the world.

But Henry's letter confirmed my suspicions. He said quite firmly that '*they*' had come to get Leo, and that I had not taken a fall of my own volition. '*They*' had made a thorough job of it, probably using a sap – a little leather bag filled with buckshot that would not leave any deep cuts and would make the attack look like a perfectly normal clumsy tumble.

He also wrote that he had a very clear and definite idea about where '*they*' had taken Leo, and that this time he wasn't planning to wait or give in. He was tired of the whole thing and was going to settle it, once and for all. Who '*they*' were, he didn't say, nor did he mention what it was he was going to settle, or where.

In general, that letter was really quite peculiar. Henry was unquestionably good at talking – he could talk his way into anything if he felt like it – but he was incapable of using pen and paper. He was dyslexic, just like the king, as he always hastened to recall.

But as soon as he took pen in hand, the knowledge that he was dyslexic meant that he would take extra pains to make everything sound as elegant as possible. He would use scores of old-fashioned, formal, anachronistic expressions, as if he were addressing His Royal Highness or a judge or some other authority who was a strict adherent of convention.

This striving for a formal linguistic cogency and his efforts to write with an elegant script caused him to seek out words whose meaning he definitely did not understand. He had evidently just heard them somewhere and was much too lazy to find out what they really meant.

And so he ended his peculiar letter to his battered friend with these not entirely unambiguous lines: 'I ask you voluntarily, so that the police might not have access to this information, to burn this letter and allow said letter to remain between us until such time as further information appears, or until such time as death should part us. In all kindness, I weep and wish you success, Yours, Henry Morgan.'

For a while everything came to a standstill. After I had spent a couple of days under observation, I was discharged from the hospital with certain restrictions: no partying, no straining and I was supposed to keep laughter to an absolute minimum. Otherwise I was free to do as I pleased. I took a cab home and managed to get through the front door of the building without being seen; my shaved and bandaged head had given me a slight aversion to light.

Things were exactly the same as usual in the flat on Hornsgatan, even though everything we had tried to build up had been lost. I walked through the enormous flat without finding any signs of life from the Morgan brothers. I planned to wait for their return, a return which, it turned out, was never going to happen.

For a while everything came to a standstill. For the first day I was on tenterhooks, expecting at any moment to hear the redemptive sound of the phone ringing or the liberating slamming of doors. Or to encounter Henry, who would tell me that the matter had been cleared up and we could now put the whole thing behind us. But nothing happened. Everything was nice and quiet, and I started getting a little restless.

My life had begun to revolve around one very sad point – the big mirror in the hallway. Approximately once every half hour I would go out there, switch on the light and stare at my shorn image in the mirror, examining the stitches under the compress and trying on various caps that might hide my embarrassing state. I decided on an English tweed number.

I was standing in front of that mirror – it was a magnificent, full-length affair with a gilded frame and cherubs at the top – when I heard a small military band booming down on the street. I was curious, so I went into the sitting room, pushed the curtains aside, and caught sight of a big demonstration moving past down on Hornsgatan. It was probably some minor political party, some less successful group that was in charge of organising the march, because the participants couldn't have numbered more than two or three thousand.

It was May Day. I couldn't for the life of me understand how I had totally managed to forget the date. The huge flat was plunged into darkness – I shied away from the light because it hurt my eyes and gave me a headache – behind the big, heavy curtains, and the depressing chiaroscuro seemed more vexing than ever. But now, at least, I saw that it was May Day, even though spring still hadn't really made its appearance yet. It looked rather cold and windy down on the street. I opened the window slightly but felt no desire to go out. I wondered for a moment what place I would have taken this year, which procession I would have chosen *if* I were in any position to choose, but I wasn't. I no longer had a choice, or so I imagined.

So I watched the demonstration until the brass section and the drums of the military band had faded into eternity. The last I saw was a big banner with a number of heads – one yellow, one black, one white and one red – that were supposed to portray oppressed peoples. The heads sat on shoulders, the shoulders held up arms with hands and the hands held guns that they would use against their oppressors.

All of a sudden a thought occurred to me. I went out to the kitchen, found the old key ring with all the mysterious keys, and then went to the wardrobe in the service corridor. At the very bottom of a sideboard, one of the drawers was locked. I unlocked the drawer and pulled it out. But of course the drawer was empty. The gun was gone.

All that was left of the submachine-gun was the rough, greasy jute cloth. The magazine and ammunition were also gone. If the drawer hadn't smelled of gun oil, I could easily have denied ever having seen that gun. But the smell was unmistakable. The gun that had lain in that drawer like a cold, gleaming reptile had finally gone away.

Whatever accounts Henry was planning to settle, he was most likely going to make a thorough job of it. There was no longer any doubt about the matter – this was extremely serious.

After a week of complete rest, I was feeling quite fidgety. Under cover of darkness and wearing a fisherman's knit cap, I had slipped out to buy supplies at grocery shops that were open late. That was all I had seen of the world in the immediate vicinity. I had carefully read every newspaper backwards and forwards, hoping I might find something that would cast some light on all the mysteries, but there was nothing. I had studied every classified ad in the 'Personals' column and tried to decipher cryptic codes such as: '79.04.28. Wait as usual, dock-berth 12'. But I decided it was unlikely that it had anything to do with me. I had also watched every single newscast on TV, but the reports dealt only with revolutions on continents entirely different from my own. There was nothing about prospective ministers of industry or their spring-cleaning. I was in the midst of a nightmare, a hallucination. I pinched myself, took deep breaths, jogged and sparred through the service corridors and tried all the classic methods to confirm that I was wide awake, although restless.

After a week of asceticism, I'd had enough. I put on my fisherman's knit cap and went down to the Furniture Man to have a chat with Greger and Birger. They had been working down in Greger's Grotto, the Shelter, and were wondering what had become of us upstairs.

'I want to thank you for your help, Greger,' I said. 'If you hadn't taken care of me, I probably would have died. At least that's what the doctor said.'

'Hey, it was nothing,' said Greger proudly. 'I just happened to find you up there in the doorway. Don't mention it.'

'I assume I was completely out of it.'

'You certainly were out of it, my boy. A hell of an unlucky fall.'

'I don't remember a thing.'

I shook hands with Greger and made him feel like he was a real life-saver. He practically had tears in his eyes.

'So when is Henry coming back?' he asked. 'He didn't say how long he'd be gone. We're starting to get a little worried about the football pool.'

'I don't know,' I said. 'But you don't have to worry about the football pool. He promised to take care of all the usual things.'

'We're used to him being gone now and then,' said Birger, winking. 'He's got that bird that he likes to see.'

'Of course,' I said, going along with him. 'He's only human, after all.'

'That's what I've always said,' replied Greger. 'He's an artist, that Henry. And an artist needs the support of a woman. He's probably got cold feet about the concert, so he needs a little comforting from a woman.'

'Of course,' I said. 'Who wouldn't?'

I couldn't stand it anymore. I could feel the sweat trickling down my forehead under the prickly knit cap, and I felt as if I might faint at any moment. I left Greger and Birger to their delusions. I discovered that I had started to lie, bluster and spout falsehoods quite deliberately, just like Henry Morgan. I was incapable of telling the truth.

I had been forced to become a fraud.

A letter arrived from chief accountant Lennart Hagberg in Borås, addressed to Leo Morgan. The accountant had made his chess move, and I was going to have to reply. Even up to the last minute Leo had kept his head and taken piece after piece away from his white opponent. Hagberg in Borås had only four pawns, a rook and a knight left, in addition to his king and queen. Leo had lost only three pawns and a knight. There was a total of twenty chess pieces left on the board, and if I didn't make a big blunder, I could probably keep playing the game a good bit into the summer. Hagberg had moved his knight to safety because it was being threatened by a black pawn – a defensive move. Since I had never been a very good chess player, it took some time to come up with something. Finally – after smoking several cigarettes and pacing restlessly, deep in thought, between the chess table and the armchairs in front of the fireplace – I consulted several old chess books from the section on games and gambling in the library. I immersed myself in some classic games that lacked any similarity to my own, and several hours later I typed up an offensive diagonal with a bishop that once again threatened Hagberg's knight. Then I sealed the envelope and put in on the shelf for ready for posting.

The daily papers kept pouring in through the letterbox, and as soon as I heard it bang shut – sleep came to me only in brief intervals – I would climb out of Göring's old bed to get the newspapers and subject them to a thorough scrutiny. Manic fortune hunters and sleazebags generally published their codes under the 'Personals' heading, but I found nothing of interest.

Not a news item, not an ad, not a marital engagement, not an obituary escaped my critical examination. Soon I had memorised even the entertainment ads. And it was then, in the first week of May, that I happened to think of the Södra Theatre. Henry was supposed to give his concert there in the middle of May, but the performance undoubtedly had to be considered in jeopardy due to unforeseen events.

At dawn I lay awake, brooding and anguished. I didn't know whether it would be a service or a disservice if I rang the theatre to cancel. The magic date was relentlessly approaching, just as unpleasant days always do, and the odds of the performance actually taking place were dismal, to say the least.

After making an attempt to think things through logically by listing all the risk factors, I concluded that it would be best to ring the theatre and cancel the whole thing. *If* Henry came back, he would most likely be in no condition to be dragged up on stage to make his debut as a composer and solo pianist before the elite of the Swedish music world. The invitations and programmes with my lyrical introduction hadn't yet been written, much less printed.

I thought it best to ring the theatre. I stated the purpose of my call to the switchboard operator, who connected me to the director. I introduced myself very politely as a personal friend of the pianist Henry Morgan, and using rather elegant phrases, I got around to the point that he would be unable to give a performance in mid-May, as planned.

'Henry Morgan?' said the programme director. 'Henry Morgan? In mid-May, you say?' he went on, apparently starting to leaf through some form of booking schedule.

'Unfortunately, I don't remember the exact date,' I said. 'But he booked it a long time ago.'

'Henry Morgan?' the programme director repeated. 'I've never heard of any *Henry Morgan*. Let's see now . . . mid-May. Guest appearance of the Russian ballet . . . the twelfth and thirteenth . . . Pupils from the Swedish Drama School . . . the fifteenth . . . Comic opera . . . the eighteenth . . . He's not part of the comic opera, is he?'

'Comic opera?' I said. 'Not as far as I know . . .'

'Hmm . . . well, let's see. The nineteenth . . . twentieth . . . twenty-first . . . Anniversary performance as a benefit for Höstsol . . . The twenty-fifth . . .' the programme director continued energetically, rattling off the PR hype for one event after another without finding any Henry Morgan.

441

'I think it was supposed to be on a Wednesday,' I said, feeling confused.

'A Wednesday, you say . . . No, I can't find anything about a Henry Morgan, and if he *had* actually booked a date, I would have noticed it before. Are you *sure* that it was at the Södra Theatre? There are so many theatres in town,' he went on as if I were an idiot.

I put down the phone without saying goodbye, without even thanking him for his help. I've felt tricked and duped many times in my life, but this was the worst.

The fire in the woodstove cast its flickering light over the darkened bedroom with Göring's old bed, the copperplate engravings of various themes from Shakespeare's plays, the photographs of my relatives, the picture of Henry, Leo and myself standing on the street which now seemed unbelievably old, and other objects that suddenly seemed terribly foreign, as if I had just picked them up at random somewhere.

I stuffed page after page, sheet after sheet into the stove, and it ignited nicely. *The Red Room* was burning brightly. I burned everything, a whole winter's toil and hard work, as if in a trance or some sort of stupor, fully aware of what I was really doing and yet completely out of it.

The Red Room was burning brightly, and I would interrupt my pyromaniac activity now and then to go out to the hallway to look at myself in the mirror. I wanted to be *seen* by someone, it didn't matter who, myself or someone else, it made no difference. Then I went back and continued to place in the stove page after page, sheet after sheet, in perfect numerical order. It no longer meant a thing to me.

Franzén the publisher didn't even sound surprised when I rang to tell him that nothing was going to come of the book. *The Red Room* had burned up and turned to ashes. He could have a sack of ashes if he liked. But he declined. He told me that he was going to spread a rumour that I had gone insane, and I told him to go right ahead. He said he would send over a contract to cancel the project and he never wanted to see me again. Then he told me, quite rightly, to go to hell.

The idea had been germinating in the back of my battered head for a long time, and now it was going to be realised. I would erect a monument to the Morgan brothers.

A warm and sultry wind was blowing. Spring had finally taken hold on the other side of the thick curtains that covered every little aperture in the flat. Over the course of a single day I proved to be extremely efficient in planning my feat with ice-cold shrewdness.

I went down to Söder Hospital to have the two stitches removed from the crown of my head and tried to act like a completely normal convalescent. Then I collected a good thousand kronor in National Health Insurance money and went to the nearest grocery shop to buy enough tins of food for a minor war – ravioli, meatballs, Bullen's Lager sausages, stuffed cabbage rolls, split-pea soup, vegetables, potatoes and other packaged provisions. I lugged everything up to the flat, stored it all in the appropriate places, and then dashed down to the Furniture Man and lied my head off to Greger and Birger. I told them that I'd heard from Henry. He was going to be gone all summer, but then he'd be home and everything would go back to normal. We were just supposed to keep digging down there in Greger's Grotto, taking the route that we'd mapped out. We had his blessing. Greger, the Flask, Wolf-Larsson and the Philatelist seemed very pleased with the news, and I got out of there with my honour intact, as planned.

Next I went over to see the Cigar Seller. He was the most difficult of the lot, that fox.

'Cute cap you've got there,' he said at once, and the pin-up dame behind the counter smiled her most seductive smile. 'They're so fashionable right now, those caps. Cuckoo's nests, isn't that what they're called? But it's a bit hot for them at the moment, isn't it? Hee, hee.'

'Not at all,' I said. 'Not at all.'

'Hmm, I see. So where's that Morgan been keeping himself? We haven't seen him in a long time.'

'Out travelling,' I said. 'Henry has gone out travelling again.'

'You don't say. And where's he off to this time?'

'Back to Paris. Paris and London,' I said.

'Ah . . . well, he's like a fish in water over there,' said the Cigar Seller, giving me that disgusting, insinuating smile of his. 'It's a sad thing about Leo.'

'What do you mean?'

'That he had to go back *in*,' said the Cigar Seller as he circled his index finger at his temple. 'That he couldn't take care of himself . . .'

'I suppose so,' I said curtly. 'In any case, I'd like five cartons of straight Camels, no filter.'

'Five cartons of straight Camels,' repeated the Cigar Seller as if it were an everyday occurrence. Then, '*Five cartons?!*'

'That's right. Five cartons,' I told him again.

The Cigar Seller winked at the pin-up dame, who rummaged around in the stock room, attired in her long, low-cut dress. She was back at once with five cartons, and the Cigar Seller gave me an incredulous look.

I didn't offer any further comment, just paid for my five cartons, no filter, thanked him and left. The Cigar Seller was shaking his head, and I'm sure that he would once again be making a circle with his index finger at his temple and then start spreading a rumour that I had gone insane and was planning to smoke myself to death.

Time passed, one day flowed into another, losing its contours; dirty dishes and rubbish had collected in squalid, mouldy, stinking piles in the kitchen; the hallway was awash with heaps of unread and untouched morning newspapers; and beneath the English cap, my hair had finally grown out to a relatively decent length.

I had set to work with the frenzy and accuracy that only a monomaniac who had first been betrayed, then manhandled and finally shorn, could possess. I had locked and barricaded the front door, drawn all the curtains in the already dimly lit flat, disconnected the telephone and isolated myself in the library on Hornsgatan in the middle of Stockholm, in the middle of May, during the election year and Year of the Child, 1979.

The desk was easily cleared. Everything having to do with my naïve and modern pastiche of *The Red Room* had gone into the fire, consumed by the flames. I piled up books and other scribblings on the floor, keeping only my own talismans, such as a fox skull that I once found in the woods, a crab shell that I'd been given by a couple of fishermen on the Lofoten Islands, a few large pebbles and an ashtray in the shape of a satyr into whose gaping mouth you flicked the ashes. I needed these talismans so as not to lose sight of myself.

Then I went to work, toiling away like someone possessed, working at least twenty hours a day with only occasional breaks for food and rest. I had smoked nearly all of my five cartons of unfiltered Camels and felt none the worse for it.

I recounted everything I knew and was able to find out about the brothers Henry and Leo Morgan, because I felt it was my duty to do so. I can be said to belong to a generation that suffers from an inadequate sense of duty – duty is such a horribly abstract concept that it must be constantly applied to the indi-

445

vidual and personal realm in order to become in any way tangible. At the very least, a person has to fulfil his duty to himself. But in this case, I felt it was my absolute duty to tell the truth about Henry and Leo Morgan. Perhaps it was also a form of therapy in order to keep going, the only means I had to endure all the waiting and anxiety, which are the unmistakable trademarks of our era.

I now knew no more than what I have already recounted, and perhaps even a bit less since occasionally I was forced to extrapolate and embellish, filling in the big gaps. The result of my efforts was that well over six hundred pages lay on the desk in the library. No one had disturbed me, the rest of the world had vanished, the words had simply poured out, and the brothers had been given the monument that they deserved. Now it didn't matter what happened; they were inviolable.

I was totally prepared, any day now, to read about Henry and Leo Morgan in the newspaper. It might be something along the lines of: the bodies of two men, aged thirty-five and thirty respectively, were found in a ditch somewhere inland; or that the disfigured corpses of two male individuals, impossible to identify, had emerged from under the ice in some damned river somewhere in Sweden. Or maybe the Cigar Seller – who read every single weekly magazine backwards and forwards – would come storming up with a big feature article in which Henry *the idiot* candidly discussed his numerous adventures in the underworld now that he was a safe distance away, from an island in the Caribbean. That was where he had always longed to go, and he had apparently managed it because of the enormous sums of money that he had come across on various byways.

But maybe I had also written all of this down because of another possibility – maybe they really were in trouble and Henry had been forced to use that old submachine-gun. Maybe he had done what he'd always wanted to do to the boundless Evil that held Leo in its grip. Maybe all of this was in defence of a crime that had already been committed, was going to be committed, or simply should have been committed. I wasn't quite sure, but the possibility existed that in court I would have to present my six hundred pages as a *plaidoyer d'un fou et son frère*, a defence for the brothers Henry and Leo Morgan, because it was highly likely that they would judged by some sort of jury.

At any rate, that was the situation on that day when I could no longer tell the days apart except by first sorting through the piles of newspapers to find the latest issue. It told me that it would soon be Midsummer and that Sweden was experiencing a heatwave. But I didn't give a damn about that.

Suddenly the doorbell rang. That damned bell broke through an intense silence that had lasted more than a month. Cold shivers immediately ran down my back.

The front door was barricaded with a heavy mahogany cabinet, and I no longer had any idea how I'd managed to move it there under my own steam. I shouted through the barricade and the closed doors, asking who it was. My voice creaked and wheezed because I hadn't used it in a very long time.

'Laundry, Egon's Laundry,' I heard from the landing.

By mustering all my strength and then some, I managed to make a crack between the mahogany cabinet and the front doors so that I could open them for the laundry delivery boy. He gave a start when he saw my capped head appear, and he gave me a very suspicious, scrutinising look, as if we'd never seen each other before. Nor did we exchange many words. I carried the box into the hallway, found some money, and paid him. I hesitantly accepted his fountain pen to sign the laundry receipt, holding it up against the door. All of a sudden I was uncertain what name to write. Finally my own name came back to me; I scribbled it down and then said goodbye to the delivery boy.

As soon as I closed the door, I went over to the big, gilded, full-length mirror in the hallway to examine my appearance. I hadn't shaved in ages, and I'd never in my life had such a thick beard. Maybe the blow to my head had upset my hormonal balance; maybe I was finally on my way to becoming more masculine, more grown-up.

By this time my hair had grown out, at least, and I could get rid of the cap, tossing it up onto the hat shelf. My face looked extremely thin under the beard, and I had acquired some ridiculous spasms, some sort of tics, under my eyes. The twitching went on incessantly but was extremely subtle. Even so, the tics seemed to disfigure my whole face, and that annoyed me. But that was presumably the price this whole business had cost me, damage that I would have to learn to tolerate. Perhaps the tics were just vexing enough that they would make my face more interesting, make me look mature and experienced. That's the sort of thing that women always appreciate.

After a general inspection of my physical state in the mirror out in the hallway, I went into the bathroom and took off my stinking blue overalls and climbed into the shower. Then I shaved with great devotion and felt myself liberated, illuminated and baptised.

Next I headed for the wardrobe, where I put on nice clean clothes. I found a shirt in the laundry box. It was a blue-and-white checked shirt with the initials 'W.S.' embroidered under the manufacturer's label inside the collar. It fit me perfectly. Strangely enough, my neck seemed to have grown bigger into the bargain. My collar size had never been this big. I didn't have a tie that matched the shirt, so I went into Henry's room and opened his wardrobe. I found a thin burgundy number that looked good against the shirtfront, under which my heart was fighting a battle that was a bit more fierce than usual.

For me nothing more remained but deep silence and a long period of waiting, or so I thought. My main interest was once again transferred to that gilded mirror with the cherubs in the hallway. I could spend hours studying my own image, trying to figure out what had happened. My hair had regained its previous appearance, my cheeks looked hollow, but no more than was tolerable, my complexion was pale and sallow, and under my eyes I had those tics.

I would soon be twenty-five years old, I had spent a quarter of a century on this earth, and perhaps I would still be here another quarter of a century later. It sounded like a very long time, but it didn't particularly feel that way. It felt as if I hadn't learned a thing, nothing at all during those twenty-five dramatic years between the Cold War of the fifties and the Iranian revolution of the seventies. I still felt ignorant and inexperienced, and it didn't matter that the image in the mirror said something completely different. It showed a lean, squinty-eyed young man who looked as if he'd been through fire, though without going up in flames.

I knotted my tie over and over again, trying to teach myself how to make that perfect Windsor knot the way Henry Morgan always did. I thought I was making progress and looked quite respectable. It felt luxurious to walk around wearing a suit and tie all day long without accomplishing a thing. I pretended not to notice that I was on my way to falling apart, that I was on my way to becoming seriously ill. If I fell apart, I was going to do it with dignity; Henry Morgan would have approved.

Not even a whole year had passed since I'd first met him, and I'd known Leo for barely six months. Everything had happened so fast that it felt as if we'd been brothers all our lives. One measly little year, I thought. Exactly one year earlier I was a whole different person, so much younger, so much more naïve and considerably more gullible. I had jumped at the chance to take the job at the golf course that my friend Errol Hansen from the Danish embassy had arranged for me. I had spent a whole summer sitting on various lawnmowers and tractors, and in the evenings I had hung out with Rocks at the bar. I had tackled huge projects that were equally noble and grandiose, just like every other angry young literary firebrand. I was bitterly forced to admit that art and history would get along fine without me.

When I later met Franzén the publisher, he managed to convince me otherwise. He assured me of my great talents as a satirist, and he got me to write an entire pastiche of Strindberg's novel *The Red Room*, in honour of the hundredth anniversary of its publication. That too had gone through the fire, but unlike myself it had burned up and turned to ashes. It felt like only yesterday, that late summer evening by the pool at the golf course country club when Franzén and I came to an agreement over drinks. We stood there spouting off about grand plans for the future as we stared at Wilhelm Sterner, the secret benefactor of the club – *non videre sed esse* – who came sailing into the cocktail party wearing his impeccable light summer jacket, like some sort of unreal zeppelin that was not in touch with the ground. Maud *the courtesan* had stood in his shadow, looking supremely indifferent. I'd never had a chance to study her at closer quarters.

And then the Trouble started. I was the victim of a burglary at my flat. During the festival with Bob Dylan in Göteborg, the thieves managed to make off with practically everything I owned, except for my two typewriters and a few odds-and-ends of little value. And then everything else happened. I hung out at the Europa Athletic Club trying to box my way out of my depression, met the whiz-kid Henry Morgan, and moved into this flat on Hornsgatan. Hardly a year later I found myself mixed up in a tragedy, a scandalous story of the highest order. I had paid a high price. The result was strange obsessions and tics under my eyes, as well as a sort of testament that was more than six-hundred typed pages in which I attempted to redress the wrongs of the Morgan brothers and create a monument to the Truth. It had turned into a bombshell, and to allow it to be published would presumably be equal to committing public suicide.

The secret would no doubt remain within the gloomy walls of this enormous flat, at least for the time being. For my part, all that was left was deep silence and a long period of waiting, or so I imagined.

The waiting turned out not to be very long at all, whatever it was that I was waiting for. I was standing in front of the mirror with the cherubs, looking at the tics under my eyes, when the doorbell rang. The sound made me shiver. I shouted through the barricade and the closed doors to ask who it was. There was no answer, so I shoved the huge mahogany cabinet aside a bit so that it was possible to peer through the glass doors at the landing. It appeared to be a woman standing there, so I dared open up unarmed. What then ensued was one of those moments of long-lasting silence when you manage to think about a lot of things – you manage to formulate your last wishes in verse, count to ten thousand, or bite all your fingernails, if that's what you want to do. I stood in the doorway, clinging to the door handle. She stood motionless on the landing and didn't say a word.

I knew immediately who she was, and she knew immediately who I was. I hated her and it occurred to me that I ought to kill her. That would be the only acceptable revenge. But death was impossible. It took only a cursory, passing glance to realise that this woman was absolutely inviolable. No matter how much you might hate her, you had to be prepared to forgive her and never harm so much as a hair on her radiant head.

She looked exactly the way I remembered her, a former *real hot number* that I had seen from a distance at the country club and in a couple of faded photos that Henry had always carried in his wallet. There really was something particularly Asian about her appearance. She might have been the most beautiful woman I had ever seen. She carried her forty years with all the mature elegance that could make a king give up his kingdom. Her long, chestnut-brown hair had a few light streaks in it, the arc of her eyebrows, her nose, mouth, chin – all her features had been sketched by an inspired God and Creator at His very best. Here stood His homage to humanity. The black dress with its two red cherries set off her deep tan, so unusual for the time of year, without making her seem overly robust in any vulgar or exaggerated way. There was a glint of restlessness in her eyes, of restrained ardour and passion, which gave her perfection a very delicate, appealing, human cast. She smelled of patchouli oil, and her appearance was as precisely balanced and chic as the role demanded. Her shoes and handbag bore the monogram of a world-famous designer, and presumably this *citoyenne du monde* had purchased her entire wardrobe from original designs, and at all the proper places. She was intimately familiar with the great cities of the world, she had practically grown up in embassies in New York, London, Paris, Vienna, Munich, Tokyo, Jakarta and so on.

It may have been several minutes that we stood there studying each other in deep silence, like two heavyweights at the weighing-in before a match, appraising the slightest move of the opponent. But there would never be any match, not between the two of us. No one would dare harm a hair on her head. I myself was already lost, punch-drunk.

She was the first one to speak, breaking the intense silence in the doorway.

'I take it that you're Klas,' she said in a deep voice, an alto.

'Um-hm,' I said. 'And you must be Maud.'

I stuck out my hand, and hers was very soft and slightly damp. She was clearly not lacking in nerve.

'We can't stand here all day,' I said. 'Would you like to come in?'

'If I'm not disturbing . . .' she said.

'How could you be disturbing me?'

'I just thought, if you were working, since you're a writer.'

'Not at the moment. Right now I'm unemployed.'

'You look as if you were going to celebrate something special, dressed in that suit. Oh, is *this* what the place looks like!'

'Haven't you ever been here before?'

'Never,' said Maud. 'Henry wanted to keep it all to himself.'

Maud's perfume spread its scent over the hallway, which was otherwise filled with rubbish and smelled terrible.

'Were you scared?' asked Maud, nodding at the imposing mahogany cabinet that barricaded the doors to the flat.

'Scared?' I said. 'Oh, I was just going to do some cleaning, as you can see.'

'Would you be willing to show me around?' she asked. 'I've always wondered what it looked like in here.'

I led the way into the dark sitting room and suddenly started chattering as if possessed, like some kind of maniac or museum guard on drugs, without thinking about what I was actually saying. I hadn't talked to anyone in more than a month, and Maud listened politely. We walked through the sitting room with the armchairs, the Chippendale furniture that old Morgonstjärna had won in a poker game from Ernst Rolf back in the thirties, the fireplace with the two statues of Truth and Falsehood, the Persian rugs, the cracked lampshades with the long dangling fringe, Leo's chess table, the ashtray on

452

a stand, the table with the top made from yellowish African *giallo antico* marble, the palms on their pedestals and everything else that filled up the room, giving it a certain museum-like quality.

Then we strolled through the dark and gloomy service corridors to the piano room with the sofa with the black tassels. There we could study Henry Morgan's composition on the sheets of music that he had strewn all over the floor, leaving them there as if for only a brief moment. Maud wanted to see his bedroom, and I showed her everything she asked to see, even Leo's two rooms, which still reeked of incense. They too had been abandoned in the greatest haste, as if at an air-raid warning or an earthquake.

I talked myself hoarse, going on non-stop about the weather, about the flat, about various details, about Henry and Leo Morgan, as well as a good deal about myself.

'The whole place is so dark and gloomy,' said Maud. 'Why do you have all the curtains drawn? Do you think there's a war going on?'

'It's just supposed to be like this,' I said curtly. 'Night exists in this flat as a perpetual possibility.'

'But it's the height of summer outside!' said Maud. 'As pale as you are, it would do you good to get a little sun.'

Without considering my view of the matter, she went over to the windows in the sitting room and opened the curtains. Light came pouring in, and I was instantly blinded and had to squint. Suddenly the flat was exposed in all its decrepitude. It had become unbelievably cluttered and filthy. The flat was in a state of decay, and of the very worst kind. Henry would have exploded with fury if he had come home, and presumably he would have thrown me out on the street. There was even an old decorated branch, withered and dried-up, left over from Lent, lying in the corner.

'Now it's starting to look like something,' said Maud. 'Although it's not at all the way Henry described it.'

'What did he say it was like?'

'Threadbare,' said Maud. 'Exceedingly threadbare . . .'

The sitting room suddenly looked quite different, in the new light. I caught sight of things and objects that I had never noticed before, possibly because it had always been so dark. Maud walked around looking at the art. She seemed to be making discoveries, finding a Lundquist here and a Nordström there. I followed her, listening to her very knowledgeable comments, as if she had taken that pleasant curving walk a thousand and one times between Bukowski's Gallery on Arsenalsgatan and Svenskt Tenn on Strandvägen – and I suppose that she probably had.

'Bric-à-brac,' she said time after time, nodding knowingly at a clock here or an Art Nouveau vase there. 'Bric-à-brac.'

She was undeniably familiar with the art field, and she found something strange behind a door that had never been displayed. It was an extremely old wooden cane with a chain attached, and on the end of the chain was a sphere with sharp spikes. It was actually the family namesake, a morning star, a type of chivalric mace. I couldn't understand how Henry had been able to resist bragging about the point.

Maud now went from room to room, opening the drapes and curtains and letting the sunlight come in through the windows. The light glittered in the glass display case containing East Indian porcelain; the light made the dark wood of the furniture gleam; the light shimmered over the polished parquet floors. And reluctantly I had to admit that this was better. The flat was more beautiful in the light.

We ended up in the library, which stank terribly of sweat, tobacco and coffee. Maud walked past the desk, which was weighed down by the burden of my magnum opus, and she pulled aside the heavy, smoke-permeated burgundy velvet curtains. Light sliced through the room and ricocheted off the many thousands of valuable volumes. And Maud opened a window to air out the stale smell. A light summer breeze drifted through the room, a gust of wind swept over the desk, catching at the well over six hundred pages and riffling through them.

'Is that a new book?' asked Maud, glancing at the stack of papers.

'I don't know what it is,' I said. 'Maybe you could call it a work in progress.'

'I've actually read all your books,' said Maud.

'You're kidding!'

'Henry talked so much about you, so of course I was curious. I liked them, all of them. But the last one was the best. It seemed more fully developed . . . And this one . . . What's it about?'

'I can't tell you,' I said. 'Not yet.'

Maud looked down at the stack of pages and boldly started leafing through them, without asking for permission. I let her have her way; she would find out for herself what it was about. She only needed to glance at a few lines here and there to realise what I had written.

'You're actually in it too,' I said. 'Here and there.'

Maud smiled, and I don't know whether it was out of some sort of conceited pride at becoming a literary heroine or whether it was from a feeling of uncertainty or fear. She asked me for a cigarette, and I handed her my last pack of unfiltered Camels.

'Would you like something to drink?' I asked. 'A gimlet, perhaps? Yesterday I found a bottle of Gilbey's under the billiard table.'

'Nothing for me, thanks,' she said. Philip Marlowe was not her type. 'There's so much that you couldn't possibly know about,' she went on. 'There's so much that you'll never be able to find out.'

'There's so much that I don't *want* to find out.' I said.

She was standing with her back to me – she had left the stack of papers on the desk – and she was looking out of the window. She was smoking quickly and efficiently, and only when she stubbed out half the cigarette did I hear that she was crying. She stubbed out the cigarette in the gaping satyr's overflowing mouth, took a handkerchief out of her handbag and blew her nose. Then she took out a little mirror and touched up her eye make-up. I didn't know what to do. I hated her, and it's hard to comfort someone you hate. I suppose there wasn't any consolation I could offer her anyway.

'I think I'll have a drink, at any rate,' I said and went out to the billiard room to get that carelessly hidden bottle of gin. I continued on to the kitchen, got out a glass, Rose's Lime Juice and a couple of ice cubes. It was supposed to be fifty-fifty. I noticed that my hand was shaking as I poured. It turned out more like sixty-forty, in Gilbey's favour.

Maud had followed me and now stood leaning against the door jamb, biting her lip.

'I . . . don't even have . . . a photo, any kind of picture to remind me of . . . Henry,' she managed to sob.

'I'll give you one,' I said, taking a gulp of my gimlet. It was excellent. 'I have one on the wall in my room.'

Maud stared at me with her tear-filled eyes, and I understood damn well why Henry Morgan and Wilhelm Sterner would do anything for her. She was so appallingly beautiful that it hurt inside me just to look at her. I felt scared and shaky.

I started walking down the corridor towards my room. Maud followed, like a child in need of company. She smelled of patchouli oil, and I was weak in the knees. Half of my gimlet splashed out onto the walls.

On the wall of my room, between the copperplate engravings with themes from Shakespearean tragedies, I had pinned up a number of personal photos of family members and various friends. There was also that picture of Henry, Leo and myself, taken down on Hornsgatan one evening a few months earlier. We were hanging onto each other like the Three Musketeers up to new tricks – three gentlemen, brimming with an appetite for life. It must have been a good day, an exceptional day.

I took down the photo, dropping all the pins on the floor, and handed it to Maud.

'Here you are,' I said. 'Keep it as a souvenir.'

Maud sat down on Göring's old bed to study the picture. She seemed pleased, or at least something that closely resembled a smile brightened her face, and I thanked God I wasn't a painter. If I were, I would presumably have devoted the rest of my life to capturing that face.

'He'll be in the cinema soon, by the way,' I said. 'He was in a film, you know.'

'Yes, so he was,' said Maud, and she smiled again. 'In a film.' She didn't sound the least bit ironic. Nor was this the proper time for irony or sarcasm.

Feeling confused, I happened to think of the fact that I still hadn't found out why this bed with the walnut knobs was called Göring's old bed. That was one story that Henry had neglected to tell me.

'It's strange,' I said, 'but that bed you're sitting on is called Göring's old bed, and I still don't know why.'

Maud lifted her eyes from the photo of the Three Musketeers and gave me an uncomprehending look.

'Göring was a Nazi and an idiot, and he was committed to Långbro Hospital, just like Leo,' I said, taking a sip of my drink. 'The world is a very strange place.'

'The day is ours, the bloody dog is dead', it said on one of the copperplate engravings from *Richard III*. It sounded beautiful but naïve. Evil always outlived its own tyrants.

'I have no idea why this bed is called Göring's old bed, nor do I have any idea what your last name is,' I said. '*Nomen nescio . . .*'

'*Nomina sunt odiosa,*' said Maud.

'How learned we can be,' I said, and laughed. I could hear that I sounded crazy. As I mentioned, this was no time for irony.

Suddenly Maud stretched out on the bed and straightened her dress. I was very surprised, sat down in the bay window and lit my very last unfiltered

Camel, crumpling up the crackling pack and tossing it into the wastepaper basket with the British hunting motif.

'It'll soon be Midsummer . . .' said Maud, apropos of nothing. 'Could I stay here a while?'

I almost fell out of the bay window, and desperately held on tight.

'If you want to,' I said. 'Although this probably isn't a very good hiding place.'

'That doesn't matter,' said Maud. 'I'll tell you everything I know, even if it means death.'

'Is that man prepared to do anything at all just in order to become a minister in some corrupt government?'

Maud nodded.

'It's more than just that,' she said. 'I've started to hate him . . . He has taken my whole life.'

I didn't say a word as I smoked my cigarette and slid away from the bay window.

'It's probably all over for me now,' said Maud, without sounding at all pathetic. 'Take off that shirt. It's his, from the beginning. I recognise it. *You're* the one who matters right now. You're so young. *You* at least have to get out of this with your life in one piece. Give me a drag of your cigarette. You didn't know what you were getting mixed up in, did you?'

'No,' I said, sitting down next to Maud on the edge of the bed, surprised at my own boldness. 'I had no idea what I was getting mixed up in.'

'What's this?' she said, brushing a finger over my cheek where the tics were worst.

'An occupational injury,' I said.